I opted for the

I tackled Sarad Nukpana from the side. He was definitely surprised. So was the Guardian. Nukpana and I hit the ground hard.

His midnight eyes widened, and then he smiled. "Mistress Benares, how good of you to join us."

My mouth dropped open, and I was too stunned to move. The goblin reached for me, but the elf got there first, jerking me away from Nukpana.

Close contact gave me a good look at the Guardian, and he was good to look at. His eyes were stunning. Tropical seas stunning—and lock up your daughters and wives trouble.

The center of my chest suddenly grew warm. It could have been my increased heart rate, but I wasn't betting on it. The Guardian's intense gaze went to my chest. I didn't think he was admiring the view. The amulet flared to life.

The Guardian's eyes widened with amazement, and he tightened his grip on me. He had my arms, so the action I was forced to take was entirely his fault. It was as direct as my previous action, but not nearly as polite.

In the next instant, the Guardian was on his knees trying to remember how to breathe.

Magic Lost, Trouble Found

Lisa Shearin

ACE BOOKS, NEW YORK

THE BERKLEY PUBLISHING GROUP
Published by the Penguin Group
Penguin Group (USA) Inc.
375 Hudson Street, New York, New York 10014, USA
Penguin Group (Canada), 90 Eglinton Avenue East, Suite 700, Toronto, Ontario M4P 2Y3, Canada
(a division of Pearson Penguin Canada Inc.)
Penguin Books Ltd., 80 Strand, London WC2R 0RL, England
Penguin Group Ireland, 25 St. Stephen's Green, Dublin 2, Ireland (a division of Penguin Books Ltd.)
Penguin Group (Australia), 250 Camberwell Road, Camberwell, Victoria 3124, Australia
(a division of Pearson Australia Group Pty. Ltd.)
Penguin Books India Pvt. Ltd., 11 Community Centre, Panchsheel Park, New Delhi—110 017, India
Penguin Group (NZ), 67 Apollo Drive, Rosedale, North Shore 0745, Auckland, New Zealand
(a division of Pearson New Zealand Ltd.)
Penguin Books (South Africa) (Pty.) Ltd., 24 Sturdee Avenue, Rosebank, Johannesburg 2196,
South Africa

Penguin Books Ltd., Registered Offices: 80 Strand, London WC2R 0RL, England

MAGIC LOST, TROUBLE FOUND

An Ace Book / published by arrangement with the author

PRINTING HISTORY
Ace mass-market edition / June 2007

Copyright © 2007 by Lisa Shearin.
Cover art by Aleta Rafton.
Cover design by Judith Lagerman.
Interior text design by Kristin del Rosario.

ISBN: 978-0-441-01505-4

ACE
Ace Books are published by The Berkley Publishing Group,
a division of Penguin Group (USA) Inc.,
375 Hudson Street, New York, New York 10014.
ACE and the "A" design are trademarks belonging to Penguin Group (USA) Inc.

PRINTED IN THE UNITED STATES OF AMERICA

10 9 8 7 6 5 4 3 2 1

Many thanks:

To my agent, Kristin Nelson, for your guidance, enthusiasm, and for believing in the magic.

To my editor, Anne Sowards, for your sharp eyes, and for always taking the time to answer a new author's questions.

And most of all to my husband, Derek. Thank you for your love, patience, and encouragement. You never doubted, and always believed.

Chapter 1

Sorcerers weren't normal, sorcery wasn't natural, and Quentin Rand didn't like either one.

Quentin had always made an exception for me, but just because you tolerated what a friend was, didn't mean you understood what they did. Nothing explained to me what Quentin was doing breaking into the townhouse of one of Mermeia's most infamous necromancers. Quentin was a thief—at least he used to be. And to the best of my knowledge, he wasn't a suicidal ex-thief. Yet there he was crouched in the shadows of Nachtmagus Nigelius Nicabar's back door, picklocks at the ready. While not the most efficient way to ask for death, it was one of the more certain.

I knew all about Nigel's house wards. The human necromancer did everything he could to inflate his reputation, but he didn't depend on it to protect his valuables. Magical wards were home security at its most basic, and Nigel had some good ones. But although they were nasty, they wouldn't kill—rumor had it Nigel liked to save that pleasure for himself. I guess when you worked with the dead for a living, your idea of fun was a little different from everyone else's. The city watch frowned on citizens taking the law into their own hands like that, but the watch was notoriously shorthanded in the Districts. They couldn't prosecute what they didn't know about, and I'd rather they didn't know Quentin was here tonight.

Quentin occasionally works for me. My name is Raine Benares. I'm a seeker. I find things. Most times the people who hire me are glad when I do, but sometimes they're sorry they asked. Personally, I think people should be more careful what they ask for. Some things are better left unfound.

Seeking isn't the flashiest occupation a sorceress can put out her shingle for, or the most highly regarded, but it pays the rent on time. I've found the formerly unfindable for the Mermeia city watch, and since I'm an elf, elven intelligence has sought my help on more than one occasion. Most of what I'm hired to find didn't get lost by itself. It had help. Help you could depend on to use blades or bolts or nastier magical means to keep what they went to all the trouble to get. When that's the case, I go by the rule of me or them.

I also apply that rule to my friends. That's why I was cooling my heels in one of Mermeia's more aromatic alleys—to keep Quentin's moonlighting from earning him a one-way trip to the city morgue.

As a former career thief, Quentin knew the underside of Mermeia better than just about anyone. That's why I hired him. Well, it was one of the reasons. Our professional paths had crossed from time to time over the years. What I had been hired to find was often something Quentin had been hired to steal. It got to the point that I just started my search with Quentin to save myself a lot of unnecessary footwork. He didn't take it personally, and neither did I. However, I always extended to Quentin the professional courtesy of waiting until the object in question had left his hands before recovering it. That way he got paid while maintaining his reputation. But when the risks started to outweigh the rewards, Quentin thought that an early end to his career might keep the same fate from befalling his life. I helped him bridge the gap between thief and quasi-law-abiding citizen.

No fact, tidbit or rumor was too small or too hidden for Quentin to ferret out—given the proper monetary motivation. Greed still occasionally whispered sweet nothings in his ear, enticing my sometime employee to seek out additional means of income. Most times he didn't tell me the details. Most times I didn't want to know. Considering where he was right now, tonight wasn't one of those times.

The city of Mermeia in the kingdom of Brenir consisted of five islands that had been forced into existence by the determination of its founders, and kept from sinking by the greed of its merchants. A powerful force, greed. It made solid ground where there had once been marsh; built palaces and trading houses where there were reeds; and inspired humans, elves, goblins, and magic users of all races to live together in a city separated only by the canals that marked their respective Districts. Sometimes we even got along.

I cupped my hands to my mouth, blowing on cold-numbed fingers. I was trying to breathe through my mouth to keep my nose from becoming any more traumatized than it already was. The cozy little alley I'd found across Pasquine Street from Nigel's townhouse held a charm all its own. I'd put a shielding spell across the entrance, so unless Quentin walked over and looked in, he couldn't see or hear me. The alley walls were slick with something dark and damp and best left unidentified. The air was chilly but still warm enough to enhance the aroma of the garbage sharing the alley with me. And the stench of the canal a block away at low tide only further enhanced my sensory experience. I rubbed my hands together, then gave up and reached for the gloves at my belt. Not that I wanted anything to happen to Quentin, but it would be nice if all this turned out to be worth my while.

"You stood me up."

I yelped. I recognized the voice, which was the only reason

my throwing knife remained in my hand, instead of being lodged in the voice's owner.

I blew out my breath. "Don't *do* that!" I sheathed my knife, though I was still tempted to use it, more from acute embarrassment than anything else.

Phaelan chuckled and stepped out of the shadows hiding the alley entrance from the street. My cousin looked like the rest of my family—dark hair, dark eyes, dark good looks, equally dark disposition. Next to them, I stood out like a flaming match at night with my long red gold hair, gray eyes, and pale skin. The hair and skin tone were from my mother. I assumed my eyes were from my father. Neither parent was around for me to ask.

Phaelan was the main reason having the name Benares was an asset in the seeking business. When looking for pilfered goods, it helped to be related to experts—professional pilferers all.

You could say our family was well known in the import and export business. The goods my cousin's side of the family imported never saw the light of day in a harbormaster's ledger, and the exports consisted of vast profits sent to secret family accounts in various banks in numerous kingdoms. Phaelan's natural talent was in acquisitions. Many times he neglected to get permission from the owners whose goods he intended to acquire; or when he did ask, his request often came from the business end of a cannon.

"Since when does spending the night in an alley rate above dinner with me at the Crown and Anchor?" he asked.

"Since Quentin's moonlighting again."

"Varek said you were staking out Nigel Nicabar's. He didn't say anything about Quentin."

When in Mermeia, Phaelan did business out of the Spyglass, and Varek Akar, the proprietor, served the dual purpose of business manager and social secretary for my cousin when he was in town. I didn't normally make my stakeouts public knowledge, but since Nigel was involved, I thought it'd be a good idea to let my next of kin know where to find me.

"That's because I didn't mention Quentin," I told him. "I'd rather the watch not get wind that he's working again."

"Varek knows how to keep his mouth shut."

"I trust Varek, but I don't feel the same way about his new barkeep. Quentin hasn't done anything illegal tonight."

Phaelan laughed, his voice low. "Night ain't over yet."

He was right, but I didn't have to admit it. If certain members of the watch knew where he was, they'd jump to conclusions, and then they'd jump Quentin.

Phaelan's ship had arrived in port late that afternoon, and the plan had been to meet for an early dinner. Early, because I knew he had plans later—plans that had everything to do with a woman, but nothing to do with a lady. My cousin had a strict threefold agenda on his first night in any port—get fed, get laid, and get drunk, in that order. Occasionally he would skip the food, but never the other two. When in Mermeia, my cousin could either be found in one of the city's less reputable gambling parlors, or enjoying the comforts offered at Madame Natasha's Joy Garden, and probably the attentions of Madame Natasha herself. This evening, Phaelan was positively resplendent in a doublet of scarlet buckskin, with matching breeches topped with high, black leather boots. At his side was the swept-hilt rapier he favored when out on the town. And unless my nose deceived me, his white linen shirt was as well scrubbed as Phaelan himself. An earring set with a single ruby gleamed in the lobe of one elegantly pointed ear. I knew all the fuss wasn't on account of me.

"You took a bath," I said. "And shaved. I'm impressed."

"Just fancying myself up for you, darlin'."

"I'm sure Madame Natasha and her girls will also appreciate your consideration."

He grinned in a flash of white teeth. It was the kind of grin that could get him anything he wanted at Madame Natasha's— or anywhere else in Mermeia—for free. He nodded toward where Quentin still waited by Nigel's side door. "So what's he doing here?"

"Asking for more trouble than he can handle."

The grin broadened. "From Nigel or you?"

"Both."

"Then walk across the street and stop him. The Crown's still holding a table for us."

"It's not that easy."

"Why not?"

"Being here wasn't his idea."

"So someone paid him well. Wouldn't be the first time. Let's go and let the man earn his money."

I didn't budge. "How much would it take for you to break into Nigel's at night?"

To his credit, Phaelan didn't have to think long. "More money than most in this city can lay hands to."

"Exactly. And Quentin's terrified of necromancers. There's more involved here than money, meaning whoever hired Quentin scares him more than Nigel does. Quentin's been trying to keep his nose clean and someone won't let him—and I don't like it."

"So ask him who it is."

"I did."

"And?"

"Quentin bought a new set of picklocks last week and started keeping to himself. I started asking him questions. He started avoiding me." I indicated the assortment of armaments and dark leather that made up my evening ensemble—all topped by a ridiculously large and hooded cloak to keep Quentin from recognizing me had he spotted me. As an added precaution, my hair was contained in a long braid and hidden under the cloak. "Hence the cloak-and-dagger routine."

"So if he won't tell you what he's up to, you're just going to follow him while he does it."

I nodded. "Exactly. And pull his backside out of the fire if need be. Afterward, we're going to have a little chat." I glanced back at the alley entrance. Phaelan hadn't brought any of his crew with him. That was surprising.

"You alone?"

"My men only want to end up in an alley after they've been drinking all night—or if they're waiting for someone. Even if they knew they'd be sharing that alley with you, I'd have a mutiny in the making."

I didn't have a response for that. I'd have mutinied, too. We settled back and waited.

A chat with Quentin was a given, but I hoped pulling his backside out of the fire wasn't going to be a part of my evening. Though with Quentin's current track record, both were probably in my immediate future.

Two months ago, Quentin had been hired to steal an emerald necklace being delivered to a local duke. The jeweler reported the theft to the duke. His Grace wasn't home, but his wife was. Unfortunately for everyone concerned, the duchess despised emeralds—but they were the favorite gem of the woman she suspected of being her husband's mistress. Bad went to worse for both the duke and Quentin. The duke simply retreated to his country estate. Quentin had to hide in the Daith Swamp for three weeks. He emerged a changed man. I guess three weeks of eating nothing but silt slugs will do that to you.

I found out about all this after the fact. When Quentin got around to admitting his career relapse to me, he also admitted that the job could have gone better. My friends on the city watch thought Quentin's flair for understatement was exceeded only by his bad luck—or stupidity—depending on who you asked.

Yet here he was tonight, about to break into the house of the nastiest necromancer Mermeia had to offer. Some people were slow learners. But I would say that if Quentin was looking for a fate worse than eating silt slugs in a swamp, he'd come to the right place.

About ten minutes passed, and Quentin hadn't so much as flinched. I couldn't say the same for Phaelan. Three months at sea had taken its toll. There was something he desperately wanted to be doing right now, and standing in a stinking alley listening to himself breathe wasn't it.

"Go on, Phaelan. Nothing's going to happen here that I can't handle."

"Not a chance. Nigel isn't known for being understanding of trespassers."

"I'm not trespassing; Quentin is." I flashed Phaelan a grin of my own. "Besides, Nigel's not home. If he were, I wouldn't let Quentin within three blocks of here."

"Then what the hell's he waiting for?"

"Him." I indicated the upstairs gallery. A tall, thin figure carrying a single lamp proceeded at a stately pace down the length of the second floor gallery, putting out lamps and candles as he went.

"Nigel's steward," I clarified. "His reputation is almost as nasty as his master's. I did some asking around. It's the same routine every night. He puts out all the lights before going to bed. Nigel won't be back until just before daybreak. He's out making housecalls. For some reason, his clients seem to think séances have to be done at night. Since Quentin's the cautious type, he'll wait until the steward gets to the servant's quarters before he makes his move."

Phaelan's expression indicated I was in dire need of a life. I wasn't entirely sure I disagreed with him.

"How long have you been staking this place out?" he asked.

"Just once. The rest came from a few well-placed bribes. If Nigel doesn't want his people to gossip, he should pay them better."

"Any idea what Quentin's after?"

"Not a clue. But if Nigel holds it near and dear, you can bet it's a short list of people who want it—or want to be anywhere near it."

"So that explains your sudden maternal urges."

"I'm just here to make sure Quentin doesn't get in too far over his head."

"I'd say he's there already. You planning to follow him in?"

"Not unless something jumps out and starts killing him."

"Then how are you . . . ?" Phaelan began. Then understanding dawned. "How did you get him to take a tracking stone?"

"Who says I asked him?" I shrugged deeper into my cloak. "Better safe than sensed. And as an added bonus, Quentin gets to go inside where it's nice and warm, and we get to stay here where it's nice and smelly."

Phaelan looked up at the now dark gallery windows. "I don't think anything in there is nice." He took a not-so-delicate sniff and looked down at his boots in disgust. "Or out here."

I followed his gaze, and took a whiff of my own. I had really been trying to ignore my boots. Though I'd rather be in a stinking alley than a necromancer's house. Especially this necromancer. I'd once heard Nigel's place described as forbidding. Just plain spooky worked for me. I think he had both in mind when he had it built. Not many people would want to live in a place that looked like a mausoleum, but then Nigel wasn't most people.

My back was starting to cramp, and I shifted my weight, trying to get comfortable. The more I squirmed, the worse it got. I hated stakeouts. My body didn't respond well to sitting or standing around for long periods of time. Then there was the boredom. I was almost hoping Nigel's steward would wake up, go looking for a nighttime snack, and find Quentin. At least I'd get to do something.

Just because I didn't really expect any violence tonight, didn't mean I wasn't prepared for it. I'm not exactly what you'd call physically intimidating. Thanks to my elven blood, I'm tall enough, but my small bones and slender build are designed more for running than fighting. For those times when speed or spells didn't discourage someone, I kept all sorts of interesting weapons, mostly the bladed variety, tucked here and there.

Quentin was even smaller than I was, and wiry—and could locate trouble faster than a lodestone could find true north.

Though considering the section of the city we were in, I'd more than likely have to call on my alternate arsenal.

I'm a magic user of respectable ability, though most sorcerers would look down their noses and call what I do parlor tricks. In addition to my seeking skills, I can move small objects with my mind, maintain an image of myself in a place I've just left, and my shields are right up there with the best. Not the most powerful sorcery by a long shot, but in my opinion, power's overrated—plus I know how to fight dirty, magically and otherwise. It's always been enough to keep me alive. Singed around the edges doesn't count.

What I can't do is manipulate the wills of others, affect the weather, communicate with or raise the dead, turn base metal into gold, see into the future, or any of the other skills other sorcerers turn into a way to make a living. Not that I haven't tried a few. I think the words "young" and "stupid" went a long way toward explaining those efforts. I even tried pyromancy once, but I almost set fire to my cat. It was at least six months before he didn't run every time I struck a match.

I couldn't see Quentin anymore, but it didn't mean I didn't know exactly where he was.

"He's inside," I told Phaelan. "And he didn't set off any wards."

"You make it sound like a bad thing."

"It's not good. Quentin's employer either had Nigel's wards disabled ahead of time, or Quentin has a ghencharm."

Phaelan didn't exactly look enlightened. "Which is?"

"A talisman that disables wards. Quentin could walk straight through every ward in that house and not make a sound. Problem is you have to know ahead of time what wards are being used. Whoever keyed it would need inside information."

Phaelan shrugged. "So someone bribed one of Nigel's servants. So did you."

"I just got the household routine. Quentin apparently got the house. Someone in there really doesn't like their boss. Nigel's not going to be happy."

"So he's not the lovable type. I'd imagine not many necromancers are. Can you track him?"

I nodded absently. I was seeing more than just Phaelan.

Quentin was in the main part of the house now. A tracking stone only lets you know the carrier's location, usually without any details as to what they see. There could be occasional flashes of image, but that only happened with magically sensitive carriers, or those you knew very well. Quentin wasn't the sensitive type, magically or otherwise. Apparently I knew him well enough, because I got a hazy vision from his viewpoint of stairs leading to the second floor. No wards. No lurking stewards. Looked like Quentin had a good ghencharm. Phaelan and I might not have to charge in to the rescue after all. But I still had every intention of sitting down with Quentin for a very long talk when this was over, and if I needed extra muscle to hold him down while we chatted, so be it.

Quentin went straight to what looked to be a formal reception area on the ground floor. He crossed the room to a wall, pushed on something I couldn't see, and exposed a hidden staircase. Interesting. Quentin activated a tiny lightglobe on the interior wall, illuminating steep and polished wooden stairs. A plush carpet of deep crimson ran up the center. It was all a little much for Nigel's taste. Maybe select noble clients saw this part of the house as well. At the top of the stairs was a door with a screened panel that was just large enough to look through. Quentin looked inside, and so did I. An ornately carved bed dominated the room. I found myself grinning.

"What?" Phaelan asked.

"Just a fun fact to know and share. Conjuring up the dead relatives of Caesolian courtiers must only pay so much. It looks like Nigel supplements his income with a little blackmail."

Quentin was searching Nigel's room, and doing a very efficient and professional job of it for a reformed thief. Someone had been staying in practice. He'd just discovered a compartment in the headboard of the bed containing a jumble of small boxes and papers. He took out a white stone box. The entire thing fit in the palm of his hand. It had been sealed with black wax, but the seal had been broken. Quentin opened the box.

The world exploded. Or at least my corner of it.

I found myself on all fours like I'd taken a giant fist to the gut. If there was any air in the alley, I couldn't find it. My vision swam, and pain stabbed behind my eyes. I heard someone whimper. I think it was me. I pitched forward, my forehead landing in something I didn't want to identify, its stench the only thing keeping me from passing out. I dimly felt Phaelan's hands on my shoulders, lifting my face out of the muck. I was dizzy, nauseous, and had an urge to make my own contribution to the pile of scraps next to me.

"Stop," I managed.

Phaelan stopped lifting, but didn't let go. I was grateful. I don't think I could have stayed upright on my own. I raised my head slowly until my eyes were level with the street. I resisted the impulse to gulp air into my lungs. I took a few steady breaths. My vision began to clear.

"Raine?" He sounded worried. That made two of us.

I tried to answer, but my mouth was too busy breathing.

"Are you all right?"

I thought about nodding, but decided against it. "Think so."

"What happened?"

"I think Quentin just found what he was looking for."

Unfortunately, I was right. Sometimes I hate it when that happens. Quentin showed no signs of putting the whatever-it-was back in the box, and my head hurt too much to maintain contact with him until he did. Fine. I broke contact. He was on his own. I assumed he had done everything he came to do, and would be coming out soon. I sat back against the wall of the alley, watched the door where he had gone in, and concentrated on breathing. Breathing was good.

No alarms went off, no lamps were lit in the servants' quarters or anywhere else in the house. The street was quiet. The few people who passed the alley with magical talent enough to see past my shields probably thought I was either drunk or had just been mugged. Either way, no one stopped to ask.

"What's keeping him?" Phaelan asked.

Glass shattered. A lot of it. It sounded like it came from the back of Nigel's house. This was followed by shouting. I recognized Quentin's voice. It sounded like he had found his good friend Trouble, and they had made their own exit from Nigel's bedroom. Phaelan helped me to my feet and then sprinted toward the back of the house. I ditched my cloak and followed as best I could. Considering how I felt, my idea of running more resembled a loping jog. No use worrying about waking the neighbors now.

Not surprisingly, Phaelan was the first to reach the back wall. He hoisted himself smoothly to the top and stopped, something my cousin rarely did. Phaelan only acknowledged one direction, and that was forward.

"Goblin shamans," he said.

That was unexpected. I heaved myself up beside him. As far as I was concerned, there were two types of goblin shamans—one good and one bad. These particular ones wore black robes lined in silver. Khrynsani. Quentin's new acquaintances were the bad kind. Why wasn't I surprised?

The Khrynsani were an ancient goblin secret society and military order, with even more outdated political ideas. The Khrynsanic credo was simple. Goblins were meant to rule, and if anyone disagreed, they weren't meant to live. Those who disagreed included every other race. Unfortunately, the minds behind the Khrynsani weren't simple, or without influence. Some of the most powerful families of the goblin aristocracy were secret Khrynsani members. The new goblin king was a Khrynsani and proud of it. So it wouldn't be long before the rest of the old blood nobility traded in their secret membership for openly fashionable affiliation.

Nigel hated all goblins, good or bad, so it was safe to say that these four weren't invited houseguests. Then again, neither was Quentin. But there they all were on Nigel's bedroom balcony. Quentin did the only thing a nonsorcerer and a human could do in his situation: he jumped. It wasn't a bad distance. Not a good one, either. But it was survivable, and his chances were better than staying where he was. Fortunately, Nigel was fond of bushes. It gave Quentin something to flatten beside himself when he landed.

The shamans didn't follow him, but four impeccably armed and armored goblins did. They effortlessly vaulted the railing and landed catlike on the ground below, missing the bushes entirely, covering the distance to the middle of the garden in about half the time as Quentin. The quartet obviously weren't street thugs, and they had made no effort to conceal their uniforms. Khrynsani temple guards. When Quentin found trouble, he didn't fool around.

Quentin was running toward the back wall, and us. He looked glad to see us. No surprise there. But the four goblins were gaining on him, and Quentin would never make it to the wall before they caught him. I swore and scrambled over the top, making a wobbly landing on the lawn below. Phaelan was right behind me. Quentin turned his back to us, leaving himself ample room to maneuver and drew a pair of long daggers.

The four goblins were larger and faster than I would have liked. But opponents, like family, were something you didn't get the luxury of picking for yourself. Realizing that Quentin's intention was to fight rather than escape, the goblins slowed, each leisurely drawing a scythelike saber. They saw Phaelan and me, but it didn't seem to have a negative effect on their morale.

Goblins were generally tall, long limbed, and leanly muscled, like elves. This quartet was no exception. Their features were angular, their large eyes dark, and their upswept ears slightly more pronounced at the tip than elven ears. Their pale gray skin set off their most distinguishing feature—a pair of fangs that weren't for decorative use only. Just because a goblin smiled at you didn't mean he wanted to be friends. The danger didn't detract from the race's appeal—some would say it fueled it. I guess all that sinuous grace and exotic beauty can make you overlook a lot, and there were plenty of half-breed children running around to prove it. Some said that elves and goblins came from a common ancestor; a theory hotly denied by the old blood of both races.

The full moon provided more than ample light to fight by. I'm sure the goblins would try to maneuver us into the shadows of Nigel's orchard. They could try, but the only place I was going was back over the wall when this was over. Not that I couldn't see well in the dark, but goblins could see better. What looked pitch dark to an elf or human was as bright as day to a goblin, which of course meant the perfect time to cross blades with a goblin was high noon in full sun. I didn't think the goblin who broke off from the group and was moving toward me would be willing to reschedule. Pity.

They fanned out to surround us. Two of the temple guards centered their attentions on Phaelan. Apparently they saw him as more of a threat. I don't think he was flattered. The one who had chosen me for a dance partner grinned, exposing an alarmingly sharp pair of fangs. His face, framed by long, black hair, bore several scars. That told me he'd made mistakes in the past. Good. Hopefully I could help him make at least one more.

He circled off and feinted a quick, stabbing attack. He wasn't serious yet, and I didn't take the bait. They didn't intend to kill us quickly. As long as things stayed quiet, and their work uninterrupted, they would want to play first. I agreed with the silence, but I had no intention of being anyone's evening entertainment. This toy had teeth.

The goblins wore tooled leather covered with a combination of blued-steel plate and scale armor. The single serpent of the Khrynsani insignia gleamed in vivid, red enamel over the heart. The etching in the steel made the armor look delicate, but I knew better. There were a few vulnerable points, but those were next to impossible to reach without getting yourself carved up in the process. Care and patience was called for here. Unfortunately, I wasn't well known for either quality. I let my breath out slowly and willed myself to relax. Let the goblin make the first move.

The first cut came at my left side, near the ribs. It was meant to annoy and test my defenses, not inflict serious damage. I parried it with my dagger, but wasn't lured into riposting. Not yet. The goblin was just out of my range, and I would have to completely turn my back on one of the two others circling Phaelan. I didn't want to find out the hard way that goblins were willing to share.

The goblin's grin dimmed. He lunged at my legs, but at the last instant flicked the blade's point up toward my abdomen. I leapt back and managed to deflect the blade, but just barely. The goblin's grin returned. He was playing again, but I wasn't.

I attacked, something he obviously didn't expect. The temple guard retreated, but not fast enough. My rapier darted out, giving me just the reach I needed. Only the top inch of the blade penetrated, but it was enough. I struck where his armor buckled at the top of the leg near the groin. The goblin's face blanched in pain and surprise, and a low hiss escaped from between his clenched teeth. His blade slashed down. He was aiming for my sword arm, but instead took a sizeable chunk out of one of Nigel's prized rose bushes. I grabbed the falling branch in my gloved left hand, and lashed out with it. The hooked thorns raked furrows in the goblin's unprotected face, and I was treated to language you wouldn't expect he learned in the temple.

I jumped back as the goblin's blade sliced through the space I had just vacated. Pain and the sudden absence of his target threw him off balance, and I slipped the tip of my rapier under the section of armored scales connecting his chest and back plates. His forward momentum pushed the blade on through. A tug and a sharp twist of my wrist extracted my blade as the dead goblin slid to the ground.

Quentin was leaning against an apple tree, dark blond hair hanging in his eyes, his normally tanned face blanched pale. I didn't see any blood on him, which was more than I could say for his opponent. The goblin was sprawled on the grass, one of Quentin's throwing daggers protruding from his throat.

Phaelan still had one goblin to contend with, and this one was showing more caution than his dead comrade. My cousin was armed with only a dagger, his rapier sticking out of a dead goblin's chest, probably caught on a rib. I was debating tossing him one of my blades when the remaining goblin attacked, moving faster than I thought any mortal creature had a right to. Phaelan dodged the first swing, and dove for the dead goblin's saber lying in the grass. He rolled as he hit the ground, the goblin's scythelike blade whistling past where my cousin's head had been an instant before. Phaelan grabbed the saber and brought it up, slicing into the creature's unarmored hip. It wasn't a killing blow, but it bought him some time.

My opponent had been scarred before I got hold of him. Phaelan's attacker had the high cheekbones and handsome, angled features of the old blood. There were no scars, and no doubt the goblin was proud of his face. That's where Phaelan struck. The goblin parried, but it wasn't a clean deflection. Phaelan's saber sliced through the creature's exposed ear. My cousin then followed the goblin's scream with a solid knee to the nethers.

Silence was no longer anyone's priority as the goblin writhed on the ground clutching his slashed ear, among other things. Dogs began barking and whistles sounded in the distance as the watch was alerted.

I felt something crawling on the air around us. I looked toward the house.

The goblin shamans had made no move to join us in the garden. They didn't need to. I couldn't hear the words of the spell they were weaving, but I could feel what it was doing. A power was building, and we didn't want to be here when they released it. It was particularly nasty, and would reduce us to smoldering corpses, if not ashes. I had no intention of being made into mulch for Nigel's roses. There were faster spells, but from the sound of things, the shamans were going for fun over speed.

I could shield us if I had to. I felt confident in my ability to keep us from being fried, but I felt less certain about being able to damage three Khrynsani shamans. This wasn't a time for a brawl—this was a time to get the hell out of here. But their spell was reaching its conclusion, so it wasn't my decision to make.

They didn't expect to be attacked, so they hadn't wasted any power shielding themselves. Their magical britches weren't going to be any farther down than they were right now. I didn't have to break their spell, just their concentration. My nose had already told me that Nigel's gardener had been fertilizing today; my eyes discovered he'd graciously left a bucket of said fertilizer for my use and enjoyment.

I could move small objects with my mind. A bucket of manure was a small object.

I tossed the bucket—and its contents—toward the balcony. As far as defensive spells went, it wasn't powerful, it certainly wasn't pretty, but it got the job done. At the very least, the goblin shamans were distracted. At the most, they were discouraged from trying to roast us. They also looked like turning me into rose mulch was the nicest thing they wanted to do, but I wasn't going to stick around and find out for sure.

Lights came on in the windows of the houses next door, and more goblins came over the wall beyond the orchard. They wore tooled leather and blued-steel armor, and wielded blades of the same fine steel—the sort of steel and leatherwork only royal retainers could afford. More temple guards joined the shamans on the balcony. Oddly enough, the goblins from the house didn't look happy to see the goblins from the orchard. Dissent in the ranks? Opposing factions? Either way, we weren't about to stay around to welcome any newcomers.

Phaelan used his foot to brace against the dead goblin's body, freed his trapped blade, and made for the wall. Getting over the top was a lot easier the first time, but then again, survival is a powerful motivator. A narrow alley ran on the other side of the wall. Once over, I had a feeling the goblins would only pursue us so far. I knew Mermeia. And Mermeia was teeming with humans and elves who would gladly serve Khrynsani temple guards their cods on a platter.

I swung myself over the top and dropped to the ground, slipping in something I didn't have the time or inclination to identify. Quentin followed, and I took this opportunity to lay hands on him. They weren't particularly gentle hands, but then after a fight with goblins who wanted me dead for no other reason than that I knew Quentin, I wasn't in a particularly gentle mood.

Quentin gasped, trying to get his wind back. "I've got to get to Simon Stocken's."

"What did you take?"

Quentin's expression was somewhere between mere panic and basic terror, probably inspired by the goblins, not me. "What do you mean?"

I gave him a shake. "What's in the box?"

He pulled a chain out of his shirt. On its end spun a plain, silver amulet. "You mean this?"

I winced, expecting a repeat of my alley experience. But there was no pain. No urge to be sick. I also couldn't believe my eyes.

"What *is* it with you and necklaces!"

Phaelan dropped down beside us. He couldn't believe we were still there.

"Go!"

Beyond going to see Simon Stocken, I didn't know what Quentin's plans were. But if it involved another extended stay in the Daith Swamp, he was on his own. Friendship only went so far.

Chapter 2

Few things stirred a man's protective instincts like ill-gotten goods.

To anyone who had no business there, Mermeia's east waterfront district was a place best avoided after dark. Chances were, if a man had killed to obtain certain objects, he had no qualms over killing to keep them a while longer, at least until he saw fit to sell them for a healthy profit.

The warehouses of the waterfront were full of valuables of questionable ownership, and manned by those whose jobs it was to guard them. Between the three of us, we knew most of them, and they us. But I wasn't holding my breath counting on any for help. If anyone brought trouble with them to the waterfront, chances were they had brought it on themselves and were expected to deal with it the same way.

Simon Stocken conducted business out of a small warehouse on the central city side of the waterfront. Prime locations backed up to the lagoon for easier and more discreet loading and unloading of cargo, but, as much of Stocken's business was conducted from the rich coffers of the central city, his less than ideal location suited his needs nicely, as did his front as a wine merchant. If it was a rare vintage, Stocken could get it for you—for a price. Like many merchants in Mermeia, Stocken's most valuable shipments were never seen by city tax agents.

Mermeia's central city also had the dubious honor of being the financial center of the seven kingdoms. And where there was money, there were creative uses, and misuses. Mermeian loans financed wars, coups, treasons, assassinations—all the building blocks of civilized society.

We were walking at a fast pace in the shadows of Belacant Way, one block over from Stocken's warehouse. While the fast pace was healthy at this time of night under normal circumstances, tonight hardly qualified as normal. Normal waterfront hazards included cutpurses and garden-variety murderers, not Khrynsani temple guards and jewelry that made my stomach do flips.

I didn't sense anyone following us. That was the first good thing to happen all night. It also made it a perfect time to start that talk I wanted to have with Quentin.

"Wait," I told Quentin and my cousin.

Phaelan stopped. Quentin clearly didn't want to.

"I need to deliver this to Stocken," he objected.

"A few more minutes isn't going to make any difference," I told him. "And I'm not convinced you should give that thing to Simon Stocken. Phaelan and I are in this, whether we want to be or not—"

"And we don't," Phaelan said.

"So I think we deserve to know what's going on."

Quentin made no move to enlighten us.

I crossed my arms. "Now would be nice."

Quentin's blue eyes darted to the warehouse behind us like he expected goblins to leap out of the walls. I had never seen him this nervous, and we had been in plenty of situations where he'd had ample opportunity. This wasn't like Quentin at all, and I didn't like it. His mystery employer just earned a top spot on my list of least-liked people.

"About a week ago, Simon contacted me about a job," Quentin said, talking fast. "I meet with him, he tells me what the client wants, and how much he's willing to pay to get it. It was good money. Real good. Then Simon tells me whose house I'd be breaking into. I tell him to forget it, no deal. That's when he hands me the letter. Tells me the man looking to hire me said to give me the letter if I refuse the job. So I read it." Quentin paused for air, and his jaw tightened. "Let's just say the letter changed my mind."

"What was in it?" Phaelan asked.

"I'm not saying. But it's got nothing to do with what happened back there."

I knew that probably wasn't true, but I wasn't going to force the issue, at least not now. "Did Stocken tell you who the client was?"

"A man by the name of Dinten Ronk," Quentin said. "Claimed to be a silversmith from Laerin. Simon had heard of a silversmith by that name. Parts of him were found last month stuffed in a barrel on the Laerin docks. The man who showed up at Simon's may have been a fake, but his gold was real enough, so Simon didn't ask too many questions." He grinned. "Didn't want to scare away a paying customer."

"Was the impostor Dinten Ronk also human?" I asked.

Quentin shrugged. "As far as I know. Simon didn't say otherwise, and he would have at least mentioned it. Not that he has anything against nonhumans. Simon does business with everyone."

"Including goblins?" Phaelan asked.

Quentin threw a nervous glance back in the direction we came from. "Not those goblins."

"Any idea why the Khrynsani want the amulet?" I asked.

"I didn't even know there was an amulet. My job was to get the box. Simon didn't tell me what was inside. I asked. He said the client either didn't know himself, or just wouldn't tell him."

"So why didn't you bring the box?" Phaelan asked.

"I dropped it, all right?" Quentin's voice went up about two octaves. "Seeing goblins appear out of nowhere can make you drop things. I had the amulet in my hand, and I figured that's what they wanted anyway. If I'm dead, the client doesn't get his goods, and I don't get the rest of my money, so I jumped out the window. Seeing goblins can make you do that, too."

I didn't doubt that, but I did doubt the part about goblins appearing out of nowhere. They had to have come from somewhere, and since they were Khrynsani, they didn't need a door to make an entrance. I knew that. Quentin didn't need to. No use scaring him any more than he already was.

"Did the goblins see that you had the amulet?" I asked.

"I don't know." He looked a little embarrassed. "It got kind of chaotic."

Quentin screaming and running and jumping out of windows certainly qualified as chaotic.

"Well, if neither Stocken nor the client is expecting an amulet," I said, carefully assuming my best rational tone, "then they won't be disappointed when they don't get one."

"What are you saying?" Quentin knew very well, and from the way his eyes narrowed, he didn't like it one bit.

"Nigel Nicabar had it," I told him. "The Khrynsani want it. I don't know what this amulet is or what it does, but if the Khrynsani want it, it would probably be bad if they got it."

Quentin started to speak, and I held up a hand. "Hear me out. Just tell Stocken about the goblins. Tell him you dropped the box, and you don't know what happened to it after that. That's not a lie."

"What about my money?"

"What about it?"

Quentin and Phaelan looked at me like I'd just uttered the most condemnable blasphemy imaginable.

"I got twenty gold tenari," Quentin informed me. "Up front."

Phaelan whistled. "I'd stroll around Nigel's house at night for that."

"I'm going to get five more when I deliver the goods, and another five if I deliver it before dawn." Quentin took two steps in the direction of Stocken's warehouse. "So I'm in a bit of a hurry. If we can move along, I can get my money, and we can all go home."

I didn't move. "Don't you mean when you deliver *the box*?"

Realization began to dawn on Quentin, and the thought that he might not get paid for delivering an amulet rather than a box was the final blow to an already bad night. I felt equally bad about breaking the news to him, but I would have felt even worse if the amulet was sold out from underneath us before I knew what the Khrynsani wanted with it—or more to the point, what Sarad Nukpana wanted with it.

Sarad Nukpana was the Khrynsani grand shaman. He was also a sadistic psychopath. I'd done work for Duke Markus Sevelien long enough to have that confirmed on numerous occasions.

Markus was the head of elven intelligence in Mermeia. I'd like to think he'd retained me as a consultant because of my superior seeking skills, but I know differently. Markus thought my being related to criminals helped me know the criminal mind. This wasn't always true, but I wasn't one to turn down a regular, well-paying client just because he wounded my delicate sensibilities. Truth be told, if it can be picked up, pried off, or in any way pilfered, my family's made off with it at one time or another. Unfortunately those pilfered goods have occasionally included people. It's not something I'm proud of, but it's not something I can deny.

Most of my work for Markus involved finding pilfered elves—diplomats, intelligence agents, assorted nobles. The kind of people the less savory members of my family would love to get their ransom-grubbing hands on. Though most of the missing elves Markus wanted me to find had been taken by the kind of people who had no interest in ransom. I guess the more money you had, the cheaper life was.

And I had it on the best authority that no one held life in lower regard than Sarad Nukpana.

I'd heard stories from some of Markus's agents who had seen the rotten fruits of Nukpana's labors up close and personal. A few of Markus's agents were goblins. They knew the Khrynsani grand shaman as soft voiced, cultured and courteous with a formidable intellect. Elven agents told a different story. One of them had been held across from another cell where Nukpana was interrogating a human prisoner. Nukpana chatted as if hosting a cocktail party—while he did a little exploratory surgery. His prisoner/patient was awake. The elven agent said the screams went on longer than he thought possible. The pleasant conversation continued, even after the screams had stopped. That story alone kept me waking up in a cold sweat for weeks.

"But it was the amulet they really wanted." Quentin was looking in growing desperation from one of us to the other. "Right?"

"Probably." I answered. "But Stocken might take some convincing. Then he'd have to get back to the client for confirmation. All of which is going to delay your payment. In the meantime, you can't turn over the amulet without proper payment. As a businessman, Stocken would understand that. It's just not good business."

"Makes sense to me," Phaelan added.

Quentin shot a betrayed look at my cousin. "You didn't have to break into that crypt Nigel Nicabar calls home." His fear from earlier in the evening had been soundly replaced by moral outrage and greed. "You didn't have goblins jump on you out of thin air. You didn't—"

"Fight Khrynsani guards to keep you from being sliced apart one piece at a time?" Phaelan's voice was soft and low.

It was the voice his enemies never wanted to hear. He stepped toe to toe with Quentin. "Something I'm beginning to regret."

Quentin raised both hands and stepped back. "It's not that I'm ungrateful, but—"

"It sounds that way." Phaelan didn't back down. Retreating isn't a concept my family's too familiar with. If we've gone to the trouble to stake out ground, or water, we're keeping it.

I blew out an exasperated sigh and stepped in. "Just tell Stocken what happened. But don't show him the amulet. Don't tell him what was in the box at all at this point. On second thought, just so you won't be tempted, why don't you give me the amulet? I'll keep it until you finish talking to Stocken."

"You sure that's a good idea?" Phaelan asked.

I knew what he was thinking, because I had already thought it. The last thing I wanted was a repeat performance of my reaction in the alley when Quentin had opened the box. But when he had dangled the amulet itself in front of my face, nothing had happened. Maybe it had been the box, or a spell guarding the box. Either way, I wanted to make sure Quentin didn't give the amulet to Simon Stocken. If Stocken dangled a pouch of gold in front of Quentin's face, the amulet was as good as gone.

Quentin looked doubtful. "You'll give it back?"

"Yes, I'll give it back." Eventually. Once I found out what it was. And if I found I needed to hold onto it to keep it out of Sarad Nukpana's hands, I'd pay Quentin the rest of his fee. Or Markus Sevelien would. For the elven duke, thirty gold tenari was pocket change. I couldn't say the same for myself. Information was a professional courtesy Markus and I had extended to each other over the years. If I happened across something that Markus might be interested in, I let him know, and the elven duke did the same for me.

I knew Markus would be interested in anything that interested Sarad Nukpana.

Quentin pulled the chain over his head and handed it and the amulet to me. I hesitated before actually touching it.

Caution had never been a bad thing for me. I took it from Quentin by the chain, and the silver disk spun slowly at the end. There were carvings on the front and back, but I couldn't make out any details. The amulet gleamed when I touched the chain. Just a reflection of the streetlamps—and the hum that I heard was just a figment of my imagination. Metal didn't make noise unless you struck it. And even if it could hum, that hum wouldn't sound smug.

"Do you hear anything?" I asked Phaelan, never taking my eyes off the amulet.

He gave me an odd look, then glanced behind us for signs of pursuit. There were none, but he knew that. "No, do you?"

"Never mind. Just my imagination."

I slipped the chain over my head, and when the amulet didn't try to burn a hole through my jerkin, I slipped it and the chain inside my shirt. The metal was warm against my skin. I told myself the heat was left over from Quentin's body. Perhaps if I kept telling myself that, I'd begin to believe it.

The front entrance to Simon Stocken's warehouse was usually guarded by at least two men. Things usually went better if they knew you. I recognized the first guard, but not the other on duty with him. Both acknowledged Quentin, and the one I didn't know opened the door for him. Stocken's guards were reliable men as long as he kept their purses full; and with business as good as it was, there was ample coin to pay for good help. Quentin went inside. We stayed outside and out of sight.

A minute or so passed. Quentin must have been halfway through the warehouse by now. Simon Stocken's office was in the far corner. I shifted my weight from one leg to the other, and adjusted my baldric on my shoulder. Then I shifted my weight back. I was suddenly uncomfortable in my own skin. I looked down at my hands. One of them actually twitched. I looked back to the warehouse. The guards were no longer by the door.

"Phaelan?"

His dark eyes were staring intently at the door. "I see it. They just went inside."

"That's not good."

"No, it's not."

That wasn't the only thing that was less than ideal. It wasn't the guards' absence that was making my skin crawl. It was something big and ugly and waiting inside that warehouse—magic, and not the good kind. Quentin was walking into trouble for the second time tonight. I knew it as sure as if it were me walking into that trap. Curious. I had a knack for sensing certain things, but big bad magical traps had never been one of them.

"Does Stocken's warehouse have a back door?" I asked.

"Of course. And two side doors and a trap door over the water." Phaelan said before dashing across the street. I was right behind him.

My cousin drew his rapier as he neared a narrow space between two stacks of crates that opened into the alley beyond. He looked through. I glanced over his shoulder, a pair of long daggers in my own hands. It was all clear to the waterfront.

"Take a right at the end of the alley," he told me. "It's the first door on the right."

"There's something waiting inside."

"Not a new shipment of Caesolian red, is it?"

"Hardly."

"One could hope."

There were no guards posted by the small side door. Things were looking up. The hinges were well oiled and opened without a sound. Even better. The warehouse's vast interior was dimly lit by lightglobes spaced at regular intervals along the walls. Only some of them were activated, throwing large sections of the warehouse into shadow. What we could see was only about a quarter full of crates, cases, and casks, which wouldn't be a sign of a healthy business in many parts of the city; but Simon Stocken based his success on the quality of the goods traded, not the quantity.

Quentin was nearing the door of Stocken's small office in the back of the warehouse. I resisted the urge to call out to him. Whatever the trap was, he had already tripped it. Getting caught with him wouldn't do any of us any good.

Quentin was completely oblivious to what he had just walked into. "Simon, I want another twenty tenari and four bottles of Caesolian red, not a drop less."

Simon Stocken didn't answer. We soon found out why.

A shadow swung across one of the lightglobes, blocking it, revealing it, and blocking it again. Along with it came a creaking sound I instantly recognized. Quentin looked up. We all did.

Simon Stocken hung from a rafter outside his office, a halter of woven hemp tight about his abnormally lengthened neck, hooked beneath the chin. His hands were tied behind his back. He was quite dead.

Quentin had his daggers half drawn when the goblins stepped from the shadows, completely surrounding him. Half of them were robed, the other half were armored—all of them were familiar.

Khrynsani shamans and temple guards.

Phaelan leaned close, his lips next to my ear. "Didn't we just leave this party?"

Some of the goblins opened lanterns and set them on crates, further illuminating Simon Stocken—something I could have done without. When they had finished, a figure robed in rich, black silk moved out of the shadows between two of the guards and into the ring of light. So much for the reason behind all my twitching and skin crawling. I still didn't understand how I had sensed it, but at least I knew why.

I also knew who the fancy robe wearer was. I'd had ample descriptions from Markus's agents.

The hood on Sarad Nukpana's robe was back and I could clearly see his face. He was only slightly taller than me, slender and compact beneath his robes. His gleaming black hair fell nearly to his waist and was held back from his face with the narrow silver circlet of his office. His features were elegant without appearing weak, beautiful without sacrificing one bit of masculinity. The reality of the goblin grand shaman didn't match the stories and nightmares I'd heard from others. But then the most beautiful serpents were the most poisonous.

There were ten Khrynsani with him that I could see, and I was certain there were more.

"Sit tight," Phaelan whispered. "I'll get some help. Tanik Ozal and his crew are two blocks over at the Rude Parrot. They live for this sort of thing."

I nodded. I agreed with him, to a point. The goblins with Sarad Nukpana were professional killers; Tanik's crew just did it for fun. There was a difference. Whether Phaelan could get back in time with Tanik and his merry band of cutthroats was one thing, whether they would be able to keep Quentin from being killed or worse was quite another.

"You took your time joining us, Master Rand," Nukpana told Quentin. His dark eyes regarded the dead broker gently swaying from the beam overhead. "Apparently the late Master Stocken tired of waiting for you."

"So you killed him," Quentin said flatly.

Nukpana smiled as if he knew the punchline to a private joke. "Master Stocken was already dancing on air when I arrived."

"To do what?"

"Inquire about a box you recently acquired from a certain nachtmagus."

Quentin didn't miss a beat. "Don't know what you're talking about."

"Considering the difficulty you had stealing it, I wouldn't think you would have forgotten so soon. My guards remember you"—Nukpana's smile vanished—"and your friends. If you need help jogging your memory, a few hours staked out on the edge of the Daith Swamp should suffice. I do have a little time at my disposal this evening. I'm certain the bog beetles would appreciate dining on something besides dead fish."

Quentin said nothing. But my mind was racing. Quentin

was terrified, but not nearly terrified enough. He had no clue who and what Sarad Nukpana was, and for once I was grateful for Quentin's ignorance. Why Nukpana wanted the amulet could wait, for now. What I needed to know was how to keep Quentin from getting himself killed in one of the many interesting ways only someone of Nukpana's ability and perversions could devise. I was feeling outnumbered. For the moment, the best thing I could do for Quentin was to sit quietly, not knock anything over, and wait. Either for Phaelan and friends to return and give me the diversion I needed to grab Quentin and run, or for an opening that had yet to present itself. It wouldn't help Quentin to get myself killed, and it wouldn't do much for me either.

Quentin remained silent.

"Tell me more about your friends," Nukpana asked in a quiet voice.

"What's in it for me? You'll kill me faster?"

The goblin smiled, a glimmer of fang peeking into view. Quentin swallowed.

Nukpana moved slowly towards him, the only sound the sibilant rustle of his robes. "I've always held the opinion that anything worth doing is worth doing correctly. From time to time, some of the gentlemen here have the challenge of extracting information. Even though I provide careful instruction to my guards, the new ones do it rather sloppily. It's unfortunate, but expected in those with little experience. Information that dies with its owner is of no use to me. Practice does make perfect."

The goblin stopped, his face mere inches from Quentin's own. "I have no doubt you will tell me all I want to know," he murmured. "Eventually. You're here to deliver the box to Master Stocken, who would in turn collect payment from his client. The client would then take possession of his new purchase. You do remember how it works in polite criminal circles, little thief?"

Nukpana was closer to where I was, but not nearly close enough for me to stick something sharp through him.

"I am that client," he said. "And I have paid Master Stocken in full." The smile vanished. "I want my property. Disarm him. Completely. Then bring me the box." He turned to leave the circle, then paused. "On second thought, if he resists, just kill him."

Four temple guards moved to act on Nukpana's orders.

Then a lot of things happened at once.

I heard a familiar whistle and thump, and one of the guards holding Quentin looked down in surprise at the crossbow bolt that had just bloomed from his chest. The goblin pitched forward to the floor, the fletching protruding from his back. At the same instant, one of the men securing Quentin's arms was propelled backwards against the warehouse wall, a bolt through his throat.

Nukpana lunged for Quentin, wrapping an arm around his neck, a curved knife at his throat. The small blade Nukpana wielded glowed sickly green with a power of its own. A pair of glowing threads snaked outwards from the tip of the blade. One curled itself around Quentin's throat; the other hovered above his heart. One word from Nukpana, and what looked like two harmless tendrils of light would instantly strike, enter Quentin's body, and end his life. I had a pair of daggers ready that would do the same for Nukpana the moment he drew breath to speak that word. I crept closer, stopping just on the edge of the light.

A strong, clear voice came from the shadows, not twenty feet away. "Don't move."

I froze. So did everyone else. The command wasn't loud. It didn't need to be. The volume was from the warehouse's cave-like interior—the authority came from another source entirely. The echo of those simple words resonated with a quiet power held in perfect check. It also doused all other magic in the room like a bucket of cold water on a candle. It looked like

Nukpana's antics had attracted a spellsinger. My night was just getting better all the time.

With the power of their voice alone —the inflection, the resonance, the charisma—a spellsinger could influence thought with a quietly hummed phrase, or control actions with simple speech or carefully crafted tune. The number of people didn't matter. One spellsinger could turn the tide of battle. Gifted spellsingers were highly prized and sought after—not to mention rare and dangerous. Judging from the way the tiny hairs on my arms were standing at attention, this one could probably do virtually anything he wanted to with his voice, and not only would his intended victim not mind in the least, they'd probably enjoy it.

Everyone froze, while Quentin was left with no choice. The voice hadn't specified who wasn't supposed to move, but one of the Khrynsani couldn't take the suspense and dove for the cover of a stack of crates. He made it, but he wasn't alive when he landed.

Nukpana shimmered with the effect of a protection spell. Its confines included Quentin. As long as Quentin was encased in that shield, he was safe from outside harm. Of course, that still left the goblin with access to Quentin, and me without.

"Have your guards drop their weapons and no one else will be harmed." The spellsinger paused on the edge of the shadows, and I could see the outline of a tall and clearly fit figure.

Shadowy figures closed in behind the goblins and appeared along the warehouse catwalks, positioning themselves to cover every goblin and every exit.

"Now." His voice was quiet, its owner a man used to absolute authority. He stepped into the lantern light.

The spellsinger was an elf in the steel gray uniform of a Conclave Guardian. I noticed appreciatively that he wore it well. He was leanly muscled, his bearing was military, and he was not happy. Large, dark eyes bored into Nukpana's. I wondered if he was as dangerous as he looked. Probably.

Conclave Guardians were based on the Isle of Mid, known

for having the largest sorcerer population on the continent. It was home to the most prestigious college for sorcery, as well as the Conclave, the governing body for all magic users in the seven kingdoms. The students were young and talented, and many were away from home for the first time. Most Conclave officials were from kingdoms where they had been big fish in little ponds. But the Isle of Mid was a big pond with bigger, carnivorous fish. Students and bureaucrats, all highly gifted, all packed together in one island city. It was a powder keg waiting to explode, and the Guardians' job was to keep anyone from striking a match.

Their sworn duty was to protect the members of the Conclave and defend Mid against any outside threat, but they spent most of their time protecting the Conclave, students and citizens, from each other. To keep the peace in a city of sorcerers took an even more talented sorcerer—and a warrior. Guardians had enough to do at home, so they only left Mid on official Conclave business—renegade mages and the like. The Seat of Twelve must want something, or someone, badly to turn Guardians loose on them. I was hoping they were just after Sarad Nukpana, but I wasn't going to hold my breath.

The elven Guardian indicated Quentin. "Release him." His words were soft, but lined with steel.

Nukpana's grip tightened and Quentin held his breath. A thin trickle of blood ran down Quentin's neck. No wonder he hated sorcerers.

"This is a Khrynsani matter and none of the Conclave's concern, elf."

The spellsinger moved farther into the light. "As a Guardian, that box and its contents are my only concern."

So much for me being able to stay out of this.

Nukpana's knife slipped deeper, and the glowing tendrils constricted. Quentin's breath came in a strangled gasp.

"Come and take him yourself." The goblin's voice promised violence; the gleam in his dark eyes welcomed it.

"Very well." There was no regret in the elf's voice, just a

calm acknowledgement of the goblin's choice. He began to whisper.

I could barely hear his voice, let alone the words, but I didn't need to hear him. Neither did Nukpana. This spellsong didn't have to be heard to work.

Neither combatant moved, but that didn't mean nothing was happening. Plenty was happening, although the only visual indication was a dimming of every lantern and lightglobe in the warehouse. While spooky, it was hardly dangerous. What was dangerous was what you couldn't see.

The power flowed beneath the Guardian's voice like a river running deep underground, its depths hidden in darkness, its deadly currents concealed beneath a calm, but swiftly moving surface. It could either sweep you away or drag you under. Either way, you'd be just as dead.

Nukpana wasn't drowning in the depths. He was busy freezing the surface.

The bottom dropped out of the temperature, and Nukpana's sibilant words came out on frosty breath. I recognized a few words of the goblin's incantation. It wasn't the words that would kill us all, it was his intent. Nukpana was calling something that had no business being on the same plane of existence with the rest of us. Why slaughter a warehouse full of Guardians yourself when you could raise a demon to do it for you? The air between the goblin and the elf crackled with blue light, the light coalescing into the outline of a figure twice the elf's height.

I'd always thought demons came from warmer climates. Looked like I was wrong.

The elf shielded himself, his own spellsong faltering momentarily in the process. And apparently demon conjuring took all of the goblin's concentration, because the glowing blade he held to Quentin's throat wavered just enough so a cut wouldn't be fatal. I didn't want to wait around to see who was going to win, and I sure as hell didn't want to stick around to see who Nukpana's demon picked first for his late-night snack.

Quentin and I needed to leave. Now. But interrupting the work of two powerful sorcerers with a spell of your own often had unfortunate consequences, aside from being just plain rude.

I opted for a more direct approach.

I tackled Sarad Nukpana from the side below the knees, where his shields were weakest. He was definitely surprised. So was the Guardian. Quentin wasn't exactly expecting it, either. As a result, the manifesting demon stopped manifesting. Nukpana and I hit the ground hard. Quentin rolled free, and I grabbed for Quentin.

Sarad Nukpana and I were face-to-face. His midnight eyes widened, and then he smiled. "Mistress Benares, how good of you to join us."

My mouth dropped open, and I was too stunned to move. The goblin reached for me, but the elf got there first, jerking me to my feet and away from Nukpana.

Close contact gave me a good look at the Guardian, and he was good to look at. His eyes were stunning. Tropical seas stunning—and lock up your daughters and wives trouble. His rich auburn hair begged to be touched, and his features were classic, strong and oh so nice. Unfortunately, he also committed my face to memory. Not so nice.

The center of my chest suddenly grew warm. It could have been my increased heart rate, but I wasn't betting on it. The Guardian's intense gaze went to my chest. I didn't think he was admiring the view. The amulet flared to life.

There was no pain or dizziness, and I didn't feel a sudden urge to be sick all over the elf. That was good, but the attention I was attracting wasn't. The Guardian's eyes widened in amazement, and he tightened his grip on me. He had my arms, so the action I was forced to take was entirely his fault. It was as direct as my previous action, but not nearly as polite.

In the next instant, the Guardian was on his knees trying to remember how to breathe.

There was a crash and the sound of wood splintering in the middle of the warehouse, following by a low rumbling. A stack of barrels, already precariously balanced, began to move. The larger of those barrels crashed into smaller casks. They began to move. Movement was not good. The Guardians and the Khrynsani shared my opinion. They all scrambled and dove for cover, including the elven spellsinger. Lanterns hit the ground, and Quentin and I ran for the door. We didn't question what or who had caused the barrels to fall; we just reaped the benefits of the distraction.

I smelled something other than spilled spirits. A dim part of my memory registered what it was—then a series of blasts lifted us both off our feet. Quentin landed unmoving against a crate. I was dazed and my hair was a little singed, but I was in one piece. Wine didn't explode, but gunpowder did. Looked like the late Master Stocken had dabbled in the arms business.

I got to my feet and staggered over to Quentin. Phaelan was already there. I should have known. Where there's an explosion, there's Phaelan. He made sure Quentin was still breathing, then unceremoniously tossed him over his shoulder.

"Sorry about that," he shouted over the din of men yelling and smaller blasts. "I didn't factor lanterns into the plan."

I could barely hear him, or myself, from the ringing in my ears. "There was a plan?" I yelled.

Phaelan grinned. "There's always a plan," he shouted back. "But I thought I'd keep it simple."

Chapter 3

"Productive evening, Raine?"

Bertran didn't really expect an answer, which was good because I didn't intend to give him one. I hadn't had dinner. Phaelan hadn't had Madame Natasha. Neither one of us were happy.

The elven intelligence agency's cross between a receptionist and a jailer sat behind a small table in the miniscule entry hall of one of Markus's safehouses. One of the perks of occasionally working for Markus was that I got the use of the agency's safehouses. I only used one if my business involved Markus's interests. I didn't have to ask myself twice whether what I wore around my neck would interest Markus. Plus, I've discovered it's not a good idea to go home when you could be leading a parade of bad guys.

This particular citadel of safety was a narrow townhouse on the less-than-fashionable side of the Elven District. The house was close enough to the waterfront for convenience, with a hidden entrance behind a sailmaker's shop for added security. I thought we'd be safe enough here for the time being. Tanik and the five crew members he had brought with him thought they'd be safer back at the tavern where Phaelan had found them. All had reasons not to be found anywhere near Simon Stocken's burning warehouse once the city watch showed up.

A stack of reports sat at Bertran's right elbow. Tonight's events certainly rated a report, but an account of what actually happened would never be included in Bertran's stack. Since I wasn't on Markus's official payroll, I wasn't required to report anything. It would be the polite thing to do, because I was using one of his safehouses, but truth be told, I wasn't feeling very polite. The amulet I wore beneath my shirt and Sarad Nukpana knowing my name made me uneasy in ways I'd never thought possible, and the fewer who knew about either, the better. For the most part, I liked Bertran, and trusted him, but only with certain things. Tonight's events didn't qualify.

Phaelan entered the house without glancing at Bertran, went straight into the back room, and with a grunt, dumped Quentin on a cot in the corner. My cousin had gone through a lot for Quentin tonight, and then had to carry him, too. And to make certain we weren't followed, we hadn't exactly taken the most direct route. I hadn't told Phaelan to be gentle. Maybe I should have mentioned it.

"Where's Markus?" I asked Bertran.

"His Grace is at a reception for the Count of Estre."

"And?"

"From there he intends to go directly home."

I reached for the pen and paper Bertran kept on his desk and started to write. I wasn't going to tell Markus everything that had happened, just the who, what, when, and where. Markus's agents made sure their boss knew everything. What had just happened at Nigel's house and Stocken's warehouse was hardly insignificant. I just had to hit the high points; Markus could fill in the blanks.

"I need you to send this message to his house," I told Bertran. "I don't need a meeting this time, just a favor."

Bertran didn't reach for the bell that would summon his assistant.

Patience had never been one of my more sterling virtues, and what little I did have had been tested to its limits this evening. I was wearing torn and blood-stained clothes. I was tired, I was sore, I was more than a little afraid, and I wasn't in the mood for any political game Bertran might be playing.

I just looked at him. "You're not moving. May I ask why?"

"His Grace requested that he not be disturbed through midday tomorrow unless it was of the utmost urgency."

I gritted my teeth against what I really wanted to say. "I can safely say what I have to tell him will more than meet his definition of urgent."

Bertran hesitated a moment more, his inner struggle apparent. He was a bureaucrat at heart, but I tried not to hold it against him. He was only using standard operating procedure, or at least trying. I never made it easy for him. Bertran hesitated a moment more, then spoke.

"Will delivery first thing in the morning be sufficient?"

That was about five hours away. What I needed from Markus could wait that long. I gave Bertran as much of a smile as I was capable of given the hour and the circumstances. Always be nice to those in a position to help you. "That would be more than sufficient, Bertran. Thank you. By the way, my friend needs a healer. Could you see if one is available?"

Bertran nodded, and rang the bell. My message to Markus and request for a healer would be relayed to Bertran's assistant. From there it would go to one of the messengers the agency employed for such purposes. Markus's messengers were good, and were paid accordingly. Some were even paid more than agents themselves.

I had some time to kill before the healer arrived, so I decided to try to get some sleep.

Unlike Phaelan, who could sleep anywhere at anytime, I

didn't have much luck with a nap. I pulled up a chair against the far wall to keep watch over Quentin and settled for trying to rest. I'd never been able to sleep in a safehouse. Go figure. I don't think it was the house; it was the events that compelled you to be there. Being in a safehouse meant you weren't safe. That certainly applied to me right now, and to a lesser extent to Quentin.

One question kept running through my mind. Why me? I knew self-pity wasn't productive, but I felt entitled to indulge myself. All I wanted to do was help a friend, and look where it got me. Then there was what I did to free Quentin. Not one of my glowing moments. But we were safe, for an hour or two, or three, if we were lucky. Both Nukpana and the Guardian knew I had the amulet. They wanted the amulet, and that meant they wanted me. I sighed and ran my hand over my face. Then there was the question I really wanted an answer to—how did Sarad Nukpana know my name?

The healer came, did her usual exceptional work, and left. Quentin had two cracked ribs, probably from being tossed into that crate. Phaelan woke up soon after the healer had gone, pulled up a chair next to mine, and used the time to clean his sword. My cousin's domestic habits would shame a pig, but he kept his weapons immaculate.

I've always found it prudent to be well out of reach when someone regained consciousness. Even if I counted that someone a friend. Especially if that friend lost consciousness in less than congenial circumstances. Considering that Quentin's last conscious thoughts included threat of torture, almost having his throat slashed, and being slammed into a crate—all my rules applied.

Quentin began to stir. This was unfortunately timed with Phaelan's use of a whetstone against a particularly stubborn knick. I didn't know how Quentin would react to awakening to the sound of a sword being sharpened, but I knew what it'd do to me.

"Phaelan?"

He never slowed or looked up. "Yes?"

"Could you stop that for a moment?"

"What?"

"Quentin's waking up. That's not exactly a soothing noise."

"What? Oh." He grinned. "You don't want to scrape Quentin off the ceiling?"

"Not really."

Quentin had stopped moving, but he hadn't opened his eyes. He was trying to keep his breathing regular, but I could see the pulse racing in his neck. Quentin had been many things, and was good at some of them, but he wasn't much of an actor. I tried to muffle a smile, and failed. Quentin was awake, but he didn't want to advertise it. I would have done the same myself. When you've lost consciousness in one place and find yourself waking up in another—usually the longer you can keep that information to yourself, the better.

"Quentin, it's us. No one is going to kill you. And I can't wait all night for you to open your eyes."

Quentin squinted in the direction of my voice. I had to admit it was a little bright in here. Maybe I shouldn't have lit so many lamps. I extinguished the one closest to the cot where Quentin lay.

He didn't need to look to know that he had been stripped to his shirt and trousers. He tried to sit up, and groaned. I put a restraining hand on his shoulder, and eased him back on the cot.

"Don't even think about it," I told him. "You had two cracked ribs, and they need another hour or so to finish setting. I'm sure the healer would appreciate it if you didn't ruin her work. Behave yourself, and you should be good as new by tomorrow night."

Quentin lay back with a ragged breath, looking a little green around the gills. "I don't feel so good."

"More than likely leftovers from Sarad Nukpana's work. Probably feels like the worst hangover you've ever had, but the dizziness should go away within the hour."

"Actually, only the second worst." His expression went from pained to puzzled. "Who's Sarad Nukpana?"

"The goblin who tried to slit your throat." I kept it simple for him. The less Quentin knew about Nukpana, the better. I admit my reasons were selfish. I was getting a splitting headache and I really didn't want to listen to Quentin scream.

He seemed satisfied with my answer. Ignorance was a state in which Quentin was content to exist. "What about the amulet?"

"Don't worry, I've still got it." I made a face. "For what it's worth."

Quentin made a face of his own. "It's not worth anything now. At least not to me."

"The goblins seem to think it's worth your life," Phaelan said, resuming his whetstone work.

Quentin's hand went to the bandage at his throat. "Don't remind me."

"They're not the only ones," I pointed out. "And none of them were in the least bit shy about being seen in uniform."

"The goblins didn't mean to leave any survivors, maybe the Guardians were thinking along the same lines," Phaelan suggested.

We all thought about that for a moment.

"How could you not know who you were working for?" I asked, leaving Sarad Nukpana's name out of it.

"In my old line of work, I almost never dealt directly with the person whose gold was paying for the job," Quentin said. "They don't want to get their hands dirty. Makes for a lucrative business for someone like Simon. Well, *made* for a lucrative business."

I pulled the silver disk out of my shirt for a closer look. It still didn't look like much. "Even for this?"

"Depends on what it does," Quentin said. "Any ideas?"

"I knew someone had set up housekeeping in Stocken's warehouse once you were inside. I knew you were in trouble."

Phaelan put away his whetstone. "You think that was the amulet's doing?"

"It wasn't anything I could do before I put the thing around my neck."

"Is it doing anything else? Besides making you sick?"

Quentin looked surprised. "It makes you sick?"

"Just when you first opened the box," I told him. "It hasn't bothered me that way since."

Phaelan slid his rapier back in its scabbard. "Regardless of what it does, or why anyone wants it, the problem is who wants it and what they're willing to do to get it. Well, cousin, what's your next step?"

Since I hadn't been able to sleep, I'd had plenty of time to think about that one. "I've sent a message to a client of mine who might be able to help," I said. "But right now, I thought I'd start by dropping in on Garadin. He's a retired Conclave mage, Conclave Guardians want this thing, so he might know something about it."

"Having a mage for a godfather is good for something, I guess," Phaelan said. "Need someone to go with you?"

I shook my head. "It's only four blocks, and I know a short-cut. I'd rather you stayed here with Quentin. You'll need to move him by midmorning."

Phaelan grinned. "I already have a plan."

"Your last plan's what put me here," Quentin growled from his cot.

Phaelan's eyes narrowed. "It got you out of Stocken's warehouse, didn't it?"

"Well, yes."

"Well, then it worked." My cousin sat back and shrugged. "Who knew Stocken had any more gunpowder?"

That was news to me. "Any more? You knew Stocken dealt in gunpowder?"

"Sure. Who didn't?"

"I didn't."

"The lanterns were unfortunate," Phaelan admitted.

I let it pass. Going down that road wouldn't do me any good.

"Did Stocken tell you anything else about the job?" I asked Quentin. "Warn you about anything—or anyone?"

Quentin smiled faintly. "Other than the usual 'Don't get caught. And if you do, don't tell them about me'? Just the information I normally need. What the client wants, where it is, and how much I'm going to be paid to get it. The rest I found out on my own. Nigel's schedule, who his servants were, where I could find them when they weren't working. Sometimes it's best not to know who you're working for."

"Or who your competition is," Phaelan added.

"Khrynsani goblins weren't on my list of possibilities," Quentin admitted.

"Don't forget about the Guardians."

"That's unlikely. I do attract interesting people."

"Quentin, people who are trying to kill you are not interesting," I said. "Speaking of Nigel's servants, which one gave you the ghencharm?"

"The what?"

"Ghencharm. That thing that let you stroll through Nigel's house without setting off his wards."

Quentin blanched. "He had wards?"

I just looked at him. When this was over, I was going to teach Quentin a thing or two or three about magic whether he liked it or not.

"Yes, he had wards. Nasty wards. Apparently they weren't there when you were. Someone did you a big favor. Any idea who? One of the servants you talked to?"

"None of Nigel's people knew a thing about me, or even suspected. Give me a little credit here, Raine. I am a professional."

Now Quentin had hurt feelings to go with his cracked ribs. Great.

"I'm not questioning your competence." Actually I was, but there was no need to say so out loud. "Someone had to know you'd be there. Why else deactivate every ward in the house?"

"If someone did know, they didn't find out from me."

Yet another question that needed an answer. If no one in Nigel's household left the magical doors standing wide open, then who did? And if Sarad Nukpana was Quentin's mystery employer, why did he feel the need to send his bully boys over to Nigel's house? Quentin was going to steal the amulet for him. All he had to do was sit back and wait for Quentin to do his job. Unless Sarad Nukpana knew he wasn't the only interested party. Was the second group of goblins more than an opposing faction? Maybe they were competition for what I was wearing around my neck.

Too many questions. Too few answers.

I knew part of why Sarad Nukpana and his Khrynsani were in Mermeia. The new goblin king, Sathrik Mal'Salin, had arrived in the city four days ago for a week of receptions culminating in a masked ball three nights from now. Nobles from surrounding kingdoms had been pouring into the city for the past week for what was being touted as the social event of the decade, and the local aristocracy was scrambling to get invitations. In my opinion, going to a party surrounded by Mal'Salins would only be fun in the way being locked in a room full of snakes would be fun.

Sarad Nukpana was King Sathrik Mal'Salin's chief counselor. From what I'd heard of Nukpana, he wasn't the party type. And judging from our little encounter in Stocken's warehouse, he had business in town other than keeping a proprietary eye on his new king. It looked like I was wearing the real reason for his visit around my neck. Small world.

I went to the corner table and poured a round of drinks. Markus saw to it that all of his safehouses were well stocked. I guess he figured that people who were in that much trouble would want alcohol. I couldn't fault his logic. I passed a brandy to both Phaelan and Quentin, and kept one for myself. I drank half of it in one gulp. I needed it even more than Quentin. He could go to ground to stay alive, but hiding wasn't an option for me. My problems were just beginning. I drained the glass.

Quentin took a good-sized gulp himself. "Did the elven Guardian manage to kill that Nukpana person?"

I winced. "He might have had other things to think about."

Phaelan chuckled softly. "Two very important things."

"Until I can find out otherwise, let's just operate under the assumption that the Nukpana person got away," I told Quentin.

Quentin was instantly alert. "Operate? I don't like the sound of that."

That made two of us.

Quentin looked around at the plain walls. "A safehouse, right?"

I nodded. Markus's idea of a safehouse looked like a cross between a barracks and a prison. My sometime client had exquisite decorating taste, but in his practicality, saw little reason to extend those talents to his safehouses.

"You said I can leave by midmorning?"

"I wouldn't be so eager if I were you," Phaelan told him. "By now those goblins probably have your name on the lips of every assassin in Mermeia. By daybreak you'll have a hefty price on your head."

Quentin wouldn't be the only one gracing a wanted poster. Phaelan didn't mention me. I was grateful. I also contemplated pouring myself another drink. Better not. I had the feeling I'd need all the quick reflexes I could get.

"I've had a price on my head before," Quentin said. "No one's managed to cash in yet. Though tonight they came close."

"Khrynsani aren't known for being a soft touch," I told him. "One Khrynsani I've heard of would throw everything he had against a human or elf just to see what would hit the far wall. The shamans on Nigel's balcony were good, but not the best they could field. And Sarad Nukpana wasn't expecting the Guardians in Stocken's warehouse. We were lucky twice tonight. It won't happen again."

Quentin succeeded in sitting up. "I've had Khrynsani try to vaporize me, feed me to the bog beetles, and slit my throat. I just want to find a nice, deep hole and crawl in for a few days until things calm down." He looked around the room. "You sure I can't stay here?"

"Sorry. If necessary, I can have the people here put you into deep hiding, but I'd rather you be where we can keep an eye on you." I turned to Phaelan. "Know where we can find a nice, deep hole on short notice?"

The smile that spread slowly across my cousin's tanned face was well known for promising bad things. If I didn't know him well, it would have made my skin crawl. I answered with a grin of my own. We're a sick family that way.

"I know just the place," he said.

"I can manage just fine on my own," Quentin protested. "I wouldn't want you two to go to any more trouble. I've been enough trouble already."

"It's no trouble at all," Phaelan assured him. "Our pleasure. You don't get seasick, do you?"

Quentin blanched. "Yes, I do. And there's no way you're getting me onboard the *Fortune*."

"Who said anything about the *Fortune*? If anyone recognized me tonight, that's the first place they'd look. No, I have another of my fine vessels in mind. And she'll be docked, so you should be able to hold down solid food after a day or so."

Phaelan's idea of a fine vessel could mean anything from a galleon to a garbage scow. But I think I knew which one he was talking about.

"The *Flatus*?" I asked, grinning wider. I liked where this was going.

My cousin nodded. "I thought it would be appropriate. Don't worry, Quentin. You'll be as safe on the *Flatus* as in your mother's arms. You don't mind the smell of dead fish, do you?"

"What's the *Flatus*?" Quentin sounded like he really could go without knowing.

Phaelan's grin kept many secrets. "She's many things. To

the harbormaster, she's a baitfisher. You know, the small fish used to bait crab pots?"

Quentin was looking pale again. "I'm familiar with them."

"She's named after the Myloran god of wind." Phaelan chuckled. "Who says I'm not cultured?"

Chapter 4

Phaelan would take care of Quentin. My job was to take care of myself. It had yet to be more than I could handle, but there was always a first time.

As an official representative of the elven crown, Markus Sevelien was more than qualified to give me the diplomatic help I might need before long, considering I was wearing the makings of an interkingdom incident around my neck. But my godfather's assistance was a lot more valuable to me right now. Markus could keep me out of trouble. Garadin could keep me alive.

The people I had annoyed tonight wouldn't go through diplomatic channels to retrieve what they all saw as their property. They would proceed straight to bolts through my back. As a former Conclave mage, Garadin might be able to tell me what I was wearing around my neck. And being a spellsinger of respectable abilities, he might be able to tell me more about the elven Guardian. I was beginning to think that both were key to my continued well-being—if not my existence.

I'd save my worries about Sarad Nukpana for the next stop on my list. One crisis at a time.

Garadin Wyne's rooms were above a parchment and ink shop on Locke Street, which ran parallel to a nameless back canal in the Sorcerers District. While he could have afforded Nigel's level of accommodations, he had the good taste and lack of pretension not to. Locke Street had everything my godfather wanted in his semiretirement: paper, ink, tobacco, a tavern that didn't water down the drinks, and neighbors who minded their own business.

A good many mages ended up in Mermeia after retirement. It was close to the Isle of Mid, but without the bureaucracy and political backbiting that Mid was notorious for. Garadin's landlord was one of the most recent to make the move. His shop did a booming business with other mage retirees. Most were scholars and needed paper and ink for recording research or for correspondence. He attracted even more business by offering bindery services for completed works.

If someone wanted to hire a mage (and had money in hand) Mermeia was the place to come, though it was buyer beware. Believe it or not, some magic users were less than honest about their abilities. I had encountered everything from complete fakes who put on a convincing show, to full-blown mages—like Garadin—who didn't want to be hired by anyone and played down their abilities to ensure they were left alone. Even if you convinced them to listen to your sales pitch, chances were you didn't have enough gold to back it up. Garadin jacked his prices up to obscene levels just so he wouldn't have to be bothered.

A narrow street between two shops on the edge of the Sorcerers District opened onto the Grand Duke's Canal—and the Goblin District on the far bank. The buildings there were stone and gleaming marble, both dark and neither encouraging to visitors. The streetlamps glowed a dim blue. The color was flattering to goblins, but it gave any other race the unhealthy skintones of a three-day-old corpse. Around the next bend in the canal was the Mal'Salin family compound, and next to that, the goblin embassy. I didn't need to see them; I knew they were there. And I certainly didn't want to get any closer to the canal. Water and I have an agreement—I don't get too close to it, and it won't drown me.

I could just make out the banner flying over the goblin embassy. I didn't need to get a good look at that, either. The House of Mal'Salin crest was a pair of entwined and battling serpents, both surmounted by a crown. They couldn't have made a better choice. Its appearance on the banner meant King Sathrik Mal'Salin was in residence—and Sarad Nukpana along with him.

I stood in the shadows, looking out over the canal, suddenly very tired. Too much had happened tonight, and I understood too little of it. I watched the reflection of the blue lamps on the rippling surface, then looked back at the Mal'Salin banner, curling and turning in the night breeze coming off the lagoon, its movement oddly soothing. I stepped out of the shadows to the water's edge, still watching. I came back to myself with a start and jumped back. What the hell was I doing?

I hurried back through the alley to Locke Street and Garadin's rooms. Garadin should be home, but if he wasn't, I'd wait and try to find something to eat. Like many bachelors, Garadin didn't stock a good larder, but I could probably scrape together enough to keep myself from starving. Potions, he could brew. Cooking was an art best left to others. My godfather accepted his lack of talent in that area, and took most of his meals out.

I wasn't quite a year old when my mother was killed. As her closest friend, Garadin took me in and found himself faced with the not so small task of raising a little girl. My mother's brother, his wife, and his family lived in Laerin. It didn't take Garadin too long to decide they were better suited for the job. Uncle Ryn was in shipping, was a respected businessman, and had done very well for himself. By the time Garadin found out that much of what Uncle Ryn called shipping was called piracy by all seven kingdoms, I was old enough to call Laerin home, and refused to budge. Uncle Ryn may be a pirate, but he ran a surprisingly moral and normal household—or at least my Aunt Dera did. It took Garadin longer to reach that same conclusion.

All things considered, I don't think I turned out half bad.

A narrow wooden stair by the parchment shop's back entrance led up to Garadin's door. I stepped over the first two stairs and onto the third. The first two creaked. Anyone Garadin didn't mind coming to visit knew that. Those that he did mind didn't know. It served as an early warning system for undesirables. I knocked and waited. No answer. Garadin was a light sleeper, so he must not be at home. I had the keys—both metal and magical—so I could let myself in. Garadin's wards surpassed anything Nigel could have ever come up with. My godfather didn't keep anything of value except his privacy, but that he held dear above all else.

Garadin had a pair of rooms—the smaller one for sleeping, the larger for everything else. Everything else consisted mainly of oddities he had collected over the years. Dried things, dead and stuffed things, things in jars, things in glass-topped cases. Then there were the books and papers. Any flat surface in Garadin's rooms was fair game. To anyone else, it looked like the place had been ransacked, but Garadin knew where everything was, and there was hell to pay if anything was moved.

The big leather chairs were overstuffed and had seen better days, but they were comfortable. To Garadin, comfort was all that mattered. I had always loved Garadin's rooms. When I had spent summers here as a child, I had never lacked for anything interesting to get into. Now all I wanted was to find something to eat and a clear place to sit down. Either was easier said than found.

After some rummaging, I found some hard cheese and a partial loaf of bread that, like the leather on the chairs, had seen better days. Nothing was growing on any of it, so I deemed it edible. Garadin didn't keep water around, but I knew where he kept the ale. It wasn't exactly a meal, but at least it was food.

A chair and footstool in a corner by the bookshelves gave me an unobstructed view of the door. I carefully moved the papers from the chair to the floor, took off my rapier and leaned it against the chair within reach. The chair creaked as I settled in. Nice to sit down, even better if no one tried to break down the door in the next five minutes.

I tore off a piece of bread and stuck it in a mug of ale to soak. While I waited for it to soften enough not to break my teeth, I took the amulet out of my shirt and looked at it again. Being a seeker gave me certain advantages when it came to finding out what an object was. What I held was a silver disk, but what it did was another matter. I knew the quickest way to find out, but the quickest way wasn't often the best or safest. The runes engraved in the silver gleamed in the firelight. It had magic; that much I was sure of. But considering who had last owned it—and who wanted it—it was probably the kind of magic I could do without. Opening my mind to Nigel's former amulet would be like sticking my arm in a hole in a swamp just to feel around. Not something sane people made a habit of doing. At least not more than once.

I considered myself sane. I dropped the amulet back inside my shirt. If no one else could tell me what it did—or if I got desperate enough—I could always go poking around later.

I ate, then located a blanket and tried to relax. Sleep would be better, but I wasn't counting on it happening. After less than a minute, I couldn't keep my eyes open.

A voice spoke my name. Softer and more soothing than a whisper, it nestled into the place between sleep and wake. I saw Garadin's room from beneath my closed lashes in half-light and shadow. For the first time tonight I felt safe. The voice slipped through the walls and windows, up through the floor and down through the ceiling, enfolding me in warmth and calming my fears. It was a low, velvety voice, a voice of intimate whispers in the secret hours of night. I made a small sound and snuggled deeper into the blanket. My heart slowed to beat in time with the wordless song. My chest grew warm.

I sat straight up, my heart pounding. I reached for the amulet. It was warm, even through my shirt. I listened. No voice, no song, only the sound of my ragged breathing—and boots on the stairs. They stopped outside the door. The doorknob turned as my blade cleared its scabbard and my feet hit the floor. I stood, but stayed in the shadows.

Someone pushed the door open, but didn't step inside. That someone was being cautious. Since Garadin taught me all there was to know about caution, I was hoping it was him at the door.

"Raine?" The voice was rich and melodious. My godfather's voice. It wasn't the voice I had just heard in my waking dream. I recognized that voice—a certain Guardian spellsinger was staying up late on account of me. I didn't think I should be flattered.

I let out the breath I didn't realize I was holding, and sheathed my blade. "I let myself in. Hope you don't mind."

"I never have before." Garadin came in and tossed his cloak over a chair. "The city's a busy place tonight. To which catastrophe do I owe this pleasure?"

"Can't I just want to visit?"

My godfather was tall and distinguished looking, his eyes intense blue, his short hair ginger, and his beard and mustache immaculately trimmed. That was where immaculate ended. His dark homespun robes swept in virtual tatters behind him. Garadin dressed for himself and comfort, and that was all.

"You could, but not at this hour," he said. "If you're out this late, the reason's usually armed and annoyed with you." He paused. "Are they?"

I chose not to answer that.

An equally tall and lanky figure came in behind Garadin, and pushed the hood of his cloak back to reveal a familiar mop of dark curls framing a boyishly handsome face that'd be turning female heads in a few years, if it wasn't already. Piaras.

Now that was unsettling. It wasn't odd that my landlady's grandson was with Garadin. Piaras Rivalin was also Garadin's student. But the young elf had just turned seventeen, and Tarsilia had set a strict midnight curfew for him. I didn't think pub-crawling with my godfather into the wee hours qualified as an approved field trip.

Piaras was a spellsinger-in-training, so puberty had been interesting at our house. I say ours because when you live in the upstairs apartment, you tend to hear and experience everything that goes on in the house anyway. As a boy, Piaras had shown signs of talent, but once adolescence set in, big feet weren't the only things tripping him up. And all hell broke loose, magically speaking, when his voice changed. Garadin stepped in at that point and promptly earned the unending gratitude of the entire neighborhood.

For me, he was just the little brother I'd always wanted.

"Speaking of someone up past their bedtime," I said. I looked from Garadin to Piaras. "Is there something I should know?"

Piaras looked to Garadin, and Garadin didn't answer immediately. He looked at the empty plate on the table. There were a few crumbs left. "Sorry I didn't have anything better to offer, though you seem to have done well enough for yourself. Considering the kind of night you must have had, I'd imagine you were hungry."

Nigel's house crawling with goblins and Simon Stocken's warehouse burning to the ground must have been public knowledge by now, but not the fact that I was involved. Or maybe Garadin just assumed I was involved. Neither assumption was good or very flattering.

"Bad news must travel fast," was all I said.

"Tarsilia sent Piaras over to the Mad Piper to tell me you might be in trouble."

I stepped a little farther into the light. Garadin and Piaras took in my blood-spattered clothes.

"I see she was right," my godfather said. "Any of that yours?"

"No. Why did she think I was in trouble?"

Piaras spoke. "Ocnus Rancil and two other goblins tried to break into your rooms. Then more goblins showed up. That's when Grandma sent me to find Garadin."

Damn.

"And considering the hour and circumstances, I didn't want to send Piaras home once he found me," Garadin added.

Piaras took off his cloak and gave me a halfhearted smile. "He and Grandma are plotting to protect me again."

"There's nothing wrong with having someone watch your back," I told him. "Phaelan was there tonight to watch mine. Who's watching Tarsilia's?" I asked Garadin.

"Parry and Alix were with me over at the Piper. They went to Tarsilia's, and I came back here with Piaras. If you had stepped in anything deep, I knew you'd come here first."

Sometimes it's nice to be predictable. I relaxed a little. Alixine Toril was my best friend, a sorceress, and one of the finest robe designers in the Sorcerers District. Parry Arne was her sometime lover, a Conclave emissary, and when it came to creative magical retaliation, he had pretty much written the book. If a fight got nasty, the big Myloran mage was good to have by your side. Tarsilia was in good hands. Ocnus and the other goblins were not.

"Going directly home didn't seem like the best idea," I told him, "though I never meant to put goblins on Tarsilia's doorstep. Were Ocnus's friends shamans or warriors?"

"Shamans," Garadin said. "Khrynsani."

Damn again.

He made himself comfortable in his favorite chair in the far corner, which oddly enough was always paper free, and lit a pipe. "And they seemed determined to get into your rooms. Apparently it was all over rather quickly. Alix just met us down the block to let us know Tarsilia had the situation well in hand by the time they arrived. Tarsilia discouraged the goblins from trying to get in your rooms, and Alix and Parry will see to it they don't feel welcome in the neighborhood. Alix said she and Parry will stay the night to make sure the shamans don't stage a repeat performance."

"What about Ocnus?" I asked.

Ocnus Rancil was a goblin sorcerer of marginal ability and maximum aggravation. He hadn't crossed my path for several weeks now. Any illegal, immoral, or just plain repugnant act committed in Mermeia usually had Ocnus's fingerprints on it somewhere. As a result, business had brought us together over the years. The results had yet to be fatal, though I had been sorely tempted on more than one occasion. I wondered if Ocnus knew about the gathering at Stocken's this evening and just hadn't managed to make the party. Considering his presence at my door this evening, that was a possibility I'd have to look into.

The smile that spread across Piaras's face reached his large, brown eyes. It was open, welcoming, and like Piaras himself, completely without guile. "Ocnus wasn't all that much trouble. Grandma let me practice on him before she sent me after Garadin."

I answered with a grin of my own. Like myself, Tarsilia believed in the importance of practice. And if Piaras had needed help, she was more than able to back him up. "What did you use?" I asked.

The tips of Piaras's pointed ears were visible through his curls. They blushed pink. "An illusion song Garadin taught me last week. I thought it'd be fun to make Ocnus think there were a pair of werehounds guarding your door."

"And?"

Piaras's smile broadened into a boyish grin. "Ocnus thought they were so real he conjured a swamp cat to lure them away. You could see through his cat, but other than that, it wasn't half-bad."

"What did you have the hounds do?"

"What comes naturally. They ate the cat. That's when Ocnus ran."

"I hate that I missed it."

Garadin nodded in satisfaction. "You just can't beat the classics."

My godfather sported a tiny smile for my benefit. I knew what it meant. The spellsong Piaras had used was one of the most advanced, and summoning realistic images of something as complex as werehounds took a level of talent that only came from years of hard work and training. Piaras could do it now. Easily. His singing voice was surprisingly deep, vibrant, filled with quiet power and impossible to ignore. He had a prodigious, natural gift. And after years of hard work and training with the right voice master, who knew what he could accomplish. The image of the Conclave Guardian instantly sprang to mind. I pushed my thoughts away from that path. That wasn't the kind of power I ever wanted to see Piaras wield.

"After Grandma sensed the goblins hiding behind Maira's bakery, she sent me after Garadin," Piaras was saying. "I wanted to stay and help, but she insisted."

"Tarsilia doesn't doubt your abilities," Garadin said, "and neither do I, but she needed to warn Raine. And Khrynsani shamans are a whole different beast than Ocnus." He looked at me, and his bright blue eyes narrowed. "Care to tell me the reason for your sudden surge in popularity?"

"I have no idea what Ocnus was doing there, but I know what the goblins were after. Have you heard what happened at Nigel Nicabar's place?"

Garadin slowly drew on his pipe, blue puffs rising toward the beamed ceiling. "We heard. Watchers coming off duty stopped at the Piper for a pint. Sounded like quite a fight."

"It was."

"You were there." He didn't ask it as a question, and I didn't take it as one.

"Phaelan and I dropped by."

A corner of his lips quirked upward. "And there stands the source of the trouble?"

"No, that would be Quentin." I hesitated before continuing. I felt more than a little uncomfortable talking about Quentin's sideline employment around Piaras. He had met Quentin, so I'm sure it wouldn't come as any great shock, but I couldn't help feeling like I was somehow tainting the innocent. "He was hired to acquire something from Nigel."

"You mean steal," Piaras said point blank.

Garadin likewise ignored my effort to tiptoe around the subject. "I take it he was successful?"

"Unfortunately, yes. Equally unfortunate is that a few people are disappointed they didn't get to it first."

I paused before continuing. I came to see Garadin to get his advice. That was going to be next to impossible with Piaras in the room. Quentin's daily struggle with morality might not be the best topic of discussion around an impressionable elven teenager, but given the proper disclaimers, it was acceptable. But Khrynsani shamans and Conclave Guardians, along with the death, dismemberment and general mayhem that had made up my evening was another matter. I didn't want Piaras hearing any of it. Knowing what had happened tonight could endanger him, not to mention I'd rather he didn't know the finer details of what I did for a living. To someone of Piaras's age and gender, my job could be perceived as glamorous. It was anything but. Though considering what had just happened a few blocks away at Tarsilia's, having Piaras wait outside while I talked to Garadin wasn't a viable option. My breath came out in a sigh.

"I don't suppose you'd be willing to stand in the corner with your fingers in your ears?" I was only half joking.

Piaras's expression spoke volumes on his feelings about that idea. "Not really."

"He's already heard most of it at the Mad Piper," Garadin said, making it clear he knew my dilemma and just wanted me to get on with it.

"No, he hasn't."

Garadin stopped midpuff. "That bad?"

"Let's just say the fewer people who know about it, the better."

Piaras was slouching against the door jam, well on his way to a good sulk. To his credit, he didn't do it often. I couldn't really blame him. I did ask him to stand in a corner. He knew I didn't mean it literally, but my meaning was clear enough. I didn't think he was old enough to hear what had happened tonight. And he wasn't. Truth be told, *I* wasn't old enough. The safest thing for Piaras was complete and blissful ignorance. If protecting Piaras meant he had to suffer the indignity of actually standing in a corner, so be it.

"I'm sorry, Piaras. But it's not safe for you to hear any more of this." Or be anywhere near me right now, my maternal instinct chimed in.

"I wouldn't tell anyone," he said.

"I know you wouldn't. I trust you. But trust isn't the issue here. Your safety is. You can't tell what you don't know."

A confused look passed over his face. "I don't understand."

I hesitated. Tact was called for here, and I didn't have any. "I'm not worried about you talking to your friends. I'm worried about those involved in this. They would want to know what was said here. If they knew you were here, they would ask you." I paused. "They wouldn't ask nicely."

The young elf's expression didn't change, but his dark eyes widened slightly. I think he got the idea.

"How long do you want me to stay in the corner?" he asked.

I smiled slightly. "Not long."

"You don't have to stand in the corner," Garadin told him. "And I can fix it so you don't have to stick your fingers in your ears." He took one last puff, then set his pipe aside. "Fingers don't work, anyway. You don't even have to face the wall, just don't try to read our lips."

"I promise."

Garadin nodded. "Good enough."

I pulled a chair over to where Garadin was sitting, and he muttered a brief shielding spell, confining our voices to that small area. It meant neither one of us could get up and move around, but I had done more than enough moving for one night. Piaras found a book and settled himself cross-legged by the fire, his profile to us. Occasionally, he would steal a quick glance. The curiosity of youth is a powerful thing.

I told Garadin the whole story, in as short a form as possible without omitting anything that might be important—which meant I told him everything. Fortunately, it didn't take as long as I thought. I had lived it once, and that was quite enough. When I'd finished, Garadin sat quietly for a few moments. He was absorbing and sorting, as I liked to think of it. I wasn't about to disturb him. He'd talk when he was ready.

"From your description, the elven Guardian and spellsinger would be Mychael Eiliesor."

I knew I'd come to the right place. "You know him?"

"I know of him. He was appointed paladin of the Guardians after I left."

I sat in stunned silence. I had just kicked the commander of the Conclave Guardians in the balls.

"What is it?" Garadin asked.

I told him.

Garadin laughed until tears were streaming down his face and he couldn't breathe. Piaras couldn't hear a thing, but the shield couldn't keep him from knowing that his teacher found something hysterical—at my expense. He grinned.

I didn't share their opinion. "It's not funny!" I said it out loud for Garadin, and towards Piaras so he could read my lips. It just made it worse.

"I'm sorry," Garadin sputtered.

I crossed my arms and sat ramrod straight against the back of the chair. "You don't sound sorry."

"I am." He snorted one last time, and wiped his eyes. "Really."

I sat up even straighter, gathering what little shreds of dignity I had left. "Well, what do you know about him?"

"Nothing bad. He was personally appointed by the Archmagus. Justinius Valerian has a knack for hiring good people, plus he's always wanted to clean house. Putting Mychael Eiliesor in as paladin sounded like a good start. He's one of the best spellsingers on Mid, and a top-notch healer. Some say the best of both."

I could have guessed the spellsinger part. "What else?"

"Paladin Eiliesor takes his job very seriously. He's honest and he doesn't play favorites." Garadin chuckled as he relit his pipe. "And don't even think about offering a bribe. Rumor has it a couple of Caesolian mages tried when he first took office. Eiliesor didn't take the offer, but he did take the mages on an extended tour of the Conclave dungeons. You thinking about setting up a meeting?"

"That's the last thing on my mind. For now I just want to find out who the good guys are. If there are any."

Garadin's expression darkened. "I can guarantee you one of them isn't named Sarad Nukpana."

"I know. I'll be seeing someone in the morning who might be able to shed some light on how Sarad Nukpana knows me."

"Nathrach?" Garadin's distaste was evident.

"Yes, I'm going to see Tam." My tone was weary in my own ears.

Garadin and I had trampled this ground before. I didn't blame him. As my godfather, Garadin felt he had certain duties. One of those duties was protecting me from inappropriate men. A couple of fond and fun memories reminded me in no uncertain terms that Tamnais Nathrach certainly qualified. But sometimes a girl likes a little inappropriate in her life. I know I do.

"Mind if I look at the amulet?" Garadin set his pipe aside, along with his animosity towards Tam. For now. Garadin picked his battles carefully with me. This was one he knew he couldn't win.

"That's what I'm here for." I reached down the front of my shirt and pulled out the chain. The silvery disk felt smooth and surprisingly cool after spending the past two hours next to my skin. I lifted the chain and the amulet over my head.

I almost didn't live to regret it.

I knew there was air in the room, but my lungs didn't believe me. Gasping didn't help. Garadin lowered me to the floor before I fell there on my own. My fist convulsed on the amulet, and pain shot up my arm as the metal bit into my palm. Garadin tried to pry my fingers open. I wanted to help him, but my body—and the amulet—had other ideas.

The air was hot, the room too small. Through half-open eyes, I saw Garadin and Piaras above me. There were others that I couldn't see. They pressed close, taking what little air remained. I couldn't see them, but I knew who they were. A Khrynsani shaman, Mychael Eiliesor, and from farther away, Sarad Nukpana. They knew who I was—and soon they would know where I was.

I felt Garadin wrench the amulet from my fingers and push the chain back over my head.

The air cleared. The presences vanished. I took a shuddering breath and tried to open my eyes more than a squint. The room was too bright. I was draped across Garadin's lap. He had one arm around my shoulders, the other clutched to his chest. He had a burn where he had grabbed the amulet. Piaras was at my side. The air was cooler now. My lungs still burned, but at least I could breathe.

Garadin was in pain. Piaras was scared. I was both.

Garadin nodded towards the shelf by his worktable. "Second shelf, fifth jar," he said between pain-clenched teeth.

Piaras hurried to comply. I decided to lie there and breathe. Not that I had any choice. My body still had a mind of its own, and I wasn't entirely convinced it belonged to me. Garadin's injury was worse, so Piaras treated him first. He applied the salve to Garadin's burn and bandaged it with a strip of linen. Then he did the same to my hand.

My godfather drew a ragged breath, and blew it out. "I don't think it likes me."

"I don't like it either, so we're all even."

Once I could sit up on my own, I held the amulet so Garadin could study it. He wasn't going to try to touch it, and I certainly wasn't about to take it off again. Piaras may not have heard the previous part of our conversation, but he saw the results. When the amulet burned him, Garadin had dropped the shield blocking our voices. Pain can make you do that. He didn't bother putting the shield up again, and I didn't bother reminding him. It'd be like shutting the stable door after the horses were gone. A little too much, a little too late.

The silver disk glittered in the firelight. To me, it looked like it was proud of itself. I swear I felt it vibrate, almost like it was purring. Glad one of us was happy. I leaned back against the side of the chair. The floor seemed relatively stable. I thought I'd stay there for a while.

"What do you think it is?" I asked Garadin.

"I don't know," he admitted without the least embarrassment. "I'd say it's quite old, and judging from the style and quality of workmanship, it is of elven make."

"Maybe that's why it likes me so much."

"Unlikely."

"One could hope."

"Objects like this don't usually ally themselves along racial lines. From its reactions to you, and the identities of those who want it, I think we can assume that it is a magical talisman of some sort."

"You think?"

"Sarcasm won't help."

"It won't hurt. And it's about all I can muster right now. I can't take it off, I don't want to keep it, but I can hardly hand it over to anybody who'd take my life to have it. And who only knows what it's doing to me."

"Do you feel different?"

"A little."

"How?"

"Twitchy, for one thing. And when Quentin was ambushed, I didn't know who had set him up, just that it was magic and it was trouble. That's a new talent for me."

"Interesting."

Everyone was entirely too fond of using that word to describe my predicament. "No, it's not interesting," I told him. "But then I'm the one the thing has grafted itself to. I just want to know what it does, and why the Khrynsani and Guardians want to get their hands on it."

"Conclave Guardians? Here?" Piaras asked, looking entirely too eager for my taste.

Great.

"Sorry. I didn't hear that," Piaras said quickly. "I didn't hear a thing." He tried getting to his feet, his long legs tangling in the process. "I'll just go stand in the corner. Better yet, I'll step outside."

"Sit," Garadin and I said in unison.

Piaras sat.

Garadin sighed. "If you hear anything you consider fascinating, just forget it immediately."

"Yes, sir."

Exhausted, I slouched back against the chair leg. "Garadin, you were once a Conclave mage. You must have some idea what that Guardian"—I shot a glance at Piaras—"who shall remain nameless, meant by 'that box and its contents are our only concern.'"

Garadin leaned back against the other side of the chair. "The Conclave has many interests, and it's been a while since I was on Mid. I still have contacts there, some I can trust. Let me ask around. In the meantime, you need to keep that trinket out of sight, and you need to be careful."

"I'm always careful."

Garadin gave me the look. You know the one.

"Whenever I can," I added.

"You're going to have to do better than that. Have you talked to your best client?"

I knew he meant Markus. No need to share that name with Piaras either.

"I sent him a note a few hours ago asking if I could use one of his safehouses as a base for the next couple of days. And after what you told me about Tarsilia's visitors, I think it's an even better idea."

Garadin shook his head, "You may want to consider arranging for more protection than that. I don't like you wandering around the city alone."

"I don't 'wander' anywhere," I told him. "I know the underbelly of this city better than anyone, and you know how I feel about someone playing shadow. I work alone."

"As long as you're wearing that, you won't be lacking for company."

"No one can sense it when I'm wearing it." I paused uncomfortably, remembering Mychael Eiliesor—and feeling his presence all too clearly in the past hour. I didn't doubt for a moment that it was his seductive lullaby Garadin and Piaras's arrival had interrupted. If he had managed to put me to sleep, then traced me here, who knows where I'd have woken up. "With the exception of my Guardian acquaintance."

I remembered another reason why I wanted to talk to Garadin. I didn't want to ask in front of Piaras, but I had no choice. "How much do you know about Gates?"

My godfather was silent before answering. "I have knowledge, but not firsthand experience, though I know some who have both." His distaste for the subject was apparent. "I don't count any of them as friends."

"I think that's how the Khrynsani got into Nigel's house tonight," I told him.

Garadin didn't say anything, but I could see his jaw tighten. Piaras had gone a shade paler, if that was possible. I didn't know how much he knew about Gates, but I was pretty sure it wasn't as much as Garadin or I knew, and I wasn't going to be the one to expand his education. This was one topic I would tiptoe around. I'm sure Garadin would agree with me.

A Gate is a tear in the fabric of reality. It's not naturally occurring. Nothing about a Gate is natural—or legal or moral. Stepping through a Gate is like stepping through a doorway, except that doorway can cover miles instead of inches. In theory, I guess any distance is possible. Gates are a convenient way to get around, if you don't mind what it takes to make one. Magic of the blackest kind, fueled by terror, torture, despair, and death—the more the merrier. It takes a twisted sorcerer to open a Gate. Luckily I hadn't had the pleasure of meeting anyone quite that sick—at least not until tonight. It sounded like something that'd be right up Sarad Nukpana's dark alley.

"I had a tracking stone on Quentin, so I saw everything he did. There were no goblins in that house before he opened that box. Quentin swears they just stepped out of thin air. I didn't want to scare him with my opinion of how that happened. He's had a bad enough night."

"Your average goblin shaman wouldn't get within a mile of an open Gate," Garadin said, "let alone create and open one."

I snorted. "I wouldn't call any of the goblins running around Nigel's place tonight average. Sarad Nukpana's certainly qualified to create and open a Gate, and considering the other goblins who took on his temple guards in Nigel's garden, Nukpana probably felt the need to be onsite to protect his investment."

Garadin raised an eyebrow. "Other goblins?"

"Expensively armored other goblins. I'm thinking they were all at Nigel's for the same reason, and I'm wearing it around my neck."

"Any theories on who they were?"

I shrugged. "Sarad Nukpana works for the new king. The new king has a brother—a brother he just recently exiled. Rumor has it little brother isn't happy with his new living arrangements and is looking to make as much trouble for big brother as possible. The prince could certainly afford to outfit his allies that well. As to why they all want what I have, I have no idea. Sibling rivalry? Revenge? Who knows?"

"You need to know."

I sat back and blew my breath out. "Tell me about it. That's one of the reasons I'm going to see Tam in the morning. He's had plenty of firsthand experience with goblin court politics."

Garadin was wearing his concerned look. I didn't know if the look was because of Tam, goblin court politics, or the mess goblin court politics had gotten me into.

He leaned forward. "I don't suppose you'd consider staying here?"

I shook my head. "Markus's safehouses are shielded well enough to resist a Gate. And if the Khrynsani do come knocking, I'll at least have enough time to get out."

"I don't like this."

"That makes two of us."

Chapter 5

Going home sounded good in theory, but so did a lot of things that ended up getting you killed.

Just because I was going home didn't mean I was staying there. Quite the opposite. I wanted anyone and everyone who might be following me to see me arrive home and then leave home—with luggage. There were things in my rooms that I needed. Once I had those things, I wouldn't be going back home until I knew I wouldn't be bringing trouble with me.

Garadin insisted on walking me and Piaras home. Normally, I would have turned down his offer. This morning I had no problem with the extra company. I had Piaras's safety to consider, and if anyone with less than honorable intentions decided to follow us, it would be nice to know that I didn't have to fight off whatever came at me and protect Piaras by myself.

I also had no problem wearing one of Garadin's old cloaks. It smelled of tobacco smoke, but it covered up the goblin blood on my clothes. For the most part, Mermeian locals are a jaded lot. But dried goblin blood tends to attract attention—especially when worn by an elf. When fresh, it's the same color as the elven variety. But as it dries it gets brighter, and unless you have a tendency to wear scarlet, there's no hiding it. I was definitely overdue for a bath. A long soak would be wonderful, but it would have to wait. I didn't have the time. Not to mention, if the Khrynsani or Guardians caught up with me, I'd rather not be in the tub when they did.

The three of us crossed the Arbor Bridge into the mainly commercial section of the Sorcerers District. The sun was just rising over the lagoon, and the streets were still hidden in shadow. Those who were up and about were either too sleepy or too intent on their own business to notice us.

I've lived in Mermeia for ten of my thirty years, and for most of that time, I've called the Sorcerers District home. Being an elf, you'd think I'd be more comfortable among my own kind, but to tell you the truth, we don't have all that much in common. I think my family might have had something to do with that. They're thieves—whether from the deck of a ship or the back of a horse, it's the same profession. Highborn elven families have galleries of ancestral portraits. Phaelan has a collection of framed wanted posters, and he's just as proud of them as if they had been rendered in oil by a fussy, overpriced court artist.

Many of the old blood made their old money much the same way as my uncle's family, but they've swept it under the nearest hand-knotted Nebian rug. My relatives flaunt it. They may be thieves, but at least they're honest about it. As a result, my family isn't exactly accepted by most members of polite elven society. But considering what I know about most polite elven society, that arrangement suits me just fine.

My stomach growled. Loudly. When the sun came up, my stomach had certain expectations. Like being fed. Those expectations hadn't been met, and my stomach was making its displeasure known. Maira's bakery was on the way home, and I saw no reason why we shouldn't stop for sugar knots. I knew Tarsilia wouldn't mind in the least if we brought some home, and it would go a long way toward improving how Garadin and I felt. Nothing like hot, deep-fried knots of sugar-dusted dough to start the morning right. Maira's it was.

Maira Takis had started out her career as a Conclave mage, but had traded it all in for the more peaceful existence of a baker. Everyone who lived on our street was grateful for her choice. The smell of Maira's sugar knots in the early dawn hours made waking up worthwhile. Maira's bakery was also popular with the city watch. Fortunately, there were no watchers in Maira's at the moment. I'd have a hard time explaining the goblin blood.

Piaras went in while Garadin and I waited outside. I smiled and waved at Maira through the window. She smiled and waved back, then her smile froze. I looked down at myself and pulled my cloak tighter. I definitely needed to change clothes. I looked back in the shop. Piaras was laughing at something Maira's assistant had said. To see him now, you'd never suspect that a few hours before, he was conjuring perfectly imaged werehounds with just the power of his voice.

"Have you or Tarsilia spoken to his parents yet?" I asked Garadin. Piaras's parents lived in Rina, but they had sent him to Mermeia to apprentice with his grandmother and to study spellsinging.

Garadin shook his head.

"Tarsilia said he's starting to get restless," I said. "I've seen it, too. You need a plan before that happens."

"I know." A tiny smile creased his lips. "I'm recommending that he study with Ronan Cayle on Mid."

I was shocked and impressed and didn't hide either. It was common knowledge that Maestro Ronan Cayle considered himself a legend who only taught future legends. It was also common knowledge that he turned out the finest spellsingers the Isle of Mid and the Conclave had to offer.

"Piaras is that good?"

Garadin's smile broadened, and there was pride in it. "He's that good."

"Maestro Cayle hasn't taken a new student in three years."

"Five," Garadin corrected.

"You've asked him?"

"I sent a messenger two weeks ago. I know Ronan from my Conclave days. My recommendation should at least get the boy an audition before classes start next term. Though I'm not worried. Once Ronan hears Piaras, he'll accept him. But I wanted to wait until I'd heard back before I wrote to his parents—or got the boy's hopes up."

An audition was more than most got. Garadin once told me that Ronan Cayle thought nothing of keeping hopeful students cooling their heels at the base of his tower for a year or more. Since most of those students had ambitions to match their egos, they tolerated the wait. I couldn't see Piaras in that kind of company. I knew talent like his didn't belong behind the counter at an apothecary shop, and I certainly couldn't see him working for a noble family singing lullabies to spoiled children, or for a pock-faced lord, singing love songs beneath some noble lady's window in his stead. Yeesh. It wasn't like I'd never see Piaras again. The Isle of Mid wasn't far, and my family had plenty of ships—some of which could still venture into Mid's harbor without inviting cannon fire.

Piaras came out of the shop carrying a bag in one hand and a half-eaten sugar knot in the other. My stomach growled in response to the sweet, buttery smell. Piaras heard and grinned crookedly.

"Me, too." He popped another knot into his mouth. "Sorry I didn't wait," he said around a mouthful. He opened the bag. "As long as we leave a couple for Grandma, I don't see why we shouldn't have some."

Garadin and I fell to without further encouragement.

Mintha Row, where Tarsilia's apothecary shop was located, was off the beaten path enough that for the most part, the only people who see me are those I trusted to see me. But this morning I wasn't going to take any chances. Like Garadin, I valued my privacy. Also like Garadin, I tended to attract undesirable elements who didn't care that I'd rather not have anyone lying in wait for me when I got home.

We slipped off Casin Street, quickly crossed a footbridge across a sluggish back canal and ducked into the alley that ran behind Mintha Row. When I'm not feeling particularly sociable, I've found this is the best way to get home. At least it lessens the opportunity for ambush. The alley was narrow and Tarsilia kept it completely clear. If you had to fight your way home, the fewer obstacles in your way, the better. What few windows looked out over the alley lacked the proper angle to get a crossbow bolt or thrown knife into a target. Perfect for a girl just wanting to get home after a long night out.

Or for your mage landlady to wait for you.

Tarsilia Rivalin stood just inside the open back door to her shop, my black and white cat Boris cradled comfortably in her arms. Boris liked Tarsilia more than he did me, but then he saw Tarsilia more, and to my knowledge, she'd never almost set him on fire. The elven mage and my cat looked at me with similar expressions in their leaf green eyes. I don't think anything I do shocks either one of them. But then it would take a lot to shock them both. Tarsilia was like a lot of people I knew in the Sorcerers District—people who had a past, and just preferred it stayed there.

Piaras gave his grandmother a light kiss on the cheek and darted past her into the shop before she could stop him. I knew I wouldn't escape questioning so easily, but then neither would he. Tarsilia would corner him later.

Tarsilia was older than Garadin. How much older, I didn't know, and I'd never seen the need to ask. I did know that I'd be happy if I aged half as well. Slender, fine boned, with barely any wrinkles visible in a still-flawless complexion, Tarsilia must have been drop-dead gorgeous in her younger days. She still turned heads of all ages. Must be a Rivalin family trait.

She took note of my blood-stained clothing. "Busy night?"

"You could say that. Piaras said you had visitors."

"I didn't have visitors," she said. "You did. No one got in, but it wasn't for lack of trying."

What my visitors had wanted wasn't in my rooms, but that didn't keep me from not wanting them there. On the rare occasion an intruder has been more persistent than my wards were powerful, nothing and no one has ever gotten past Tarsilia. She may be small, she may be old, but I wouldn't cross her.

"Are Alix and Parry still here?" Garadin asked.

"They just left," Tarsilia told him, turning to go inside. Her silvery hair swung in a practical braid down the length of her back. "Alix has to open her shop in a few hours, and since she's been on shaman watch all night, she wanted to get some rest."

Garadin and I followed her. I closed the door, latched it, and passed a hand over the lock to reactivate Tarsilia's wards. Someone who trusts you enough to have you know their wards trusts you a lot. My movement wasn't lost on her.

"Feeling a little skittish?" She took a not so delicate sniff. "I guess goblin blood does that to a person."

"And goblin shamans on your doorstep."

"Open your cloak. Let's see how bad it is."

I did as told.

"Any of that yours?" she asked.

"No."

Tarsilia dumped Boris on a nearby chair and pulled a burlap sack from under her worktable. She tossed it to me. "When you go upstairs to clean up, put any clothes you can't salvage in that. My last shipment of newtwort came in it. The stink from that will cover up anything. Tom's coming by this afternoon to pick up some things I need for him to burn. He'll dispose of it."

I just loved her. "Thank you, Tarsilia."

She shrugged off my sentiment. "Can't have you leaving evidence lying around for the next goblins who pay us a visit to find."

"Hopefully there won't be any more."

"You holding your breath on that?"

"Not really."

"Good. I'd hate to see you disappointed."

She shut the door leading into the shop. She needn't have bothered. Piaras already had a pretty good idea of what was going on.

Her green eyes leveled on me. "Now what are Khrynsani shamans doing visiting you at nearly two in the morning?"

"I have something they want."

"Is it in your rooms?"

"No."

"Do you have it on you?"

"Yes."

"Do you want to give it to them?"

"I can't."

"Then you have a problem."

I had to agree with her on that one. "Yes, I do."

"Want to tell me about it?"

I thought for a moment. The last thing I wanted to do was drag everyone I cared about into the mess I found myself in. The fewer people who were in this with me, the better. Piaras knew some of it, but not enough to get him into trouble. But what little Piaras knew, Tarsilia would soon know. A Conclave inquisitor was nothing compared to Tarsilia when she felt she ought to know something. She was relentless. On the other hand, she might be able to help. Like most mages in the District, Tarsilia had a Conclave background and had spent more than her share of time on the Isle of Mid in her younger days. She didn't talk about it much, but I know she didn't learn to fight dirty behind an apothecary's counter.

"Don't worry about me getting myself hurt," Tarsilia told me, as if reading my mind. She probably had. "I've survived a long time stepping in things I should've stayed away from. I've just made more enemies tonight. Those Khrynsani know where I live. If they want me, they know where to find me."

That statement would concern me coming from almost anyone else. But Tarsilia wasn't anyone else. If the shamans were smart, they wouldn't come back.

"And if I'm lucky, they'll give me another chance," she said with an evil little smirk.

Or if they were suicidal.

"She's just not a good tenant to have, Tarsilia," Garadin said. He grinned and draped an arm around my shoulders. "You should have evicted her long ago. Better yet, you should have never let her in to begin with." He planted a light kiss on the top of my head. I detected pride in his voice. "She's bad to know and worse to be around."

"Of course she is," my landlady retorted. "Why do you think I like the girl? When you get to be my age, you take your excitement any way you can get it. Having Raine around keeps me from getting slow." She turned back to me. "You sure you don't want to tell me what's going on?"

I sighed and pulled the amulet out of my shirt. The metal was warm and smooth beneath my fingers, almost as if it were trying to make up for its behavior last night. I dropped it against my shirt. I wasn't buying.

Tarsilia reached for the amulet. I pulled back.

"You don't want to do that," Garadin warned her.

"Why not?"

Garadin and I held up our bandaged hands.

Tarsilia lowered her own hand. "Good reason."

She settled for a close study. I turned it so she could see both sides. It behaved itself perfectly.

"Not much to look at, is it?" she finally said.

"It's not my usual taste in jewelry."

"How did you come by it?"

I gave her the short version of last evening's events. I was getting better at it with each retelling.

"If they're after this, they'll definitely be back," Tarsilia said when I'd finished.

I felt a small surge of hope. "You know what it is?"

"Not a clue."

Hopes dashed. "Thanks."

"It was obviously made to do something," she said. "It certainly isn't attractive enough to wear for any other reason. Considering the lengths those who want it are willing to go to get it, I'd say it has a more practical purpose. You're sure you can't take it off?"

"Not if I want to continue breathing. Meaning if anyone takes the amulet, they have to take me along with it. And I don't plan on going anywhere with anyone I ran into last night."

Tarsilia thought silently for a few moments. "If the Guardians are involved, it stands to reason that the Seat of Twelve is involved."

That sounded reasonable enough to me. Not good, but reasonable. The Seat of Twelve was the name given to the twelve most powerful mages who made up the governing Conclave council. Not exactly people I wanted to notice me. I looked to Garadin. He nodded in agreement. Great.

"Well, I know a man who should know what this thing is and what it does," Tarsilia said, "but it's been over twenty years since I last saw him."

"Who?" Garadin asked.

"Justinius Valerian."

My godfather looked stunned. It was a look I didn't get to see on him very often.

"You were a student of the Archmagus?" he asked, clearly impressed.

"No, we were business partners for a time. That, and I slept with him."

I didn't even try to stop my jaw from dropping. One man had absolute authority over the Isle of Mid and everyone on it. The Archmagus. And Tarsilia had slept with him.

"For about five years," Tarsilia added. "The sex part, that is. The business partnership dissolved long before that. We just couldn't seem to agree with each other."

"Sounds like you agreed with each other just fine," I said.

Tarsilia winked. "That's a different kind of agreement, dear."

Garadin recovered quicker than I did. "Think he would remember you?"

She gave him a flat look. "I can guarantee it."

That was more than I'd ever wanted to know about my landlady.

"As nice as getting information about this necklace would be," I told her as diplomatically as I could, "there's the small matter of time. I don't have any. Not to mention, the Guardians take their orders from Justinius Valerian. If he wants the amulet, he'd just have the Guardians drag me back to Mid along with it. Let's see what we can do to avoid me surrendering to the Guardians, shall we?"

Tarsilia shrugged. "Suit yourself. But until you get rid of that trinket, things are going to be busy around here."

"They're not going to be busy, because I'm not going to be here," I told her. "The Khrynsani will be watching my rooms. When I make it obvious that I'm moving out, I should take my trouble with me."

Tarsilia bristled. "You're not letting goblin shamans run you out of your home."

"It's just temporary," I assured her. "I can't have Khrynsani visits becoming a nightly event around here. I won't endanger you or Piaras. Don't worry, I'll be going somewhere safe."

Tarsilia didn't look convinced, but she decided to let it drop. I knew it wouldn't stay that way.

My rooms above Tarsilia's shop were small, which I preferred to think of as cozy. Cozy also had the added benefit of less to clean. I've never been one for clutter, so what furnishings and possessions I had were there because I either needed or simply wanted them. Less clutter also made it obvious from the moment I opened the door whether anyone had been there while I was gone. Everything I owned had a purpose and a place, and if it had been moved, I'd know about it.

Nothing had been moved.

As a Benares, I had an eye for the finer things in life, and I saw no reason why I shouldn't have a few of them. Nothing too terribly expensive, just nice. I liked warm feet, so why shouldn't I keep them toasty on a Nebian rug or two? I bought one; Phaelan gave me the other. I knew where mine had come from; I couldn't say the same for Phaelan's gift. As to furniture, I had a preference for warm-colored fabrics and dark wood. And on one occasion, Markus Sevelien had paid me with a particularly beautiful painting I had often admired in his office. It was of a fog-shrouded landscape with the ruins of a temple. Not the most cheerful subject, but I liked it.

These rooms were my home. I was being forced to leave, and that made me angry. Now all I wanted was someone to take it out on.

Tarsilia had come upstairs with me, my self-appointed bodyguard for the morning. Piaras was downstairs opening the shop. Garadin had left once I promised him that I would get myself to one of Markus's safehouses. It wasn't a lie. At some point during the day I was sure I'd find my way to a safehouse. I needed answers, and answers were difficult to come by when you were hiding. By no stretch of the imagination was I that good a sorceress even on my best day, strange amulet or not.

Boris darted around my legs and ran straight for his basket by the fireplace, no doubt to make sure his favorite toys were still there. Satisfied, he began kneading the old blanket I used to line his basket. At least one of us was going to get some sleep.

"Could you keep Boris with you for a few days?" I asked Tarsilia. "I don't want him here in case someone gets really serious about breaking in."

My landlady shrugged. "He stays with me most days anyway. Are you going to put a seal on the doors and windows when you leave?"

I hadn't thought of that. As much as I disliked the thought of anyone in my rooms, using a sealing spell would just make any potential intruder think there was something inside worth taking—like the amulet hanging quietly around my neck.

"I don't think so. No one will actually expect me to be staying here. If I'm not here, no one else should come sneaking around. Unless it's Ocnus, then you can just sic Piaras on him."

"You know how to spoil an old woman's fun, don't you?"

I went into the bedroom to change clothes and gather what I would need over the next few days. Nothing appeared to have been moved in here, either. I looked over at my dressing table. My one and only mirror was where I had left it—face down. When it came to getting from one place to another, Gates weren't the only alternative to the front door. Mirrors would work in a pinch, and some sorcerers made a specialty out of spelling things through them. The one mirror I had was small and wasn't on my wall. I'd seen firsthand the kind of nastiness that could make its entrance through a big wall mirror.

I took off the blood-stained clothes as carefully as I could. The leather jerkin was a total loss. The shirt could be washed, but I wasn't going to be here to do it, so the shirt would have to go, too. Everything else was salvageable. As much as I would have liked to, I didn't think sending a bill to the goblin embassy to replace my favorite jerkin would be a good idea. From what Tarsilia had just told me, I was sure I'd get other chances to collect.

I chose a blue shirt and my favorite brown leather doublet. It was my favorite because it had steel links woven between the outer leather and inner lining. It wasn't light by a long shot, but those steel rings had saved my bacon on more than one occasion. The doublet also had leather sleeves, better for hiding what I wasn't leaving my rooms without—a pair of slender daggers in forearm sheaths. They were also some of my favorites, for the same reasons. I topped it all with a pair of short swords strapped to my back. They fit nicely under a cloak, and wielded nicely in tight spaces. I now felt armed enough to set foot outside my front door.

"How close of a look did you get at the shamans?" I called to Tarsilia through the partially closed bedroom door.

"As close as I needed to. Those two were fresh from under a rock. Alix, Parry, and I took turns standing watch. He's nice to have around the house when undesirables come to call."

I found two clean shirts and put those in my pack along with my other things. "Did he go home with Alix?"

"Of course. But he told me he was just going to walk her home." She chuckled. "He can put on the airs, but he's no gentleman."

I smiled and buckled the leather strap on my pack. "I think that's what Alix likes about him."

I came out of my bedroom and tossed the burlap sack with my ruined clothes next to the door. I flopped into a chair. Boris decided I was now acceptable for physical contact, and after a tentative sniff, rubbed his head against my hand, demanding to be scratched. I obeyed.

"A lovely couple," Tarsilia concluded.

I knew she wasn't talking about me and the cat. To her credit, she didn't say anything else, or toss any meaningful glances my way. In this instance, even I could read her mind. But regardless of what Tarsilia wanted for me, it didn't change my reality. The men I attracted didn't have rooms or homes. They had lairs. Or lived in an island fortress and gave guided tours of the dungeons for fun.

I had a spotty history as far as the opposite sex was concerned. Any and all of my prior relationships had been at the mercy of my family, or more accurately, at the mercy of my family name. There was no middle ground. Men either ran for the hills when they heard who my family was, or they were just using me to get in with my uncle. Sissies or scoundrels—that was all I'd gotten in the past, and I didn't want either one. I grinned at a couple of particularly pleasant memories. A couple of those scoundrels hadn't been half bad at first.

Tarsilia had brought the sugar knots upstairs with us. She popped one in her mouth. She could do that all day and never gain an ounce. The thought of food made me remember something. I grumbled under my breath.

"What is it?" Tarsilia asked.

"I'm supposed to meet Alix for lunch today."

"You're afraid she won't remember?"

"No, I'm afraid she will. Considering what's happened, she'd be better off not showing up. I don't want to attract more attention to myself than I have to. Having lunch with Alix might not be the smartest thing for me to do right now."

"You don't want to sit in an outside café at midday?" She finished off another knot and wiped her fingers on her work apron. "Where's your sense of adventure?"

"Replaced by survival instinct. Though a public place might be safe. Generally sorcerers don't blow each other away at high noon in a public square." I stopped. "I just described a duel, didn't I?"

"Yes, you did." Tarsilia grinned. "Mind if I join you two? Sounds like fun."

Dueling is forbidden in the city, but that doesn't stop sorcerers from doing it. And a watcher's meager salary doesn't exactly inspire local law enforcement to get between two sorcerers bent on obliterating each other. The chronic offenders are usually mediocre talents fighting over a choice client—or looking to enhance their reputations. Charlatans don't have the talent to survive a duel, and a mage doesn't want to be bothered with such childish pastimes. Of course there are exceptions. Then there are the suicidal types—mediocre talents who try to goad a mage into a duel. I guess they think it looks good for them to have fought and defeated a mage. What few of them fail to remember is that duels have winners and losers. Losers tend to be dead. That memory lapse is the reason why there always seem to be rooms available for rent in the Sorcerers District.

"Don't worry, I'll let Alix know you can't make it," Tarsilia was saying. Her little face grew solemn. "If you promise me you'll be careful."

I gave her an impulsive hug. "I promise." I draped a hooded cloak over my shoulders, followed by my pack. I didn't raise the hood. I wanted to be seen leaving. Later I'd see what I could do about a little vanishing act. "And if careful doesn't work, maybe I'll just be lucky. Luck has to start speaking to me again sometime."

Chapter 6

You know it's going to be a bad day when you can't get privacy inside your own head.

I knew it'd only be a matter of time until someone came looking for me. When that time came, I had hoped that someone would trail me at a discreet distance. Aside from being invasive and rude, mind touching was just icky. Not to mention having somebody popping into your head starts to wear on you after a while. It makes you wonder which thoughts are yours and which ones have been planted and fertilized by someone else. After last night, my own imagination was doing a fine job of shoveling fertilizer all by its lonesome. It didn't need any help.

Since it wasn't an actual speaking voice, I couldn't put a name to it. But the slimy trail it left behind left no doubt that it was a Khrynsani shaman. A certain elven Guardian had already put in an appearance, so why should the goblins be left out?

Ignoring it wouldn't make it go away. As uncomfortable and disgusting as it felt, I let whoever-it-was putter around for a little while. Too long and he would see everything I saw—and know precisely where I was. He wasn't going to be there that long. But the longer he was there, the easier it would be for me to slam my mind's door on his figurative fingers. I was overdue for some fun.

I ducked down a side street and stopped. It was early, so it was empty. I'd never been able to dispel a mind intruder and walk at the same time. Not coordinated enough, I guess. I stilled my thoughts and waited. My visitor was impatient, so I didn't have to wait long. My action was rewarded by a pained shriek from the other side.

Visitor gone. Problem solved. For now. I knew he'd be back, and he'd probably bring a friend or two with him—or his boss. Sarad Nukpana must have either been a late sleeper or busy getting in a little prebreakfast torture. Before he had some time to spare for me, I was going to do everything I could to make sure my mind wasn't such an interesting destination, or myself such an irresistible target.

One big way to do that would be to take off the amulet. Not recommended under normal circumstances, but I had been thinking. If I had the white stone box the amulet came in, half of my problem might solve itself. Quentin had dropped the box when the Khrynsani shamans came through the Gate. Through my link with Quentin, I had seen that there were runes carved into the surface—runes that were probably containment spells. If I could find that box, I might be able to take the amulet off. I'd worry later about what to do with an amulet-in-a-box. One problem at a time.

First stop, Nigel's house. I'd done work for the city watch, and counted several officers as friends. I didn't think it'd be all that difficult to talk my way into the house. Finding the box and having my idea work was another thing, not to mention a slim hope, but at this point I'd take what I could get. At the very least, it put a spring in my step for the rest of the way to Nigel's house.

I took a shortcut through Brightleaf, the Elven District's

oldest and most elegant section. Trouble rarely came to Brightleaf, and on the rare occasions when it did, it had the decency to use the back door. The old blood disliked disruptions to their well-ordered lives, and maintained bodyguards to ensure it didn't taint their doorsteps. High-walled gardens further insulated them from the baser elements. If they couldn't make trouble go away, they at least went to great lengths to pretend it didn't exist.

Just because I didn't care to be around most elven aristocrats, didn't mean I couldn't appreciate their taste. Mermeia was built on a marsh, but a stroll through Brightleaf convinced you otherwise. It was amazing what a lot of money and a little magic could do. Aristocratic elves had a thing for trees, and the more the merrier. Since this section of Mermeia didn't have enough for them, the elves had planted additional trees. Now Brightleaf looked like a woodland park in the middle of the city. The flowers of the kembaugh tree attracted fireflies, and I had to admit it made for a pretty sight at night with all the twinkling lights. All in all, a nice way to live if you could afford it.

As I walked along the cobbled and tree-lined avenue that ran next to the Old Earl's Canal, I caught an occasional glimpse of shaded courtyards through ornate—and securely locked— gates. Mermeia's canals rose and fell with the tide, and the smell along with it. Not in Brightleaf. An elaborate system of filters had been installed at the entrance to every canal where it entered Brightleaf. The water was always pristinely clean, and smelled the same way.

A lone boatman leisurely poled his way down the canal. He sang as he went, a simple tune I had heard boatmen sing on canals all over the city. His voice was pleasant enough, but not really all that memorable. That was what I heard. What I felt flowing quietly under his song was something else entirely. Paladin Mychael Eiliesor was up early. I wasn't the only one with a morning mind visitor, but the boatman seemed oblivious. Unlike the Khrynsani shaman, Eiliesor didn't invite himself into my head, and using the boatman's voice wasn't all that invasive either. As far as doing something like that went, it was actually quite polite. It was also sneaky. The Guardian wasn't inside *my* head, so I couldn't do a thing to get rid of him. Eiliesor could follow me anywhere in the city using the same trick with any susceptible passerby.

I didn't feel like being followed. Time for a little sneakiness of my own. I felt bad about involving the boatman, but I'd feel worse if Eiliesor tracked me long enough to locate me physically. I didn't know if I could break Eiliesor's contact with the boatman, but I could sure give him something else to think about. I could move small objects with my mind, and a gondola pole was a small object. I concentrated, yanked, and the boatman took a swim. When the baffled boatman managed to heave himself back into his gondola, his sputtering sounded a lot like a certain Guardian commander.

I grinned and darted around the corner and out of sight. Mission accomplished.

Nigel's townhouse must be crawling with city watch by now. Considering who and what Nigel was, Janek Tawl would probably be in charge of the investigation. And the hands-on type that he was, Janek would be overseeing things himself. If that was the case, I should be able to talk my way into the house for a little investigating of my own.

After that, I'd put myself out of circulation for a few hours at one of Markus's safehouses. The peace and quiet would be welcome. A nap, a bath, and a decent meal wouldn't hurt, either.

I ducked out of sight once I crossed the canal at Wormall Mews. This part of the Sorcerers District was a rabbit's warren of twisting streets and alleys that no one was going to follow me through—at least no one using feet. And if someone did pick up my trail, it was broad daylight, I was armed in more ways than one, and if my follower wanted a fight, I was more than willing.

The bridge across the canal to Pasquine Street was busier than usual for that time of day. Hardly surprising considering what had happened there last night. I stepped to the railing to allow a cart to pass, and a flash of red caught my eye. Pasquine Street had the dubious distinction of being the closest point in the Sorcerers District to the goblin embassy. The Khrynsani banner had joined the royal standard already flying over the compound. I guess after last night, there wasn't much use in Sarad Nukpana denying that he and his boys were in town. The amulet thrummed under my shirt.

"Oh, shut up," I muttered.

Wormall Mews was thick with small businesses popular with nonsorcerers. Fortune-tellers, alchemists, astrologers, and the like did a healthy business parting the local Mermeian population from their coin. Most of the proprietors were only marginally talented, but a convincing performance went a long way toward building a successful business.

I walked the two blocks down Pasquine, keeping to the side of the street opposite Nigel's house. I spotted Janek talking to someone who looked like he might be one of Nigel's wealthy merchant neighbors. Janek saw me about the same time.

Chief Watcher Janek Tawl was human, Brenirian by birth, and a watcher by natural talent. People trusted Janek, even people who weren't particularly trustworthy themselves. His knack for getting results had put him on the fast track to second in command of the watch in the Sorcerers District. That was as far as he wanted to go. Janek liked being on the streets with the people. He looked like a watcher. It wasn't just that he was built like a soldier, all ropy muscle—it was an attitude. An attitude that said "Don't even think about trying that in my District."

Janek had helped me in the past, and I had given him more than a few leads. He was probably hoping for one or two more this morning, but I didn't see myself being helpful, at least not yet. Janek could toss me in jail for where I had been last night, what I had done, what I was wearing around my neck, and how it had gotten there.

I crossed the street. One of the watchers charged with keeping the curious away moved to head me off. I pushed back my hood just enough for him to see my face, and he waved me through. Sometimes it's nice to be recognized.

More than a few seekers found their way onto the city watch. Logical enough, I guess, since things and people manage to get themselves lost on a daily basis. The money seekers made on the watch wasn't good, but it was steady. I'd admit to being tempted from time to time, but never any more than that. I've always had problems with orders—especially the taking and following part.

From what I could overhear, Nigel's neighbor didn't realize what had happened until this morning. Janek took a few notes, thanked the man for his time, and strolled over to me, shaking his head in amazement.

"Goblins demolish the bedroom, break most of the windows on the back of the house, and have a full-scale battle in the garden, and Master Owen doesn't hear a thing."

It was my turn to be amazed. "He was home?"

"Yes. He said he slept through the whole thing."

"You believe him?"

"No one could sleep through that. Though from what we found in the garden and canal out back, part of me can't blame him for wanting to turn a blind eye."

"That bad?"

Janek tucked a small notebook into his belt. "Pretty grim. No one liked Nigel, but more than a few powerful people are suddenly interested in his well-being now that he's missing."

"Nigel's missing?" That was news.

The watcher nodded. "And when powerful people are interested, the commissioner's interested. Which means I'm supposed to find Nigel, and fast."

"Easier said than done this week."

"Yeah, he picked a hell of a time to make himself vanish,"

Janek said. "The city's crawling with foreign nobles, so it's not like we don't already have our hands full. Everyone's working overtime, and the local criminals are the only ones who don't mind." He chuckled. "To add insult to injury, they're making more money at it than we are. First time to the big city for a lot of the nobles, and they don't have the sense to keep their purses and jewels to themselves. Our locals just can't resist that much temptation."

I could attest to the craziness. Alix had been run ragged for the past month with costume fittings for Mermeian social climbers invited to the goblin king's masked ball. Costumes weren't her normal business, but most of the better robe designers had expanded their services to meet the sudden demand. It was the only chance some would get to rub elbows with goblin royalty, and they weren't about to miss the opportunity. It was the aura of danger even more than the prestige that drew many of them to the ball, but they'd be better off— and a lot safer—if they just stayed at home.

"Where was Nigel last night?" I asked.

"He was scheduled to do a séance for the Marquis of Timur. The marquis' gondola arrived at Nigel's dock at nine bells last night. Nigel got in, the gondola pulled away. Neither he, the boatman, nor the gondola have been seen since."

"What did the marquis have to say?"

"All he could do is complain that he was missing his best gondola and boatman. I think he was more upset by losing the gondola."

"Kidnapping?"

"That's my guess. I've got men out looking for Nigel, the boatman, and the gondola, but so far we've come up empty on all counts. When I got here this morning, I found my men busier keeping people out than gathering evidence."

"The curiosity factor's bound to be high," I said.

A grin spread across Janek's unshaven face. "I wouldn't call these people curious. Desperate is more like it. Riggs said they were doing a pathetic job of covering it up. A couple of them turned out to be servants of some rather highborn ladies—and a few highborn gentlemen. If Riggs was the bribe-taking type, he could have earned his retirement this morning."

I remembered the viewing screen concealed in Nigel's bedroom wall. I was willing to bet Janek's men were going to find all sorts of interesting evidence, and most of it probably wouldn't have a thing to do with last night. Good for me. Bad for the local aristocracy.

"You heard what happened?" Janek asked.

"Everyone's heard."

I didn't give anything away with that. One good thing about lack of sleep, you only had one expression—tired. Janek was wearing the same one.

"Nigel's not too popular with the locals, goblins included," the watcher continued. "There are probably more than a few people waiting to help him into permanent retirement."

"You think the goblins expected Nigel to be at home?"

Janek shook his head. "I'd say the break-in was for robbery, but with Nigel missing, there's no way to find out for sure just what was stolen, if anything. One hell of a fight is about the only thing we can say for sure happened."

He'd get no argument from me on that one.

"That and a Gate ripped into Nigel's upstairs front hall. Messy one, too. Rush job, and they didn't stay around to clean up the residuals."

I knew it. "Any idea who made it?"

"The Khrynsani are in town, so they're definitely suspect. But they're not the only ones in Mermeia capable of creating a Gate."

"Any mages or sorcerers missing lately?" I asked. "Besides Nigel?"

Janek knew where I was going with that. The person killed to fuel a Gate's creation didn't have to be magically talented, but it made for a stronger and more stable Gate if they were. If Sarad Nukpana had gotten his hands on a magic user, punch-ing a hole into Nigel's townhouse would have been a lot easier. The pickings were plentiful in Mermeia. Retired Conclave mages, sorcerers, seekers, healers, mediums, exorcists, conjurors—the list went on and on, from truly gifted individuals making an honest living, to the mediocre only looking to part the gullible from their coin. In Mermeia, there were ample customers for both—and both offered ample victims if a goblin grand shaman was out gathering Gate fuel.

Janek's expression darkened. "Nigel's the sixth to vanish this week."

I blinked. "The sixth?"

"A medium vanished two days ago and a healer was reported missing just this morning. The other three were street magicians, simple folk the watch know." Janek's jaw clenched. "Regardless of who they are and what they do, they're my people, my responsibility, and all the paper pushers downtown care about is making a good impression on the dignitaries in town for the week. I get pressured to solve the cases, and do it quick, but stay quiet while I do it."

Anything could have happened to any of them, but this week Sarad Nukpana had come to town.

In addition to being one of Mermeia's best watchers, Janek Tawl was a respectable, and respected, sorcerer. It was one of the reasons he worked in the District. Crimes involving sorcerers were best investigated by someone with more than a passing knowledge of magic, and compassion for its practitioners. Janek had both.

I looked around at the onlookers swarming around Nigel's townhouse. Give it another hour and it'd be a full-fledged circus. "Good luck."

"We'll need it."

"Any chance you'll be able to trace the Gate back to its source?"

"Possibly. It wasn't that messy of a job. But anyone talented enough to open a Gate would have enough talent to clean up after himself better than that—or so you'd think."

Unless he were annoyed or injured—or just didn't care.

"The goblins who ripped the Gate must have taken their casualties back with them," Janek said. "There's too much blood for the number of bodies we've found. Apparently they tore a Gate right into the house to get in and left the same way."

"That took a lot of effort," I said.

"Blew every house ward Nigel had right to hell."

So much for why Quentin hadn't set off any alarms.

"Once all hell broke loose, I'd imagine neatness didn't count for much," I said.

"True." Janek agreed. "Where were you last night? You've never struck me as the curious onlooker type."

It was a casual question, but Janek never did or said anything casually. I let an easy smile spread across my face. It's a talent I've developed over the years. "You suspect me of being in Nigel's garden with a small army of goblins?"

He shrugged. "You know a lot of goblins. If there was trouble, and if you weren't in it, you'd at least know about it." His green eyes narrowed slightly. "But, if you knew something you could tell me, you would."

Over the years we'd known each other, we had on more than one occasion known something about what the other was investigating. And on more than one occasion, we couldn't immediately share that information. Once circumstances untangled themselves, we shared what we knew. My circumstances were about as tangled as they could get. Janek's weren't much better with the watch commissioner breathing down his neck.

"If I find out something myself, I'll share it if I can," I promised.

It wasn't a lie, because I didn't know anything that would help Janek with his investigation of Nigel's disappearance.

"Any chance I could see the bedroom and hall where the Gate was opened?"

Janek shrugged. "I don't see any reason why not. You might find something we missed."

That's what I was hoping for. Something along the lines of a small, white box.

•   •   •

Janek wasn't joking when he said the bedroom was destroyed. Raised on the streets of Mermeia, Quentin knew how to fight and fight dirty. When cornered, the dirtiness escalated tenfold. That he was surprised by several Khrynsani shamans only made matters worse. After Quentin left the room through the nearest window, the Khrynsani and their underlings had conducted their own search. Judging from the destruction, they had to be quick about it, and they weren't happy with what they didn't find. Janek was lucky he had a room left to investigate. But he didn't know what he was looking for. I did.

The floor was covered with broken bits and pieces of what were once Nigel's personal possessions. I gave a low, impressed whistle for Janek's benefit, then scanned the floor between the bed and shattered windows for the white stone box.

Nothing. I tried not to make my disappointment too obvious. Fortunately, Janek was talking to a young watcher posted by the door and didn't notice. The compartment concealed in the headboard was open, the contents strewn across the bed.

No white stone box.

The bed had been moved at an angle and searched. It was massive, so I knew Quentin hadn't moved it, and that left only the Khrynsani and their temple guards. They knew that Quentin had taken the amulet, so the object of their search could only be one other thing. The same thing I was looking for. And from the absence of that thing anywhere in the room, I'd say they found it. Damn.

A gleam of blue metal caught my eye next to the bed. I walked over and knelt next to it, but was careful not to touch it. Things were looking up. Maybe I could tell Janek who his culprits were without incriminating myself.

"What did you find?" Janek asked.

"Your house wreckers left a calling card," I told him.

Janek knelt next to me. "It's a medallion. Nigel has a lot of those."

"Not one like this."

"Like what?"

"This is goblin."

He started to reach for it.

"Khrynsani," I said.

Janek's hand stopped midreach. My friend didn't get to where he was by being stupid.

"You're sure?"

I could feel the malice oozing from it—and so could the amulet around my neck. I was also treated to some sibilant goblin chanting. I could hear it. Janek couldn't. I knew goblin. I knew what they were saying, and it wasn't anything I wanted to hear. That particular piece of jewelry had been worn by a very bad goblin while he did some very bad things. And recently. My guess was Sarad Nukpana's Gatekeeper. Or Nukpana himself. The chain was broken—maybe Quentin had helped him remove it.

"Unfortunately positive," I said.

"Someone was careless."

Janek turned to the watcher who remained steadfastly by the door. For the most part, Janek's people were either sorcerers themselves or sensitives, those who were acutely aware of the presence of sorcery, but without talent themselves. From his clear desire to be elsewhere, I'd guess the young human was the latter. I didn't blame him in the least. Khrynsani magical leftovers gave me the creeps, too.

"Willem, go downstairs and have Riggs bring up a containment box." As the young man left, Janek lowered his voice so only I could hear. "So, you think I should pay a visit to the goblin embassy this afternoon?"

His words said one thing. His tone said something else entirely. Janek wasn't asking my professional opinion. He was asking my opinion based on what I had seen when I was here last night, or my close association to whoever had. I glanced at him. He was wearing his best fess-up look.

"You wouldn't happen to have an opinion on why the

Khrynsani would bother to rip a Gate into this house, would you?" he asked.

I indicated the wreck of a bedroom. "They seemed to be looking for something."

"Know what it was?"

"I have no idea what the thing was, or why they want it." That definitely wasn't a lie. Other than an amulet, I didn't know what it was, what it did, or why they wanted it. But finding out had become my new life's goal.

Janek took a small sealed envelope out of his cloak's inner pocket. "Considering who sent this, I thought you might."

I took the envelope from him. There was no return address and the seal had the outline of a dove in the center. That told me who it was from. Markus Sevelien. No one who knew Markus would ever equate him with a dove. Maybe that's why he used it; maybe it was just his twisted sense of humor. My vote was for the latter.

"That red-headed messenger of Markus's brought it," Janek said. "Wonder how he knew to bring it here?"

I cringed inwardly and broke the seal and opened the envelope. "You know Markus is good."

"Yeah, he's good. So good he knew where you were going even before you got here."

From what I'd told him in the note I'd sent from the safehouse, Markus had to have known I'd come back to Nigel's. I'd be willing to bet an identical note had been delivered to the senior-ranking watcher working the crime scene at Stocken's warehouse. Markus liked to be thorough.

I tried to ignore the scowl that had taken up residence on Janek's face and scanned the note. After a quick read, my face must have been a perfect match for his.

Those few words scratched on parchment made me officially homeless. There were no safehouses available as of this morning. They were all being used by elven diplomats and their retinues arriving in town for the goblin king's masked ball. No doubt Phaelan and Quentin had been asked to leave if they hadn't already cleared out. For his sake, I hoped Bertran had asked Phaelan nicely. I sighed. The pack that hung over my shoulder was small, but it had suddenly gotten a whole lot heavier.

Janek drew breath for the question I knew was coming. Just then we heard someone running up the stairs. It was Riggs.

"Sir, come quick. They've found a body in the canal."

I blew out my breath. Saved by the corpse.

The corpse in question was Nigel Nicabar.

The watchers had collected the bodies found in Nigel's house, garden, and canal, and put them in the greenhouse located at the back of the garden. The necromancer's talents weren't with living things, so the greenhouse's tables were pretty much empty—at least of plants. Dead goblins lay under sheets and tarps. I couldn't help but feel that Nigel would have approved. What he wouldn't have approved of was being included among them. Nigel wouldn't have been caught dead surrounded by goblins, yet that's exactly how and where he was. I don't think he would have appreciated the irony.

Apparently the watch had run out of things to cover bodies with. From what I saw in that greenhouse, our fight with the temple guards was a lovers' spat compared to what the goblins had done to each other after we left. Part of me wanted to run out of there screaming, but the other part couldn't help but notice that while elves turn light gray after death, like living goblins; dead goblins turn pale, like living elves. Interesting. Also interesting was that all of the bodies wore Mal'Salin house badges on their armor, a detail I couldn't see last night. That confirmed that I'd stepped in the middle of a bad case of sibling rivalry.

"They're all Mal'Salin." I tried to sound surprised. Act ignorant, get information. It'd worked for me before.

"Yep," Janek said.

"I know the Mal'Salins aren't exactly one big, happy family, but isn't this a bit excessive?"

He ran his hand over his eyes. "Yep."

The weariness evident in that one little word told me that something else had just been dumped on Janek's already overflowing plate.

"Care to elaborate on that 'yep'?" I asked.

"Rumor has it the king's little brother is in town."

Crap. Sometimes I hated it when I was right. So much for it being just the prince's allies acting on his behalf. Looked like Prince Chigaru had decided to make a personal appearance. The goblins have a saying about their royal family: blood is thicker than water, and Mal'Salins aren't shy about drowning each other in either.

"You think half of the dearly departed belong to the prince?" I asked.

"That's my theory. Like I need an assassination attempt this week. Though if Prince Chigaru is in town to take down his big brother, at least he'll probably do it in the Goblin District." Janek flashed a grim smile. "Not my jurisdiction. Unfortunately their guards brought their feud across the canal into Nigel's garden, which is my jurisdiction."

When Sathrik Mal'Salin took the goblin throne after his mother's death, one of the first things he did was clean house. That cleaning involved exiling anyone and everyone who could possibly pose a danger to his rule. His younger brother Prince Chigaru Mal'Salin was at the top of the list. The prince hadn't been pleased to be swept out with the trash.

Janek pulled back the tarp covering the necromancer and we both blew out our breath at the stench. I looked over his shoulder at the corpse and was glad I hadn't eaten a big breakfast. Nigel hadn't been much to look at on his best days, and soaking in a canal hadn't helped him any.

"That's Nigel, all right," I said, trying in vain to breathe through my mouth.

Janek put on a pair of healer's examination gloves. He peeled back what remained of Nigel's collar to look at the throat. "Who found him?" he asked Riggs.

"A silk merchant by the name of Eleazar Adlai," the watcher replied. "Apparently Nigel bobbed to the surface about an hour ago."

That earned Riggs a sharp look from his superior. "Why wasn't I notified before now?"

Riggs tried not to grin and failed. "It took the merchant that long to recover from the sight of Nigel popping up next to his dock, sir. We just found out ourselves. Master Adlai had just arrived to open his shop and was tying off his boat. He was still screaming when we got there." The grin grew. "I didn't know a man could scream like that. He's heavily sedated in his shop at the moment. I could question him later if you'd like."

"Were there other witnesses?"

Riggs nodded. "And they all corroborate his story."

"Then I think we can leave Master Adlai alone," Janek said, still intent on the dead man's throat. "Raine, what do you make of this?"

I bent to look where Janek indicated. "It looks like he was strangled, but the windpipe wasn't crushed. But then it also looks like a severe burn."

"Does that mean what I think it does?" Janek asked.

"If you're thinking that Nigel was killed by another sorcerer, then yes, that's probably what it means."

Riggs spoke. "If you don't mind my asking, ma'am, how do you know that?"

"Some sorcerers can generate a shock internally, kind of like lightning, but not as strong," I explained. "They can conduct that shock into an object, or a body, through touch. Given enough power behind it, it's usually fatal."

"So someone didn't want him coming home last night," Riggs said.

"Raine, do you think the goblins may have arranged to have a chat with Nigel, then used him to fuel a Gate when they were finished talking?" Janek asked.

"If he left at nine bells, that would have been enough time for almost anything—from anyone. There's a long list of people who would like to see Nigel dead." I had run into some of those on a shorter list last night, but this wasn't the place to tell Janek.

Riggs cleared his throat uneasily. "A Gate? Are you saying that he was sacrificed? Wouldn't they want a virgin or something? Or even a nice person?"

Janek laughed. I settled for a snort.

"That's an old wives' tale, Lieutenant," Janek said. "Nice doesn't matter, and I don't think anyone could ever mistake Nigel here for an innocent."

A rope had bound Nigel's ankles together. There was evidence of a frayed knot at the end. "Whoever the culprit was, they wanted to hide their work for as long as possible," I ventured. "This rope was probably attached to a weight of some sort. The killers wouldn't have to look far to find something large enough to keep their work submerged. How long do you guess he has been underwater?"

"Not long," Janek said. "The knucker bites and the sludge from the canals just make it look longer."

I had seen the knucker bites on Nigel's body, and had been doing my best to ignore them. Knuckers were smaller, distant relatives of the dragon family that thrive in Mermeia's deeper canals. They're scavengers, feeding on whatever meat they find. The city's canals were teeming with them at one time. The city's engineers had decreased the population, but had not eradicated it, much to the delight of the local criminals. Quentin once remarked that an assassin acquaintance told him that nothing disposed of a body like tossing it into a nest of knuckers.

Janek pulled the canvas back up over the necromancer's body, and turned to me. "Let's go where the air is more breathable. We need to talk."

Chapter 7

We need to talk.

Innocent enough words coming from most people, but rarely a good thing from a chief watcher. Too much talking right now on my part, especially honest talking, and I'd end up in the city jail. I'd killed a Khrynsani temple guard last night. Most people would consider that worthy of an award, not jail time. Still, I've never been one to tempt fate.

We were in Nigel's study. I had seen it before, though not in person. Quentin's viewpoint last night had been more than sufficient—and I was spared knowing what it smelled like. The air was cloying, sweet, and reminded me of dead things. Nice.

Janek sat down behind the massive desk. I took a seat in one of Nigel's guest chairs. Janek looked exhausted. That made two of us. He reached into his pocket and pulled out a collection of colored beads and wood held together with some bits of copper wire.

"What can you tell me about this?" he asked.

He made no move to give it to me, and when I saw the runes

carved on the bits of wood, I made no move to take it. It looked like a primitive charm. Most things like that were innocent enough, but looks could be deceiving. I learned that lesson the hard way a couple of years ago—and was wearing a refresher course around my neck right now.

Janek turned it over in his hand. "It belongs to a street magician by the name of Siseal Peli. He never lets it out of his sight. We found it yesterday morning at the foot of the Herald Bridge."

"No Siseal?"

"Not a trace." A muscle worked in the watcher's jaw. "Siseal said it protected him against curses. Looks like it's worthless against anything else."

He put it on the desk between us. I let it sit there.

I knew what he wanted me to do. I just didn't know if I wanted to do it.

Something to understand about seeking: sometimes finding people involved handling objects that belonged to them. The closer the person was to those objects, the better. Better for connecting with that person, but mostly better for seeing stuff you'd rather not know existed. Problem was, you never knew if you'd get visions of fluffy bunnies, or creatures from the lower hells snacking on said bunnies—or on the person you were looking for.

Siseal Peli had been carrying the charm when he was grabbed. Therefore, it was probably chock full of nice, fresh, horrific visions. Mine for the watching. Though at least I wouldn't have to listen. Some seekers could get sound, smells, sensations, basically everything the victim experienced. I wasn't that gifted—or that unlucky. I didn't know Siseal personally, but I had seen him on the steps leading up to the Herald Bridge. He spent his days there selling the charms he made to passersby. He was always smiling.

I picked up the charm.

I didn't expect to see anything at first; a connection usually took a few seconds to establish. Not this time. The amulet I wore thrummed to life and I immediately saw Siseal Peli's final moments.

I knew they were final. I smelled his fear. Heard his screams. Felt his death.

I never considered shadows lethal. Siseal must have known something I didn't.

His killer detached itself from the darkness of a doorway. It was tall, almost hobgoblin in shape—if hobgoblins were made of black ink. Siseal's breath froze, then came in panicked gasps. He knew what was about to kill him. He tried to run, but his killer was fast. Blink-of-an-eye fast. The magician's fists sank into a body warm and pulsing like living quicksand. The blackness flowed up his arms and legs, paralyzing his muscles and taking Siseal's life as it went. The magician found breath to scream just before his head was pulled inside.

Swift and simple. And sickening.

For the second time since arriving at Nigel's, I was glad I hadn't eaten a big breakfast. As a result, the only thing I tossed on the desk was Siseal's charm. But it didn't stop me from having a serious case of the whirlies.

"Are you all right?" Janek looked concerned. All three of him.

I think I might have nodded. Head direction was questionable right now.

"Well, did you see anything?"

So much for concern. I gripped the arms of the chair as the whirlies faded. "Nothing nice."

The watcher swore. "He's dead?"

"I assume so."

"What's that supposed to mean?" he snapped.

I met his snap and raised him a snarl. "It means he was there, then he wasn't."

Neither one of us meant it, and we knew it. That and friendship also meant not having to apologize. Saved a lot of time with hurt feelings. While I was feeling entitled, I decided not to mention the screaming, among other things. Janek knew what I was capable of. I'd rather not answer any awkward questions, like how I acquired my new talent.

"Just gone?" Apparently Janek had problems with that part. "Like through a Gate?"

"No. Gone as in ceased to exist. I'd say that qualifies as dead."

His eyes narrowed. "What did you see?"

I didn't particularly want to recount it, but Janek wasn't going to let it go until I did.

"It was big, black, and fast."

"Hobgoblin? Nebian?"

I let out a bitter laugh. "I wish."

"What was it?"

"I don't know, but I think he did."

"Describe it."

"No features, no face, no limbs, tentacles, claws, or anything remotely resembling something used to kill. Just shadows. Solid black shadows. Then nothing."

I couldn't express what I had felt. Which was fine, because I didn't want to think about it.

"Were there any Khrynsani around?"

"Not that I could see." That was the truth. I wish I had seen Khrynsani. It'd be better than knowing that some nameless, faceless, soulless creature was on the nighttime streets of Mermeia sucking sorcerers from the world of the living.

But I had to give Janek something. I owed him that much.

He needed to know about Simon Stocken and Sarad Nukpana, and their connection to what happened here. I just couldn't spill my guts without revealing my involvement, at least in part. Nothing like being indirectly involved in a pair of murders to test a professional relationship—and a friendship. But I knew where I could start.

Sorcerers at the level of mage had to register with the city watch on entering Mermeia, as well as several other larger cities. It let local law enforcement keep track of people with that kind of power. Public safety, and all that. Interestingly enough, Guardians didn't have to register. They're the ones local law enforcement reported their registrations to. Sarad Nukpana was a grand shaman, the goblin equivalent of a mage. He also had diplomatic immunity, which didn't do anyone any good except Sarad Nukpana. The most powerful and dangerous mages were often employed by governments and their officials. They were encouraged to register as a courtesy to the city they were visiting. But if they chose not to, there was nothing the local watch could do about it. I wonder if Sarad Nukpana had been courteous. I was willing to bet he had.

"Did Sarad Nukpana register when he arrived?" I asked Janek.

Puzzled lines appeared between his eyebrows at the shift in topic. "Yes, he did."

"You registered him?"

"Riggs did."

"Did he give his business while here?"

"Advisor and counselor to His Royal Majesty, King Sathrik Mal'Salin."

"Figures," I said. "Did Riggs believe him?"

"Not a chance. A goblin grand shaman usually has business in town other than what they list on their registration—and Khrynsani are never up to any good anytime. I've had Nukpana watched. He's due to leave after the ball."

The amulet felt icy cold and hard against my chest. "I wouldn't be surprised if he applied to extend his visit for a few days," I said. "Know where he was last night?"

"The report said neither he nor any of his shamans left the goblin embassy—at least not through the front or back door. I have to admit, for a Khrynsani trying to sneak out after curfew, a Gate would be the way to go. Perverted and sick as hell, but an efficient way to get around town."

I knew I was going to regret this, but Janek needed to know, at least some of it.

"I think Nigel's house was just the Khrynsani's first stop of the evening," I said.

The watcher sat motionless. "The first. You think."

I nodded. "Simon Stocken's warehouse was probably second."

Janek's face was devoid of any expression. It was his watcher's face. I found I didn't like being on the receiving end.

"Is this your opinion, or do you know it as fact?" he asked.

"I was at Stocken's warehouse and sensed the remnants of a Gate. A few minutes later I ran into Sarad Nukpana and a handful of his shamans."

"A Gate, Sarad Nukpana, a murdered Simon Stocken—and you."

"Well, and a few other people, but they don't enter into the equation."

"Why don't you let me decide that?"

"I'd rather not."

Janek took a deep breath and quietly let it out. Then he just sat there for a few moments. He looked at me. I looked back at him.

"And this is related in some way to how Nigel ended up in the canal."

I shifted uncomfortably in my chair. "More than likely."

"Are you going to tell me or do I have to wait a couple of days for the next installment?"

"Simon Stocken was fencing what the goblins came here to steal."

"Except the goblins didn't manage to steal it."

I nodded. "Right."

"Do you know who did?"

"Yes, but I can't tell you, and I promise this person's identity has absolutely no bearing on this case."

"It wasn't you, was it?"

"No." I sat up straighter. I was insulted, but only mildly. Considering my family and professional connections, I could hardly blame Janek for his conclusions.

Janek sighed. I almost felt sorry for him. I knew this was

driving him crazy. Or more to the point, I was driving him crazy. Sometimes I had that effect on people.

"The person who stole this object escaped from Nigel's house and took it to Stocken to collect the rest of the fee," I said. "But I think the Khrynsani were there first."

I opted to leave the Guardians out of it. It was confusing enough. Besides, Janek was law enforcement; Mychael Eiliesor was law enforcement. I didn't want to find out the hard way that they had been old school buddies.

"Let me get this straight," Janek said. "I have Nigel and Simon Stocken, two prominent Mermeian citizens dead, and in all probability, the murderer not only has diplomatic immunity, but cannot be physically placed at either crime scene." He paused. "Does your nameless thief still have the thing that everyone's after?"

"No."

"Do you know where is it?"

I knew enough to keep my mouth shut.

"I could jail you on obstruction of justice and withholding evidence," Janek told me.

"Possibly. But you won't."

"Give me one good reason why not."

"I'm more valuable to you outside a cell than in."

"As what?"

"Bait."

Janek slowly walked around to the front of the desk and perched on it, directly in front of me. He leaned forward. "Raine, you're in possession of stolen goods—either literally or by knowledge of location. In the eyes of the law it's the same thing. Why don't you just turn it over to me?"

That was true. I was in possession of stolen goods—stolen goods I couldn't hand over even if I wanted to. One, said goods would probably kill me if I tried; and two, Janek was in no way qualified to defend himself against said goods or those who wanted it. While I wasn't any more qualified than Janek, I just didn't dump magical amulets on my friends then run away while every baddie in the city jumped them. I had to take the moral high road sometime.

"Believe me, Janek, I'd like nothing more, but truth is, I can't."

"Can't or won't?"

"Can't."

"Do you think you'll be able to turn it over to me in the near future?"

"Nothing would make me happier—and that's the honest truth."

Janek sat back. "You're going to be popular."

"Too late. I already am."

"I can spare a few men to stay close to you," he said quietly.

I almost said I didn't need protection, but that was absurd. I needed all the protection I could get. But I wasn't going to take it from Janek's already depleted resources. The watch commissioner was notoriously stingy with his men, especially in the Districts. It was a sincere and very generous offer.

"I appreciate the offer, but we both know you can't spare the men. Not now. Besides, I've made other arrangements."

Though with no room at any of Markus's safehouses, my arrangements had just gone up in smoke. But I wasn't about to tell Janek. He thought jail cells were safe; I knew jail cells were death traps when someone like Sarad Nukpana was after you.

He kept his eyes on mine. "The offer still stands. Just let me know."

"Thank you."

Janek stood. "Tell me one thing."

"What's that?"

"If you turn up on a table like Nigel, who do I go after first?"

"Good question."

Chapter 8

In my opinion, the best source for information on Sarad Nukpana would be from a former member of the goblin royal family—especially from a primaru, or shaman of the royal blood. I considered Primaru Tamnais Nathrach a friend. Tam wanted to be more than friends. I wasn't sure what I wanted. I figured that friends or more than friends don't normally kill each other, regardless of the Mal'Salin duchess they used to be married to, so I felt relatively safe paying Tam a visit.

Tam was one of those scoundrels who'd come into my life and actually stayed there. I knew him well enough to trust him—to a point. There were things about Tam that I'd probably never know, and I wasn't sure I wanted to. I think that was part of his appeal.

In addition to locating missing people, I was often hired to find missing objects. Some of those objects were magical; most were mundane—and small and valuable and shiny. Mermeia was more than a favorite retirement destination for mages; it was a playground for mages and nobles alike. The kind of playground where if you wanted to play, you had to pay. Tam owned Sirens, the most exclusive and notorious nightclub and gambling parlor in the city. Most of the money that found its way onto Tam's tables came from the healthy bank accounts of the mages or nobles placing the bets. Some of those bank accounts were less than healthy. Tam wasn't directly involved in stolen goods, but he did have clientele who routinely came into unexpected bounty. Tam had no problem with that bounty being spread around his establishment—even if that bounty had yet to be converted into the coin of the realm.

Tam and I met as a result of yet another cash-strapped noble working his way through the remains of his wife's inheritance to support his gambling habit. One wife in particular drew the line at her grandmother's favorite ring. She hired me. I tailed her husband right to Tam's high-stakes card table. The husband tried to compel me to look the other way. I don't compel, and I sure as hell don't look the other way. Tam's been known to avert his eyes, as well as have troublemakers like me tossed into the canal behind his club. Tam may be a scoundrel and an opportunist, but he's also a savvy businessman. It looked good for him to return the lady's ring. He told me later he did it to impress me.

Tam considers me a challenge; I consider Tam a work in progress. I also think there's a gentleman lurking under that calculating exterior. Tam thinks "gentleman" is a dirty word.

I talk dirty to Tam every chance I get.

This morning I wanted to talk to Tam about his former in-laws—and whether they had contacted him when they had arrived in town. After his wife's death, Tam had asked to leave the royal family's service. I had always suspected politics played an equal role in his decision. I wanted to know if someone had tried to pull him back in. Working for the Mal'Salin family wasn't usually fatal, but telling them you were quitting almost always was, even if you were family. Especially if you were a talented shaman who had once provided a valuable service. Many felt Tam's talents were wasted on a nightclub. I disagreed. Tam had had more than one bad experience in his former line of work, and he'd left that life behind to do what he enjoyed. Good for him.

I knew Tam wasn't a loyalist when it came to King Sathrik Mal'Salin. I also knew there were many in the Goblin District who shared Tam's political leanings. And with the king and his Khrynsani in town, it was healthier to keep those leanings to yourself. The politics of Tam the business owner was that if it was good for business, he was in favor of it. I couldn't see the Khrynsani being good for anyone's business, except possibly an assassin or an undertaker. I wasn't so sure about the politics of a primaru and former member of the Mal'Salin family, but I did know I trusted him enough to ask.

I crossed Heron Row a block down from Tam's place and stopped. Sirens was closed during the day, but apparently that didn't stop Tam from having visitors.

This wasn't just any visitor. I knew this lady. Or at least knew of her.

Primari A'Zahra Nuru had a direct connection to, and the ear of, the Mal'Salin family.

The primari, or shamaness of the royal blood, had taught the goblin queen mother, as well as the late queen. She had also been Tam's teacher and mentor. When Sathrik, the queen's eldest son, took the throne after his mother's sudden death, he encouraged Primari Nuru to retire. He provided her with a modest house and annual income in Mermeia, far removed from the goblin court. It seemed the new king didn't want his dead mother's tutor underfoot. Hardly unexpected considering A'Zahra Nuru's rumored abilities and Sathrik's recent activities, most notably the questionable circumstances of his mother's death.

Primari A'Zahra Nuru was hardly retired. According to Markus, she was Prince Chigaru Mal'Salin's most trusted advisor. And now here she was visiting Tam. Chigaru's retainers had taken on King Sathrik's Khrynsani guards in Nigel's garden last night. A'Zahra Nuru drops in on her former student this morning. The odds were against a coincidence. If I wanted answers, it looked like I had come to the right place.

The diminutive goblin wore a simple gown of pale mauve silk, and her silvery white hair was elaborately styled and held in place with tiny, jeweled pins. More pale gems glittered on the lobes of her upswept ears. As with Tarsilia, the years had been kind to A'Zahra Nuru. Her pale gray skin was still smooth over high cheekbones and fine features.

The primari must have wanted to see Tam very badly to be out on a bright, sunny morning. Goblins were mainly nocturnal, by preference bordering on necessity. They could be out during the day, but their dark eyes were painfully sensitive to sunlight, and most chose to just remain inside. Shops and businesses in the Goblin District were open during the day, but kept extended hours in the evening for the convenience and comfort of their clientele. During the day, the windows were kept shuttered and the interiors dimly lit. Any human or elven customers had to make do the best they could. If goblins ventured out during the day, they wore dark-lensed spectacles. A'Zahra Nuru wore a stylish pair of these perched on the bridge of her patrician nose.

The amulet tingled in the center of my chest, and I had the sensation that someone had just woken up from a long nap. It knew something I didn't, and I suspected the goblin primari had everything to do with it. She hadn't hesitated in her progress down Heron Row, but I knew that she had sensed me, the amulet, or both. My hand instinctively went to the disk, and I pulled farther back into the shadows of a side street. What she was using weren't shields. It was a searching spell, completely silent and more complex than anything I could have attempted, let alone pulled off. It spread toward me like surface ripples on a pool.

Sensing something that subtle was another first for me.

I didn't try to stop it. I knew better. A block or deflection would have announced my presence like slamming a door in Nuru's patrician face. My stomach fluttered as the spell flowed through me. The primari hesitated a fraction of a second, then continued on her way. I continued breathing again. The amulet was proving to be as good a watchdog as it was a nuisance. But just because it growled at strangers didn't mean I was going to trust it with my own neck.

I waited until the primari was well down Heron Row before crossing the street to Sirens' front door.

Tam's bouncers weren't on duty, but Tam's wards certainly were. And they were at full power. Tam's wards at half-strength were something to behold, full power would take care of anything short of a magical tidal wave. It looked like a certain goblin primaru was feeling a little insecure this morning, and I was willing to bet that insecurity started last night and intensified with his mentor's visit this morning.

I knocked, even though I was sure Tam's wards had already announced me. After a few moments, a small section of the door slid open, just large enough for the pair of amber eyes that looked out. I recognized the eyes and the elf they belonged to. Lorcan Karst, Tam's floor manager. I heard the sound of locks being unfastened and wards being shifted. The door opened.

Lorcan was tall and lithe, and like most elves, deceptively slim and much stronger than he looked. Lorcan in particular was more dangerous in other ways than most realized. Rarely did anything happen that he couldn't control—one way or another.

"Mistress Benares, what a pleasant surprise. What can I do for you?"

He didn't look surprised to see me—pleasantly or otherwise.

"Is your boss in?" I asked.

"He is."

"If he's not too busy, I need to speak with him." I paused. "And if he's busy, I'm willing to wait."

Lorcan stepped aside and ushered me into the dimly lit interior. "I will ask. May I have Kell get you anything from the bar while you wait?"

The barkeep looked up from his work and waved in greeting. I smiled back.

"Nothing, thanks," I told Lorcan. "Morning, Kell," I called across the empty dance floor.

The big goblin continued to put away glasses. "It's been too long. Where have you been keeping yourself?"

"Here and there. The usual."

I paused to let my eyes adjust to the dim lighting. Many of Tam's employees were also goblins, and Tam wanted his people to be comfortable. I had been here often enough to know where everything was, but I wasn't in the mood to trip over a wayward chair. To my left, next to the long, sleek bar, was an area with only a pair of elaborately carved doors behind a small desk. Tom had commissioned the doors from a local artist. I had looked closely at the panels. Once. I don't blush easily, but suffice it to say what the carvings look like from across the room are entirely different from what they really are. Behind those doors, and up a flight of stairs was the most exclusive gambling parlor in Mermeia.

Gambling wasn't illegal in Mermeia, but exploiting certain magical advantages was. Combining gambling and sorcerers was either a very good or a very bad idea—depending on which side of the table you were on. For sheer profitability, a fancy Conclave education had nothing on what a moderately talented sorcerer could learn and earn in an upscale Mermeian gambling parlor. Nudging a pair of rolling dice, manipulating a deck, compelling your fellow players to study the insides of their eyelids while you did a little reconstructive work on the game board. The possibilities were nearly endless. Tam ran a legitimate establishment, or at least that's what the city watch believed. I didn't buy it for a minute.

Lorcan escorted me to my favorite booth against the back wall. I knew the way, but the elf was a gentleman and a good manager, so I let him do his job.

"I will let Primaru Nathrach know you are here," he said.

I nodded. Tam already knew I was here, but I was willing to let protocol take its course.

Lorcan vanished behind a discreet set of velvet drapes concealing the narrow hallway leading to Tam's private office, and Kell had disappeared into the back room, so I made myself at home. Other booths in Tam's place were better for being seen, but this booth was better for seeing—and leaving. Even in Sirens' relatively safe surroundings, having access to the back door, and to the alley and canal beyond was occasionally useful. Tam liked keeping behavior in his place as civilized as possible. An occasional discreet vanishing act on my part did wonders for sustaining our friendship.

My gaze drifted to the stage. The evening's entertainment was setting up. One of them, a young goblin, had stopped and stood openly watching me. I watched him right back, and considering how easy he was on the eyes, it wasn't hard work. He had the body of a dancer, all sleek muscle, and he was dressed to accentuate every angle. Knowing a thing or two about muscle tone and what it takes to acquire and maintain it, I knew that his hadn't come entirely from dancing, though no doubt he did that well enough or Tam wouldn't have hired him.

He looked toward Tam's office and bowed slightly. "My primaru."

I turned to find Tamnais Nathrach watching us both with amusement.

Seeing Tam always made me breathe funny.

Like many goblins, Tam wore his black hair long. Normally it was pulled away from his face with a silver clasp. This morning it was loose, slightly disheveled and fell in a shimmering wave to the middle of his back. Looked like someone had spent the night here. Tam crossed the floor to me like a big, beautiful, and dangerous cat that had just awakened from a very satisfying nap. If I listened closely enough, I could probably hear him purr. He wore trousers and matching boots of dark, soft leather. Over that was a long silk dressing robe woven with an intricate pattern of silver and blue. He let the robe fall open, treating me to a view of smooth, silvery chest. Tam noted my appreciative glance with a sly smile and a bit of fang peeking into view.

He nodded toward the stage. "I see the two of you have met."

"Not really," I said.

"We are ready, my primaru, if you would like to listen," the young goblin said.

"Very much so." In a whisper of silk, Tam slid into the booth next to me.

While the musicians prepared, Tam took my hand and barely brushed my palm with his lips.

Seeing Tam made me breathe funny; touching Tam made me forget how.

"It's been too long," he whispered, his dark eyes shining in the half light.

Kell had said the same thing. Somehow it was different coming from Tam. I didn't have to be told why.

After the night I'd had, on top of virtually no sleep, I thought I'd probably spook horses and scare small children. From the look I was on the receiving end of, Tam didn't agree. Though knowing Tam, he probably hadn't noticed anything going on above my neck.

Tam and his voice were like fine, dark silk—he was provocative, his voice was seduction itself, and both made you feel completely decadent. I wasn't entirely immune to his charms, and I didn't entirely mind. I had always told myself that Tam didn't mean anything personal by it. It was a harmless little game that we both enjoyed. Perhaps if I told myself that long enough I'd begin to believe it.

The music began. Drums and two other percussion instruments established a languid beat, and then the low, vibrant tones of a goblin flute joined with the melody. The tempo increased slightly to the pulsing rhythm popular for the current mode of dancing. The young goblin began to sing, his body moving in perfect time to the drums. It was a love song that only a goblin could love, full of seduction, deception, and betrayal with just a touch of death thrown in for good measure. But it wasn't the words that held my attention; it was the singer, or more to the point, his voice. His rich tenor gave meaning to the song far beyond the words. As the music increased in energy and intensity, so did his voice and his dancing. If I hadn't been acutely aware of what he was doing, I could have easily found myself enchanted.

Although he was not in the same class as Mychael Eiliesor, the young goblin was a spellsinger of impressive power and control. It wasn't unusual for establishments like Tam's to employ spellsingers—a little subliminal singing to compel patrons to order more drinks, or to convince them they're having the time of their lives was fairly common. This goblin's skill was a little much just to raise bar tabs. If he had wanted to, he could have done much more. But then, Tam had never been one for doing things halfway.

The song concluded, and we both applauded, Tam with more enthusiasm than I.

"He's good," I murmured.

"Yes, he is," Tam agreed.

"Too good."

Tam looked over at me, a slow grin playing with the corners of his mouth. "I offer only the best. My clientele expects it from me. If they want shoddy spellsinging, they can go down to the Troubadour."

"I wasn't talking about his singing. I meant what's going on under it."

"He wasn't aiming at you, darling, so where's the harm? Spellsingers have to make a living, too."

He wasn't aiming at me, but he easily could have been. And after last night, I was a little more sensitive about that sort of thing. Not to mention, a spellsinger that gifted could easily find work more suited to his level of talent and probably better paying, though I knew Tam wasn't cheap. He paid his people well, and then some. The result was an intensely loyal staff.

"That was well worth the wait, Rahimat," Tam told the spellsinger.

The young goblin looked pleased. "Thank you, my primaru. With your permission, we will perform it tonight."

"You have my permission and my blessing."

With a bow to Tam and another glance at me, the spellsinger turned and began speaking in low tones with his musicians.

Tam was standing by the booth. I hadn't seen him move. "You wish to speak with me privately?"

I looked away from the spellsinger and stood. "I do."

Tam slipped his long-fingered hand to the small of my back. "Kell has brought refreshments to my office."

The narrow hallway leading to Tam's private domain was lit by illuminator globes set into recesses in the wall. The resulting light was pale golden, and very flattering, the same as the lighting in the main room. Everything and everyone looked better in low, soft lighting. Throw in a couple of strong drinks, and even Tam's hobgoblin bouncers would look irresistible. I'd always found the glow to be a little too perfect. I'm sure Tam had added a few magical touches to enhance the effect.

Tam opened the door and stood aside for me to enter. A warm caress passed over my skin as I stepped across the threshold and through his shields. Being on friendly terms with the proprietor helped. Tam made sure his shields knew I was always welcome. Trust was a wonderful thing.

A door was open behind the mahogany desk. Through it I saw the corner of a bed, with pale sheets spilling into a pool on the floor.

"You would welcome a few extra hours of sleep." He didn't ask it as a question.

"I would welcome a few hours of sleep, period."

"That could be arranged."

From the sound of his voice, that wasn't all that could be arranged. "Tam, I'm serious."

"So am I."

The goblin went to a small sideboard in the corner and poured Nebian jasmine tea into a pair of gold-painted porcelain cups so fragile they looked like they would shatter if you looked at them wrong. I could smell the delicate floral brew. Nebian jasmine was rare, and importing it was prohibitively expensive unless you had the money or the contacts. Tam had both.

He handed me a cup, deliberately brushing my hand as he did so. "What is so important that you cannot spare a few hours for me?"

I slid into one of the two overstuffed velvet armchairs facing the desk. "I don't have a few hours. I have a problem."

"Don't you always? You need to make time. Play is important."

"Play is your business, Tam, not mine." I took a sip of tea, closed my eyes and inhaled. Night-blooming jasmine. A moment of pure and complete bliss. It'd be nice if I could make it last.

"It's also my business to make people happy." His voice dropped to a low, suggestive purr. "What would make you happy this morning?"

"Other than a few hours of sleep, the same thing that always makes me happy. Knowing things that the bad guys want to keep secret."

"Those aren't the fun kind of secrets."

"They are to me. Now more than ever."

"I'm probably going to regret this, but is there anything I can do to help?"

"Without endangering yourself or your business," I finished for him.

"That would be nice, but with you, it's usually not possible."

I paused before continuing, taking both my time and another sip, and sniff, of tea. "You heard about Simon Stocken?"

"I heard."

I didn't say how I knew, and Tam didn't say how he heard. Tam would never betray me, and I extended the same courtesy to him. But at the same time, we didn't share anything we didn't have to. Our relationship operated strictly on a need-to-know basis. I think there are things about Tam that I'd rather not know; and I'm positive there are things about me that I'd rather Tam not know. It's not a lack of trust, just good sense. I've always been a practical girl.

"I received a shipment of Caesolian red and some vintage liqueurs from him just last week," Tam said. "I have two other sources, but they lack Master Stocken's particular acquisition skills and attention to detail. I suspect my cellars will suffer before I find a suitable replacement." His expression darkened. "*If* I can find one. Do you know who was responsible?"

"Why? Want revenge?"

"Possibly."

"Sarad Nukpana."

I like to give little gifts to my friends, and to myself. If Tam could somehow cut short the goblin grand shaman's trip to our fair city, it would make a lot of people feel better— especially me.

Tam was silent for a moment. "More than a few individuals in the Goblin District would love to send Sarad Nukpana home in a large box, in small pieces. But just because they want it, doesn't mean they're going to volunteer to make it happen." He regarded me soberly. "Is your interest professional or personal?"

"Both."

Tam sighed. "Who hired you?"

"You know I can't tell you that." Especially since I had become my own client.

He shook his head and took the chair opposite mine. "Are you willing to take some advice?"

"I'm willing to listen."

"Find another case."

"I've already been given that advice."

"You'd be wise to take it."

"Too late for that."

"It's only too late when you're dead." Tam exhaled slowly and settled back in his chair. "I heard his shamans paid you a visit last night," he said.

"You've always said I need to get a social life."

"Raine, you've never met him. I have. Trust me, this isn't anyone you want to have notice you."

Too late for that. "I hear he's quite the nutcase," I said.

Tam voice was steady. "He's also brilliant, skilled, sadistic, and utterly insane. He's a monster, Raine. Do us both a favor and walk away from this one."

"I can't. At least not without help."

He was wary. "What kind of help?"

"Just information."

"And you think I have this information."

"It would certainly make my life easier—and possibly longer—if you did. The Khrynsani also paid Nigel Nicabar a visit last night."

"What did Nigel have to say?" Tam asked.

"Not much, because he's dead."

That seemed to be news to Tam. "Nigel's dead?"

"Bobbed to the surface just off the Grand Duke's Canal this morning."

The tiniest smile creased Tam's lips. "You have to admit that's not a grievous loss to the necromancer community." He paused and the smile vanished. "You think I know something about this, don't you?"

"I think there's a better than average possibility."

To someone who didn't know him that well, Tam's face was an expressionless mask. But I knew him that well. There was plenty going on behind those large, dark eyes, and most of it had to do with deflecting my questions.

"I have nothing to do with Nigel," he said. "And even less to do with the Khrynsani. I have my vices, and while some are arrestable offenses, it's nothing I would burn in the lower hells for."

"Some people would say that's open for debate," I said. "I

know you like to watch those you don't want watching you. The Khrynsani definitely qualify."

Tam waved a negligent hand. "King Sathrik's throwing himself a party two nights from now. Someone has to see to the catering."

"I don't think Sarad Nukpana's minions are here to make tiny sandwiches or arrange flowers, and neither do you. Try again."

"Unless it affects me, there are some things I'm content not to know. You should do the same more often."

"Maybe next time."

"The direction you're heading, there's not going to be a next time. The Khrynsani have come for whatever reason, they'll do what they came to do—and then they'll leave. When they do, Mermeia's goblin community is going to let out a collective sigh of relief."

"Not exactly welcoming their new king and his counselor with open arms?"

"Let's just say many of us are reserving judgement. Anyone that chooses Sarad Nukpana as his chief advisor isn't going to win many loyal subjects in this city. As long as Sathrik and his pet shamans are in town, I'll be spending as little time as possible in the Goblin District. Too many Mal'Salins there who are best avoided."

"Not eager for a family reunion?"

"I loved my wife," Tam said point-blank. "I've never had similar feelings for her relatives. I'll be staying here for the rest of the week."

Time to put my cards on the table. "Sarad Nukpana wants something that Nigel had. Nigel doesn't have it anymore and neither does Sarad Nukpana. I need to know what that something is and what it does. And I need to know it sooner rather than later."

Tam sensed my mood shift. Playful, it wasn't.

"I don't know what they were looking for," he told me.

"But if Sarad Nukpana wants it, it would be best if you weren't in his way when he finds it."

I put my cup and saucer on the side table. "The only people who know I'm asking questions are people I trust not to betray me." I paused meaningfully. "Or lie to me." I threw that in for good measure. I was sure Tam had a perfectly good reason for not being totally honest. Quentin hadn't been totally honest with me either, and look what kind of trouble that had caused. I was tired of getting the runaround, and was feeling a little spiteful. What I was wearing around my neck earned me the right to instill some guilt. If I was lucky, it might bear useful fruit.

Tam's dark eyes widened beguilingly. "You trust me?"

For a brief instant, he looked sincere. I was touched. Almost.

I couldn't help but smile. "With my life, yes. But not with the rest of me."

His answering grin exceeded my own. He looked almost boyish. "Do you have somewhere safe to stay?" He indicated the pack at my feet. "It looks like you're running away from home."

I made a face. "You're closer to the truth than you think. I had accommodations, really good ones, but they fell through. And I won't be responsible for putting Khrynsani on Tarsilia's doorstep again."

"Then I insist that you stay here."

"I thought you were staying here."

His dark eyes shone. "I am."

"You don't give up, do you?"

The smile vanished. "I'm almost as persistent as Sarad Nukpana."

I stood and picked up my pack. "I know. That's why I won't stay here. I need sleep, not a wrestling match."

Tam raised his right hand. "I promise to be the perfect gentleman."

"Gentlemen—perfect or otherwise—don't make promises they have no intention of keeping."

Tam stood smoothly, his expression solemn. "I never do." Then solemn turned to something else as he reached out and tucked a wayward strand of hair behind my ear. "Would you like a bath as well?"

Getting naked in Tam's immediate vicinity didn't seem like the best—or at least not the most direct—way to get to sleep, but I couldn't deny that I needed and desperately wanted a bath.

"Is that a polite way of telling me that I *need* a bath?"

Tam stepped closer, his fingers trailing from my ear to lightly brush my throat. "I smell goblin blood on you." His voice had turned husky.

I didn't move. "He was asking for it."

"No doubt, especially if the blood is Khrynsani."

I saw no reason to deny it. "The blood is." I paused. "Its owner was."

Tam looked at me then laughed quietly. "So I assumed. I'll have the tub filled."

Tam's tub was a wonderful place to think.

Even if Tam wasn't a gentleman, at least he was trying. Tam was a businessman, and he considered me an investment. Tam never made an investment unless he knew it would pay him full dividends later. I reached for the soap. That was fine with me, later wasn't now. For now, Tam had left me alone in his plush little apartment to make myself at home.

There was more to Tam's private domain than a bedroom behind his office. There was a sitting room with a plush couch and more overstuffed chairs; there were rugs you could sink in up to your ankles, one of which was strategically placed in front of a carved marble fireplace, along with the tub. I had looked at the carvings before getting into the tub. Same people, same activity. Apparently wooden doors weren't the only medium Tam's naughty artist friend worked in.

Soaking in the hot, scented water made me realize just how

tired I was. But it also helped me think a little more clearly about my encounter with Sarad Nukpana.

It stood to reason that since Nukpana had hired Quentin, he might have heard of me. Quentin worked for me. A natural, logical chain of progression. No scary conspiracy there. What it didn't explain was why the goblin grand shaman had seemed downright tickled to see me. Maybe he was just the friendly type. Yeah, right. Just your friendly neighborhood psycho.

I leaned back in the tub to wet my hair. I didn't think Tam knew about the amulet and why Nukpana wanted it. But based on Tam's reaction to the mere possibility of my path crossing Nukpana's, if I told him, I'd be locked in his bachelor hideaway until the Khrynsani left town. I looked around. It was really very nice. The throw on the bed looked suspiciously like Rheskilian sable. I grinned. Only one way to find out for sure, but I'd have to dry off first. Not a bad way to spend a couple of days, but it wouldn't do a thing to explain what I was wearing around my neck, what it did, what it was doing to me, and why I couldn't take it off. And most importantly, how the hell Sarad Nukpana knew me.

I sank lower into the tub. Drowning would solve all my problems.

"Turned into a mermaid yet?"

I jumped, water sloshed. Tam was closer than he should have been. No big surprise there. Though at least he was dressed. I relaxed a little, but was still careful to keep the amulet, as well as some other things Tam would find intriguing, well below the waterline. Just because Tam was dressed didn't mean he couldn't take off what he had just put on, and from his expression, he looked like he was giving that some serious thought.

He was dressed for going out, and armed for staying there awhile. A goblin with a mission. I had a feeling that mission involved me. What a sweetheart, though I knew better than to tell him that to his face.

"Going to see anyone I know?" Or had just met.

Tam's expression gave nothing away. "I doubt it."

I didn't.

"Does it have anything to do with me?"

Silence.

Wonderful. Tam is going to get himself killed and it's going to be my fault.

"When was the last time you ate?" he asked, nimbly changing the subject.

"Let's see . . . dinner last night at the Crown & Anchor. Didn't happen. Ale and dried bread at Garadin's in the middle of the night. Unfortunately that did happen. Then there were sugar knots from Maira's this morning. Delicious."

Tam just shook his head. "I figured as much."

There was a discreet knock at the door. It was Kell with a tray of something that smelled like heaven. The big goblin was trying to avert his eyes from the sight of me in the tub, but he wasn't having much luck. I slipped deeper into the water to help him out.

He left the tray and the room, both quickly. I giggled.

Tam smiled and met my eyes. "What is it?"

"I wouldn't have pegged Kell the easily embarrassed type."

"It's not every day he finds a beautiful woman in my tub."

"It's not?"

Tam's eyes were unreadable. "No, it's not."

He turned away and removed the plates from the tray and set them up on the table and opened a bottle of wine I was sure cost more than I made in two weeks. It looked like a feast. If Tam hadn't been standing there, I'd have been out of the tub and at the table, naked or not.

Tam tossed the robe he'd been wearing earlier across the chair next to the tub. "If you do not wish to get dressed immediately, you may wear this while you eat."

"You're leaving now?"

"I've already dined, and I have business to attend to."

Oh yeah. Killing or getting himself killed on account of me.

"If you need anything, Kell will get it for you," Tam added.

He bent and placed an almost chaste kiss on top of my head. Though the bending gave him ample view of everything under the water. "Sleep well. I'll be back by eight bells tonight."

And he left. Very sudden, very un-Tam like. I didn't trust it.

I got out of the tub, dried off, and slipped into Tam's silk robe. It was still warm and smelled like Tam. Nice. I sat down at the table and devoured everything Kell had brought. By the time I'd finished, I could barely keep my eyes open. I put my clothes—and my blades—next to the bed where I could reach them, then slipped out of the robe and into bed.

Oh, and the throw on the bed? Definitely Rheskilian sable.

Chapter 9

When I woke up, I knew it was far later than I wanted it to be, though the extra sleep was much needed and worth it. A glance out the window confirmed the late hour.

I planned to be gone before Tam returned. I had errands of my own to run. While I couldn't march myself to the goblin embassy and demand that Sarad Nukpana explain himself, I could do something almost as productive and a lot less dangerous. I could ask Ocnus Rancil, and I wouldn't ask nicely.

Ocnus Rancil may not be the most gifted goblin sorcerer in Mermeia, but pound for pound, he was the sneakiest. Nothing happened in the Goblin District that Ocnus didn't have his fingers in one way or another. Everyone knew that, including the Mal'Salin family. As a result, Ocnus was what you might call the royal family's chief weasel about town. And Ocnus's presence at Tarsilia's door with several Khrynsani shamans in tow told me that his weasel duties had expanded to include tour guide. Ocnus needed to understand that my home wasn't a stop for visiting tourists; I needed to understand what Sarad Nukpana wanted with me. Ocnus might not know everything, but I was sure he knew something. I was also sure Ocnus and I could reach an agreement.

But I wasn't counting on knives or threats to get the results I wanted. I knew a curse and I'd use it if necessary. Generally I stayed away from curses. They had a tendency to backfire, aside from being just plain mean. I had made an exception for this little beauty. I had used it only once, and it had been more than effective. Ocnus had been on the receiving end that time, too. It was repugnant, even by his standards. I had put a three-day time limit on it—fire fleas reproduced after four days. I'm not completely without compassion, even when it came to Ocnus.

I don't think he wanted a repeat infestation.

It didn't take long for me to get dressed and armed. I knew where Ocnus spent most of his days. It was in the Goblin District, in a section I normally avoided, but avoidance wasn't an option if I wanted to talk to Ocnus.

Tam's staff had arrived to set up for the night's clientele. A few didn't recognize me; most did. There were more than a few surprised looks and knowing smiles when I stepped out of Tam's office. They knew the boss's office wasn't the only thing behind that door. After the bath, meal, and nap I'd had, I felt wonderful and couldn't care less what anyone thought.

"Mistress Raine."

It was Kell. I walked over to the bar.

"Was the lunch to your liking?"

"It was wonderful. Just what the doctor ordered."

He nodded, pleased. No signs of blushing. I guess it helped that I was wearing clothes.

"This arrived for you while you were asleep." He reached down behind the bar and handed me a sealed envelope. "Since the boss had said you weren't to be disturbed, I waited."

I looked at the seal. It was plain and the paper wasn't top quality. Definitely not from Markus.

"Who delivered it?"

"Lorcan took it at the door," Kell said. "But I got a look at the messenger."

"Goblin?"

He shook his head. "Human."

I did a quick scan to check for any unpleasant surprises. Normally a wax seal was just a seal, and breaking it just opened a letter. Sometimes it opened a nasty spell. Better safe than struck. It felt clean, so I opened it.

What a coincidence. Ocnus wanted to talk to me, too. I'll bet he did. Probably had a nice, cozy little chat planned. Just the two of us—with a dozen or so of his new Khrynsani best friends. Though where he wanted to meet was surprising. Dock Street at the north end of the Smuggler's Cut Canal. That was on the waterfront in the Elven District, a long way from Ocnus's usual haunts. The Ruins was at the north end of Dock Street. I didn't like to be anywhere near The Ruins this close to dark, but it beat the hell out of the Goblin District any time.

It was Ocnus's chosen topic of discussion that interested me most. He claimed to know why Sarad Nukpana wanted me and the amulet. But the last line of his note baited the hook and I couldn't help but bite.

And the location of the artifact he plans to use you and the amulet to find for him.

I could smell the setup from here. For Ocnus, information was currency. Apparently I didn't have any information he wanted in exchange, because he was asking for fifty gold tenari.

He wanted to meet at seven bells. I knew that when Ocnus was anywhere near the Elven District waterfront, he had an early dinner at the Flowing Tide, and he always dined alone. Usually because no one else wanted to dine with Ocnus. It was just before six. If I hurried, I could keep him company.

I tucked the letter in my belt. "Tell Tam I went out for dessert."

•　•　•

The sun had just dipped below the horizon, bathing the lagoon in golden light. It was my favorite time of day. Too bad I didn't have the time to enjoy it. I wanted a quiet night, with more than a few hours of sleep. Wanting it didn't mean it was going to happen, but I could hope. After talking to Ocnus, I could always come back and take another bath—especially since after talking to Ocnus, I'd want to.

A pair of city employees leisurely made their way down the bank of the Smuggler's Cut Canal, lighting streetlamps. It was the dinner hour, and people were hurrying home to the evening meal. I turned the corner at Dock Street just in time to see Piaras forced into an alley by a pair of cloaked figures. Part of me wondered what Piaras was doing anywhere near The Ruins at dusk. The other part knew it wasn't his idea. The young spellsinger looked afraid. I looked down Dock Street in both directions. The lamplighters had vanished and there wasn't a city watcher to be seen. Figures. Just when I could have used some backup.

I had a pair of blades in my hands and a spell on my lips, and I was familiar with the alley Piaras had been shoved into. Unlike many alleys in Mermeia, this one had two exits. The trick would be to get to the closest exit first. Maneuverable space in any street near The Ruins was at a minimum. Not the safest place to cross swords with anything. Halfway down the block was another alley that ran parallel. An opening between a pair of buildings connected the two. In addition to not going in blind, it might earn me the element of surprise. Surprise may not always be necessary, but I've found it's a good thing to have. Sometimes it's the only thing you can get.

I ran as silently down the alley as I could, checked around the corner and proceeded to the end. I stopped and listened. It was virtually dark between the buildings and completely silent. Great. My hackles went up along with my suspicions. There should be some kind of noise. Piaras may be young and inexperienced, but he wouldn't go without a fight. I flexed my fingers on the grips of my short swords to ease the tension. Nothing left but to take a look.

Piaras and his captors were standing where I could clearly see them. They were facing the alley, obviously waiting for me. Damn. Piaras had given them a fight, but had come out on the losing side. There was a line of blood from one side of his mouth, and the side of his face showed signs of a fist-sized bruise. One of his captors was big, cloaked, hooded, and had one leather-covered arm firmly around Piaras's throat, choking off all sound and most of the air. His other hand held a long, slender blade pressed under Piaras's third rib, just below the heart. His hands were bare—and gray.

The goblin didn't move and neither did I.

Two more goblins emerged from the shadows. Their elegant clothing and leather armor all but blended in with the increasing dark. Street thugs they weren't. I knew one of them: Rahimat, the spellsinger from Tam's nightclub. He stopped to stand beside Piaras, a slender stiletto at the ready. Whether Tam had anything to do with this remained to be seen, but if I got out of this alive, Tam had some explaining to do—and he'd better talk fast, before he couldn't talk at all.

A slight figure lurked on the edges of the shadows. I couldn't see his face, but I didn't need to.

"You skipped dessert," I told Ocnus.

"Business comes first. I can always have dessert later." He turned to the goblin holding Piaras captive. "I kept my end of the bargain."

The hooded goblin nodded to Rahimat, and the spellsinger distastefully tossed a pouch of coins at Ocnus's feet. Unless my Benares ears deceived me, it sounded suspiciously like fifty gold tenari. The pouch vanished into the folds of Ocnus's robes almost before it hit the ground.

The little goblin's smile was full of fang. "It's always a pleasure to do business with you, Mistress Benares." Then he scurried out of the alley.

Other goblins even better armed started coming out of the

woodwork. Under normal circumstances I would have run, but normal circumstances didn't have Piaras with me and at the mercy of goblins who carried themselves and their weapons with the confidence of professional killers.

The hood of the goblin who held Piaras captive slipped back, exposing the high cheekbones and handsome, angled features of old-blood nobility. A trio of goblins approached me from behind and began relieving me of my weapons. They managed to find everything, and I had no choice but to let them. I looked at Piaras, willing him to a calmness I didn't feel. His dark eyes reflected equal measures of pain, fear and helpless rage. The leader stared unblinking at me, his dark eyes hard and flat. Piaras was no more to him than a means to an end.

When I was completely unarmed, he spoke. His voice was calm and measured, and he expected nothing less than my full cooperation.

"You will come with us, or the boy will die."

Chapter 10

There were two types of ground in The Ruins—that which was solid, and that which only looked that way. I hoped our captors knew the difference.

Few remembered what The Ruins' real name was. It had once been the most exclusive address in Mermeia—until about a hundred years ago, when a personal vendetta between a pair of retired Conclave mages got out of hand. It had been a lush island park in the middle of the city, home to only the most wealthy. When creatures out of a nightmare began haunting the dead mages' estates, Mermeia's social elite decided to take their high living elsewhere. Grand villas and sprawling gardens fell into piles of stone and swamp as the trees and lagoon reclaimed their own. Ruins were all that remained of the once beautiful mansions, and the name had stuck.

Since then, The Ruins had become a favorite haunt of criminal gangs and rogue sorcerers looking for a hiding place and privacy for their work and experiments The descendants of a few of those magical experiments gone awry still roamed The Ruins' depths. In the course of my work, I'd seen a few of them firsthand, and had secondhand knowledge of others. I was in no hurry to repeat either experience.

Several unfortunate incidents had forced the city's leaders to take action. A high, iron fence topped with spikes was erected to keep The Ruins' inhabitants in, and the general populace of Mermeia out. Protecting the stupid from themselves hadn't been a popular use for taxes. Many citizens, myself included, felt that if someone wasn't bright enough not to go wandering into The Ruins, they had every right to cut themselves from the herd, and we shouldn't go wasting taxpayer coin trying to stop them.

A walk through The Ruins was bad enough without being bound, blindfolded, and led by armed goblins. I had been here before, though it wasn't my first choice then and it certainly wasn't where I wanted to be now. I couldn't see a thing either through or underneath the blindfold, but my other senses were telling me that things hadn't improved any since my last visit.

Daytime in The Ruins was generally quiet, as most of the things that made their home there needed the dark in order to venture out. As soon as the sun set, those things began to wake up—hungry things whose first order of business was to find food. Unfortunately, Piaras and I qualified as food. Muffled shrieks and calls erupted from nearby. A guttural moan materialized from above us, only to be abruptly silenced. I wasn't sure which was worse, whatever the goblins had planned for us, or being an evening snack for what was now growling to my immediate right.

Escaping wasn't an option I considered for very long. Even if we could get away, it was dark, we were blindfolded, our hands were securely bound behind our backs, but most importantly, I knew what was out there. When it came to The Ruins, I'd consider our captors the lesser of two evils until they proved otherwise.

Piaras was being herded by a second group of goblins on the trail behind us. They didn't want me talking to him. That became obvious to me the moment I tried. My jaw still ached from where a goblin fist had abruptly made its acquaintance. Apparently a punch hurts a lot more if you don't have the advantage of seeing it coming.

The goblins set a quick pace. Apparently they didn't like leisurely nighttime strolls through The Ruins either. I was grateful for the speed, but it didn't make it easy to keep my feet under me. My captors didn't care. With a firm grip on my upper arms, they just lifted me over whatever obstacle lay in their path. I guess it was faster than letting me fall down on a regular basis.

Our captors finally slowed down. From that, and the feel of flagstones beneath my boots, I guessed we had arrived at one of the abandoned villas. I hardly expected to find a goblin who could afford the muscle accompanying us camping out in a fisherman's hut, and I had to admit it was the perfect hiding place.

I heard more goblins as we were led up a short stair and into what I assumed was our destination. I dimly saw flickers of light beneath the cloth of my blindfold as we were taken down a long corridor. I heard goblin voices. One suddenly drowned out the others in a flash of anger. I couldn't make out the words, but the voice's owner clearly wasn't happy. A door grated open on long-unused hinges, and my arms involuntarily tensed in my captors' grip. The voice abruptly lowered to a terse, sibilant whisper. We were pushed forward and the voice fell silent.

A gloved hand removed my blindfold. Once I finished blinking against the light, I found myself in what looked to have once been a gentleman's study. The dark wood walls were dull with age and neglect. What furniture remained was of the finest quality, before time and damp swamp air had taken their toll. Much of it was covered with either sheets or equally pale and filmy cobwebs. That told me that the goblins hadn't been here long, and they weren't planning to outstay their welcome. The room was lit by candles, and the sole source of heat was a small fire dwarfed by the massive marble fireplace that contained it.

Our host stood before the fireplace. He was a tall goblin, his beautiful face a carefully emotionless mask. Except for its blue black shimmer, his waist-length hair was unadorned. His eyes were dark and intense, with hardly any white exposed. He took a breath and a forced calm settled over him. I wasn't fooled. I also knew exactly who he was. Prince Chigaru Mal'Salin may be a fugitive on the run from his brother, but he was going to do it in style, and he could certainly afford the muscle that had brought us here and now loomed directly behind us.

Some of the goblins in the room with him also wore their black hair loose, while others wore theirs in braids, elaborately entwined with silver chains and caught at the base with jeweled clasps. They wore earrings with fine chains linking them to cuffs attached to the ear near the pointed tip. All were stylishly attired in dark silks and velvets; and like their prince, some wore intricately tooled leather and blued-steel armor in addition to their finery. All were armed.

Street thugs they weren't. They looked like what they probably were: a royal court in exile.

I inclined my head to the tall goblin by the fireplace. "Your Highness."

"Mistress Benares."

Sarad Nukpana *and* a Mal'Salin prince knew my name. That was more than a little alarming.

"Yes, I know who you are," the goblin prince said. His gaze landed on Piaras. "Who is this?"

"Bait," one of the guards told him.

Piaras's dark eyes flashed in anger. Good for him. He hadn't panicked, and he had been given ample opportunity. From what I'd heard about the Mal'Salins, things would probably get worse before they got any better. If they got any better.

The prince's black eyes locked with mine for several long moments. "Untie them," he said quietly.

One of the guards approached and sliced through my bindings. I rubbed my wrists to restore the circulation. Piaras did the same.

"I apologize for any inconvenience or affront to your dignity. I assure you neither was intended. I needed to speak with you, and you have been most persistent in avoiding me."

Avoiding him? I didn't even know he was looking for me. Though I shouldn't be surprised. It seemed like everyone else in Mermeia was looking for me. The prince's voice was polite, but strained. He was under control, but only because he wouldn't allow himself to be otherwise, at least not yet. Something was going on here, and I didn't think I wanted to know what it was.

"I regret I had to resort to such crude means to bring you here, but I am running out of time, and you left me with no choice. It was fortunate that you happened along when and where you did. If you had not, we would have had the regrettable task of proving that we had your young friend. We probably would have had to do something drastic." He paused. "That would have been unfortunate."

Piaras paled. The prince took no notice. I fumed.

"Well, we're all lucky today, aren't we, Your Highness?" I knew I was in enough trouble without comments like that, but I couldn't help myself.

The prince ignored it. "May I offer you a drink?"

"No, thank you."

He gestured with a long-fingered hand to a high-backed chair opposite the fireplace from himself. "Then sit. If you please."

Not seeing the harm in it, I accepted. Better to save my strength for when I needed it later. He took the chair opposite me. Piaras was left standing, flanked by a pair of guards. The prince had made his status clear. I would cooperate, or Piaras would suffer. I had known Chigaru Mal'Salin for less than three minutes and I already disliked him. Not that I really expected to feel any other way.

The goblin prince gestured to a figure standing on the edge of the shadows. "Jabari?"

"Yes, Your Highness?"

"I want you and Sefu to stay. The rest of you may go."

He may have been addressing his guards and courtiers, but he never took his eyes from mine. I made it a point not to look away. If there was any blinking to be done, I wasn't going to be first.

"I understand you met Sarad Nukpana last night."

I saw no reason to deny it. "I wouldn't exactly call what happened between us a meeting. More like an avoidance."

"Only on your part," he murmured. "Sarad Nukpana is most eager to make your acquaintance."

I shrugged. "I seem to be having that effect on men lately."

"Yes, there is something about you that is oddly bewitching."

I tapped my heel against the floor, knocking some of the mud from my boots. "Must be some indescribable quality I have."

"I can describe it quite well. A silver medallion of elven make, carved with runes that do not seem to mean anything—except to a dead elven Guardian who had it forged nine hundred years ago. Does that sound familiar?"

I shook my head, which wasn't easy to do around the lump that had taken up residence in my throat. "Not in the least. But then it doesn't sound like my taste in jewelry either."

The goblin prince leaned forward, close enough for me to catch his scent. Sandalwood mixed with spices. His voice was soft and low. "Sarad Nukpana knows you have it—as do I. Your secret is out, Mistress Benares."

I let the silence grow for a few moments, and when I spoke, my voice was steady, which was another surprise. I made no move to show him the amulet, and I certainly wasn't going to take it off, even if I could.

"I really think you could afford better," I told him. "Mermeia has some of the finest silversmiths in the seven kingdoms. What's so special about this particular chunk of metal?"

It was the prince's turn to grow some silence. He did it well, and he did it for longer than I did. As the silence expanded, so did his smile. It was genuine. He found something amusing, and I think I was at the business end of his joke.

"You actually do not know what you carry." There was a note of wonder in his voice. "How can that be?" Then he thought of something that tickled his funny bone even more. "I could tell you," he teased, "but your stay here would have to be longer. I could not risk you interfering with my plans."

I wasn't about to give him the amulet, so he could plan on keeping me here for as long as he liked. I had yet to be locked up anywhere that I couldn't get out of.

I settled back in the cushions, and leisurely crossed my legs at the ankles. "Enlighten me." Chigaru Mal'Salin wasn't exactly the information source I had in mind, but since no one else was willing to talk, I'd take my knowledge where I could get it.

The prince's black eyes glittered in the dim firelight. "What do you know of the Saghred?"

I knew it was goblin. When Garadin had taught me goblin history, he had concentrated on the crazies—which meant I had a more than adequate knowledge of the Mal'Salin dynasty. The Saghred had been temporarily in the possession of Omari, a Mal'Salin king who had elevated insanity to an art form.

"A legendary talisman first heard of in your peoples' Fifth Age," I said, as if reciting from Garadin's lesson. "It was said to be a black rock that fell from the sky. It was incredibly heavy, but it was only the size of a man's fist. Rumor had it King Omari wanted to use it to destroy anyone and anything he didn't like, which was pretty much everyone and everything. Rumor also had it the rock was more than capable of all of the above and then some. Only shamans of the highest order could wield it—at least for a while. Eventually they all went insane and destroyed themselves. The Saghred was contained in a specially made casket of white stone from the Sorce Mountains. The Guardians took it away from King Omari. They tried to destroy it and failed, so they hid it. It was never seen again." I paused, mostly for air. "I couldn't walk all that well if I had a rock that heavy hanging around my neck, Your Highness."

"No doubt," the prince agreed. "And the Saghred is not an object safely transported. Which is why the Guardian charged with protecting it had a beacon made to enable him to watch his charge without having to keep it with him, or remain in the Saghred's hiding place for the rest of his life."

I realized where this was going, and it wasn't anyplace I wanted to be. "Let me guess, you think his jewelry commission was a silver medallion."

The goblin prince didn't answer. He just smiled.

"A beacon with which to locate the Saghred," he told me. "In my people's language, the word Saghred roughly translates as 'Thief of Souls,' something else it is said to do. According to legend, shamans who had fallen from royal favor were sacrificed to the stone. The shamans doing the sacrificing received enhanced powers from the stone in exchange for their gift. Those enhanced powers came with an extended life and insanity; being sacrificed meant your soul was trapped for eternity inside the stone."

The prince leaned forward in his chair. "And if I may correct you, Mistress Benares." His silken voice was little more than a murmur. "While all the shamans who used the Saghred did go insane, only a few actually destroyed themselves. Most were taken by the stone."

The only sound was the crackle of the fire. "Taken?" I whispered.

"While using the Saghred. If the stone hungered, it would feed to sustain itself. Those shamans were absorbed, Mistress. Their powers and souls added to those already trapped inside—trapped for eternity with the very colleagues they had sacrificed with their own hands."

"Not much of a welcoming committee."

The prince smiled. "No doubt. Goblin armies that carried the Saghred before them were indestructible—and their adversaries were annihilated. My brother and Sarad Nukpana want the Soul Thief very badly. I do not want them to succeed in acquiring it. My wants are simple, Mistress Benares. You have the beacon. You are a seeker. You will help me find the Saghred first. Once I have it, you and the boy will be allowed to leave here alive and whole."

I had the lodestone to an ancient soul-stealing rock hanging around my neck. Wonderful. I had no intention of being caught in the middle of some twisted sibling rivalry. And under no circumstances was I going to help a Mal'Salin, any Mal'Salin, or anyone working for a Mal'Salin gain possession of something with the pet name "Soul Thief."

"My skills in the craft are marginal at best," was what I said. "I'm hardly qualified to help you."

"One does not need to be a mage to use a beacon—or for the beacon to use you. I had been told that this particular beacon was keyed to its maker. Yet, according to my teacher, you have been able to tap its power quite effectively."

So much for wondering if Primari A'Zahra Nuru sensed me outside Tam's nightclub this morning.

"I am curious to know how you can do this," the prince continued, "but that's not important at the moment. Finding the beacon was one problem for my brother, finding someone who could wield it was another matter altogether. So now I must not only keep the beacon from my brother, but you as well. And since there is the possibility that Sarad Nukpana will be able to locate the Saghred on his own, we must find the Soul Thief first."

"And if I refuse?"

As expected, he cast the barest glance at Piaras. I needed no further elaboration, and I hoped the prince didn't see the need to give it.

"Sathrik murdered our mother with his own hands, Mistress

Benares. He killed or exiled her most trusted counselors, and he has tried to kill me on numerous occasions. Now he has brought that shaman from the lower hells to rule beside him." He paused, and I could see the muscles working in his jaw. "Even more that his diseased mind desires will be his once he has the Thief of Souls. Sarad Nukpana only needs spilled lifeblood to open it, and a soul sacrifice to tap its power." His voice dropped to the barest whisper. "My brother has everything, with even more to gain. I have nothing left to lose."

His eyes were jet orbs. Not only was he determined, he was desperate—and probably willing to do things a normal person would find just a little bit insane. Unfortunately his brother wasn't here for him to take it out on. After being brought up in the same house as Sathrik Mal'Salin, I could almost understand the mentally unstable part. And on a certain level, I could understand and almost sympathize with his motivation, but not with what he was trying to do.

"Your decision is quite simple in my eyes," he continued. "You are either for my brother, or you are against him."

"I don't see myself ever being for Sathrik Mal'Salin."

"Then you will find the Saghred for me."

I hesitated. Not the best move, but I didn't want to get what I was about to say wrong. Such things have a way of blowing up in your face. Especially when I say them.

"From what I have heard of your brother and Sarad Nukpana, and from what I have been told of the Saghred, getting the three of them together in the same room is the last thing anyone wants to happen."

"Then we are in agreement."

"Understand my dilemma, Your Highness. I've heard what your brother and Sarad Nukpana are capable of. I do not know you, or your plans."

"My plans are no concern of yours. Regardless, you are hardly in a position to bargain."

"True. But you say that my friend and I will not be harmed, that we will be released once you have what you want. You're asking for my complete trust on your word alone. I've never dealt with you, so don't take this personally, but the elven people have had bitter experience with the word of a Mal'Salin. It's often been open to interpretation, usually by the Mal'Salin who has just given their word."

There was an angry hiss behind me, and the sound of a blade clearing its scabbard. The prince didn't move. The guard next to Piaras didn't move. I certainly wasn't going to move. I also wasn't going to get too excited about my chances for long-term survival. I didn't hear the blade go back where it came from, and I really didn't want to turn around and find out where it was.

The prince had been resting one of his hands on an intricately carved armrest. It snapped off under the pressure of his grip. I hoped it was wood rot, though I knew better. I tended to have that effect on people.

When the prince spoke, his voice was calm. "Unlike most of my family, my word is my sacred bond. You can believe that or not. But I had you brought here at great risk to my people and to myself because my brother gets close to his goal, and the Guardians grow increasingly desperate, as do I. So you see, Mistress Benares, neither one of us has any choice."

I didn't consider getting cozy with an object nicknamed Soul Thief much of a choice.

Prince Chigaru's dark eyes drifted down to where the amulet rested against my chest beneath my doublet.

"Remove it."

I made no move to comply. "I can't take it off."

"I am not interested in what you want, Mistress Benares. I have given you every opportunity to end this without any actions we would both find distasteful."

"She can't take it off. It won't let her." Piaras's voice was strong and quavered only slightly.

Like a spark beneath cold embers, I felt the power flare to life under the young spellsinger's words. The danger was there, and it was real, palatable in the room's chilled air. I didn't know if Piaras realized what was happening, but the prince knew something was different. He had been schooled in the magical arts too well not to know. But I don't think he recognized Piaras as the threat he was. Yet. The last thing I wanted was for Chigaru Mal'Salin to see Piaras as anything other than harmless. I needed a distraction.

I pulled the amulet from beneath my shirt.

Piaras's response was immediate and impassioned. "No!" He lunged for me, but was restrained by the two guards.

I forced myself to ignore him. Fortunately, Prince Chigaru didn't have that problem. His attention was instantly riveted to the amulet gleaming in the firelight. I took a deep breath. Mission accomplished. It brought up a whole new problem, but I was prepared to deal with that any way I had to. I had a feeling it wasn't going to be pleasant for anyone in that room, including myself. I didn't care. My hands were untied, there was a window in the room, and I was more than ready to leave. I could feel the amulet stir, its warmth spreading through my body. I think it had had enough, too.

The prince had stood and was now leaning over me, his hands resting on the armrests of my chair, effectively pinning me in my seat. His hair fell in a dark, silken curtain around us both, concealing us from sight. He made no move to touch me, or take the amulet. He just stared at me in a way no one had ever looked at me before. It was awe mixed with recognition of elemental power and an overwhelming desire to possess it. I didn't like his look one bit. I stared back. Out of the corner of my eye I saw a large dust-covered vase on a side table. It wasn't close enough for me to get my hands on, but I didn't need my hands to introduce it to the back of Prince Chigaru's head. It was a pleasant image and I treated myself to a small smile. The goblin misunderstood it entirely. His problem, not mine.

"It has bonded to you," he breathed. "The Soul Thief itself shines through your eyes. You glow with the power of death."

I recoiled, more from his words than from a Mal'Salin prince only inches from my face.

There was a scuffle in the shadows, then a grunt as Piaras hurled himself at the goblin prince, taking both of them to the ground in a tangle of limbs. The guards, no longer distracted by their prince's attention to me, tried to pull Piaras off, only to receive kicks for their trouble. One flick of thought and the vase flew from the table into my hands. It was large and metal and made a satisfying solid sound when it came in contact with the guards' heads. The wrestling mass parted briefly and I was rewarded with a clear shot at Prince Chigaru's shoulder. It wasn't the body part I had in mind, but I wasn't in a position to be picky, so I took it. The doors crashed open and more goblins poured into the room—armed goblins who weren't happy to find their prince on the floor. Armored hands slammed me back into my chair, and a sword point made sure I stayed there. Piaras was jerked upright, both arms wrenched behind his back.

The prince stood and slowly wiped blood from his lip. His eyes were blazing. Piaras didn't flinch or look away.

Prince Chigaru addressed the guards. "Secure our guests in the room upstairs, post guards, then report back to me."

Chapter 11

The door closed and locked behind us. The lock sounded all too substantial, and the footsteps of our guards didn't fade away down the corridor as I'd hoped, but not really expected. Prince Chigaru's guards were following his orders to the letter. I was considered too valuable right now.

We were in what had probably been a guest bedroom. It had been finely appointed in its day. Now, the brocade upholstery was threadbare, the velvet bed hangings thin and tattered, and the heavy smell of damp and mildew hung in the air. There were a few other pieces of furniture, but most were covered with dingy sheets, dust, or both. Two lamps had been lit on the mantle, but the fireplace was dark and cold, as was the room. The only other source of light came from a sliver of moonlight peeking through a pair of etched glass doors.

I made my way around the room, knocking on walls, checking for hidden doors. All activities anyone watching would expect of a new prisoner. My stroll ended at the glass doors. They led out onto a small balcony, and were locked, but the lock could be easily picked. Another Benares family talent.

It also had other attractions. I moved on, not wanting to draw attention to our most likely exit. Apparently Prince Chigaru hadn't planned too far ahead for holding prisoners. Lucky for us. It was probably also the reason why we were being held in the same room. Lucky for me. I didn't want to escape only to have to search for and free Piaras.

When I had looked down into the garden, I saw that our host had made up for any oversight. Five armed Mal'Salin royal guards were posted below to make sure things didn't get interesting. I didn't sense any surveillance in the room itself, but there would probably be someone watching or at least listening to us soon. There were too many places in the wall that would perfectly conceal a pair or two of prying eyes. But I wasn't going to wait around for them to arrive. I was going to remove us from Prince Chigaru's royal hospitality as soon as possible.

The prince assumed that between the guards and The Ruins, that I would be disinclined to try to escape. My first rule was never assume. This went nicely with my second rule—always try to escape. While I occasionally failed at the first, I had always succeeded in the second. Tonight wasn't going to be an exception.

Piaras was standing perfectly still in the center of the room by a settee at the foot of the canopied bed. While this sort of thing didn't happen to me all the time, it wasn't exactly a rare occurrence. But I thought I could safely assume that Piaras had never been taken prisoner by Mal'Salin royal guards, led bound and blindfolded through The Ruins at night, threatened with torture by a goblin prince, then topped off the evening by attacking the aforementioned royal. I felt my lips curl into a quick grin. Come to think of it, those were all firsts for me, too.

Piaras was watching me, his liquid brown eyes wide and intent. I knew he was probably scared to death, and with good reason. Prince Chigaru wasn't happy with him, and I know the guards he kicked were less than amused. Piaras was still alive because the prince thought he could use him to compel me to find the Saghred for him. And he was right. I wouldn't allow them to hurt Piaras. That left one option: get out of here as quickly as possible. I went to the settee and sat down, motioning to Piaras to sit beside me. We were facing the outer wall. No one could be watching from there and reading lips. Then I used my version of the spell Garadin used last night to keep Piaras from overhearing our conversation. If anyone was spying on us, I was going to make them work for it.

Piaras sat, opened his mouth to say something, then stopped. I think he was more than a little overwhelmed. I was feeling a little that way myself.

I took his hand and gave it a light, reassuring squeeze. "I'm not happy here either," I said in the barest whisper, my lips close to his ear. "Don't worry, we won't be staying long."

"How?"

"Through the glass doors. There's a trellis on the outside wall that should hold our weight."

"Are there any guards?" he asked.

That question surprised me. Good. He may be scared, but he was keeping his wits about him.

"Five."

He started to stand, probably to take a look for himself. I tightened my grip on his hand.

"Someone could be watching. Let's not give ourselves away yet."

He sat back down and drew a deep breath. It shuddered as he exhaled. Probably the first good one he'd had since we were brought here. The hand I held trembled slightly, as did the shoulder touching mine.

"I'm sorry," he finally managed.

"For what?"

"For being worthless."

I just sat there for a moment, waiting for that one to make sense. It didn't. "Where did you get that idea?"

"I haven't done anything. All night, I haven't done anything to help."

"What do you call what you did downstairs?"

"Stupid. I just made things worse. I could have gotten us both killed."

No, just you, I thought. Prince Chigaru needed me—at least for now. I didn't say that out loud, but I'm sure Piaras was well aware of how close he had come. Besides, he was feeling bad enough.

"It was a little impulsive, but you were just trying to protect me." I draped a sisterly arm around his shoulders, and gave him a quick hug. "It was also very brave. There just happened to be a couple dozen goblins on the other side of the door when you did it. Not your fault." I tried to give him a smile. "Neither one of us was hurt, so don't worry about it."

He looked down at the floor. "I wasn't brave; I was scared."

"You were scared and you still attacked the prince to protect me." I grinned. "Sweetie, I hate to be the one to break it to you, but that's called brave."

He looked up. "It is?"

"If you *weren't* scared and attacked the prince, that'd make you suicidal and a couple of other things you don't want to be."

Piaras almost smiled. "Thanks. Though none of this would have happened if I hadn't gotten myself caught."

"True," I admitted. "But they wouldn't have been after you to begin with if the prince hadn't wanted me. So all this is my fault. If there's any apologizing to be done, it should come from me." I tried a weak grin and another hug. "Sorry."

He tried a grin of his own. His didn't make it either. "It's okay."

"No, it's not. But it will be."

I had an idea, and if it worked, it would not only get us out of this room, but it would go a long way toward giving Piaras back some of his self-respect.

"So, how are your sleep spellsongs coming?" I asked casually.

I felt his hand go ice cold beneath mine, and his shoulders

went rigid. He knew exactly what I had in mind. So much for the no-pressure approach.

"I can't put five goblins to sleep!"

"Ssshhh!"

"I can't!" he mouthed.

"Can't or just never tried?" I stopped. That was stupid of me. When would he have had a chance to put goblin guards to sleep? Garadin said Piaras had the gift, and I had seen proof firsthand, though not to the extent I was asking. Trial by fire wasn't the best kind of final exam, but we didn't have any other options available.

"Do you need to see your subject while you work?" I made my voice all business and no doubt.

Piaras had his face in his hands, his elbows resting on his knees. He glanced sideways at me and gave a single shake of his head. I couldn't help but notice that he looked a little pasty.

"Good," I said, trying to sound encouraging. "You can do this."

"How do you know?" He sounded as close to miserable, and sick, as possible.

"I don't." I wasn't going to be anything other than totally honest with him. He deserved that much. Besides, he would know if I was lying to him, and that would ruin any chance of this working. "But Garadin does, and I trust Garadin. He said he's never seen anyone with such a powerful gift."

Piaras lowered his hands. I saw a flicker of what may have been hope in his dark eyes. Hope and surprise—and a healthy quantity of doubt. After all, this was Garadin we were talking about.

"Garadin said that?"

"He did. He told me how you put everyone in the Mad Piper to sleep in just a few measures."

That at least earned a crooked grin from Piaras. At this point I'd take any progress I could get.

"They were bored and drunk," he said. But the grin had widened.

"According to Garadin, they weren't bored, and Salton Oakes didn't get his shipment that day and had to water down the ale. So they weren't drunk, either. They were bespelled— by your voice. Garadin told me he was very impressed."

"He didn't tell me."

"You expected him to? Garadin doesn't give out praise lightly. Trust me, I know." My godfather probably wouldn't appreciate me telling his student how brilliant he was, but if anyone needed a big dose of confidence, and needed it now, it was Piaras.

I could use some myself. Piaras couldn't do his work until I did mine. Now that we were away from the press of courtiers downstairs, I felt the ample wards Primari A'Zahra Nuru had left behind to protect her beloved prince. If I failed to block those wards completely, Piaras wouldn't get past the first few notes of his goblin lullaby. My job was to let the guards enjoy a sleepsong serenade while covering the figurative ears of Primari Nuru's wards.

Piaras swallowed. "I'll do my best." His voice was firm and his eyes determined.

And I would do mine.

"I'll shield you while you work," I told him. "Once the guards are out, we'll have to move quickly. Once we're on the estate grounds, stay close to me. Once we're off the grounds, stay *very* close to me."

He nodded solemnly. "I understand."

He didn't, but I wasn't going to be the one giving him the gruesome details of what was waiting for us outside the estate walls—and probably inside as well. He'd find out for himself soon enough.

My part was almost as challenging as weaving a lullaby for five Mal'Salin royal guards. More than five, actually, but I wasn't going to tell Piaras that either. I would shift my shields to let his song extend to the guards outside our door. I didn't want to be climbing down a potentially rotten trellis at night with goblins at my back. I could feel Primari Nuru's wards around and inside the house. Once those were disturbed, Prince Chigaru would have every guard on the estate after us. There were enough things out there without Mal'Salin royal guards to deal with. I estimated it was about three hours until midnight. During my previous visit to The Ruins, I had found out the hard way that this was the height of feeding time. Not the best time to be out and about, especially when those doing the feeding considered you tasty.

The amulet, beacon, or whatever it was had been helpful until now, at least when it came to shielding me. If it helped with what I was about to do, I would gladly overlook its previous attempt on my life.

While it wasn't necessary for the goblin guards to actually hear Piaras's song, it was necessary that there not be any magical barriers in his way. Master spellsingers could blast through just about anything, and while Piaras might be able to do the same, the less work he had to do right now, the better. The shields I was about to put up wouldn't be a problem. They were to keep nosy wards from listening in—Piaras's song just needed to get out.

It took a few minutes of concentration on my part to nestle my shields into place just above the goblin primari's wards. It was a good fit. Nothing disturbed. Nothing activated. Everything shielded. Too well shielded. I did good work, but this was way beyond my capabilities. Even Garadin might have been impressed. It looked like the beacon was up to its new tricks, but I'd have to worry about that later.

Now it was Piaras's turn.

He was hesitant at first—not from any lack of knowledge of his craft, but from too much knowledge of our situation. He knew what was at stake, and the pressure showed. His first few notes were tentative as he felt his way through the melody, concentrating hard to get just the right blend of tone and intensity. Concentrating too hard. The song suffered as a result. It might cause a few yawns down below, but that was about it.

I held up a restraining hand. "Wait."

He stopped midnote, his face pale and strained. His breath seemed to stop as well. This wasn't going to work, not like this.

"You're trying too hard. I know you don't want to hear this, but you need to relax."

"Relax?" Piaras's tone and expression were equal parts panic and disbelief.

"I know. Easier said than done."

"Yes," he said, as if I couldn't have uttered anything more obvious.

"You're going to have to ignore the goblins," I told him.

"I'm singing to them. The spell doesn't work without an audience."

"You know what I mean. Ignore who and what they are. Think of them like the people at the Mad Piper."

"No one at the Piper wanted to kill me."

I hated it when logic reared its ugly head.

"The goblins don't want to kill you either. At least not right now. That leaves you free to think happy, peaceful, sleepy thoughts at them."

Piaras looked at me like I had lost my mind. I wasn't entirely sure he was wrong. But I was entirely sure that if he didn't get this right, the goblins would kill both of us, and there wouldn't be anything happy or peaceful about it.

He thought about it, decided something, but didn't look happy with his decision.

He sighed. "You're right."

I'm glad he thought so.

I took both his hands in mine. "You can do this. I know it, and so do you."

He began his song again. Quietly, shyly, but without the fear of his first effort. The soft, gentle melody rose to weave a vision of warm spring evenings, the golden pulse of fireflies, and the scent of night-blooming flowers. The song rose and fell like rolling swells of a ship in a calming sea, or a mother's hand at a cradle. Floating above it all was the heartbreakingly beautiful song of a nightingale.

I was glad he wasn't aiming at me.

I casually strolled over to the window and looked down into the garden as if admiring the view. I was. Goblins were dropping like flies. It started gradually. A spear dropped from relaxing fingers. A head bobbed to an armored chest. A goblin body leaned against the outer wall. Piaras accomplished it all with extreme care and control. Garadin was right; Piaras had a genuine gift. Tonight I was grateful for it.

I returned to the settee. I couldn't help but smile. "Good work," I said in the barest whisper.

For the benefit of anyone who either looked or came into the room after we were gone, I left an image of Piaras and I still seated and passively awaiting our fate. Another shield would keep anyone from seeing us leave through the balcony doors. My usual mirages looked solid enough, but they wouldn't stand up to touch, and would dissipate in about ten minutes—good old smoke and mirrors magic.

What sat looking back at me wasn't my usual work.

If I hadn't known I was standing by the glass doors, I would have had a hard time believing that wasn't me sitting at the foot of the bed. Piaras looked similarly challenged.

"That's good," he said, looking a little wild-eyed.

I swallowed. "Yeah, it is."

I tried to ignore myself sitting behind me and picked the lock on the glass doors. The beacon apparently deemed me qualified, and let me do that all by my lonesome. I was right about the trellis. It was iron, bolted to the house, and built for the ages. I was grateful for the builder's attention to detail. The guards slept peacefully on the ground around us.

We had to cross an expanse of lawn to get to the forest. It was windy, and the clouds raced overhead. In a few seconds, I estimated a large cluster would pass in front of the moon, giving us better cover for a dash across the lawn.

At that moment, a goblin sentry came around the corner of the house and plowed into Piaras. It was one of the guards who had pulled him off of Prince Chigaru. Unfortunately, he remembered us, too. So much for quiet.

"You!" he roared, and lunged for Piaras.

Piaras jumped back with a startled yelp. He didn't think, he just reacted—with a solid right hook to the goblin's temple. The guard dropped like a rock, a surprised look frozen on his face. I was surprised, too, but for different reasons entirely.

Piaras stood over the sprawled form, stunned by his own handiwork. "That's for calling me bait," he finally managed.

Someone had been teaching Piaras bite to go with his bark. "Where'd you learn that?"

Piaras winced and shook his fist against the sting. "Phaelan thought it was something I needed to know."

I might have known. "What else has he been teaching you?"

Piaras flashed a sheepish grin. "You really want to know?"

"Probably not." I peered out into the gloom. It looked as clear as it was probably going to get, but not nearly clear enough. There were things out there. And considering the hour, chances were better than average that we were going to be meeting some of them. I stripped the goblin of his weapons and handed Piaras a long dagger.

"Phaelan teach you to use one of these?"

He looked uncertainly at the blued-steel blade in his hand. "We're working on it."

"Hopefully you won't get a chance to practice tonight."

I took a curved sword and a pair of throwing knives. The guard probably had more on him, but I didn't want to take the time for a more thorough search.

We ran across the lawn and into the cover of the trees. They were low and dark and more than adequate to hide us. After we had gone about fifty yards, I stopped and listened. No one was following. But that didn't mean something wasn't following. I was quite sure something was, and I didn't need the beacon humming against the center of my chest to tell me about it. The hair on the back of my neck was doing a fine job.

I took us in a direct line away from the estate. Distance was more important than direction right now. We were in The Ruins, so I could safely assume that anything following us wanted to kill and eat us, and probably not in that order. When I no longer felt anything breathing down my neck, I'd stop and get my bearings. Our pace was even faster than the goblin guards had set bringing us into The Ruins. Survival was a powerful motivator.

After my last trip to The Ruins, I had asked Janek Tawl for a map and committed it to memory. I had sworn I would never get lost here again. With the amount of criminal activity in The Ruins, the city watch had commissioned the best maps money could buy. Hopefully I would live long enough to tell Janek it was a good investment.

The ground sloped upwards, and we followed it. There were only two areas of The Ruins that could be called high ground. We were fortunate to have found one of them. It wasn't the way out, but it would go a long way toward helping me find one. At the top, there was a low grouping of stones surrounding a rock slab where the ground leveled off. I knew exactly where we were. That slab had seen various uses over the years, none of them good.

Piaras stopped beside me. "Where are we?"

That wasn't a question I wanted to answer. "It doesn't have an official name."

"What's the unofficial name?"

"The Butcher Block."

He looked at the slab. "Because of the rock?" he asked uneasily.

"Yeah, because of the rock."

The spellsinger stepped in for a closer look. I didn't stop him. There was enough light to see where dark stains had seeped into the stone, becoming a permanent part of it. Piaras didn't need to be told what those stains were.

He quickly returned to my side.

The lower Ruins spread out below us. In the distance, I

could see the lights from the Sorcerers District and the harbor. So close, yet so far. Unseen from the forest floor, the tops of the trees twinkled with light when seen from above. In the canopy, pale lights of blue and white glowed, died, then reappeared farther away, until the forest was alive with fairy light. I had to admit it was possibly the most beautiful, and surprisingly peaceful, sight I had ever seen. And I didn't let myself believe it for one second.

"How do we get out?" Piaras asked.

"The closest exit is a little over two miles that way." I indicated the mostly overgrown path to our left, and the lights in the all-too-far distance. "That'll put us out at the south end of the Sorcerers District."

"That's a long two miles."

Two tiny pinpoints of light appeared through the trees. I thought they were eyes, until they separated. In the next few seconds, more delicate pink lights appeared, singly and in groups of two or three. They darted around us on translucent wings. The illumination seemed to come from the creatures themselves.

Piaras turned slowly, following their flight. "Are they moths?"

I tried to see one clearly as it dove in front of my face and then away. I caught the briefest glimpse of miniature arms, legs, torso and head—all no larger than my thumb, and all without a shred of clothing. There were both males and females.

"They look like some type of sprite or fairy," I said.

Tonight was full of firsts. Possibly not everything living in The Ruins wanted us for a late supper. If it were true, it would be a welcome change.

One of the fairies darted on hummingbird wings around Piaras's upheld hand. She was definitely female. She lightly brushed the spellsinger's hand with her feet. Once. Twice. Piaras remained perfectly still and waited with breathless anticipation. The fairy landed.

More fairies appeared. Their glow was brighter than before,

the colors deeper, more of a rosy orange than pink. I noticed a slight cut on Piaras's wrist where the bindings must have broken the skin. The fairy had noticed, too.

"Piaras," I warned.

"But they're beautiful," he protested, enthralled with the ethereal form perched coyly in the palm of his hand. His face was illuminated by her pale pink glow. She looked rather taken with him, too.

"Yes, they're very pretty. Now, say goodbye to the nice, naked lady and let's get out of here."

The naked lady smiled, and suddenly she wasn't so nice anymore. Razor-sharp teeth glittered in a tidy row a split second before she hissed and sank them into Piaras's wrist. With a gasp, Piaras jumped back and swatted at her. Her pink glow flared to red as she and the others dove at us.

I'd seen enough. "Run!"

Piaras didn't have to be told twice.

Run we could do, but escape was not happening. The forest had upright trees, fallen trees, rocks, brambles, and vines. The blood-sucking fire pixies just darted over or around anything in their path, flames spreading out behind them like the tails of tiny comets. The ground grew soggy, then wet beneath our feet. If memory served me, there was a shallow pond just ahead. Nothing like a little water to dampen fire pixie ardor. At least that was what I was hoping. It was the best I could come up with on no notice.

We burst into the clearing and were instantly knee-deep in pond water.

I quickly waded toward the center, and told myself that being drained dry by fire pixies was a worse death than drowning. I didn't buy it for a minute, but for Piaras's sake, I'd at least try not to think about it.

"Get a deep breath and stay under for as long as you can," I called over my shoulder.

The pixies could just hover above the surface until we were

forced to come up for air, but I'd deal with that stumbling block when I came to it. One problem at a time.

The center of the pond was chin deep on me, chest deep on Piaras. I took all the air my lungs would hold and went under. Piaras followed and did the same.

The pixies were on us immediately. They looked like torches waving over the surface. They darted about, searching. I thought my lungs were going to burst, but I didn't move. Then as suddenly as they had arrived, they were gone. Not trusting luck of any kind tonight, especially the good kind, I waited a few extra moments before sticking my head above the surface. It was hard not to noisily gulp air.

No pixies. No lights.

Piaras's head popped up beside me. "They're gone?" he gasped, once he had filled his own lungs. He seemed as doubtful of our good fortune as I was.

I scanned the surrounding trees. No glow. "That's what it looks like."

"Why?"

"Tastier offer?" I didn't really believe it, but it would have to do until something else came along; but in the meantime, I wasn't going to question it too closely. "Let's get out of here."

I felt heavier coming out of the pond than I had going in. I knew I was taking some of the pond with me soaked into my clothes, but I was listing a little too far to the right. Piaras looked at me, his eyes as big as saucers.

"Raine." His voice was tight.

I stopped and looked down at myself. I didn't see anything. "What?"

He grimaced and pointed to my right side.

I lifted my right arm to get a good look and bit back a scream. It came out as a squeak.

A black, shiny leech was working hard to attach itself to my ribs. It was easily a foot long. And from the enthusiastic way it was squirming to get through my leathers to my skin, I must have been the best thing to come along in quite a while.

I cleared the water and was on the bank with my knife out in record time. The only thing I wanted worse than to have that leech off was to scream. I couldn't remember ever wanting to scream and run that badly.

"Soul-stealing rock, razor-fanged pixies, blood-sucking leeches," I hissed as I struggled to get my knife wedged under the thing's blindly seeking mouth and pry it off. "When this is over I'm going to treat myself to a screaming fit. I deserve it, and I'm going to have one."

I sliced the leech from my doublet and checked myself for others. I stopped. Something was very wrong. Even more wrong than foot-long leeches. Piaras coughed twice from swallowing water, and then it hit me. The noise Piaras had just made was the only sound I could hear. It was as if every creature, living or whatever, was holding its collective breath in anticipation of something. The pixies had known what it was, that's why they had given up so quickly. I suspected we didn't want to wait around and find out what the pixies knew. Piaras realized it at the same time.

"Which is it?" he whispered.

I assumed he was referring to my litany of this evening's monsters.

"None of the above. We need to move." The amulet felt like it was trying to slice its way through my doublet to free itself. "Whatever it is, it's coming at us fast."

I doubled back toward the hill with the intention of skirting its base. That would put us back in the direction of the closest way out. The newest threat was coming from the opposite direction, so every step in our present direction took us farther from the whatever-it-was and closer to home. Worked for me.

I stopped suddenly just before the edge of a large clearing. Piaras plowed into me from behind, and we both went down in a tangle of limbs. I looked up and froze.

Prince Chigaru Mal'Salin stepped out of the shadows about fifty yards to our right. He wasn't alone. I didn't expect he would be. He had neither seen nor heard us, though I imagined that would change soon enough. He was well armed and armored, which was more than I could say for myself or Piaras. Looked like someone was a little put out by our early departure.

Rahimat, the goblin spellsinger, drifted wraithlike out of the trees to stand beside him. Neither of them had sensed us, and I didn't know if it was the beacon shielding us, or the presence of whatever was coming up behind us. What I did know was that we were trapped between the goblins and something the amulet and my own instincts were telling me was infinitely worse.

Chapter 12

"*Mistress Benares. I know you are here. I promise I will not harm* you or your spellsinger, which is more than I can say for the creatures living in this forest. You will not make it out alive without my protection."

Spellsinger? I swore silently. So much for keeping Piaras out of this.

The goblin prince paused, listening. He gestured, and his guards spread out to surround the area where we were. They didn't know our exact location, but it wouldn't take them long, especially if they stepped on us.

My hands were sweating against the leather dagger grips. I forced my breathing to remain even, and released the shielding spell I had been holding, quietly I hoped, to cover both of us.

The goblin prince and his guards moved closer. They didn't make any effort to be quiet. They didn't need to. They weren't the ones hiding.

"I give you my word, both of you will be released unharmed once I have the Saghred."

That's what the prince was saying, but that wasn't what I

believed. I kept my hand on Piaras's shoulder, and willed him not to move. I need not have bothered with the warning. Piaras remained flat on the ground, peering through the thick reeds, eyes alert to the goblins moving toward us. The long dagger was in his hand, and the look on his face said that he wasn't going anywhere else with a goblin tonight—and if any goblin tried to make him, they were going to regret it.

Prince Chigaru's guards were armed mainly with swords. There were a few crossbowmen. Not nearly few enough, but I would take any advantage I could get. I wouldn't exactly call what I sensed approaching us an advantage, but if it gave the crossbowmen something else to shoot at besides us, they were more than welcome to join the party.

I didn't know what scared me worse: the goblins, what was stalking us, or what I wore around my neck. If metal could have emotions, I would say that the beacon was having some strong ones, and it was doing everything it could to compel me to share them. My mind knew I was outside and there was plenty of air for everyone. My body wasn't convinced. The air was getting thick. Only one thing could do that. Magic. The bad kind. And there was entirely too much of it.

I was being hunted, and not just by the prince.

I looked up. A richly robed goblin stood on the far side of the clearing, halfway between us and Chigaru Mal'Salin. The prince's guards froze. I didn't blame them. I also didn't need a formal introduction to the newcomer. We'd met last night.

Sarad Nukpana stood alone, completely unprotected from Prince Chigaru's guards. Any one of them could have put a bolt in his chest. Not a one of them tried.

The grand shaman's head turned, his gaze leisurely taking in every goblin in the clearing. Some of the prince's guards shifted uneasily, some looked away. I heard branches snapping as a few goblins back in the trees bolted in terror.

"I should have expected a traitor to be hiding in the wild with the animals," Nukpana said.

"Or Khrynsani to be consorting with monsters," Prince Chigaru replied, his features expressionless.

Others emerged from the shadows behind Sarad Nukpana, some robed, others in royal Mal'Salin armor. They had no intention of attacking immediately. They were waiting for something, and I for one, could go through the rest of the night without knowing what.

A solitary goblin stepped forward as the others deferentially made way for him. This was unexpected. The beautifully intricate scrollwork on his chestplate clearly identified him. Twin serpents twining around one another, battling for dominance, both surmounted by a crown. He looked like a slightly older version of the prince.

King Sathrik Mal'Salin.

"Brother," he said.

Prince Chigaru remained motionless. "Sathrik."

"You will address your king as Your Majesty." Nukpana's voice was still and quiet, but the menace was clear.

"He is not my king, and he is no longer my brother," Chigaru said. "He is worthy of neither my respect nor my honor, so I may refer to him in any manner I choose." He laughed softly. It was hollow and without humor. "He should count himself fortunate I use his given name rather than others that come to mind."

Piaras and I didn't need to be anywhere near this reunion. If we ran, we would be shot. If we stayed, we would be found, and then shot. And that was if we were lucky. Clearly, the ending would be bad either way. At the moment, I didn't know which Mal'Salin brother was worse, and I didn't even want to think about Sarad Nukpana. I suspected Sathrik Mal'Salin lacked the power to call his grand shaman to heel if he wanted to play with us a while before he had us killed. Still, if his words to me last night were any indication, Sarad Nukpana wanted me very much alive. That might be even worse.

The prince inclined his head in somber acknowledgment of his brother as he slid his saber free of its sheath. The hiss of escaping metal was instantly repeated on both sides. From the eager faces around us, this was a confrontation a long time in the making. I so did not want to be here when it happened.

The night was suddenly split by a feral goblin war cry. I couldn't tell which side it came from. It was immediately answered in kind by a raw voice. Bolts were loosed from both sides as the goblins eagerly charged each other.

I didn't wait to see any more. I pushed Piaras to his feet and we ran back into the trees. I couldn't see where I was going, and until we put the sound of goblins killing each other well behind us, I didn't care. I found spaces between the trees, but more often I found brambles and vines. My face and arms stung with tiny cuts. The ground abruptly dropped away into a ditch. Piaras's long legs took him to the other side. Mine weren't as long, and I wasn't as lucky. I landed just short of the rim, and my knee slammed hard into the ground. Tears came to my eyes, but I pulled myself up and kept running.

Piaras suddenly stopped. It was my turn to run into him. Fortunately for both of us, he didn't fall down.

I saw what had stopped him in his tracks. I agreed with his decision. Sarad Nukpana wasn't what I had sensed hunting me.

A black mass loomed before us. I had seen it before—through Siseal Peli's dying eyes.

More of them glided from the trees, surrounding us. I felt rather than heard something move behind me. I spun, going back-to-back with Piaras, my daggers held low. I was face-to-whatever with one of them. I slashed where an abdomen should be, but the blade passed straight through it. An oily finger extended to touch me. The beacon kicked against my chest like a hammer. My chest tightened until I couldn't breathe past the pain, and my vision blurred. The things drew back.

Someone was running toward us through the trees. Moments later four Khrynsani shamans burst into the clearing. Like Piaras and me, they stopped dead at the sight of the monsters. But unlike us, they didn't seem surprised to see them. They didn't exactly look relieved either. The shamans moved to surround them, chanting in low, sibilant whispers. I recognized some elements of a containment spell, but of a sort that I had never been taught, nor would ever want to learn. Perfect for monsters.

It had no effect.

It was the goblins' turn to be surprised. I felt their fear, and the creatures' hunger. They wanted us more than they wanted to obey the shamans, and the goblins' spells just seemed to annoy them. Maybe it was me, but annoying these things didn't seem like a good idea. The shamans didn't see it that way and kept chanting. Two of the creatures turned toward them. The eyes of the goblin closest to us widened in disbelief.

Two of the things glided toward him. The goblin stopped chanting and drew breath to scream, but the creatures reached him before he had the chance. They flowed over the spot where he had stood. Nothing remained.

A static charge like the aftermath of lightning hung in the air. Two of the creatures had now fed, and the others shifted restlessly, eager to do the same. The remaining three shamans were more experienced. They didn't run—and they should have.

Some of the creatures drifted closer to me and Piaras, their caution giving way to hunger. I fought back in every way I knew. Garadin's lessons hadn't left me unprepared. My repel and shielding spells were of the highest level, but nothing worked. The more I threw at them, the tastier a morsel I became. Magic didn't stop them. It fed them.

The final goblin shaman managed to scream before they took him. Then Piaras and I had their undivided attention.

Garadin had taught Piaras protection spells, but because of his age and inexperience, I had assumed they were only the most basic. I was wrong.

Piaras sang. His normally warm, rich baritone turned harsh and dark, the notes booming and discordant. He sang in goblin, the language the creatures supposedly obeyed, the language of dark magics. I didn't like hearing it from Piaras. But the monsters just ate it up. Literally.

Spells didn't work, sung or otherwise. Shields didn't work. They just swallowed them whole. The beacon thrashed against the center of my chest like a wild horse fighting a bridle. I froze, suddenly more afraid of what I was thinking than what the monsters were about to do. Prince Chigaru said the beacon was connected to the Saghred. If I was connected to the beacon, I was connected to the Saghred. The creatures ate everything I could give them. Could they eat everything the beacon—and the Saghred—could give them? It didn't seem to think so. And with my life in danger, I didn't have a choice, regardless of what the Saghred might do to me.

There was an opening just beyond where the creatures circled us. Both of us wouldn't have time to reach it, but if I could distract them long enough, Piaras might.

"Get behind me," I told him. "When they come after me, I want you to run."

"I'm not leaving you."

"Do it!"

Piaras glanced sharply at me, his mouth forming the word "no." The sound never made it out. He saw my face and froze. His own reflected disbelief—and fear. He was afraid of me. I didn't know how he saw me in that instant, and I didn't want to. Prince Chigaru's words came back to me. Death. He saw death reflected in my eyes. Was that what Piaras saw now?

The Saghred's power was building. I couldn't stop it any more than I could stop the goblin-spawned things that closed on us. I couldn't resist the power and found that I didn't want to. My hand went to the center of my chest. It felt like it belonged to someone else. The leather of my doublet was no barrier. I didn't feel the beacon, I felt what lay beyond it—wild and whole and wide awake.

Its power became my power. I was its instrument, but the tune was still my own.

My ribs heaved against the pressure to keep breath in my

body. The power tore its way to the surface, a complexity of magic I never knew existed until now. That power became a part of me, as did knowledge of a way to destroy what threatened us. Thoughts not my own flashed like lightning through my mind, too fast for comprehension, too complex for reason—but not too inaccessible for action.

One of the creatures rushed us, crazed with hunger. I threw myself in front of Piaras and into the creature before it could reach us, and before it was ready to feed. The instant of contact opened a floodgate, releasing more power than a thousand such creatures could consume, and threw us both to the ground. The thing tried to separate from me to save itself, but it couldn't. There was a blinding flash of light, then all was still. The pressure holding me down lifted. I opened my eyes.

The creature was gone. They were all gone. There was nothing left.

I felt raw and exhausted and I had the worst headache of my life. I also felt the urge to be sick. I groaned, rolled over, and threw up. It felt like there were hundreds of voices inside my head. Wonderful. Every magic-sensitive within miles must have heard what had just happened. The volume was deafening. I held my head with both hands. It didn't help. I rolled over onto my back, gulping air. The ground was cool and damp. Maybe if I could just shut my eyes for a little while.

Piaras was kneeling over me. "Raine, can you hear me? Are you all right?"

I opened my eyes to a squint, and moved my head in what I thought was an up and down motion. It hurt, so I stopped.

Piaras started lifting me to my feet. "We need to go. Now."

I didn't want to be on my feet, but I tried to help him as much as I could. "Something's coming?" I heard myself slur.

"Yes, something's coming."

My legs would have been perfectly content to wait for every Mal'Salin and goblin in The Ruins to converge on us. The rest of me just wanted a nap. From the sounds of things, company wasn't going to be long in coming. It didn't matter if they belonged to the king, the prince, or the psycho—Piaras and I would be just as dead.

"I'm okay," I told Piaras, standing on my own. I was a bit wobbly, but at least I was upright. The ground was still looking awfully good.

He didn't look convinced. "You're sure?"

I managed a weak smile. "I can sleep when I'm dead, and that's not going to be tonight. Dead, that is. Sleep I'm still hoping for."

"Perhaps we can help you with that."

I knew that voice.

Paladin Mychael Eiliesor stood squarely in the middle of the path that I judged to be the best way out of this nightmare—and he didn't look inclined to move. A full complement of Guardians moved quickly and silently through the trees, putting themselves between us and the goblins. That action I could agree with and even be grateful for, but I doubted the same was true of Eiliesor's intentions. The beacon rested quietly against my skin. Coward.

A blond human Guardian ran back to the paladin from the direction of the goblin pursuit. "More Khrynsani shamans, sir." The big man grinned. "Almost enough to make it worth the trip."

He held a curved battle-ax in his hands, and I could feel the magic he held in check. I think he wanted a chance to use both, though he looked like he would enjoy using the ax more. I hoped he got what he wanted. Everyone deserved a little happiness. He was bearded and sections of his shoulder-length hair were braided. Myloran sea-raider stock. Uncle Ryn had a few Myloran berserkers on his crew, and the Guardian had a familiar maniacal gleam in his eyes. He looked like he'd fit right in with Uncle Ryn's boys.

"Take the men and cover our exit," Eiliesor told him. "Do not provoke an attack."

"What if they attack first?" the blond Guardian asked eagerly.

"Defend yourselves."

The Guardian saluted and vanished into the trees.

I took a step back. "*Our* exit?"

"You do know how to find trouble, Mistress Benares."

Eiliesor hadn't moved, but his posture told me he would be on me in an instant if I moved again. I decided to stay put, for the moment. I let my breath out slowly and relaxed my shoulders, ready to spring. His movements perfectly mirrored mine.

"It's not like I have to look far," I said. "Trouble usually finds me, especially lately."

The Guardian smiled, and I had to admit the effect was startling. He managed to look boyish and dangerous at the same time. "I told myself the next time I found you, I was going to be on dry land," he said.

I couldn't help but smile back at him. "I won't apologize for the dunking in the canal yesterday morning. A girl's got to protect her privacy."

"I'm no trouble, Mistress Benares. At least not to you." His smile vanished, replaced with something surprisingly like concern. "You would do yourself and your spellsinger friend a great service if you would believe that. For your own safety, I need the two of you to come with me."

I glanced at Piaras. Everyone recognized what he was. Did he have "spellsinger" written on his forehead or something? Piaras was looking at the elven Guardian with wide-eyed awe. Great. I didn't need this now.

"She plays a dangerous game, Guardian," came a smooth and cultured voice from behind us. "As do you."

Sarad Nukpana was standing not ten feet away, looking at Piaras and me with bright-eyed interest. Still darkly beautiful, still just as deadly.

I used my arm and body weight to shove Piaras behind me. It took what little strength I had left, and I was sure he didn't appreciate the gesture. I didn't care.

The Guardians and the goblins had found each other among the trees, and judging from the sounds, neither group was playing nice. It didn't concern me, not now. With everyone else occupied, it was just the four of us here in the small clearing.

"I'm not playing anything," I told the goblin. "Games are fun, and I'm not having any."

"Then you're not playing the right ones." Nukpana's voice was soft, reminding me of something slithering through dry leaves. "Though what you did to my Magh'Sceadu was entertaining enough. Or should I say, what the Saghred did to my Magh'Sceadu. Either way, it was very impressive, but you should be more careful. Raine, isn't it?"

My skin did a full-body crawl at the sound of my first name crossing Sarad Nukpana's lips.

He spoke, his tone pleasant. "I have long looked forward to our meeting." He considered me, his intense gaze holding me where I stood. "You have your father's eyes."

I just stared at him, shocked into silence, my breath stopped. I didn't know who my father was, but I did know I didn't want him to be anyone Sarad Nukpana knew and remembered.

He noted my reaction, absorbed it, then discarded it.

"Playing with the Soul Thief is dangerous," he chided. "I would not want you to damage yourself prematurely. I have need of you later. I agree with you, games should be enjoyable." His attention fixed on Piaras, and his smile spread, fangs clearly visible. "A hatchling nightingale. The power in your song was unexpected, but hardly unwelcome."

Mychael Eiliesor circled off to the left, putting himself firmly between me and Piaras and the Khrynsani grand shaman. With his Guardians in the forest all around us, he probably wasn't too concerned with us escaping.

"You would have done better to have remained in your embassy," the elven Guardian told the goblin. "As would your king."

"Our quarry has been as elusive as she is desirable," Nukpana said, glancing at me. "Like you, I have been forced to seek her out." One side of the goblin's lips quirked upward as if from a private joke. "What are the odds? The two of us competing for the attentions of the same fair lady."

"There is no competition." Eiliesor's voice was low and intense, and I felt his power building. So did the amulet. The slaughter in the forest around us was nothing compared to what the spellsinger had ready to unleash.

"Are you that confident in your success?" the goblin said. "Listen all around you. I do not hear many human or elven voices."

I could see Eiliesor's profile, and caught the slightest hint of a smile.

"You're right, those screams are goblin."

"Then we should hurry to conclude our business," Nukpana said, completely unruffled. "Mistress Benares, you have something that belongs to me. I hired your human employee to recover it, but my attempts to retrieve it have been plagued by unexpected complications." A hint of fang again glimmered from a slow smile. "Complications that for the most part have been eliminated."

Simon Stocken. Nigel Nicabar. Me. Piaras, for standing next to me.

"You presume much, Primaru Nukpana," Eiliesor said. "Such as ownership. The beacon is a Conclave artifact. That ownership has not changed—nor will it."

"Ownership is possession," the goblin said, his black eyes lingering on me.

Both Nukpana and Eiliesor were suddenly closer. I hadn't seen either one of them move.

The elf's eyes narrowed. "That's far enough."

"On the contrary, Paladin Eiliesor, I'll be going much farther."

I knew what was about to happen. Sometimes a girl doesn't mind being fought over. This wasn't one of those times. I was in no condition to fight my own battles right now, but I wasn't about to stick around to become someone's spoils of war.

Mychael Eiliesor didn't move; he just dropped the glamour

that had kept his power masked. The air around him rippled like the surface of deep water in the wake of something large just below the surface, something dangerous. The elf's magic reached Sarad Nukpana. The goblin flinched. If you blinked, you'd have missed it. I didn't blink, and I didn't miss it.

I wasn't the only one who sensed it. I was also certain Mychael Eiliesor had no illusions about who and what he was dealing with.

"Take the boy and go."

Eiliesor's voice was calm—and inside my head. Piaras was as transfixed on the scene before us as I was. I wasn't about to wait for the Guardian to change his mind. I began backing away, pulling Piaras with me. I was sure Mychael Eiliesor could take care of himself. You didn't get to be paladin if you couldn't. I was in no condition to take care of anyone right now, and it wasn't just me who was in danger. I had Piaras to think of.

"Go. I can deal with this."

I hesitated a moment longer, then we ran.

Chapter 13

We found our way out of The Ruins at the south end of the Sorcerers District near the canal at Rowan Street. It wasn't close to where I wanted to be, but since what I wanted most was to be out of The Ruins, I wasn't going to quibble about the details.

The streets were deserted, which I expected for both the hour and section of town. Rowan Street was largely residential, and the residents were asleep. I would like to have been asleep in my bed, but for the moment I was just grateful to be breathing.

Piaras and I were doing our fair share of that. Once I got my bearings—and my legs back under me—the final sprint through The Ruins was uneventful, but we were both more than a little winded. Running, combined with multiple near-death experiences, will do that to you.

Once over the bridge separating The Ruins from the District, we quickly crossed Rowan Street and stopped well out of the lamplight next to a vacant townhouse. We needed a moment to catch our breath, but the last thing I wanted to do was set off anyone's house wards.

"We can't go home, can we?" Piaras asked. From his tone, he knew the answer to that one as well as I did.

"Not yet. We're not far from Phaelan's ship. We'll go there first. I'll have him send word to Garadin. I need to talk to him. We'll also let Tarsilia know that we're safe."

"But we're not safe."

I got the feeling Piaras really wanted me to tell him he was wrong. Unfortunately, I couldn't do that.

"Safe is relative," I told him. "We're not within a mile of Sarad Nukpana or anyone named Mal'Salin. That'll have to do for now."

I knew what was hanging around my neck. Now I needed to know how to get rid of it, without it or anyone else getting rid of me. Mychael Eiliesor was best qualified to tell me how. He would be looking for me, but I was going to find him first. Enough was enough.

Piaras didn't say anything else, but I could virtually hear the wheels turning in his head. He had done a lot of growing up tonight. You didn't get to choose the events that boosted you into adulthood. If you were lucky, it was an event that in the future would trigger pleasant memories. If you weren't lucky, you got nightmares. What I said next might keep the awakening-to-your-own-screams part to a minimum for Piaras. No doubt he was trying to make sense of everything he had seen tonight—including me. But I thought I owed him the assurance that, unlike the things that had attacked us, I wasn't a monster. It'd be nice if I could believe it myself.

I wanted to ask Piaras about what he'd done to the Magh'Sceadu, or what he'd tried to do. It was a repelling spell, something every magic user should know for their own protection, but it was in goblin and Piaras had done it very well. Almost too well. I wanted to be sure it had been either Tarsilia or Garadin who had taught it to him, but I decided it would be better not to bring that up right now. The less Piaras dwelled on what had almost happened to us, the better.

That brought up something I wanted to forget completely. *You have your father's eyes.*

Suddenly, a cloaked and hooded figure came running around the end of the next block. This time of the night, anyone in that big of a hurry couldn't have been up to any good. He spotted us immediately, and Rowan Street really didn't offer any places to hide.

The man, or whatever, had come from the direction of the outer city, not The Ruins. That was one point in his favor, though I wasn't ready to award him any more. I stood my ground, and Piaras did likewise. We had more than had our fill of cloaked and hooded figures, and were sick, quite literally, of running. Besides, there was only one of him. After Nukpana's pet shadow monsters, I felt able to deal with anything one lone figure could dish out. And if magic wasn't enough, there were always my favorites—fists, knees, or steel. I drew my ill-gotten knives. I was armed and ready. He might as well know it.

The figure stopped about ten feet away from us and threw back his hood.

"I thought you two would be happier to see me," Garadin said.

When finally I found my voice, it was a little higher than usual. "Are you trying to get yourself skewered? Don't run at people like that!"

Garadin went to Piaras first and enfolded him in a crushing hug. I still had bare blades in my hands, so I guess I couldn't fault his first choice. I sheathed them.

"How did you find us?" Piaras asked, when Garadin let him breathe again.

"How could I *not* find you?" My godfather gave me the same bone-crushing hug. "I'm surprised you two didn't wake up the entire District." He held me at arms length and gave me an accusing look. "You took the amulet off again, didn't you?"

"Not exactly. By the way, we can add a couple of names to

the list of people who want this thing. Chigaru Mal'Salin is one of them."

That tidbit surprised Garadin.

"Piaras and I were his guests for the evening," I said. "He told me what the amulet is and what it does. We'd still be there, but we didn't want to outstay our welcome, so we left. The prince thought we were being rude and invited us back."

"His invitation involved swords and crossbows," Piaras clarified.

"And I ran into Sarad Nukpana again," I continued to Garadin, who still looked a little stunned. "He has his new pet king with him. I'll give you all the details, but we might want to go somewhere less public first."

Phaelan's ship was moored in the deepest part of the lagoon. Though Mermeia had ample deepwater docks, Phaelan had exchanged his dock in Whitaker Creek for a mooring after our encounter at Nigel's. He valued his ship and his crew, and always said he felt safer surrounded by water. I thought it was a good idea then. I thought it was an even better idea now. Anybody can walk down a wooden dock; no one I knew could walk on water.

Oddly enough, my fear of water didn't extend to a fear of being on a ship. Boats were another matter. Boats were small. Boats could tip over. To me, a ship was like a big wooden island. As a general rule, islands didn't sink. I applied the same rule to ships. I knew ships could sink, but since one had yet to sink under me, I saw no reason to change my rule.

Garadin went to arrange transportation while Piaras and I waited hidden behind a stack of crab pots awaiting repair. Drake's Landing was home to the majority of Mermeia's fishermen, and was bustling and noisy as the boats were coming in from a night of fishing. There was more than enough controlled chaos going on to hide a pair of newly fugitive elves.

The sunrise was still hours away. I had seen the sunrise yesterday and had hoped to avoid being awake for it today. Now I was just grateful to be alive.

"Some of Maira's sugar knots would be nice right now," Piaras said wistfully.

From his uncertain glance, food wasn't all Piaras had on his mind. He just wasn't sure how to bring it up.

I had a pretty good idea what he wanted to talk about.

"Sugar knots would be good," I agreed, looking out over the harbor. Part of me was perfectly willing to wait for Piaras to bring up the subject in his own time; the other part just wanted to get it over with. I didn't know what to tell him. I didn't understand what had happened to me either, so I certainly wasn't qualified to explain it to anyone else. But once we got out to the *Fortune*, I was going to be explaining it to Garadin, or at least trying to, so I might as well start practicing now.

Piaras beat me to it. Patience wasn't high on the list of teenage virtues. It wasn't at the top of mine, either.

"Are you all right?"

His voice was quiet and the question tentative, as if he already knew the answer, but didn't really want to hear it. He wasn't inquiring about my health. He wanted to know if the Raine who had come out of The Ruins was the same Raine who had gone in. It was a good question. I wished I knew the answer.

"I don't know."

He just stood there, looking at me with those big brown eyes, and in one terrible moment, I thought he was going to cry. Psychotic goblin brothers, Khrynsani shamans, various creatures of the night, even Sarad Nukpana—those I could take. What I could not take was Piaras going to pieces on me. At this point, I'd probably join him.

I waved my hands frantically. "No, no. Don't cry." I blinked back misties of my own. "If you cry, I'll cry, and I don't want to cry."

Piaras didn't cry, but he took a shuddering breath, which was just as bad. "It's all my fault. If I hadn't gotten myself caught, none of this would have happened." His voice was on the verge of breaking. "We'd both be home right now, and you wouldn't have had to use . . ." He gestured vaguely and helplessly at where the beacon rested beneath my shirt. ". . . that thing, and . . ."

I was going to put a stop to this right now, before the salty sting in my eyes went any further.

"That thing's the reason we're still alive. I don't know what happened to me, but it's not your fault. It's nobody's fault, except maybe a nine-hundred-year-old dead Guardian who couldn't keep track of his own necklace. But he's not around for us to yell at."

Piaras sniffed, then wiped his eyes on his shirtsleeve. I resisted the urge to do the same.

He swallowed, and took a deep breath, steadying himself. "What are you going to do?"

"The only thing I can do. Contact Mychael Eilicsor and find some way to give him this thing. If he wants it, he can have it. Guarding the Saghred is his job, so I'm going to help him get on with it."

"Do you think you can trust him?"

"I can't trust any of the others who think they should have it. They all want me dead, or worse. He doesn't seem to. It's not much, but it's a start."

Piaras sniffed. I sniffed.

I heard Garadin's low whistle. I peered around the crabpots. The *Fortune's* dinghy was pulling up to the dock.

Saved by the boat.

Two of Phaelan's crew rowed us out to the *Fortune*. The dinghy had a section covered by a tarp. Piaras and I slipped under the tarp unnoticed by the fishermen and unseen by any goblin.

The short trip out to where Phaelan's ship was moored gave me a few minutes to think. Those thoughts kept coming back to the Guardian. Mychael Eiliesor could have forceably taken the amulet from me as soon as he'd found us in The Ruins, and in my condition, there wouldn't have been much I could have done to stop him. He didn't. What he did do was put himself between me and Piaras and the danger of Sarad Nukpana and told us to go. He wanted the amulet, but he wasn't going to endanger our lives to get it. In short, he was being the perfect paladin and gentleman. I felt a little smile coming on. It wasn't what I'd expected, but it was something I could definitely get used to.

We got out to the ship without incident.

For the first time tonight, I felt safe. As with most of his possessions, Phaelan didn't bother with flash—with the *Fortune*, fast and nimble was all he wanted. She delivered both. She also delivered forty guns, and men and elves who knew how to use them.

Aeryk Galir, Phaelan's first mate, met us as we boarded on the port side. It faced the barrier islands, well away from any curious eyes.

"The Captain doesn't get many visitors at this hour," Aeryk said, grinning as he helped me over the side. "He was surprised to hear you were coming aboard."

"This wasn't exactly planned. I won't be staying long. It wouldn't be safe for me or anyone else here."

"Whatever trouble's after you, ma'am, we can handle it."

"Right now *I* can't handle the trouble I have after me, and I'm not going to make my problems anyone else's. I plan to be gone before anyone knows I'm here."

Aeryk shrugged, then nodded. He'd had firsthand experience of the trouble I occasionally managed to attract, and he wasn't going to give me any arguments.

"The Captain asked me to have you all join him in his cabin."

We went below. Phaelan was at the table in the center of the cabin, the remains of some kind of meal in front of him. With Phaelan's night owl tendencies, who knew which meal it was supposed to be. I crossed the cabin in three strides and greeted my cousin with a big hug. Phaelan wasn't the touchy-feely type, and normally I respected his personal space, but things hadn't been normal for days so I felt entitled.

Piaras had to duck his head to get through the door, and my

cousin's smile vanished when he saw the young elf's bruised face. The color hadn't faded, but at least the swelling had gone down.

"What happened?" Phaelan's voice promised many bad things for whoever had caused that bruise.

"Nothing good," I told him. My voice suddenly sounded as exhausted as I felt. I think it was the sight of somewhere to sit, and no one standing between me and there, waiting to kill me. I pulled up a chair and sat down, my muscles tight and protesting from a night of running and other less healthy activities. "I should probably start from when I left home yesterday morning."

Phaelan ordered food and clean clothes brought for both of us. Mine were still more or less in one piece, but the smell left something to be desired after the dunking in The Ruins' pond, so I took my cousin up on his offer. When I'd changed, I told them all about my day—starting with my talk with Janek at Nigel's townhouse, then to my spotting of A'Zahra Nuru and subsequent meeting with Tam. I finished with Ocnus's setup and how Piaras and I had spent our night.

By the time I stopped talking, Piaras had excused himself from the table and stretched out on Phaelan's bunk. He was now sound asleep. I was hard pressed to keep my own eyes open.

Garadin had his elbows on the table, his forehead resting against the palms of his upraised hands. It was a thinking position he used when there was more of a problem than infor mation to solve it. Glad he agreed with me.

"In a twisted way, it being a beacon makes sense," he said. He lifted his head and leaned back in his chair. "It would certainly explain its popularity—and yours."

"Nothing makes sense to me, least of all why it picked me to attach itself to," I told him. "Guardians guard the Saghred. I'm not a Guardian. I'm only a passable sorceress."

Apparently I was also my father's daughter, and while I wanted to talk to Garadin about it, I thought I'd wait until we were alone.

"The beacon doesn't seem to mind," Phaelan noted.

"Well, I do."

"It doesn't seem to care what you think, either."

I let that one pass. He was right.

"I have an idea of what you did." Garadin's blue eyes were solemn as he looked back at me. "But I have no idea how you were able to do it."

It was only as much as I knew, and didn't know, myself.

"How much do you know about the Saghred?" I asked him.

"Enough to know that you don't want anything to do with it."

"Too late for that." Now for the question of the night. "What can contact with it do to me?"

Garadin didn't want to answer that one. That much was obvious.

"Legend has it the Saghred can level armies or kingdoms," he said. "Though there's no historical record of the Saghred linked with any destroyed army or no-longer-existing kingdom. So it's probably safe to say those are false claims."

"Probably safe?"

"More than likely."

"But not definitely."

"No."

I sighed and took a sip of coffee. Phaelan served it laced with whiskey, and it burned its way down my throat.

"Though the Great Rift in Rheskilia was said to have been caused by the Saghred in a Khrynsani experiment gone wrong," Garadin added.

The Great Rift was a mile-wide, nearly fifty-mile-long tear in the mountains of the Northern Reach. That was some experiment.

"But what would it do to *me*?" My voice sounded rather small.

"I've only read about Khrynsani shamans using the Saghred," Garadin said. "And they weren't too sane to begin with, so I don't think they're your best point of reference."

"For what?"

"The Saghred affecting mental stability."

My coffee stuck in my throat. I managed to swallow. "I've heard that one, too."

"Just another claim, probably false," Garadin hurried to assure me. "I'm sure what you experienced tonight was the beacon, or the shielding spells protecting the Saghred."

That was easy for him to say. He wasn't the one possibly on the verge of going off the deep end.

"Mychael Eiliesor would be the one to ask," Garadin added. "The Guardians play anything to do with the Saghred close to the vest. You've decided to meet with him?"

I nodded. "As soon as I've had some sleep. I have a feeling I'm going to need it."

"Do you know where to find him?"

I smiled, though it probably looked more like a grimace. "That's the only easy part of this whole mess. I don't have to do a thing. He'll find me. He's been popping into my head on a regular basis lately, so the next time he does it, I'll just make a date. I was going to find him first, but I'd rather have a few hours of sleep."

"Do you want some company when you meet with him?" Phaelan asked.

I took another swig of whiskey coffee. It didn't burn now, but then I couldn't feel my tongue anymore, either.

"All I can get," I told him. "I don't want any misunderstandings. When I tell him he can have the beacon, he needs to know that I'm not part of the deal."

Phaelan drained his own mug. "I think we can help him understand that."

"Tell me more about the creatures that attacked you and Piaras," Garadin said.

"What Sarad Nukpana cooked up?"

"Those are the ones."

"More like shadows than anything," I told him. "That is, if shadows were solid, and if ink could eat people." I fought a shiver and failed. "Nukpana called them Magh'Sceadu. I know goblin, but I've never heard that term before. Do you know what they are?"

Garadin nodded. "They're a Khrynsani creation, supposedly made out of goblin elemental magics. They function much like a sponge. They absorb magic in those who have it, and the life force of those who don't. The shaman who created them can then use the harvested power for other purposes."

If Sarad Nukpana was their creator, I wasn't anxious to hear about those other purposes, or think about how close Piaras and I came to finding out firsthand. The first order of business when I met with Mychael Eiliesor should probably be a thank you.

"They can take any form their creator chooses," Garadin continued. "But as with most conjurings, you can make them as elaborate or simple as needed. Elaborate takes time and effort. From your description, what you encountered were Magh'Sceadu at their most basic. A quick and dirty version. Apparently the Khrynsani are more concerned with getting a specific job done rather than making them look pretty."

I didn't need to ask what that job was. Or more to the point, who that job was.

I looked over at Piaras. He was still asleep. Good. I didn't want him to hear what I was going to ask. I didn't want to know the answer, but I needed to. I had seen what they had done to Siseal Peli and the goblin shamans who had tried to rein them in, but I didn't know what had actually happened to them. If I ran into Nukpana's beasties again, I wanted to be better prepared, though I really didn't think it would help. The shamans thought they were prepared, and look what it got them. But I'd take a little knowledge over a lot of ignorance any day. At the very least, I'd die knowing what killed me.

"I don't think Sarad Nukpana intended the Magh'Sceadu for you or Piaras," Garadin said, not completely misreading my thoughts. "Considering what they were made to do, sending them after you would have been heavy-handed, not to mention wasteful in Nukpana's opinion. You have the beacon, he wants the Saghred, so he wants you alive."

Garadin didn't need to tell me that. I had figured out that sickening fact all by myself.

"Nukpana probably turned them loose in The Ruins to feed on the magical creatures there," Garadin continued. "Less chance of attracting the city watch that way."

Made sense to me. "The shamans lost control of them and paid the price. If I hadn't been able to do whatever it was I did, we probably would have ended up the same way."

"Possibly."

I fought down a wave of nausea. No, probably.

"I'd say that you and Piaras together attracted their attention. You certainly got mine. One whiff of your magic and they probably snapped their leashes, so to speak, to get at you. Once they were on your trail, all the shamans could do was chase them down and try to regain control."

"So the shamans were eaten?" Phaelan asked.

I didn't like the sound of that last word at all. But from the horror that I had witnessed, that was the most apt description.

"Absorbed would be more accurate," Garadin said. "Once a Magh'Sceadu has had its fill, a Khrynsani shaman uses what was taken to power their own sorceries. Then they turn it loose to fill its belly, or whatever, again. As to what a shaman does with that power boost, it's generally big, nasty, and something even a group of the most talented shamans couldn't, or wouldn't want to, do alone."

That sounded too close to the Saghred's idea of fun for my taste. I suddenly wanted more whiskey in my whiskey coffee.

"That 'big and nasty' wouldn't extend to opening Gates by any chance?" I asked.

Garadin nodded. "That and a whole bevy of other nice, wholesome activities. I haven't exactly gone out of my way to get direct knowledge. Like Gate creation, the rituals said to be used to make a Magh'Sceadu are repugnant to say the least. Blood, torture, and living sacrifices—it's unclear whether any of these are actually required, but it gives the Khrynsani an excuse."

A kidnapping could leave a trail. Absorbing didn't leave anything. It went a long way toward explaining the sorcerers who had vanished recently without a trace. Magh'Sceadu didn't leave leftovers.

I had a lot to think about, and I had a feeling no one I had run into this evening was going to wait patiently while I sorted everything out. I looked up. Garadin was watching me intently.

"What are you going to do about . . . ?" He nodded in Piaras's direction, not wanting to say his name out loud for fear of waking him.

Piaras was curled under the blanket, his breathing deep and even. I knew exactly what Garadin meant. Too many people knew what he was capable of. Too many of the wrong kind of people. I wasn't the only reason those Magh'Sceadu came after us. I may not have even been the main reason. After putting the goblin guards to sleep, and then confronting Nukpana's pet monsters, Piaras had glowed with power, and it hadn't diminished until we had left The Ruins. He had left a trail for just about anything that wanted to follow us.

"He did good work tonight," I said quietly.

"I know," Garadin said. "I heard him."

"So did a lot of other people."

"You weren't exactly discreet yourself."

"But I've dealt with crazies before," I said. "Some almost as bad as Sarad Nukpana. It's what I do for a living. It's my choice. Piaras didn't have a choice." I lowered my voice further. "Piaras used a repelling spell against the Magh'Sceadu. In goblin. You taught him that, right?"

Garadin's gaze met mine unflinchingly. "I thought it was something he might need to know. How did he do?"

"Very proficient. Almost too much so."

"Those spells are complex. Especially in goblin. The boy kept his head." Garadin nodded his own in approval. "Good."

I agreed it was good that Piaras kept his head. But I wasn't happy that he had been put in a situation where he risked losing it in the first place.

"I'd just rather he not have to make a habit of defending himself against creatures like that. Normally I could arrange for him to stay in one of Markus's safehouses, but they're all full. Besides, I'd rather he be with people he knows. Any suggestions?" I asked Garadin.

"Home would be the best place for him."

"But is it safe?"

"Tarsilia has some of the strongest house wards in the District," Garadin said. "And I'll move in until all this is settled."

"Hopefully that'll be soon, and with a win for our side." I finished off my coffee. "Now, if everyone will excuse me, I need to take a nap and make a date with a Guardian." I indicated the cabin's other bunk, presently buried under maps and papers. "Can I borrow that for a few hours?" I asked Phaelan.

In response, Phaelan stood and started cleaning it off. Except his idea of cleaning involved mostly transferring the pile from the bed to the top of a nearby trunk.

I pulled back the blanket and sat down on the edge of the bunk. "Wake me if we're about to be slaughtered." I meant it as a joke, but it didn't quite come out that way.

Phaelan probably meant to smile. It didn't quite make it either. "Other than Eiliesor, don't worry about any interruptions. We'll make sure it stays quiet for you."

From his serious tone, I had no doubts. But as I lay down and pulled the blanket over myself, my last thought before drifting off hoped those wouldn't turn out to be famous last words.

Chapter 14

Sleep didn't take long finding me, and I didn't take long finding Mychael Eiliesor. I had no idea how I found him, but if the beacon could talk, I was sure it could tell me.

I found myself in an unfamiliar and lavishly decorated bedroom. Only the best and most expensive furnishings and linens, and my eye for such things was very accurate. I'd come to realize that if I liked it, it was expensive. Another Benares family trait. I heard movement from the canopied bed. The embroidered bed curtains were pulled back, and the occupant shifted in sleep. I stopped breathing.

Mychael Eiliesor lay on his side with a pale sheet draped loosely over his waist. One arm was curled under the pillow, and the other stretched across the bed. His coppery hair gleamed in the light of a single bedside lamp and one loose curl brushed his temple. My eyes were drawn lower, down the leanly muscled torso and beyond. If he was wearing anything, it wasn't obvious to me. He moved and the sheet slipped farther. Nope, he definitely wasn't wearing anything. I felt my face flush, which shouldn't have been possible considering that I wasn't really there. I looked away. Then I looked back. I couldn't help myself.

His glorious sea blue eyes were open and watching me. I didn't like water, but I could drown in those eyes and die happy. I froze in shock. *He could see me.* I looked down at myself. *I* could see me. But I was asleep onboard the *Fortune.* I couldn't be in both places at once. Or could I? But how?

Eiliesor was now propped up on one elbow. He was still watching me, but now there was the beginning of a smile tugging at the corners of his mouth. Heart-stopping.

"This is unexpected," he said.

He was telling me.

"We need to talk," I heard myself say. It didn't sound quite like me, but then I wasn't quite here, or there. I had a fluttering moment of panic and disorientation. Actually, I didn't know where I was.

His smile had turned into a grin. "We *are* talking." Then his eyes widened slightly. "You've never done a sending before, have you?"

I shook my head. "The past two days have been full of firsts." I swallowed, and looked back down at my hands. "I'm not supposed to be this solid, am I?"

"I know of only two mages on Mid who can manifest that well, and you're doing it through three layers of my best shields."

That did it. I had just gone from being merely creepy to truly scaring myself. I wondered if I could faint. I think it must have showed, because the Guardian started to get up.

I waved my hands. "No, no. Stay." Seeing him get out of bed, now or anytime, would *not* soothe my rattled nerves. Quite the opposite.

He stayed. But he moved so that he was sitting on the edge of the bed, the sheet gathered around his waist. He motioned me to a chair. I looked at it and wasn't exactly sure if it would work; that is, whether I could actually sit down when I wasn't really there. I gingerly sat down—and didn't fall through. A pleasant surprise, disturbing, but pleasant. Much like the unob-structed view of the elf's smoothly sculpted chest.

Having never done this before, I wasn't sure how long I would be able to stay, so I thought I'd better get to the point.

"I have questions; you have answers."

"I have some questions myself," he said.

I'll bet he did. "I'll make you a deal," I told him. "You answer mine, and I'll answer yours."

"I'll tell you what I can."

I nodded. It was as much as I would be doing myself. There were some things about myself I'd rather a Conclave Guardian didn't know.

"I'll start," he said. "Sarad Nukpana hired your partner to steal the beacon. He called you by name. You can use the beacon. This isn't a coincidence."

"You get right to the point, don't you?"

"I don't have time for anything else. Neither do you."

Looking at our mutual situation from his point of view, I guess my involvement did look rather shady. To a point he was right. I couldn't exactly walk the moral high road here. But knowing a thief didn't make me one; and a psycho knowing my name didn't make me one of those either, so I felt entitled to get on my high horse, however briefly.

"I didn't steal anything, Paladin Eiliesor. And I resent being treated as if I did. I deemed you the most likely to help me solve my problem, and the least likely to try and kill me afterward. That's why I'm here. It's not how I normally choose sides, but it'll have to do."

He just looked at me. "Then how did you get the beacon?"

I told him. However, I completely neglected to mention Quentin by name at all, or Phaelan or Piaras or anyone else I cared about. Amazing how little details can get glossed over in relaying the bigger picture. I'm certain Eiliesor wanted to know the details, but I didn't think they were necessary. If he felt otherwise, he didn't show any sign. Apparently only one thing was important to him, and it was hanging around my neck.

When I had finished, he just sat there, watching me, no doubt weighing my words against his own version of the truth. My tone had betrayed no emotion, nor doubt as to my sincerity. And I knew he didn't believe me for a minute. His problem, not mine. Yet.

He finally spoke. "So you know what you have."

It wasn't a question.

"More or less. Chigaru Mal'Salin told me last night. Though I think he told me because he didn't expect I'd be going anywhere."

"Probably. How much do you know about the Saghred, Mistress Benares?"

"More than I did yesterday, which is a hell of a lot more than I ever wanted to know. I know what it is, some of what it supposedly does, and that a lot of people want to get their hands on it, yourself included."

"Let me tell you what I know, Mistress Benares. Your partner"—he paused and smiled slightly—"who apparently has no name, discovered the beacon the night before last in the home of a prominent Mermeian necromancer. The moment he opened the containment box was obvious to me, as it was to many in this city. I know the beacon passed into your possession at Simon Stocken's warehouse. I sensed it again, a few hours later on the edge of the Sorcerers District. The signal was subtle. I sensed it only because I knew what I was listening for."

He stood, and holding the sheet loosely around his waist, reached for a long dressing robe draped across the foot of the bed. "What I heard last night in The Ruins was not subtle, nor was it the small magics innate to a beacon. I followed it and found you and a spellsinger far too young to be that powerful. You had just destroyed six fully formed Magh'Sceadu. A casual observer would say you had accomplished this feat all by yourself." He paused. "I'm not a casual observer."

He turned away from me, put on the robe, and let the sheet drop to the floor.

I swallowed.

He tied the sash, and turned to face me. "Forgive me, Mistress Benares, but your natural gifts are marginal at best—at least they used to be. What you accomplished last night is a level of craft you should not be capable of. You reached through the beacon and used the Saghred. How, I do not know. I've never agreed with Sarad Nukpana on anything, but in this instance he is correct. You're playing a dangerous game."

I didn't know whether to be insulted at his less-than-glowing assessment of my former abilities, or concerned by his accuracy. But it was his last opinion that struck the nerve.

"No one ever asked me if I wanted to play, Paladin Eiliesor. I'm a seeker. A good one. Aside from that, I can defend myself, and I have a couple of parlor tricks up my sleeves. That's all I knew until two days ago. Many in this town wouldn't mind having what I have now. I'd like nothing better than to pitch this piece of metal in the nearest canal, but I can't."

The Guardian looked puzzled. "Can't?"

"Can't. Remember an hour after I left Stocken's warehouse? You said you sensed the beacon again?"

"Yes."

"That's when I tried to take it off. It was like having a lightning bolt strapped to my neck. It almost killed me. I've had to wear it ever since."

Eiliesor searched my face for signs of something only he knew. He took his time doing it, and the intense scrutiny of a gorgeous, silk-robed Conclave Guardian made me want to squirm. I resisted that impulse, as well as some hands-on urges that were trying to get my attention. I really hoped Eiliesor wasn't a mind reader, too. I'd had enough embarrassment tonight.

"That's impossible," he said after what seemed an eternity. "Eamaliel keyed it to himself. No one else should be able to use it."

"I'm not trying to use it. And I don't know this Eamaliel person or care about his taste in jewelry. I just want to know how to get this thing off without it killing me."

"And you can't?"

For some reason, that single, simple fact just wasn't getting through to him.

"I think we've established that," I said, rapidly losing what little patience I came with. "Why shouldn't I be able to take it off?"

"From what I've learned, your partner, whose name is Quentin Rand, since you seem to have forgotten, is a gifted thief, but not the best. Sarad Nukpana could have done better. A goblin loyal to the Khrynsani cause would have been a more logical choice. I don't think Nukpana chose your partner, Mistress Benares. And neither do you. He called you by name in that warehouse for a reason." He took a step toward me. "I want to know what that reason is."

I didn't move, but I was more than ready to. "So do I. I have no idea how Sarad Nukpana knows me. I don't want to know him. That's the truth."

"Your involvement in this goes much further than you believe." Eiliesor's voice had lost some of its edge. Maybe he had some sympathy that my world had been kicked upside down and that a couple of those kicks had been his. "Sarad Nukpana knows the full extent of that involvement. I don't. I don't believe you do either, but I will find out."

I had no doubt that he would.

His eyes were on mine. "Tell me about your father."

Sarad Nukpana's words from just hours before came back to me. I didn't want them to.

"I never knew him, and my mother died when I was less than a year old. What does that have to do with anything?"

"It has much to do with everything. If you're linked by blood to Eamaliel Anguis, it's possible that the beacon would respond to you. It would also be possible for you to have direct contact with the Saghred without any of the usual side effects."

"Side effects?"

"Contact with the Saghred causes delusions, insanity, then death. But during that time, the wielder is capable of channeling the stone's full power. You've used the Saghred, yet you're completely unaffected. That tells me only one thing."

"Only one?" I heard myself ask. Then again, maybe I didn't hear it. Maybe I was being delusional.

"That you are somehow related to Eamaliel Anguis. It would have to be a close link, within at least two generations, closer would be more effective. Did Prince Chigaru tell you anything about him?"

"Only that he's been dead for about nine hundred years. That's a little old to be related to me by less than two generations."

"Eamaliel's missing, not dead," Eiliesor corrected. "In addition to being a link to the Saghred, the beacon is a lifemarker. Eamaliel had the beacon keyed only to him. If he died, the link to the beacon would be severed, as would the beacon's link to the Saghred. Events of the past two days have shown that link remains. If the link remains, so does Eamaliel."

That remark had implications I wasn't prepared to deal with anytime soon. I knew who my mother was; and according to Garadin, she wasn't a nine-hundred-year-old elven mage turned Conclave Guardian. She was a talented sorceress, but she hadn't been that good. If she'd been better, she would still be alive. That left the possibility that Eamaliel Anguis was my father. That possibility was disturbing, but the other was too horrible to contemplate. Unfortunately, I contemplated it before I could stop myself.

"Nine hundred years old?" I whispered.

"It's not unheard of for links with objects of power to lengthen life. The Saghred is known for it."

Not unheard of in his world maybe. It was a good thing I was sitting down. Thoughts and questions darted in panicked circles in my head, running into each other. One question managed to stay on its feet. I wondered how my blood could run cold if I hadn't brought my blood with me.

I heard Mychael Eiliesor's voice as if from another room. "Mistress Benares?"

"Raine," I finally heard myself say. "Call me Raine. You might as well."

Eiliesor knelt in front of my chair. "Are you all right?"

"Sure." I spoke from a daze. I was everything but all right, and I didn't think I'd ever be all right again. I forced myself to take a deep breath. I didn't ask for any of this, I certainly didn't want any of this, but I had it, and there was nothing to be done but to deal with it. My screaming fit would have to wait a little longer.

"Tell me," I said, forcing my voice to be steady. I wished I felt the same.

"Excuse me?"

"Tell me everything you know about the Saghred and Eamaliel Anguis." My fear was giving way to anger. I welcomed it with open arms. I knew what to do with anger. "You know, Nukpana knows, the Mal'Salins know. I even think one of my goblin friends knows. I don't like the dark and I'm tired of being kept there. So tell me."

Eiliesor considered me for a moment. I patiently waited, and looked back at him. His sea blue eyes were just as beautiful, but no longer as intimidating. I wasn't surprised by my sudden calm. It's easy to be patient when you're about to get what you want.

He stood and went to sit on the corner of the bed closest to me, his back against the bedpost. "You know the events that led up to the Guardians taking the Saghred from King Omari Mal'Salin." It was a confirmation, not a question.

I nodded.

"Eamaliel Anguis led the team who recovered it. When he returned to Mid, the survivors of that team and a few select Guardians tried to destroy the Saghred. They failed. Lucius Cavan, the Conclave Archmagus at that time, ordered Eamaliel to hide the Saghred to keep it out of the wrong hands. Eamaliel didn't want to spend the rest of his life sealed in a vault, so he had a beacon made so he could guard the stone from a distance. But rather than an open beacon, which would allow anyone who wore it to find the Saghred, he had it keyed to himself."

"Not very trusting."

"He had reason," Eiliesor said.

"Lucius Cavan tried to take it?"

"He wasn't even the first in line."

Garadin always said a man didn't have to have power to be corrupted, but it sure happened faster when he did.

"Eamaliel expected it," Eiliesor said. "But when he hid the Saghred, he did the same with himself. Lucius charged Eamaliel with desertion, but Eamaliel didn't see it that way. The Saghred was his charge, his duty. There were others on Mid to take his place there, only he had the connection to the Saghred. So, he devoted his life to guarding it. That was nine hundred years ago. Neither have been heard from again, until rumors surfaced a few months ago. As a protector of Eamaliel's legacy, I take those rumors—and my duty—very seriously."

His expression was just as serious. Cancel that, it was downright grim.

"And that duty is?" I wasn't sure I really wanted to know.

"Find the beacon, find the Saghred, and return both to Mid."

A question occurred to me. "If only Eamaliel can use the beacon, how were you planning to find the Saghred—that is, until I came along?"

"Eamaliel keyed the beacon to himself," Eiliesor said. "So we've had to do it the hard way. As a seeker, I'm sure you're aware that when something is moved, it leaves a trail, both magical and mundane. We followed both. They led us here."

"And your mundane trail included . . .?"

"People see and hear things. People talk."

"In other words, old-fashioned footwork. I do a lot of that myself."

The Guardian shrugged. "Time consuming, but it gets the job done. Unfortunately the Khrynsani know as much as we do. And as far as your connection to Eamaliel goes, it appears Sarad Nukpana knows more. We've traced the Saghred to Mermeia, but no farther."

"Mermeia's not small."

"We've noticed." He paused. "There's only so much more we can do on our own. Will you help us find the Saghred?"

I leaned back in the chair. "Chigaru Mal'Salin asked me to do the same thing last night."

"I'm not Chigaru Mal'Salin."

"I noticed."

"The only way to remove the beacon is to find the Saghred."

I kind of thought it'd be something like that.

"Just out of curiosity, what do you want with the Saghred?" I asked the Guardian. "Everyone else has plans once they get their hands on it. What are yours?"

"To keep it out of anyone's hands," he said. "If you agree to help us find it, we'll decide if it's secure in its present resting place. I would rather not disturb it unless it's absolutely necessary. To move it means drawing attention to it."

"And that would be bad."

"Very much so. Lucius may be long dead, but there are others eager to take his place. If the Saghred is secure, we will leave it where it lies, along with your beacon, of course. If the beacon behaves normally, once it is touching the object to which it was keyed, you will be able to remove it."

"Let me see if I understand this. I have to touch something called Soul Thief before I can take this thing off?"

"That is the way a beacon typically works."

"That's not the way I work, typically or otherwise."

"The other option is to go though the rest of your life,

greatly abbreviated though it would be, with the beacon hanging around your neck. I wouldn't advise that option."

"And if it isn't in a secure location?" I asked, though I was almost certain I didn't want to know the answer.

"Then we have the means to take it with us," Eiliesor said. "There is a chest which held the Saghred during its time on the Isle of Mid. We brought it with us."

"The Saghred and the beacon both in the chest."

"That is correct."

"But not me." I wanted confirmation on that point.

Eiliesor's lips creased in a smile. "Your presence would not be required."

"And I would be free to go."

"Yes."

Best news I'd had in days.

He stood in a whisper of silk. "May I see the beacon?"

Unlike the goblin prince, Mychael Eiliesor asked nicely enough. I stood and pulled the beacon from its hiding place under my shirt, and held it by its chain. It was completely solid and it shouldn't have been. I wasn't here, so it shouldn't be either. That should have bothered me, but it didn't. I was already way beyond bothered.

Eiliesor closed the distance between us in two strides. I would have backed up, but there was the small matter of a chair behind me and only his silk robe between us. It was a very nice robe. Matched his eyes.

He reached out to touch the slowly spinning disk, but stopped just short of making physical contact. Like Janek, Mychael Eiliesor didn't get to where he was by being stupid.

"Not very impressive, is it?" I managed. Suddenly there wasn't nearly enough air in the room. "Looks can be deceiving."

His blue eyes were on mine. "I'm not easily deceived, and I am impressed."

I was talking about the beacon. I don't think he was.

He looked down at the disk. "Eamaliel chose a perfect disguise," he murmured in admiration.

I closed my fingers around the disk and dropped it into the front of my shirt. For a moment, I thought Eiliesor was going to go in after it. My look stopped him.

"A disguise isn't worth much if everyone knows what it is," I told him. "Too many people want to get their hands on this thing. Since I can't take it off, they want to get their hands on me. I can't let that happen."

"And it won't," the Guardian assured me.

I didn't like his tone. Or the narrowing of his eyes. It painted pictures of me being tossed over his shoulder like a sack of potatoes and carried off to Mid. I chose to ignore that thought for now, and tried even harder to ignore that I think I liked that thought. For now I had the very real and immediate problems of getting Eamaliel's handiwork from around my neck and keeping myself from becoming anyone else's permanent guest.

Too much to do in one night. And too much to do by myself. I was good, but I did have limits. I looked up at the Guardian. I didn't need the beacon's help to tell me exactly what he was thinking.

"I want to put you under protective custody," Eiliesor said.

There was a lot of that going around.

"That would involve me locked in a room with a bunch of Guardians outside, right?"

One corner of his mouth tipped upward. "I believe two would be sufficient."

"I've made other arrangements."

"The same arrangements you had last night?"

"No, these are new and improved arrangements." It wasn't exactly the truth, but it'd have to do until I came up with something else.

"I should hope so," Eiliesor said. "As long as you wear that beacon, I can't allow you to remain unprotected. I can't risk Nukpana capturing you."

"You mean capturing the beacon."

"Unfortunately, you and the beacon are one and the same."

"Unfortunate is right," I muttered.

"Nukpana knows what you're capable of now. He was caught off guard once." Eiliesor gave me a level look. "He won't be caught unawares again."

He was right. I didn't want to admit it, but I certainly couldn't deny it. I just nodded. A couple of Guardians to watch my back might not be all that bad. The blond one I had met last night seemed like a nice, homicidal sort. And it wasn't like Eiliesor could act immediately on any impulse he might have toward keeping me prisoner. Since my body was still onboard the *Fortune*, he couldn't keep me here against my will. At least I didn't think so. Then again, a lot of what I deemed impossible two days ago had turned out to be all too possible. The way my luck had been running, this would turn out to be one of them. And if I looked in those blue eyes for much longer, I might decide house arrest was a simply wonderful idea.

"I'm not opposed to a little extra protection," I said. "The only way I can protect myself from Nukpana and his like is by running or using the Saghred, or more accurately, letting it use me. It happened last night, and I never want it to happen again."

"Then we're in agreement. I'll have a few of my men keep you under surveillance."

"A tentative agreement," I clarified, like I could stop him from having me followed. "I have family and friends who I won't endanger any longer. Some are capable of protecting themselves; some are not. Nukpana wouldn't hesitate to use them to get to me. I can't allow that to happen, either."

"The young spellsinger?" Eiliesor asked.

I nodded. I didn't like the way Sarad Nukpana had looked at Piaras last night. I liked it even less knowing what I knew about Sarad Nukpana.

"I can provide protection."

"Thank you," I said, and meant it. "My family is taking care of it. But I do appreciate your offer."

"I appreciate your cooperation." His voice was oddly gentle. At least he seemed to realize that he had just turned what was left of my life upside down. I think he expected a fight from me. I would have liked to have given him one, but the truth was I needed to save my fight for when it was really necessary. Sarad Nukpana was out there.

"I'll meet you tonight at a nightclub called Sirens off Heron Row in the Sorcerers District," I told him. "Do you know it?"

"I do."

"I'll be there at nine bells." I managed a grin. "With a few family members, of course."

"Of course."

I had one more question, but was more than a little embarrassed to ask.

The Guardian sensed my dilemma. "Yes?"

"How do I get back to where I am?"

I heard voices talking.

At first there was one, then I could distinguish two. Thankfully, I knew them. It meant I was waking up in the same place where I had fallen asleep. I liked it when that happened.

"Let me get this straight," Phaelan was saying. "You tackled Chigaru Mal'Salin, kicked his guards, and later decked a sentry?"

I slowly opened one eye. The other side of my face was still firmly buried in the pillow. Phaelan was grinning from ear to ear. From the other side of the cabin, Piaras's own expression was a perfect match as he nodded.

He was sitting cross-legged on Phaelan's bunk. The bruise was fading nicely, the swelling all but gone. It looked like Phaelan's ship's healer had been in while I slept. Considering what had happened last night, he looked amazingly calm. While I still had the urge to keep him safe, I no longer felt as much of a need to protect him, if that made any sense. The Piaras who woke up on the *Fortune* was a more mature version. He wore it well.

So much for the kid being scarred for life.

Then I remembered where I had been, whom I had seen, and how I had seen him. I sat up, gasped and pulled my own covers up under my chin.

"What is it?" Phaelan wasn't sure whether he should be alarmed or not.

"Nothing."

"It doesn't look like nothing."

I glanced under the blanket, and breathed a quick sigh of relief. At least *I* wasn't naked under the covers.

"Determined Guardian?" Phaelan chuckled, misinterpreting my reaction entirely.

"No."

"Didn't he try to contact you?" Piaras asked.

"He didn't have to."

Phaelan's eyes went wide. "*You* contacted *him*?"

"I didn't mean to, but I did."

"Well, was he expecting you?"

I had an entirely welcome flashback to the sight of Mychael Eiliesor naked in bed. I felt myself flush. "I don't think so."

Phaelan noted my reaction and his grin turned wolfish. "Sounds like you had yourself some fun, cousin. Good girl."

"Did not."

The grin grew wider. "Liar."

"Well, are you meeting him?" Piaras asked.

"I suggested tonight at Tam's club. It's public enough. I told Eiliesor I'd be there at nine bells, but I'll be there earlier. After last night, I want to have a little talk with Tam about Ocnus and a certain goblin spellsinger."

I looked out the porthole next to my bunk. It occurred to me that I had no idea how long I had been asleep. The low clouds outside didn't help my guesswork any.

"What time is it?" I asked Phaelan.

"Just past two. You slept through lunch."

Lunch. There was another wonderful idea. It ranked right up there with the promised safety of a certain Guardian's protective custody. Custody that I'd turned down. I sighed and tossed back the blanket. While safety would be nice, I'd settle for lunch.

"Do you think you might be able to trust the Guardian?" Piaras asked. He sounded hopeful. So was I.

"I just might."

Chapter 15

Phaelan and a few of his more socially presentable crew were my chosen escorts for the evening. I knew they wouldn't be much of a deterrent if we ran into Sarad Nukpana, but everyone else we encountered suddenly preferred to be on the other side of the street. When we got to Sirens, Phaelan and two of his crew came inside with me and made themselves at home at the bar; the others stayed outside and covered the exits. Considering the way my luck had been running lately, it wasn't all the precautions I wanted to take, but it'd have to do.

I thought I had arrived with plenty of time to have a heart-to-heart talk with Tam, but apparently I'd have to get in line. A reunion was underway in my favorite booth. Tam and a certain elven Guardian were chatting away like old friends.

I sauntered over. "I see you boys know each other."

Neither looked guilty at being seen with the other, nor did they look surprised to see me. Normally, I'd smell a setup, but I was the one who suggested the meeting place, and it definitely hadn't been under compulsion. But something was going on here, and I suspected it had everything to do with me.

"I know Paladin Eiliesor tolerably well," Tam said with an easy smile. "The good Guardian helped me out of a sticky situation once."

"And Primaru Nathrach once assisted me with a minor inconvenience," Eiliesor said.

"Tonight, Mychael and I are sharing war stories," Tam offered, his grin widening until his fangs were showing. "Raine Benares war stories."

"Though Tam has more to share than I do," Eiliesor said.

"But yours hurt more," Tam countered. He looked at me, his expression pained. "You didn't really kick him *there*, did you? I'm certain that wasn't called for."

"It was completely called for," I assured them both, pulling a chair up to the end of the booth and sitting down. And I was thinking about doing it again.

"I have some questions for you," I told Tam. "I was going to speak with you alone, but since you and the paladin seem to be such good friends, I'm sure you won't mind if I just ask them here."

Tam knew I was not amused, and I was rewarded with a flash of uncertainty in his dark eyes. Seeing them here together had thrown me a sharp left hook. The least I could do was return the favor.

I pushed on, not giving either one of them a chance to respond. "Has Paladin Eiliesor told you how I spent last night?"

"No, he hasn't," Tam said, his eyes on mine. "And you left before I returned. Kell's explanation of your whereabouts was hardly enlightening."

I looked at the stage, even though I already knew what was there—and who wasn't. The musicians from the day before were playing, but one of them was conspicuously absent. I wasn't surprised.

"Your new spellsinger isn't here," I noted.

"It's early yet," Tam said.

"Then he's performing tonight?"

The goblin's dark eyes narrowed suspiciously. "Of course.

It's the busiest night of the week." He paused. "Why wouldn't he?"

I shrugged. "I just thought he might have somewhere else to be. A second job, perhaps." I watched Tam's face carefully. "He didn't show up last night, did he?"

The goblin's uncertainty was blooming into something else, something darker. "No, he didn't."

"Did he tell you why?"

"I haven't seen him—or you—since yesterday afternoon."

"I was unavoidably detained, thanks to your missing spellsinger." I kept my voice low. I wanted answers, but I didn't want everyone in the place to know my business. "We were in an alley last night. He had a dagger aimed at Piaras Rivalin's ribs."

Tam went utterly still. "Perhaps you should tell me about your evening."

"Perhaps you should tell me what the hell you're trying to pull." My voice was just above a whisper. I didn't have to shout to attract attention. I already had it. Lorcan Karst had moved to stand a few feet behind his boss. A good manager knew the signs of trouble, and I wasn't bothering to hide how I felt. Out of the corner of my eye, I spotted a pair of Guardians. I recognized the overeager, blond ax-wielder from last night. I didn't recognize the equally large, dark-haired Guardian with him. Phaelan and his boys had left the bar and spread out to cover the Guardians.

Unless anyone sneezed, there shouldn't be any fatalities.

Tam still hadn't moved. "Piaras was harmed?"

"You care?"

He flinched as if I'd slapped him. "I do."

I let out a breath, and leaned back in my chair. I released the edge of the table. My knuckles had clenched themselves white. I didn't believe Tam was directly responsible, but when a Mal'Salin asked a favor, saying no wasn't an option. They were Tam's family. They were in town. And they probably had asked.

"He's black and blue today, but he'll heal." The edge faded out of my voice. A little. "No thanks to your spellsinger. Or Ocnus Rancil. Or the Mal'Salin prince they're both working for."

That got the Guardian's attention. "Tam, perhaps we should take this into your office."

"I agree." The goblin started to stand.

I stayed where I was. "I don't. You have more than one exit from your office, Tam. I'd rather not be near any of them. I value my safety over anyone's feelings right now." I looked from one to the other. "I'm sure you gentlemen understand." I gestured to the seats they just vacated. "Please, make yourselves comfortable."

They sat.

Tam spoke first. "I had no part in whatever happened to Piaras last night."

He didn't mention me, just Piaras. A good sign that he wasn't up to his neck in this, but it didn't mean his hands were clean.

"But you knew about it," I said.

"No, I didn't."

"I'd really like to believe you," I told him. "There aren't too many people I can trust right now. I'd like for you to still be one of them."

His expression softened. A little. "I am."

"Then I need you to start being honest with me."

"Honesty is dangerous right now."

"So are secrets."

Mychael leaned forward. "We really shouldn't discuss this any further in the open."

I didn't like it, but I had to agree with him. I waved Phaelan over.

"Would you join us in Tam's office? Paladin Eiliesor feels the need for a little privacy."

•   •   •

Tam was sitting behind his desk. I think he felt the need to have a solid piece of furniture between us right now. He knew what I'd done to Eiliesor. Phaelan let the two crew members who had come with us into Sirens know we wouldn't be coming out for a while. They stationed themselves near Tam's office door. I was sure they'd have plenty of Guardian company.

Tam had offered the hospitality of his personal bar, and Phaelan was taking him up on it. "Can I get you something?" he asked me.

"Sure." A drink sounded like a wonderful idea. I was perched on the edge of one of Tam's plush, overstuffed chairs and was feeling a little tense. Wonder why. I didn't really think Tam had ordered me kidnapped last night, or that Mychael Eiliesor was going to do the same tonight, but caution had never been a bad thing for me.

I took the glass and a sip. The tang of Caesolian port burned with a cool fire. I had to hand it to Phaelan. When invited to help himself to a connoisseur's private stock, he knew enough to go straight for the good stuff.

My cousin and his drink made themselves at home in another chair.

"Kell told me you went out for dessert," Tam said quietly, his hands folded on his desk. "Would you care to elaborate?"

I looked at Mychael Eiliesor, my question unspoken, but obvious.

"Tam knows why I'm here," Eiliesor told me.

I blinked. "He does?"

Tam was wearing a similar stunned expression. It was a look I'd never seen on him before, and unfortunately, I wasn't in the mood to enjoy it. Apparently my involvement was news to him, too.

"Raine and I will be working together on this," Eiliesor told Tam. He glanced at me, his eyes unreadable. "At least I hope that's still the case."

The beacon picked that moment to wake up and say hello. Tam's eyes widened even farther. There was nothing like having a secret that wasn't so secret anymore. Actually, it was a re-lief. And since everyone in the room knew my hand, I might as well put my cards on the table. I pulled the amulet out of my shirt.

Tam's dark eyes were instantly riveted to my chest. It was familiar territory for them. "No," was all he could manage.

I smiled. There was no humor in it. "Ta-da."

"That's impossible." Tam found more words.

"It should be, but it's not," Eiliesor said.

"You knew?" Tam asked Phaelan, who amazingly enough was sitting quietly through all this.

My cousin grinned. "It'd be difficult not to. I was there when she got it."

I stared hard at Tam. "I might ask you the same."

"What?"

"How you knew."

"That depends on what you mean by 'knew'?" Tam's re-sponse to a question was very often another question. It wasn't one of his more endearing qualities.

"Tam," I warned.

He glanced at Eiliesor.

"Tell her," the Guardian said.

I set my drink aside. "Tam, I'll make you a deal. You tell me all about yours, and I'll tell you all about mine."

The goblin's lips curved into a slow, wicked grin. "And in front of everyone."

My lips narrowed into a thin, angry line. "Just spill it."

Tam sat back in his desk chair. "About two weeks ago, my former teacher arrived in town. She asked to meet me for din-ner. Since we hadn't seen each other in a few months, I didn't think much of it. During dinner, she asked a favor. She needed a safehouse, something isolated and easily defensible. My family owns property that I thought would fill her needs. The other morning she was here asking to extend their stay."

"You really need to hire a cleaning service, Tam," I said. "Other than that, nice house, very impressive."

The goblin raised one dark brow. "I beg your pardon?"

"Piaras and I were guests at your out-of-the-way cottage last night."

His expression darkened. "I suspected who would be staying there, so I thought it prudent to ask her a few questions. Apparently, I should have asked more. What she did tell me, I really didn't like, but it wasn't enough to refuse her request. I probably should have. Was she there last night?"

"Not that I know of," I said. "But her wards were. She left her prince in a cozy, well-protected nest."

Tam frowned.

"Did she mention what they were doing in town?" I asked.

"She was predictably elusive on that point. Knowing about Sathrik's visit told me that the less I knew about Chigaru's visit, the better."

"Did she ask anything of you other than your house?"

"No."

"So she didn't mention the beacon or the Saghred."

"Not a breath. I found that out from Mychael."

"Thanks in part to you," Eiliesor told me, "things have moved faster than we anticipated. We've had to catch up. Fortunately, the Khrynsani are still a few steps behind."

"I'm sure my former teacher thought I'd refuse to help if I knew the entire plan," Tam continued. "She would have been right. She's honorable and would never knowingly harm anyone, but she has the misfortune of thinking that Chigaru Mal'Salin shares her morals. I've met the prince, and while he's a far superior alternative to his brother, he's still a Mal'Salin. My teacher has been known to turn a blind eye in some instances."

"He told me he only wants to keep the Saghred from his brother," I said.

"You spoke with him?"

"It wasn't my idea."

I gave him the shortened version of last night's events.

Tam was incredulous. "And you came walking in here by yourself?"

Phaelan cleared his throat indignantly. "Me and eight of my best men hardly constitute 'by yourself'."

"Could you or your eight best defend Raine from a Khrynsani attack?" Tam snapped.

"Could you get a spell past your front teeth when there's a fist coming at it?" Phaelan shot back.

"My escort was more than adequate," I told them both. "And Paladin Eiliesor has arranged for a pair of his Guardians to become my new shadows. The two waiting outside, right?" I asked Eiliesor.

"That was the plan."

I spread my hands. "See, plenty of protection."

"Why her?" Tam asked Eiliesor.

"I have a theory," was all he said.

Since that theory involved a nine-hundred-year-old Guardian being my father, it was a theory I didn't want to think about, so I changed the subject.

"What about your spellsinger?" I asked Tam.

"What about him?"

"Who, what, when, and why did he take up kidnapping as a second career? He paid Ocnus Rancil to set me up. Since when is Ocnus working for him?"

"Ocnus works for the Mal'Salins," Tam reminded me patiently.

"Yes, I know that; but what is Ocnus doing working . . . " I paused, thought and concluded in the span of two seconds.

"Your spellsinger is a Mal'Salin?" My voice felt the need to rise a couple of octaves; I felt the need to let it.

"Rahimat is my late wife's nephew."

I couldn't believe what I was hearing. Then again, I could.

"*Uncle* Tam?"

"Well, yes."

"And you didn't tell me."

"I didn't see where it would improve the situation any; so, no I didn't."

"You mean improve *your* situation."

"Same thing."

"Hardly."

"I had no idea Rahimat was working for Chigaru Mal'Salin, if that's what you're getting at," Tam said. "Though I'm sure his being in Mermeia isn't a coincidence. Planting him to spy on me isn't like Primari Nuru, so I'd imagine it was the prince's doing. She trusts me; the prince does not. Rahimat was on summer break from the Conclave college. He's a spellsinger, and he told me he wanted to earn some extra money, so I put him to work."

I had to bite my tongue. Uncle Tam wasn't Rahimat's only source of summer fun money. Most kids get a normal summer job. Mal'Salin teenagers kidnap and dabble in world domination. I guess they had to get on-the-job training somewhere.

"I wonder if he'll show up for work tonight," was what I said.

"From what you've told me, it's unlikely," Tam said. His eyes darkened even further. "But if he does, I can guarantee he'll wish he hadn't."

Eiliesor sat on the edge of Tam's desk. "I'd like to know more about the note you received from Ocnus Rancil."

"Sure. Which part?"

Tam snorted. "The part that compelled you to abandon all common sense to go meet with him."

I squared my shoulders. "That would be the same part where he claimed to know the location of the Saghred."

"What?" Eiliesor was suddenly like a hound on a scent.

"Except he didn't directly refer to the Saghred," I added. "He called it an 'artifact.' Knowing what I know now, I think it's the same thing, right?"

"It is. Do you remember his exact words?"

"Don't have to. I still have the note." I handed it to him.

The Guardian read it. "It sounds like Master Rancil may have stumbled into some very valuable and dangerous information."

Tam grinned. "From what I heard last night in the Goblin District, Ocnus didn't just stumble; he fell face first. He ran out of the District this morning and hasn't been seen since. Word has it Nukpana is looking for Ocnus. Hard."

"If Rancil knows the Saghred's location, why wouldn't he just sell the information to Sarad Nukpana?" Eiliesor asked.

"Knowing Ocnus, he probably made the offer," Tam said. "But if he's up to his usual tricks, Nukpana wasn't the only potential buyer. And with the Mal'Salin family split into two camps, working for the family has become even more complicated than it used to be."

Phaelan tossed back the last of his drink. "Sounds like he's holding out for the highest bidder."

"Ocnus is known for playing both sides of the fence, so that wouldn't surprise me," I said.

Tam chuckled. "Sarad Nukpana doesn't like to be played."

"Anything from the rumor mill on where Ocnus has gone to ground?" I asked. If Tam didn't know, I had a real good idea.

"Not a peep."

"Considering who's after him, Ocnus has every reason to claw his way under the nearest rock," Phaelan noted.

I smiled. It was a slow smile, and it was borderline malicious.

"I think I know just which one to turn over."

Chapter 16

No doubt Ocnus had always wanted to be popular. Now I wanted to talk to him. So did Sarad Nukpana. But somehow, I didn't think that was the kind of popularity Ocnus had in mind.

Tracking the goblin snitch was simple enough. From time to time, Ocnus found it prudent not to be among his own people. Nothing like having a deal go sour to compel you to make yourself scarce. When the Goblin District was the last place he wanted to be, Ocnus had three favorite places to drown his sorrows: the Blind Bandit, the Sly Fox, and the Sleeping Giant. The Blind Bandit had burnt to the ground last month, the owner of the Sly Fox wanted to get his hands on Ocnus almost as much as Sarad Nukpana did, so that left the Sleeping Giant. Sure enough, Ocnus was in residence at the bar with his two hobgoblin bodyguards in tow.

Bodyguard work came easily to hobgoblins. When you're huge, furry, fanged, and yellow-eyed, you don't need much else as a deterrent. Ocnus's muscle-bound bookends were good at one thing—being big. To their credit, they did it very well. But speed, either of thought or action, wasn't a burden either one carried.

The Sleeping Giant was a dockside dive located on Cutthroat Alley. I know what it sounds like, but the locals liked the name. In fact, they thought they were being downright civic-minded by calling it what it really was. It told the non-local what was likely to happen to them if they dawdled there. If a nonlocal chose to ignore the warning that was their business, or life.

Phaelan was waiting for Ocnus with two of his crew and a pair of Guardians in an alley off the aforementioned alley that ran beside the tavern. Tam was back at Sirens. He had a business to take care of. I told him I would take care of Ocnus.

Mychael Eiliesor was taking care of me.

There was no way the Guardian was going to let me out of his sight. I guess I should have been grateful he didn't take the hardline security solution of locking me up somewhere. I was sure he still considered that an option, but since there was no way he could get the Saghred by himself, it was in his best interests to stay on my good side. And that's exactly where he was. Really close. While Eiliesor's proximity was rather nice, it wasn't very practical. If I needed to draw a blade, I'd have to knock him out of the way first. And considering his size in relation to mine, I knew that wasn't physically possible.

I'd join Phaelan in a minute, but I wanted to talk to Eiliesor now. I had some questions. Nagging questions of the life and-death variety. Eiliesor and I were behind some crates around the corner from Cutthroat Alley. Phaelan would let me know when Ocnus put in an appearance. I wanted the first hands around Ocnus's throat to be mine.

Eiliesor stood an arm's length away, utterly still, his hands relaxed—and where they could immediately draw either sword or dagger. Always the Guardian, always on duty, always ready for anything. I wondered if he even knew how to relax. Not that I wanted him to start now, but I did wonder what a playful Mychael Eiliesor would be like.

He must have felt me watching him. He looked down at me, his dark eyes unreadable in the alley's faint light.

"What are you thinking?" His voice was a husky whisper. Raising your voice in this part of the waterfront was never a good idea. Maybe he knew that. Or maybe it was just for me. Either way, it was a very nice whisper.

"Nothing," I lied.

"You were smiling."

"Was not."

One corner of his mouth turned upward. "Yes, you were. What is it?"

"I was wondering if you're ever off duty."

"I am."

"Do you ever act like it?"

His blue eyes shone in the half-light. "I've been known to. Is that what prompted the smile?"

"It was. I just can't imagine you being anything other than a Guardian."

"I don't know what you may have heard about me," he began.

"By the book and all business."

The smile broadened slightly. "I do hold myself and my men to a higher level of accountability than some of my predecessors. It's earned me a reputation that has its uses. Sometimes it makes my job, and the jobs of my men, a little easier." The smile faded. "I take my position—and my responsibilities—very seriously. You're in danger because of an object that is my responsibility, something I'm asking you to help us find."

I shifted uncomfortably. "My reasons for agreeing to help aren't exactly honorable, you know. I'm one big bull's-eye for a lot of bad people until I can get this thing off of me, so I have a vested interest in helping you get what you want."

"That doesn't lessen the danger you'll be in over the next few days, nor does it lessen my appreciation for your help—

and my admiration of you." The Guardian paused awkwardly. "Mistress Benares?" His voice was oddly formal.

"Yes?"

"I would like it very much if you would call me Mychael."

I felt a smile coming on. I didn't try to stop it. "I think I can do that."

If the light had been better, I would have sworn he had blushed. I felt a little warm myself.

Now for the question of the night. "Do you have a plan?" I asked, my voice small and quiet even to me.

Mychael seemed genuinely puzzled. "Pardon me?"

"A plan. Say Ocnus actually knows where the Saghred is, and we get him to cough it up. Do you have a plan that's going to get this thing off my neck while leaving my head attached to my shoulders?"

"I do, but the details depend on where the Saghred is."

Now for the question I really didn't want to ask. "What if the weasel's lying? What if he doesn't know a thing, and he just tried to con the wrong people? It wouldn't be the first time. What then?"

Mychael was silent for a little too long.

"You are a seeker—and your father's daughter."

I thought it'd be something like that.

He moved a step closer to me. I didn't move, and I didn't mind.

His voice was low. "If there is the possibility, however remote, that Ocnus Rancil knows where the Saghred is, I would prefer to get that information from him and then confirm it through more mundane means."

I swallowed. "Because the Saghred's dangerous."

"That's one reason." Mychael paused uncomfortably. "No doubt you are a fine seeker, but your father had the beacon created to his skill level. He was an exceptionally gifted mage, one of the best our order has ever produced. He knew how to use the beacon to keep track of the Saghred. Unfortunately, that information vanished with him. But I am knowledgeable of how a beacon such as yours works—"

"So you can walk me through it, if necessary."

He smiled slightly. "If necessary. Hopefully it won't be."

"What are the chances that Eamaliel Anguis is my father?" I finally asked. "Really."

"From the beacon's reaction to you, almost a certainty."

I was quiet for a longer moment, for an entirely different reason.

"A nine-hundred-year-old elven Guardian is my father." I said it as much to myself as to the much younger elven Guardian standing in front of me. Like saying it would make it more believable. Or less terrifying.

"He was connected to the Saghred," I said. "I'm connected to the Saghred. He's nine-hundred-years old and still alive. I'm going to be . . . ?"

"Just fine," Mychael assured me.

"How do you know that?"

"Eamaliel had nearly continuous, daily contact with the Saghred for almost two years before he ever had the beacon made. And he wore the beacon for nearly a decade before anyone noticed he didn't seem to be aging. You've never touched the Saghred, and you've only worn the beacon for two days. We're going to find the Saghred, get the beacon off of you, and you're going to be just fine."

"No magical leftovers?"

Mychael was silent.

"You've been reassuring until now," I said. "More of the same would be nice."

"There could be some residuals."

"Residuals?"

"When Eamaliel keyed himself to the beacon, he essentially keyed himself to the Saghred. The beacon acted as a conduit, and transferred some of the Saghred's power to him. You experienced a taste of that last night with the Magh'Sceadu.

With beacons and objects of power, any link is usually severed when the beacon is removed."

"Usually."

"With something as powerful as the Saghred, the residuals can be significantly more than mere magical leftovers."

"So some of what I can do now could stay with me?"

"It's possible that all of what you can do now will stay with you."

"Great. Every couple of hours I'm finding something new I can do." I had a thought, and it made me faintly queasy. "Would Sarad Nukpana know this?"

"He is a leading Saghred scholar," Mychael said. "Yes, he would know."

I didn't need to know that.

Phaelan's low whistle came from the alley. Show time.

I slipped into the alley next to Phaelan. Mychael stayed around the corner. I'd told him before we'd left Sirens that I wanted a shot at Ocnus first. I was the one he had set up; I was the one with the beacon stuck around my neck. I felt that earned me certain rights and privileges. Before tonight, I'd never thought of strangling Ocnus as a right or privilege, but the past few days had been full of firsts.

I looked around. No Ocnus. "Where is he?"

Phaelan's smile flashed in the dim light. "He's finishing off his last pint now. I had Norleen giving him free ale. He'll have to stop here before he leaves."

"Here?" Understanding dawned, and it didn't smell good.

Phaelan grinned. "Yeah, right here."

"Am I standing in . . . ?" I looked down at my boots in disgust.

His grin grew to wolfish proportions and he tapped his own boot in something wet. "Highly likely. Payback is hell, cousin. From Nigel's stinking alley to Ocnus's."

Now I remembered why I avoided alleys in this part of the

waterfront. I was glad it was a cool night. In high summer, the smell would have been unbearable.

Never think a night can't get any worse. There's all kinds of worse.

"Who's Norleen?" I asked, trying in vain to keep my mind off my feet.

"The brew mistress here. I knew her when she worked at the Beggar's Back. Brews fine ale, but the dwarf who owns this place is too cheap to sell the lady's nectar at full strength. He thinks he can make more profit if he waters it down. But I understand you can get it full strength if you slip Norleen a little extra."

"Ocnus is no use to us drunk," I reminded him.

"No problem. Norleen made sure he filled his bladder before his brain. He'll be just relaxed enough to make him receptive to questioning." He grinned. "Or you could always speed things up and do a mind link."

My expression and accompanying gesture let him know what I thought of that. Doing a mind link on someone like Ocnus was akin to turning over a rock and finding squishy things underneath. With Ocnus, finding something squishy was always guaranteed.

Phaelan nodded toward the shadows Mychael had blended into. Literally blended into. Eerie. Phaelan's look wasn't entirely approving. "What do you think about that one? I don't trust him."

The two Guardians from Tam's place were standing not five feet away. Phaelan didn't seem to care. If his goal for the evening was to have the blond Guardian's ax embedded in his skull, he was off to a fine start.

"I don't expect you will," I told him. "His job is to uphold the law. Yours isn't. If I want to get rid of this thing, I'm going to need some help. He's my top candidate." I looked at the tavern's door. "Are Ocnus's pet goons still with him?"

"Never three feet from his side," Phaelan said. "It's enough to make me claustrophobic. He must be nervous tonight."

I snorted. "I wonder why. I hope Norleen gave them free ale, too. The less sober people we have to deal with, the better."

"Full strength to one, but the other's not drinking. She tried, but no dice."

"Not a problem," the blond Guardian rumbled.

I jumped. I'd almost forgotten they were there.

The Guardian grinned down at me. "Not to worry. We'll entertain those two while you and the captain talk to Master Rancil."

He sounded only too happy to help. I could develop a soft spot for the ax wielder.

Phaelan was right. Ocnus, and his bladder, had more than their fill of Norleen's brew. We slipped farther into the alley. Apparently there were only so many places Ocnus's twin mountains of muscle would go with him. Alleys that doubled as public urinals didn't make the cut. Maybe they weren't as dumb as they looked. The two Guardians drifted silently to either side of the alley entrance, and literally blended into the shadows like their commander. It was spooky. Ocnus came into the alley. His guards didn't. I heard their boot scuffs. Then I didn't. Like I said, spooky.

Phaelan had done this sort of thing before and deemed it prudent to wait until Ocnus had finished doing what he came to do before apprehending him. Something to do with the possibility of accidents. Unlike most of Phaelan's plans, I didn't question the wisdom of this one.

Once Ocnus was actually in the alley, I found a simply fascinating spot on the wall that warranted my complete and undivided attention. Phaelan would handle the more physical aspects of securing Ocnus. I was here in case Ocnus was still capable of defense of the magical variety.

I heard a thump followed by a strangled squeal. So much for Ocnus being capable.

Phaelan had him neatly pinned to the alley wall. "Hello, Ocnus."

"Captain Benares," the sorcerer squeaked.

I stepped out of the shadows, my most serious I'm-going-to-hurt-you-now look on my face. I was hoping Ocnus would buy my bluff and I wouldn't actually have to do anything. Especially anything that involved touching him. From the widening of Ocnus's eyes, I guessed I was the last person he expected to come face-to-face with tonight. Then again, Ocnus's bulging eyes may have been due to Phaelan's forearm on his throat. I told myself it was me. It helped keep the evil glint in my eye.

Ocnus was still alive and walking around the city because certain people found him useful. Like now. Those same people had also allowed him to live because it would be difficult to explain to the city watch that they'd killed Ocnus just because he was annoying. While the watch all knew Ocnus and would understand the reason, the law wouldn't let them approve of it.

"Spending the Mal'Salin gold you earned last night?" I asked.

"Last night was just business, nothing personal."

"Piaras Rivalin was beaten and we were both kidnapped." I stepped in closer to Ocnus than I wanted to be. For people like him, intimidation and proximity went hand in hand. It was crude, but it worked. "Last night was everything personal."

Ocnus managed to shake his head. "You don't understand."

"I think I do. Word has it that Sarad Nukpana is looking for you."

Ocnus tried a smile, but it just came off looking queasy. "He gave me the night off."

Phaelan sighed regretfully, though I knew he didn't regret one thing he was prepared to do. "Ocnus, you really need to work on your lying. You've been here less than an hour, and you've finished off five pints all by yourself. Even one of your guard dogs was hard pressed to keep pace."

The pudgy sorcerer looked around wildly.

"They found something else to do," I told him. "You might see them later."

"I think you're having a bad night," Phaelan surmised, "and you're trying to drink yourself into a better one. It doesn't work that way. Trust me, I know."

"I don't think you have the night off," I told Ocnus. "I think you've run away from home."

Phaelan adjusted his grip. "You running away from home, Ocnus?"

The sorcerer squirmed a little and squeaked.

"I think that's a 'yes'," I said.

"Your Mal'Salin friends wouldn't get within a mile of this dump," Phaelan said. "We think that's why you're here. You must have done something extra naughty to put an entire city between you. Care to share with us?"

I leaned in close. "I'll settle for where the Saghred is. Since Chigaru Mal'Salin already paid you the fifty tenari you were going to charge me, I'll just take the information."

Ocnus's eyes flickered to my chest. He suspected the beacon was there, at least that's what I told myself. If I let myself think otherwise, Ocnus wouldn't be in any condition to tell me anything. One of my fists flexed involuntarily. Then again he didn't need all his teeth to talk.

"The Saghred has always belonged to the Mal'Salins," Ocnus managed. Phaelan hadn't lightened the pressure on his neck, but I could hear a faint note of smugness. The smugness of someone pleased with a job well done.

"Which one? King Sathrik or Prince Chigaru?"

Ocnus squirmed some more.

"Yeah, I thought so. That has to be a problem for you, especially considering that the king brought Sarad Nukpana along on his little goodwill trip. Psychos don't have much of a sense of humor when it comes to being double-crossed."

"Professionally speaking, there's nothing wrong with having two clients vying for the same prize," Phaelan noted. "But it's risky, and takes a certain level of skill to get away with their money and your life. Ocnus here just isn't that gifted."

I narrowed my eyes and twisted the corner of my mouth

into what I'd been told was a smile that promised many bad things. Considering the anger I had bubbling just beneath the surface, I didn't have to try very hard to look mean. I slowly drew my favorite dagger for good measure. It was thin and slightly curved. Ocnus had heard what I had done with it last year. Little of it was actually true. When it came to maintaining a reputation, facts were fleeting, but you could ride a rumor for years. It wasn't facts that had Ocnus shaking in his puddle.

"And I don't think you're much of a risk taker," I said, fighting back several violent urges. Phaelan looked similarly challenged. "I think you know where the Saghred is. So does Sarad Nukpana. You can tell us here, or we can go somewhere quiet and we'll ask you again, and we'll keep asking until you tell us. It's entirely up to you."

"Nukpana won't allow this," Ocnus squeaked around Phaelan's arm.

Phaelan chuckled. "You actually *want* him to know? You're crazier than he is. If you don't tell her everything, either I'll kill you, or she can put that filleting knife of hers to good use. And as long as we have you, Nukpana will think you talked. Either way, your night's going to go from bad to worse unless you tell us where the Saghred is."

Ocnus's ferret eyes darted to me. There was a crack in his bravado, but I could tell it wasn't ready to open. Not yet. I was tired of standing in a stinking alley, and I knew just the thing to turn that crack into a chasm.

I had no intention of using the knife, so I put it away. But I kept the smile. I knew just the thing to get Ocnus into a conversational mood. Ocnus worked for the Mal'Salin family, but he also feared them, with plenty of good reasons. The royal family's closets were packed with skeletons, but one skeleton in particular pushed Ocnus's panic button.

My grin broadened. Not all Mal'Salins were in the Goblin District tonight, and one of them owed me big time.

"Ocnus, there's someone I want you to meet."

•   •   •

Tam just looked at me. "Tell me you're joking."

"Sarad Nukpana wants the Saghred. I want my life back. Ocnus knows where the Saghred is. Need I say more?"

We were in the storeroom at Sirens. Phaelan was back on the *Fortune*. After delivering Ocnus into Tam's clutches, he considered his work with me for the evening done. Chivalry wasn't dead, but sometimes when it got around Phaelan it took a nap.

Mychael Eiliesor was in the next room. Since the plan was to let Ocnus go after we had the information we wanted, the Guardian chose to lie low. Ocnus hadn't seen him, and Eiliesor wanted to keep it that way. Mainly he didn't want Ocnus running around with the knowledge that at this moment, Mermeia was positively teaming with Guardians who were after the same thing as the Mal'Salin family and Sarad Nukpana.

I knew Tam kept a spell around the storeroom to make it soundproof. I suspected it was used as an interrogation room almost as often as it stored glasses and tablecloths, but I really didn't want to know the details. Ocnus was inside the room and couldn't hear us.

"You set me up," Tam accused.

There was a lot of that going around.

"Turnabout's fair play," I told him.

"You're not going to let me forget about Rahimat, are you?"

"Should I? Your nephew's up to his pointy ears in dumping me and Piaras at Chigaru Mal'Salin's feet, and you tell me I should let it go?"

"I didn't have a thing to do with that, and you know it." He smiled slowly. "Besides, you like me too much to stay mad."

There wasn't much by means of contrition in that smile, but this was Tam we were talking about. Besides, it was true. I did believe him, and Tam was way too charming to stay mad at for long. Since he was right, I did the only thing I could do. I changed the subject.

"Markus's dockside safehouses are all occupied at the

moment, so this was the most convenient place to bring him. Will you help me or not?"

Tam glanced at Ocnus through a gap left intentionally in the door boards. He opened his mouth to say something, then stopped. He shook his head and laughed softly.

"I don't have to say how much you'll owe me for this."

"I owe you nothing. You owe me for last night."

"It wasn't my fault."

"It was your house. You didn't have to let A'Zahra Nuru and her princeling stay there with his closest, most heavily armed friends."

Tam almost looked sheepish. "Actually, I did. Refusal would have been, how shall I say, difficult for me."

Tam obviously didn't want to expound on that, not to mention, I didn't have the time.

"Help me get Ocnus to talk and I'll set you up with the best spirits distributor in Greypoint."

The goblin's dark eyes flickered in interest.

"She keeps Markus Sevelien's cellar stocked."

That got Tam's attention.

"We'll discuss the details later," I added. "Ocnus first. Fine wines later."

Tam glanced at the little sorcerer and took a deep breath. I didn't blame him. I wouldn't want to breathe Ocnus's air either.

"The things I do for my customers."

I smiled, stood on tiptoe, and gave him a light kiss on the cheek. "And your friends."

"Them, too," he whispered. His breath was warm against my cheek—and his hands even warmer on my waist.

His lips found the tip of my ear, then his tongue made the discovery. I discovered I only had one breath, and it wasn't going anywhere. And neither was I. One of Tam's hands encircled my waist, pulling me tight against him. I tried unsuccessfully to remember why I was here. The question flittered around my head in search of an answer. Oh yeah, Ocnus. If that didn't dampen Tam's ardor, nothing would.

"Ocnus." It came out on what little breath I could spare.

"Mmmm?" Tam's lips were busy working their way south, and his free hand was doing likewise.

I tried to point to the interrogation room, but my fingers had somehow tangled themselves in Tam's hair. Traitors.

"Ocnus." I said with only slightly more insistence.

"Let him get his own girl," Tam murmured. Then he kissed me, a devastating meeting of lips and warm breath, topped off with just a nibble of fang, all guaranteed to liquefy the knees of any woman. I didn't need the Saghred's help to know what Tam wanted to do next.

With Mychael Eiliesor in the next room.

I found my breath, inhaled half of Tam's, and pushed myself away.

"Mychael's in the next room," I managed.

His hold tightened. "He can get his own girl, too."

I raised a warning finger. "That's not what we're here for." I swallowed and tried for more air. It just came out as a gasp.

Tam slid smooth fingers beneath my chin, tilting my face up to his. "Plans can change." The sly grin on his lips had worked its way north to his dark eyes, eyes that had somehow gotten even darker.

"Perhaps." I swallowed again, hard. "Later."

Tam reluctantly released me, but took his sweet time doing it. I stepped back and straightened my shirt—and tried to do the same to my thoughts. Prying and kicking them all out of the gutter they'd fallen into wasn't easy, but I managed.

Tam and I stepped into the storeroom. From Ocnus's expression when he saw Tam, I knew this was going to be easy and a little enjoyable. I felt a twinge of guilt about the last part, but the thought of Piaras's bruised face, along with fire pixies, giant leeches, and Magh'Sceadu—and that Ocnus had played a direct role in causing it all—was enough to make it go away.

"Since you don't want to speak to me, I thought you might

like to talk to Primaru Nathrach." I paused meaningfully. "You're aware of his relation to the Mal'Salin family, in addition to his previous position as the late queen's chief shaman." I didn't ask it as a question. Ocnus knew who Tam used to be even better than I did—or wanted to.

Ocnus's nod was punctuated by a squeak. So much for confirmation of Tam's past activities, or at least his reputation.

"He's also a good friend of mine."

"A very good friend," Tam added, his voice low and smooth—and completely devoid of mercy. It spoke volumes about what he would be willing to do, and it promised torments beyond Ocnus's feeble imagination. It gave me the creeps. I could only imagine what it was doing to Ocnus.

I turned to leave the room. "Just let me know if you need anything," I told Tam cheerfully.

The goblin nodded slowly, his face expressionless. I fought back a shiver. Could I pick my friends, or what?

Ocnus's worst fear about the Mal'Salin family centered squarely on what they did to servants who had displeased them. They ate them. Of course this wasn't true. Well, at least not anymore. But when it came to maintaining prejudice, or a reputation, a little rumor went a long way. Especially if the rumor involved rotisserie cooking. The rumored antics of the Mal'Salin family multiplied those fears a hundred fold.

"Wait!" Ocnus's voice was thin, shrill, and appropriately terrified.

Now we were getting somewhere.

Once Ocnus started talking, there was no shutting him up. His double-dealings had multiplied into a veritable web of intrigue. I knew greed could make you stupid, and I thought I'd seen and heard it all, but Ocnus's antics appalled even me.

Sarad Nukpana wanted the beacon, and an expendable human thief to get it for him. Ocnus had never liked Quentin, so he topped Ocnus's list of expendables. Once Chigaru got wind of what his brother and Nukpana were after, he wanted in, too. At this point, things got sticky for Ocnus. He couldn't refuse Sarad Nukpana's order without exposing his dealings with Chigaru Mal'Salin. Ocnus knew the double fee he stood to collect wouldn't do him much good if he were dead, and he was desperate to shift the blame. He told Sarad Nukpana that Quentin was going to double-cross him and fence the beacon through Simon Stocken. It sounded like Stocken hadn't died quietly, naming Ocnus as the main source of Nukpana's inconvenience. Then there was last night. Ocnus had been watching Piaras and told Chigaru's retainers exactly where to find him. Then he sent the letter to me at Sirens. So the entire evening in which Piaras and I were nearly killed on numerous occasions had been orchestrated by the quivering mass of goblin seated not five feet from my clenched and eager fists. I heard a growl. I think it was me.

"Raine." Tam's voice was low and warning. "Even Sarad Nukpana would be challenged to extract information from a corpse."

I unclenched my fists and my jaw. "That's fascinating, Ocnus. And I can put all that information to good use, but it still doesn't tell me where the Saghred is."

"I can't tell you!" he wailed. "He'll kill me!"

"Who?"

Ocnus's lips quivered with muffled sobs. I found it increasingly difficult to keep my rage at a respectable level. It would be a lot easier if Ocnus weren't so pathetic.

"Nukpana," he snuffled. "The king, the prince. It doesn't matter, I'm just as dead."

Even if I could put my decency on a shelf, I didn't have the stomach for torture, or the patience for a long interrogation. Good thing I didn't have to make a living as an inquisitor. I'd starve. Tam sensed my frustration and stepped in, bless him.

"Very well, if you refuse to be useful to my elven friend, you can still be useful to me. You are from Mipor, are you not?"

Ocnus paused, then nodded cautiously, seeing no harm in the question.

"Good. I don't know if you are aware, but Miporian flesh is

a delicacy in our family." Tam popped the button off of Ocnus's shirt cuff with a sharp snap, and slid the dirty linen above his elbow. He glanced distastefully at the grime. "Naturally, you'll have to be washed first," he muttered under his breath.

Ocnus looked to me in wide-eyed panic.

I made no move to stop Tam. "Where's the Saghred?"

When Ocnus didn't answer, Tam lifted one of the little sorcerer's arms speculatively. "Probably a bit stringy beneath the fat, but an overnight marinade should take care of that." His dark eyes became dreamy as he ran a fingertip smoothly down the pasty underside of Ocnus's arm. "Grandmother had the most delectable recipe," he breathed. "The meat all but fell off the bone."

"The goblin embassy," Ocnus squeaked. "The mausoleum."

"How do you know this?" Tam half pulled Ocnus from his chair, the sorcerer's arm clutched tightly in his fist.

"A year ago there was an elf who wanted to get onto the embassy grounds."

"Describe him," came Mychael's steady voice from the now open doorway.

Ocnus swallowed and looked from me to Tam.

"Do it," I growled.

The goblin sorcerer licked his lips. "Gray eyes, gray hair, but he wasn't old. He had more than enough gold, so I didn't ask questions."

Ocnus was panting. Just my luck he'd hyperventilate and pass out.

He took a deep, shuddering breath. "I brought him onto the grounds through The Ruins. He went into the mausoleum. He never came back out. I went in to look. He wasn't there. There's only one way in and I was watching it the whole time."

I looked at Tam. "Mausoleum?"

"There's a mausoleum on the property from the previous owners."

"How do you know he carried the Saghred?" Mychael asked.

I felt the pull of a spellsinger in his words, compelling Ocnus to tell the truth. He need not have bothered. Ocnus was telling the truth, or at least what he thought was the truth. I think the beacon was helping things along. Once again, I was grateful.

"He had a small box made of white stone," Ocnus said. "Like the box Nukpana had me hire Quentin to steal. Only this one was larger and square." He held his hands about four inches apart, no easy task considering Tam still had one of those hands.

"How do you know there was anything inside?"

"Something was glowing, like a big firefly. Red, flickering."

Mychael put a box of translucent white stone on the table in front of Ocnus. "Anything like this?"

Ocnus licked his lips again. "Exactly."

"And Nukpana doesn't know?"

Ocnus swallowed and shook his head.

Tam released Ocnus, but didn't move away, instead looming ominously over the goblin snitch.

"I find it difficult to believe that you found a way to get even more gold out of Sarad Nukpana and yet you passed up the opportunity."

Ocnus seemed to shrink in his chair. "Not at first. I overheard why he needed the beacon. You know, what he hoped to find with it. That's when I remembered the elf and the stone box." A twitching had taken up residence in Ocnus's left eyelid. "So I set up another meeting with him. To make him an offer. That's when I heard he knew about my deals with the prince. I didn't go to the meeting."

"Smart move," I muttered.

"I was leaving town."

"Even smarter."

"My ship wasn't leaving until the morning tide, so I went to the Sleeping Giant." Ocnus tried his trademark oily grin on for size, but it just came off looking sick. "I've told you what you wanted to know. How about just letting me go? My ship leaves within the hour. I'll be on it, I swear." He looked from me to Tam, then to Mychael in growing desperation. "If I stay here, he'll kill me."

"If you're lucky," Tam told him.

Mychael looked into Ocnus's eyes. The goblin snitch couldn't look away. Mychael held the gaze for nearly a minute, until beads of sweat formed on Ocnus's forehead. "I think he tells the truth. Raine?"

The beacon vibrated beneath my shirt, if I hadn't known better I'd say someone was excited. I nodded and put my hand over the beacon. "It seems we agree."

"You could go to the mausoleum now," Ocnus told me eagerly. "Nukpana's not in the embassy tonight."

"Where is he?"

Ocnus's eagerness changed to confusion. "I heard he was going nightingale hunting."

Chapter 17

I couldn't get back home fast enough.

Patience wasn't my strong point even when I didn't have reason to hurry. Time wasn't on our side. We had to use the canals; Sarad Nukpana just had to order another sorcerer tortured and killed to make another Gate. My legs wanted to run all the way home, even though my head knew that cutting through the center of the city on the Grand Duke's Canal would be faster; not to mention if I ran, I'd be out of breath and useless to Piaras once I got there.

What seemed like an eternity later we arrived at the Mintha Row dock. I didn't wait for the crew of Guardians to tie us off, and neither did Mychael, nor Tam in the boat behind us.

My legs finally got to do what they wanted. It was two blocks to Tarsilia's and I ran the whole way. I rounded the corner and saw her shop. No Khrynsani shamans lounging by the door. That was a good sign. The lights were on. Not normal for nearly two in the morning, but when Garadin was protecting something, he always liked to see where it was.

I reached out to push open the door, and ran smack into the

one-two punch of Garadin's shields and Tarsilia's wards. I might as well have hit a wall with my face. Through the pain, I remembered they did good work. I staggered and lights flickered before my eyes. I dimly heard the musical sound of metal clanging, and wondered if I'd hit my head that hard.

I looked up.

Garadin stood in the now open doorway. The metal sound was the chimes Tarsilia had hanging from the beam just inside the door. I shook my head to clear it. Pain immediately followed. Not the best idea.

"You ever think of knocking, girl? Hurts a lot less." He motioned and the shield parted for me.

Tarsilia was standing behind the counter, hands braced on the polished wood, eyes leveled on the doorway. I turned and saw Mychael and Tam still standing just beyond the threshold.

"You're home," she said to me, but her gaze had settled on my two escorts. Perhaps settled was too mild a term. A slab of granite landing on something doesn't exactly settle. No doubt Garadin had told her who Mychael was and what he wanted—and Tarsilia was already all too familiar with Tam. And from the gorgon stare both of them were on the receiving end of, Tarsilia held Mychael and Tam personally responsible for everything that had happened to Piaras and me over the past two days. It was overdone and completely overprotective—and I loved her for it.

"It's all right," I assured her. "They're with us."

She didn't look entirely convinced, and unless she gave her permission, there was no way, short of using a magical battering ram, that Mychael and Tam were getting inside. Tarsilia had to invite them to cross her threshold. Her scowl told me she'd do it, but she wasn't happy about it.

"Mychael Eiliesor, Paladin of the Order and Brotherhood of Conclave Guardians, and Sacred Protector of the Seat of Twelve," she pronounced formally. Then she stopped and looked at me.

"Tarsilia, they need to get inside. Now."

She sensed my urgency. "You and your guests may now enter my home," she finished quickly.

There was an audible pop, and the shield parted and Mychael and four of his Guardians came inside, Tam bringing up the rear guard. The rest remained outside. The shield and wards resealed themselves seamlessly and without sound.

"What happened?" she asked me.

"Where's Piaras?"

"He couldn't sleep; he's in the workroom."

I brushed past her, and headed for the back of the shop.

Tarsilia was right at my heels. "What's wrong?"

Suddenly, everything was. The air grew heavy with power, and it felt like the atmosphere before a lightning strike, prickling my skin like a thousand hot needles. Sarad Nukpana wasn't looking for a way around Tarsilia and Garadin's wards—he was punching his way through them.

Tarsilia and I were closest to the workroom door. We were the only ones who made it inside the room. As soon as we crossed the threshold, the force of the opening Gate sealed the room like a trap door slamming over our heads. Piaras looked up from where he had been grinding dried herbs, his eyes wide, like a deer caught in a hunter's sights. I swore and reached for every shield I had. The Gate and the dark magic that fed it ate them like a late night snack. There was no way Mychael or Tam or anyone else could get in. And we weren't getting out.

Sarad Nukpana's Gate opened simply, no mouth of hell, no brimstone stench, just a parting curtain of silvery fog. I tried to draw my blades; I wanted to push Tarsilia behind me. Neither one was going to happen. The same dark sorcery that sealed the room held the three of us immobile. A sickly sweet smell came from the Gate and the sibilant chanting of combined goblin voices came from beyond it. I knew the chanting and what was feeding its power was worse, much worse. I heard the screams in the background to prove it.

Tarsilia was next to the Gate when it opened. She was the first to be taken.

"No!" Piaras's anguished scream was in my ears and my mind.

A trio of black-robed goblin shamans crossed through the Gate into the room. A fully formed Magh'Sceadu drifted silently behind them. I couldn't do a thing to stop any of them—and neither could Piaras. They grabbed him and pinned him to the floor, the Magh'Sceadu floating eagerly within touching distance. Piaras's wide eyes tracked the creature's every move. He knew what to be most afraid of.

Sarad Nukpana stood just on the other side of the portal. He made no move to come through. He didn't need to. His shamans and Magh'Sceadu were doing a fine job all by themselves. And if he had created the Gate himself, he'd have to stay on the other side to keep it stable and open. It had taken an obscene amount of strength to punch a hole through the shields and wards surrounding Tarsilia's shop. Nukpana had the strength, and from the sudden silence behind him, he had taken the lives.

"Welcome, Mistress Benares. This is a pleasant surprise. Just when I thought you were going to be elusive again, you've become most accommodating."

His voice was just as I remembered: crisp, cultured, and skin-crawling creepy. I could see his eyes and I didn't want to. Reflected in those dark eyes was something quiet, something ageless and malignant. If eyes were the windows to the soul, Sarad Nukpana's soul had never seen the light of day.

Here was a goblin who enjoyed his work way too much.

To him, Piaras was little more than a boy, and what magic I had of my own would be hard pressed to mess up his hair, and he knew it. The Saghred was capable of more—much more. He knew that, too. He smiled slowly.

Then he extended his hand through the Gate to me. Dark blood was smeared on his palm. I knew it wasn't his. As his hand passed over the Gate's threshold, the pressure holding us immobile lifted. I treated myself to a deep breath. Piaras drew a ragged gasp. I guess if a hunter wanted his prey, he had to open the trap.

"Come, Mistress Benares. We have much work to do, and time is short."

A reasonable request, in a reasonable tone. No maniacal laughter, no gleeful wringing of hands. None of the usual hallmarks of evil. Then why did I want to scream and run, and not in that order?

I swallowed the scream. "Let him go."

That confused Nukpana. I guess he wasn't too familiar with demands.

He realized what I meant, and glanced down at Piaras. You think I'd have asked him to give up a favorite lab animal. "I'm afraid that's not possible."

"That's the deal, take it or leave it."

He smiled again. "You are in no position to bargain, Mistress."

"Neither are you."

I could let the Saghred use me, but it would take my breath, what was left of my strength—and would bring me one step closer to whatever awaited me by using it again. I didn't want any of those things. Yet if I did nothing, the goblin would get everything his blackened heart desired, including two of the people I held most dear.

Easy decision. Some things are worth any price.

I knew what I wanted to do. I just had no idea how to do it. Fortunately, the Saghred knew both. My heart hammered in my chest, and my breath came quick and shallow from the awakening power. The goblin's smile widened. I knew why I couldn't breathe. He didn't. Let him think I was terrified. I was. But not only of him.

The Gate was in my home because of Sarad Nukpana. I wanted to hurt the goblin grand shaman very badly. Hurt him, hurt the Gate. It was simple and brutal, but then I'm a simple and brutal kind of girl. If he wanted the power of the Saghred, he could have it. I hoped he choked.

At that moment, Piaras wrenched himself free of one of his captors, kicking the shaman under the chin with the heel of his boot. Sarad Nukpana's attention went from me to Piaras for a fraction of a second. It was the only chance I was going to get. I took it.

I had the brief satisfaction of seeing the goblin's black eyes widen in shock as the impact hit him. It lifted him off his feet, propelling him backward out of my line of sight. I felt the tremors, saw the chunks of stone fall from the ceiling in the room beyond the portal. The screams of pain I now heard were goblin. Over it all I heard Sarad Nukpana's voice, calling for order, weakened, but hardly dead.

He wasn't dead? I had vaporized six Magh'Sceadu in The Ruins. The Saghred could level armies, but it couldn't kill one goblin? My throat constricted and I tasted blood in my mouth. I continued forcing the power that coursed through me into the Gate. Black flowers bloomed on the edge of my vision. If I lost consciousness, I was dead.

Piaras roared.

His terror was compounded by a rage that had been born last night in an alley, grew in The Ruins, and now ripped itself fully formed from his vocal chords in an apothecary's workroom. I'd seen him angry, but never like this. The power within him fed off of that anger.

His wordless scream was filled with pent-up rage and fear—and was aimed in a straight line through the Magh'Sceadu to the Gate that had just swallowed his grandmother. The three shamans and the Magh'Sceadu were unfortunate enough to be in his path. The force of Piaras's voice blasted them back through the Gate's mouth, and slammed it shut behind them.

I slid down the wall I found myself against. Piaras lay sprawled on the floor. The force field vanished with the Gate that spawned it, and Mychael, Tam, and Garadin all but fell into the room.

I crawled over to Piaras and knelt beside him. He scrabbled back as far in the corner as it was possible to get. He would have pressed himself through the wall if he could have. Anything to get away from the things that he had banished, from me, and from himself.

"Don't touch me!" His dark eyes were haunted and his breath came in short, shallow bursts.

The remnants of his magic crackled in the air around him. I was sure he saw the Saghred's leftovers all over me. I didn't want to be near me, either. I lowered my hands and slowly sat back on my heels, utterly exhausted. I knew how he felt. When you feel like your skin is trying to crawl free of your bones, the last thing you want is someone touching you, regardless of how badly you may want to be held.

I sensed Mychael and Tam's solid presence on the floor beside me. Garadin stood just behind me. The beacon had stopped burning. I didn't need it to tell me that the danger was over. For now. Sarad Nukpana may not have gotten what he came for, but he had stolen enough.

"We'll get her back," I told Piaras. "I'll do whatever I have to."

I said it like a promise, but I couldn't promise Piaras anything right now, least of all the safe return of his grandmother. But that didn't mean I wasn't going to do everything I could to make that happen, even if it meant turning myself over to Sarad Nukpana.

"That won't be necessary," Mychael said, his voice close. "Even if it were, I wouldn't let you do it."

I turned my head toward him with an effort. My thoughts must have carried, or Mychael was just that good. Probably the latter.

"Do you have a better suggestion?"

"He will contact us, with the terms for Tarsilia's release—"

"Release? You mean trade." I saw no reason to dance around what was essentially an exchange that would never happen. Sarad Nukpana had no intention of trading Tarsilia for anyone. He would have other uses for her. I didn't say it out loud. We all knew it, and if Piaras didn't know, he didn't need to.

"That's what he'll ask for," Mychael said, "but it's not what he's going to get."

"And just what is he going to get?" I snapped.

Mychael's face was grim. "More than he bargained for."

"I just tried to give him 'more than he bargained for' and it didn't work." I looked to Garadin for the answers I didn't have. I knew he didn't have them either, and that just fed my rage and frustration. "Why didn't it work? It felt the same as it did in The Ruins. The power was there. There was nothing left of six Magh'Sceadu. How did he survive?"

"I don't know," my teacher admitted. "But we're dealing with a Gate, the darkest of magics, and the Saghred. Who knows what kind of magic is at work there? But they're both magic, so the same or similar rules should apply." He looked genuinely concerned and didn't try to hide it.

Nice to know it wasn't just me, but that was nowhere near the answer I wanted.

"All I want to know is, how are we going to get my grandmother back?" Piaras asked from the corner. "And when." There was a steely edge to his voice that I'd never heard before. His question, and his stare, were aimed directly at the Guardian.

"Sarad Nukpana is in the goblin embassy," Mychael told him. "I can't imagine him holding your grandmother anywhere else."

"And the Saghred is in the mausoleum on the grounds," Tam said.

"Convenient one-stop shopping," I muttered.

"Do you have a plan?" Piaras asked Mychael point blank.

"I do."

"What is it?"

Mychael looked at him in silence for a moment. "Not now."

"Why? You don't want to talk in front of me? You think I'm too young?" Piaras's eyes were the darkest I'd ever seen them. They were a match for Mychael's intensity, and then some.

"Not until you've had a chance to recover." His tone said he'd tolerate no argument.

I agreed with him completely.

"You just closed a Gate, from the *outside*," Mychael continued. "Do you have any idea how difficult—no, how impossible—that is?"

Piaras's own voice was subdued, but only slightly. "No, I don't."

"Which is probably why you could do it," Garadin said.

Mychael continued to look at Piaras. I didn't know if he was sizing him up, testing him, or just seeing if he would blink first. Piaras didn't blink and he didn't look away. Apparently satisfied with something, Mychael broke the contact.

"We can't talk here. There's a place the Khrynsani can't tear a Gate into."

"And just where would that be?" I asked.

"We Guardians have a safehouse of our own."

Chapter 18

Piaras was pacing.

We had arrived at the Guardians' safehouse in the central city just before dawn. I had already seen the master bedroom in my previous visit, and the rest of the palazzo was just as lavish. It belonged to the Count of Eilde, a cousin of Mychael's who was conveniently away on his honeymoon at the moment.

Our trip to the count's home had been uneventful. And not much had happened since. That was Piaras's problem. Nothing was happening at this particular moment to rescue his grandmother, and he was not happy about it. The beacon, on the other hand, seemed to know that there was a reunion with the Saghred in its immediate future. It hadn't stopped purring since we'd arrived.

"If not now, when?" Piaras asked.

"Before midnight, tonight." I was just repeating Mychael's timeline, and truth be told, I liked saying it about as much as Piaras liked hearing it, which wasn't much. But unlike Piaras, I saw the wisdom in waiting. Piaras had been forced to watch Khrynsani shamans drag his grandmother through the ugliest

Gate I had ever seen or heard of, so wisdom and waiting weren't a big part of his thinking right now.

"Sarad Nukpana will kill her before then." Piaras swallowed and looked away, but not before I caught a glint of tears in his eyes. "Or worse." The Piaras of two days ago wouldn't have cared all that much if I had seen him cry. The Piaras standing with his back to me now in the Guardians' safehouse was trying desperately to show no signs of weakness. I personally didn't see tears as a weakness; but being in his late teens, and male, Piaras viewed the world a little differently, especially now. I guess I couldn't blame him.

"He won't kill her—or hurt her," I said.

I expected him to react angrily, or at the very least demand how I could possibly know. But he didn't. He understood all too well why Sarad Nukpana wanted to keep Tarsilia alive and whole. The goblin had other sorcerers he could use to fuel a Gate. Tarsilia was more valuable to him as a hostage. At least for now.

Piaras was looking at me. I knew he saw me for a brief moment as Sarad Nukpana saw me. A commodity to be traded for, used, and discarded. Piaras did not like seeing me that way. That made two of us.

"And he's not going to kill or hurt me either. Or you." I said it as much for my own benefit as Piaras's. Seeing Piaras getting misty triggered the beginnings of a salty sting in my own eyes. I concentrated really hard on making it stop. Mychael would be here any moment, and he was not going to see me cry. It wouldn't do Piaras much good either. Mychael had promised to fill us in on the details of this plan of his. A little enlightenment would go a long way toward improving morale right now.

The door opened, and I was instantly on my feet. Not that I expected anything bad to come through the door, but old habits—and recent events that had reinforced those habits—were hard to break.

It was Garadin, which was a relief to both of us.

I sheathed the dagger that had found its way into my hand.

"Was Calchas at home?" I asked him.

"He was."

Garadin had come with us to the Guardians' safehouse, but had left soon after with an escort of two Guardians to see Calchas Becan, a nachtmagus who had the largest private collection of books on the higher dark magics, including Gates. An exorcist and demonologist by trade, Nachtmagus Becan was a nice enough gentleman by all accounts, but I wouldn't want to sleep in the same house as that library. Still, research was good. I was going to be seeing Sarad Nukpana face-to-face tonight and I wanted to know what had happened and why—or more to the point, what had *not* happened and why.

Garadin was taking his time helping himself to cheese, meat, and ale at the sideboard.

"Well?" I asked impatiently. "What happened to me . . . it . . . whatever?"

"Gate got in your way," he said around a mouthful of cheese.

"What? It was a Gate. It was open. I was on one side, Nukpana on the other. Nothing between us but air. No problem."

Garadin held up a hand, stopping me. "Big problem. About four miles worth. You're forgetting about distance. Apparently distance is very important, critical even."

"What distance? We were in the same room." As soon as I said it, I knew I was wrong. "He was on the other side of the city from me."

"Correct."

"But I had a clear shot," I protested.

"Through a Gate," Garadin clarified. "The distortions on that threshold were violent enough to diffuse all but a small part of what you threw at him."

I had a sick feeling in the pit of my stomach. "How much got through?"

My godfather shrugged. "Maybe five percent, maybe less."

I flopped down in my chair. "Just enough to piss him off."

"Probably."

No, definitely. The rest was so simple. I would have pounded my head against the wall if Nukpana hadn't already done it for me. I was so stupid.

Piaras spoke. "Then what I did worked because I aimed at the Gate itself, not anything on the other side."

"Precisely."

I knew what it meant, and I didn't like it in the least. "So if I want to do any damage to Sarad Nukpana of the permanent variety, I need to be in the same room with him."

Garadin took a swig of ale. "Just close by will do."

No, close by wouldn't do. I didn't want to be close to Sarad Nukpana or a soul-stealing rock either. But what I wanted didn't seem to matter much this week. Though if there was one thing to be grateful for, the goblin had experienced the same problem I had, otherwise I wouldn't be standing here to feel stupid.

"So other than closing the Gate, I didn't do much good either," Piaras said.

"You did the equivalent of slamming a very big, very heavy door in Nukpana's face," I told him.

"Then why do I feel so . . ." he struggled to find the right word. "Helpless?"

Garadin and I both stared at him in disbelief. Mine was the open-mouthed kind. Garadin kept his closed. He was busy chewing again.

"Helpless is the last word I would use to describe you tonight," Garadin told him, after he swallowed. "I'm sure Sarad Nukpana doesn't see you as helpless. And just because Tarsilia isn't here with us doesn't make you helpless or ineffective."

"But I couldn't save her. I failed."

I spoke up. "You didn't fail. I couldn't save her either. If you failed, that means we both did. But blaming ourselves isn't going to do us or Tarsilia any good. We did our best."

"And it wasn't good enough."

I sighed. I felt the same way, but I was going to keep that one to myself. Piaras was just another perfectionist in the making. Nothing he ever did would be good enough, at least not for him. And while I could warn him off that path that I had well and thoroughly trampled myself, I knew it wouldn't do any good. I hadn't listened either. I glanced at Garadin. The tiniest smile curled the side of his mouth facing me.

"Oh, shut up."

His smile widened. "I didn't say a word."

"But you were thinking plenty."

"And I would deny every one of them."

Piaras was looking from one of us to the other. We'd completely lost him. "What are you talking about?"

"Garadin was just thinking how much you remind him of me at your age. And he finds it funny that I'm getting back some of what I gave him."

The young elf was still baffled.

Garadin chuckled. "Payback is hell."

"You'll never find a worse critic than the one inside your own skin, or a more difficult one to silence," I told Piaras, by means of explanation. "The best you can hope for is to teach it some manners."

"It was you against three Khrynsani shamans and a Magh'Sceadu," Garadin told him, "and who knows how many more on the other side of that Gate. Sarad Nukpana doesn't travel with incompetents. You kept yourself from being taken prisoner—"

"And me, too," I chimed in. I believe in giving credit where due. "You saved both of us. Our situation would be a lot different right now if you hadn't slammed that Gate in Nukpana's face."

The shadings of a gratified blush crept up the young spellsinger's neck. "But Grandma—"

"Was beyond your reach," came Mychael's voice from the doorway.

"Unless someone is keyed to a Gate during its construction, once you cross the threshold, you cannot come back across," the Guardian told him. "Once Tarsilia was on the other side, it would have been impossible for her to return. There was nothing you could have done."

Piaras considered what Mychael had said for a moment, then nodded. I guess having your conscience absolved by a legendary spellsinger carried more weight than your friends and family, regardless of their qualifications.

"What exactly did I do?" Piaras's voice was subdued, as if he needed to know the answer, but wasn't all that sure he really wanted to.

"Your instinct told you the Gate needed to close," Mychael said. "It had harmed someone you love. You wanted that Gate, and anything that had come through it, gone. You channeled that desire—rather intensely—through your voice. The Gate obeyed and collapsed on itself. In simple terms, you used your voice to make your wish a reality."

Piaras just stared at the paladin. "But I don't know how to do that."

"Apparently you do. On a deep level, you knew exactly what needed to be done, and you did it." Mychael paused, his blue eyes calmly searching Piaras's face. "The sight of that Gate opening terrified you beyond thought."

He hadn't asked it as a question, but he expected a response. Piaras nodded mutely.

"Beyond thought lies instinct. That which tells us to fight and protect, or flee and survive. It's primal and we all have it at our core. Your instincts were telling you to do both. But you couldn't run and you couldn't use your body to fight, so you struck out in the only other way you knew. It was raw and primitive, but it accomplished what you wanted."

Mychael paused. I could tell he wasn't comfortable in the least with what he was about to say.

"A master spellsinger would have been hard pressed to do what you did tonight," he said. "You destroyed in an instant what it took Sarad Nukpana and his best shamans hours to construct. You have an incredibly powerful instrument, Piaras. Though I'd imagine Sarad Nukpana thinks of it more as a weapon. In this one instance, I agree with him. Either way, for your own safety and the safety of others, you need to learn to harness and control that power, or at the very least guide it. And you need to learn it now. Who's your teacher?"

"I am," Garadin replied. "Though not for much longer, I suspect. He's never done anything close to what he did tonight, though I've suspected for some time he had the potential." He grinned crookedly. "I just didn't think the boy would bloom so soon. Two weeks ago, I sent a letter to Ronan Cayle asking that he accept Piaras as a student next term. Ronan's a former colleague of mine, and a friend, so I think my recommendation will carry sufficient weight to persuade him."

The last remaining bit of color drained from Piaras's face. He knew only too well who Ronan Cayle was. Anyone who had any aspirations to spellsinging did. Everyone also knew that it was virtually impossible to get an audition, let alone be accepted as a student.

I smiled. I think Piaras was even more stunned that Garadin thought highly enough of his abilities to recommend him, even with what I had told him in The Ruins. From the expression on his face, the combination of the two scared him almost as much as Sarad Nukpana had.

"I think that's a good idea," Mychael told Garadin. "Have you heard back from Ronan?"

Garadin smiled. "I had a letter waiting for me at home this morning. On my recommendation, Maestro Cayle will grant Piaras an audition."

"Based on what I witnessed tonight, I'll add my recommendation to yours." Mychael grinned. "And when I return to Mid, I'll drop by and talk to Ronan. He was my teacher, too, Piaras. Between Garadin and myself, I can virtually guarantee he'll open his tower to you."

This was all too much for Piaras. He started to say something, then stopped, flushing to the tips of his ears. He was still having a bad night, but at least now he had some happiness to go along with it.

Mychael was now looking at me. Unlike Piaras, I knew with an absolute certainty that I didn't want to be told what I had done tonight. Mychael could save his breath. I already knew. First obliterating six Magh'Sceadu, then trashing Nukpana's Mermeian laboratory. Thanks to the Saghred, I was alive; but also thanks to the Saghred, I now possessed a largely unknown, potentially unlimited power—one that drew sorcerers of questionable character to me like lodestones to north. I didn't want either the power or the crazies, but I knew that even if I could get rid of the power, there was no guarantee the crazies would leave me alone.

Mychael must have seen that knowledge in my eyes, because he didn't say a word. I wish I could deny what had happened to me, and keep my mouth shut, too. But I had to ask.

"Was the elf Ocnus described my father?"

"Yes."

"We're going to the embassy after the Saghred tonight, aren't we?"

"Yes."

"I just made myself *completely* irresistible to Sarad Nukpana, didn't I?"

"Undoubtedly."

Not what I wanted to hear, but what I expected.

"And Sarad Nukpana will hunt me for the rest of my life unless I hunt him down first."

"Yes."

"Can you answer me with more than one word?"

A smile tugged at the corner of his mouth. "If necessary."

Piaras was not smiling. "We're not going to rescue my grandmother tonight?"

"The moment the Saghred is secure, we will go after your grandmother," Mychael assured him.

"And Sarad Nukpana," I added.

"Have you ever been inside the goblin embassy?" he asked me.

"Once or twice." I didn't particularly care to dwell on those occasions. I hadn't been an invited guest either time.

"Good, that will be helpful. Are you familiar with the grounds?"

"I haven't had the pleasure." Considering what I'd heard about what the goblins considered gardens, I didn't think I had missed out on much.

"The embassy is the newer building on the property," Mychael said. "The royal residence is considerably older. The mausoleum and the ruins of a temple are between the two. I have Guardians staking out the goblin embassy and the Mal'Salin family compound. One wall surrounds them both."

"How convenient."

My sarcasm didn't go unnoticed. Considering my present and future circumstances, I thought everyone would understand my lack of enthusiasm.

"Ocnus says the Saghred is in the mausoleum," I said. "There's probably not a sign pointing to where it's hidden. I do hope you're not planning on opening crypts until we hit the jackpot."

"The beacon will let you know when we're getting close."

"How?" I asked warily. The beacon's previous communications hadn't exactly been subtle. I could really go without another near-death experience.

"The same way that most beacons work. An insistent tugging, becoming stronger as you get closer to the object to which it's keyed."

I could handle tugging.

"Between your attack, and Piaras slamming the Gate on him, Sarad Nukpana isn't going to be back to full strength in the next day," Mychael continued. "And I plan to take full advantage. He will still be dangerous, but perhaps not as deadly. It's an advantage we didn't have before."

"Getting in should be easy enough," I said. "Considering who I am and what I'm wearing, they'll welcome me with open arms. Leaving will be the hard part."

Mychael's expression turned sly. "Not if you leave with everyone else."

I didn't like his plan already. "Everyone else?"

"The goblin king's masked ball? The social elite of your city are in a frenzy. You might have noticed."

"The masked ball," I said, without enthusiasm.

"Tonight at the goblin embassy," Mychael finished for me. "It couldn't be more perfect—everyone will be wearing masks."

I didn't think anything about it was perfect. Not only would I be going into the equivalent of a dragon's den, I had a feeling I'd be doing it wearing something I ordinarily wouldn't be caught dead in. Though if I was lucky, or if Mychael was as good as everyone seemed to think, I'd end up neither caught nor dead.

"I, and a few of my men, will be attending as representatives of the Archmagus." Mychael backed off a step, and executed a courtly bow. "I would be honored if you would accompany me as my guest."

All I could manage was, "Is this a date?"

That must not have been the response he was used to. He thought for a moment. "You could call it that. If you're concerned about your reputation, we'll both be masked so no one will recognize us."

"The only damaged reputation would be yours," I told him. "I'm a Benares, remember?"

"That doesn't concern me."

Another surprise. A really nice one. "It doesn't?"

"Not in the least. However, you're also probably an Anguis."

Of course. That meant I was only half criminal. My father was a Conclave Guardian. That made the other side of my family marginally acceptable. I was sure he didn't mean it like it sounded. Few people did, but that didn't stop them from saying it—or more often, thinking it. Either was just as bad. Snow in the Nebian desert. The paladin of the Conclave Guardians with a Benares. Both ranked in probability right up there with the lower hells freezing over. I looked around for something to kick. Where was Ocnus when you needed him?

There was a knock at the door.

"Come," Mychael called.

It was the blond ax wielder, whose full name I'd discovered was Vegard Rolfgar. "Sorry to interrupt, sir. But we have a message from the Khrynsani."

Mychael stepped forward to take the wax-sealed paper. "How was it delivered?"

Vegard came in and shut the door behind him. "It wasn't. Hugh and Teris were on watch at the goblin embassy when two shamans stepped outside and tacked this to the gates." He grinned. "Hugh kind of thought it might be for us, so they retrieved it. It's addressed to the lady," he said, indicating me. The blond Guardian removed a long, narrow cloth-wrapped bundle from his belt. "The goblins used this for a nail."

Mychael took the bundle and carefully unwrapped it. From his expression, he knew what it was. I had a good idea myself. The last fold of cloth fell open. It was a Khrynsani ceremonial sacrificial dagger. I hate it when I'm right. Judging from the dark gems encrusting the grip above the nearly foot-long triangular blade, and the single ruby topping the pommel, it probably belonged to Sarad Nukpana himself. I knew then that whatever words were written on the parchment, it was just an invitation to play. The real message was the dagger. Though if Nukpana had ordered this one used to tack a note to a gate, at least he couldn't use it for more twisted purposes. But I was sure he had a spare. The crazies always did. The dagger was a personal challenge, and I took it as one.

Mychael studied the envelope. It was sealed with black wax, and appeared to be harmless enough. But we both knew better. Nothing that Sarad Nukpana produced could be harmless. I let Mychael finish his inspection. He included a scan that made me feel more confident about his results. After another moment or two he passed it to me, his distaste apparent.

"It seems to be safe," he told me. "Not clean, but safe."

It was as much as I expected. I accepted it, and to Mychael's bemusement, still did a scan of my own. I valued my life more than the Guardian's feelings, but I got the impression that considering the author of the message, Mychael didn't take my caution personally.

The pale cream parchment felt smooth beneath my fingers. I had my suspicions regarding its origin, and looked up at Mychael. His lips were pressed into a tight line. So much for his distaste. I was pretty sure I knew what kind of skin the parchment was made from. I steeled myself and took out a small dagger to use on the seal. Just because I had to open it didn't mean that I couldn't touch it as little as possible. I needed to read the message, and that would be difficult to do with the letter in the fireplace and me cringing in the opposite corner of the room. I could tell myself that the elf or human whose skin had been used for Sarad Nukpana's personal stationery was long dead. It didn't make it any better, just almost bearable.

I broke the seal. Nothing happened. No doubt Nukpana was saving all of his unpleasant surprises for a more personal encounter. The letter was written in goblin, which wasn't a problem for me. His choice of ink was another matter altogether. I had a big problem with that. It was blood, and it had to have been fresh. Focus on the message, I told myself, not the ink source.

I read it. I didn't want to focus on the message either. I felt more than a little lightheaded at the words scratched on that parchment. Sarad Nukpana wrote them to terrify me now, so I wouldn't be able to fight him later. He wanted Piaras at our meeting. If he wasn't, the deal was off, Saghred or no Saghred. He went on to assure me that killing a spellsinger so young and gifted would be a waste and was the last thing on his mind. Then he told me exactly what was on his mind, in calm, clinical detail. I clenched my jaw, sending my rage back to the hard knot in the pit of my stomach where it had come from. I wasn't going to keep it penned up for long. Venting would come later, when I had Sarad Nukpana's throat between my hands.

"What is it?" Mychael asked.

I handed the letter to him. "He's getting greedy. Do you read goblin?"

"I do."

"Good." I wasn't about to read it to him, not with Piaras in the room, or even with Piaras out of the room. I didn't want to give life of any kind to the goblin's twisted words.

Mychael scanned the page. From the expressions that flowed across his face, his reaction was much the same as my own. The Guardian just went up a couple of more notches in my estimation. Protective instincts in a man could sometimes be more of a hindrance than a help, but considering who and what Sarad Nukpana was, I'd take all the protective instincts from others that I could get, especially if that someone was a Guardian paladin.

"What is it?" Piaras was on his feet, and walking toward Mychael. "What does it say?"

I blocked his way. "No!"

My vehemence shocked even me. It froze Piaras in his tracks. From the look on his face, you'd have thought I had slapped him.

"I'm sorry, but you don't need to read that." My volume backed off, but not the intensity.

I had taught Piaras to read goblin myself. But I had taught him for mixing herbs for medicines, not to read the perverse ravings of a monster.

The young elf's expression hardened. "Why not? If it's about Grandma—"

"The only mention of your grandmother is to set up the trade."

That wasn't entirely true, but I didn't want to tell Piaras that either. Sarad Nukpana had made another reference to Tarsilia, detailing precisely what would happen to her should we not promptly comply with his wishes. Then at the point of her death, he would use what remained of Tarsilia's life to fuel another Gate to come and get Piaras and me himself. Piaras was not going to read that.

"The trade for you?" Piaras asked quietly.

"Yes." I told myself a half truth was better than none at all.

Piaras didn't respond immediately. He just looked at me. He knew there was more, and he didn't need any magical talent to tell him. If I had reacted that strongly, chances were he really didn't want to know. But he felt he should. And as much as I didn't want to admit it, I wasn't all that sure he was wrong. The world was full of ugliness. Piaras was going to have to find out about it sooner or later. I just didn't want it to be now, and like this.

"What else is in it?" he asked. His voice was quiet, but firm. He wasn't going to back down. Part of me was glad.

I didn't answer immediately. It wasn't a comfortable silence for anyone, but most of all for me. "I would rather you didn't see what he wrote," I said at last. "It's the product of a sadistic mind, and you won't gain anything by knowing what's in it. I don't even want you to touch the letter. Just trust me this once, and don't insist."

"Is some of it about me?"

I hesitated only briefly before answering. "Yes."

"He wants to hurt me, doesn't he?" Piaras knew the answer to that question as well as Mychael and I.

"Yes, he does."

My response sank in, and full realization came close on its heels. Piaras handled it well.

"He wants both of us," he said.

"Wanting doesn't make it happen," I told him.

"We're going to do everything within our power to keep both you and Raine safe," Mychael said. "And get your grandmother back alive."

Piaras carefully considered his words before he spoke. "Then I don't need to know the details of the letter. But if there's anything in it that I need to know before tonight, please tell me."

I was confused. It was a welcome change of emotion. "Before tonight?"

"When we rescue Grandma. If there's anything that I should—"

"*We*? No, no. There's no 'we.' You're staying here."

"No, I'm not."

"Yes, you are."

"Actually Raine, it's best that he go with us," Mychael said.

"What?" I couldn't believe what I was hearing. If all went well, I was going to be strangling Sarad Nukpana in a few hours, but there was a real possibility I was going to do the same to Mychael Eiliesor right now.

"To retrieve the Saghred and go up against the Khrynsani is going to take every Guardian I brought with me," Mychael said. "The safest place for Piaras is with us."

I couldn't fault his logic, but that didn't mean I agreed with him. I had protective instincts of my own, and those instincts wanted to take hold of Piaras and not let go. My more practical side knew that wasn't possible. At the very least, I'd have to let go of him to kill Sarad Nukpana. My second set of options involved locking Piaras in the deepest cellar in the city, or have Phaelan set sail with him immediately for the center of the closest ocean. Appealing, but hardly practical. And neither would put Piaras beyond the reach of a creature who could rip a Gate to anywhere he wanted.

So I just met Mychael with stony silence. Sometimes I hated it when I was right, but I always hated it when someone else was. Especially when their being right made me wrong. I'm irrational that way. It's something I'm working on.

Chapter 19

Sarad Nukpana wanted the exchange to happen at midnight in the temple ruins near the Mal'Salin family compound. The Saghred was in the mausoleum on the embassy grounds. It sounded simple enough. Go to the party, take home one soul-stealing rock as a party favor, and while we were in the neighborhood rescue Tarsilia. Simple. Right.

Things were getting entirely too complex. Mychael's plan for sneaking us unnoticed into the embassy involved wearing what I considered to be entirely too noticeable clothes.

King Sathrik Mal'Salin's theme of choice for his debut in Mermeia was a masked costume ball. The masked and disguised part I could understand and completely agree with. Walking into the goblin embassy with a mask on appealed to me on many levels, and all of them involved my continued survival. But the fancy costume part went a couple of big leaps too far. I knew that highborn goblins and elves alike were jumping at any chance to attend and outdo each other in extravagance and drama, but that didn't mean I had to join them.

Mychael said I did.

"So you propose we all just stroll in through the front door?" I asked.

"That's the preferred way to enter when you have invitations."

"Uh, Mychael, don't those invitations have your name on them? Being Justinius Valerian's official representative and all?"

I might have seen the beginnings of a sly grin. "They do. Which is why we won't be using them. One of my men will be posing as me for the evening."

"Does he know what he'll be walking into? Aside from me and Piaras, you're probably next on Nukpana's most-likely-to-die list."

"He knows. He volunteered. Three more of my men will be accompanying him."

"Then whose invitations are we using?"

"In addition to his home, the count is graciously allowing me to assume his identity for the evening. Gavril and I are cousins, so we're similar enough in build and coloring. Add a mask and costume to that, and no one will know that I'm not him. Gavril, his bride, and four guests have invitations. They were due to arrive back this morning, but I sent word last week that considering the state of affairs here, he and his new wife might want to extend their honeymoon a few more days. They thought it was a wonderful idea."

I heard only one thing. "We're posing as newlyweds?"

"Yes."

For one of the few times in my life, words failed me.

"The new countess is from Rina," he said, mistaking the source of my concern entirely. "No one here has ever seen her, so no one will know that you're not her."

"Except Sarad Nukpana."

"You'll be masked."

"I'll be wearing the beacon."

"You'll be with me," he said. "And we'll be surrounded by my men."

I couldn't argue with that. Mychael already had two wins in his column against the goblin grand shaman.

"You and I, in addition to Piaras and Garadin, will be using four of the count's invitations," Mychael said. "Vegard and Riston will be using the other two. My men without invitations will get onto the grounds another way."

"How many men?"

"All of them."

Finally, something I could agree with.

Though Mychael could have emptied out the Guardian citadel on Mid, and I wouldn't have felt secure. The Guardians might be able to protect me from Sarad Nukpana, but there wasn't a thing they could do about the Saghred. That was my adversary to face, and when it came down to it, I'd be going it alone, just me and the Soul Thief. Not my idea of a fun date.

That made me remember something else. Prince Chigaru Mal'Salin wanted the Saghred almost as badly as he wanted to kill his brother. When you've been feeding a hate as long as Chigaru and Sathrik, you get good at it. Nothing like a potential reunion between homicidal brothers to add spice to the evening.

"I don't think we'll be the only ones using someone else's invitations," I told Mychael. "I can't see Prince Chigaru being in town and sitting this one out. He seems to think any opportunity to get his hands around big brother's throat is one worth taking."

"I wouldn't be surprised if he were there."

I wouldn't be surprised either. Concerned, yes. Surprised? Definitely not.

"Though for a distraction, there's nothing like a nice, public assassination attempt," Garadin said from the doorway. He walked a couple of steps into the room and executed a slow spin. "How's this?"

My godfather looked like he had just stepped out of a Nebian pasha's throne room. His long, sapphire silk tunic flowed over full matching trousers. Both were completely encrusted with silver embroidery. The tunic was fastened down the front with a profusion of silver and pearl buttons. It was topped with a wrapped-silk turban with a jeweled pin at the front. It was a bit overdone, but on the whole tasteful and suited Garadin perfectly.

I wish I could say the same about my chosen ensemble for the evening. When I say chosen, I don't mean by me. I would never have selected the extravagance of bronze velvet, ivory Pengorian silk, gold embroidery, and jewels that spilled across the chair beside me as either my first or last choice. Mychael had picked our costumes personally. I was pretty sure I could trust the Guardian paladin with my life, but I knew now that I couldn't trust him with my wardrobe choices. If Mychael said that fancy dress was necessary, I'd go along, but only to a point. I had to draw the line somewhere.

"Can I at least wear black?"

"No," he told me point blank.

"Why not?"

"It says so on the invitation, along with the no weapons request. Only Mal'Salin royal guard and retainers will be wearing black. Not having any guests in black cuts down on any confusion or misunderstandings. As to weapons, we'll carry, but they'll have to be small."

I didn't want another misunderstanding with a Mal'Salin guard, but I did want to blend in with the woodwork. With the attention that gown was guaranteed to attract, I'd have trouble not being the center of attention.

Costumed balls were a staple of the wealthier classes in Mermeia, so the trunks and armoires of the count's palazzo yielded a bumper crop of what Mychael deemed appropriate attire for the evening.

I looked at the costume again. Judging from the feathered mask and golden hooked beak, I think I was supposed to be a hawk. There were worse things I could be, and a bird of prey was oddly appropriate for the evening's activities.

The gown's flowing skirt and short train were bronze velvet, with an elaborate feather pattern painstakingly embroidered in gold thread, and sprinkled the entire length with tiny, golden jewels. The skirt was slit in the front to reveal the same treatment in ivory Pengorian silk, with what looked to be diamonds. The tight sleeves were similarly done in ivory with embroidered bronze velvet oversleeves attached at the shoulders and falling to the floor to represent wings. The bodice was ivory leather and intricately tooled with gold to resemble smaller feathers. I approved of the leather and even the corset I'd have to wear underneath. I wouldn't be comfortable, but at least I'd have marginal protection against pointy steel objects that went stab in the night.

While I had to admit it was beautiful, the gown wasn't appropriate for anything I had planned this evening. For one, I liked breathing. Between the corset and the gown's low-cut bodice, air would be the only thing that wasn't ample. Second, my legs needed to be free for life-extending activities like fighting and running—neither of which I have ever been able to do in a gown. And from the looks of things, the bronze oversleeves almost brushed the ground. First whiff I got of trouble, those sleeves were history. Though if worse came to worse, I could slash my bodice laces if I needed more air, and hike up my skirts if I needed to run away from something.

I sighed in resignation. Mychael took that as a yes.

"Sarad Nukpana knows I'm a woman." It was my last line of defense, but I'd take it. "That's what he'll be looking for. Can't I at least wear trousers?"

"There will be plenty of women there in all manner of dress," Mychael assured me.

"And probably undress," Garadin added. "I've heard the Nebians are sending a delegation with the pasha's son. He's brought at least ten of his wives with him. I can't imagine them staying at home tonight."

"And the count's new bride would hardly wear trousers to her first public appearance in her new home city," Mychael said. "Trust me, you won't attract undue attention. Unless, of course, you do something to draw attention to yourself."

"I'll be on my best behavior," I promised. Like I had a choice in that dress.

For some reason, I don't think he believed me.

In addition to the mask, there was a hat: I picked up the bronze velvet concoction with its sweep of plumes. I think it was supposed to look like the hats noble women of fashion had taken to wearing while hunting. I didn't want to think about all the birds that had given their tail feathers, along with their dignity, so that some Mermeian noble could scare away game, or make a grand entrance. I just hefted the hat and looked at Mychael. If push came to shove, I could always use it as a club.

"Something has to hide your hair, even after you put it up," he said. "It is an unusual color."

Mychael Eiliesor. Guardian paladin, sacred protector, master spellsinger, fashion consultant.

I felt a smug little grin coming on. I wasn't going to admit defeat. Not yet. I had an idea. An idea that wouldn't get me out of going to the ball, but it would get me out of wearing that gown. "What about the beacon?"

"What about it?"

"It's on a chain. This gown has a low bodice." I glanced at the gown again and swallowed. "A very low bodice. Everybody's going to see that chain. A few are going to know what's attached to it. Plus, the chain's silver; all the jewels on this gown are set in gold. That'll make it even more noticeable. The only thing worse than wearing a plain silver chain at a royal ball is wearing a plain silver chain that clashes with one's outfit."

Mychael didn't just match my grin, he raised me a smirk—and a rope of sparkling diamonds dangling from his hand.

I stifled an unladylike word. The Benares in me made a small sound and reached for the strand. Maybe the gown wasn't so bad after all.

I pulled my hand back. "But I can't take the beacon off."

Mychael moved behind me with the diamonds. "You don't have to. If I may?"

I swept my hair up and away from my neck. I didn't know what he was doing, but he seemed to, and since what he was doing involved the most diamonds I'd ever worn in my life, I decided to give him the benefit of a doubt.

"Pull the beacon out of your shirt," he said.

I did.

"Hold it against your chest and remove the chain."

I turned my head and looked at him. "Are you sure?"

"Yes. It'll be fine."

"I'm not worried about it; I'm worried about me."

He was grinning like a little boy again. Irresistible. "Just do it."

I held the beacon against my breastbone with one hand and slipped the chain out of the loop at the top of the beacon with the other. Mychael's hand came around from behind and handed me the end of the jeweled rope. I looped it through. It could have been my imagination, but the beacon's happy purring sounded just a little bit happier. Looked like I wasn't the only one who liked diamonds.

Mychael fastened the clasp, his hands warm against the back of my neck. That felt even nicer than the weight of the diamond rope. I lowered the beacon back into my shirt, my hand lingering on the diamonds. A masked ball might not be so bad.

Piaras wasn't going to be spared the indignity of fancy dress either. Mychael had suggested a substitute. One of his Guardians was about the same height and build as Piaras, and in costume, would pass as the spellsinger until it was too late for Nukpana to do anything about it once, or if, he found out. Piaras didn't insist on reading the letter, but he had insisted on this. He said that the goblin would know instantly that it wasn't him, and he wouldn't endanger his grandmother by unnecessarily angering the goblin grand shaman. I agreed with his reasoning, but I didn't like having him within a hundred miles of Nukpana. Piaras said that he was willing to take that risk.

Everyone else would be risking their lives, he wouldn't be an exception.

The door opened. We all turned to look.

It was a six-foot-tall peacock.

"Tell me you're joking, sir," the peacock said to Mychael.

The voice was Piaras's, but I didn't recognize anything else. I just stared in open-mouthed astonishment. My second of the evening. Mychael and Garadin just looked stunned.

Piaras was dressed in golden brown, vibrant blue, and iridescent emerald green. His doublet was rich blue velvet, short and formfitting with delicate silver embroidery representing peacock feathers and a dark jewel at the center of each feather's "eye." The cloak was a matching blue silk covered entirely with actual peacock feathers. It was tied dueling cloak style with a silver cord, under his sword arm and over the opposite shoulder. Of course with the goblin king's request, Piaras wouldn't be carrying a sword. The trousers were formfitting golden brown suede with matching high boots. The silver mask was inlaid with sapphire and emerald enamel, and was adorned with more feathers that curved to conceal some of Piaras's dark curls.

To say the costume was a bit much would have been the ultimate understatement, but both it and the young elven spellsinger were breathtakingly beautiful.

I had to say something. "Now you can't tell me *that* won't attract attention."

Mychael looked like he was reconsidering his grand scheme, or at least Piaras's part of it.

A victory. Yes. At this point, I'd take what I could get.

The goblin king's masked ball was being touted as the event of the social season. Call me a pessimist, but I couldn't help but think of it as hunting season, with me as the prized catch being delivered dressed and trussed to the hunter's front door.

The beacon seemed to think it was about to get what it wanted. At least that was the impression I got. It was hard to believe it had only been three nights since Quentin had stolen the beacon and given it to me for safekeeping. Ever since then, the beacon had either been completely silent, or trying to kick a hole in my chest. After we set out from the count's palazzo, the beacon had settled down to a gentle hum in time with my heartbeat. Glad to know one of us was happy with our destination.

To help keep gondola traffic moving on the canals, and to avoid any flaring tempers that might result from gridlock or clashing cultures, classes, or magic, the mayor of Mermeia had ordered all members of the city watch, not otherwise assigned, to traffic duty. I know the watchers loved that. They were angry, they were armed, and most importantly, there were five of them at every major waterway intersection. There were more than a few aristocrats in town for Sathrik's little get-to-gether; aristocrats who felt entitled to go where they wanted, when they wanted, and to answer to no one when they went there.

Our city's finest were there to tell them otherwise.

In an elaborately draped and gilded gondola to our port side, a Pengorian noble was being issued a stern warning for failure to yield to a smaller vessel. It probably wouldn't have gone any further than a warning, but when the indignant Pengorian in question started shrieking about his privileges in this and any other city, the watcher said nothing else and promptly began writing him a ticket. As we turned the corner at the bell tower, I could still hear the noble's shrill protests.

It warmed my heart.

Though what filled me with less than a glowing feeling was the rolling motion caused by the heavier than normal traffic on the canals. My normal—and entirely rational, I might add—fear of drowning had little to do with my present discomfort. I tried to focus on the unmoving building in front of us, rather than the all-too-moving water undulating below me. My eyes believed the deception. My stomach didn't buy it for a second.

In addition to his house and invitations, the count had given

Mychael the use of his gondolas. While thankfully not as extravagant as some of the floating palaces attempting to make their way to the embassy without tipping over, the count's gondolas were sleek and tastefully elegant. Some of Mychael's Guardians were outfitted in the count's house livery of blue and white, and were piloting the gondola Piaras and I were in along with Mychael. The count's other formal gondola was to our starboard, also with a full complement of Guardian oarsmen with Garadin and Vegard looking miserable in his borrowed finery.

Weapons wouldn't be allowed in the embassy, and any who tried to defy the royal edict would be denied entrance. We all needed to get inside, so we played by the rules—to a point. Elaborate costuming allowed for all kinds of places to conceal a small blade or two, or three or four, or more in my case. I was wearing enough steel to make me feel as comfortable as possible, considering the circumstances. And I made sure Piaras was similarly armed. The problem being, I was sure plenty of King Sathrik's guests were thinking along the same lines. So unless Sathrik wanted to kick most of his guests out, he was going to have to make a few concessions.

Piaras and I were both masked and wore dark, hooded cloaks. Mychael had determined, and Garadin agreed, that with most of the high nobility from the seven kingdoms in attendance, Piaras's costume wouldn't stand out in the least. Besides, it was the only costume in the count's trunks that fit him. I took a wait-and-see attitude. I had to admit that this was one time I didn't want to be able to say "I told you so." However, as an extra precaution, Mychael had asked us to sit in the section of the gondola near the stern that was draped from view. Neither of us had objected.

"Raine?" Piaras ventured from the plush upholstered seat next to me.

"Yes?"

I couldn't see his face, but I didn't need to. Just hearing him say my name told me he probably looked as scared as he sounded. I squirmed in my bodice in a vain attempt to get a decent lungful of air. If I looked as uncomfortable as I felt, we were quite a pair.

"How much farther?"

From the sound of his voice, he didn't want to be any closer. The only place he wanted to be was home. I'd like to be there myself. Under my bed sounded like a nice, cozy spot. Piaras had never been into the heart of the Goblin District. Piaras had never wanted to go, even on a dare from his friends. Not that his friends would go themselves, or would many other elves, for that matter.

"We're almost there." I reached out and gave his hand a squeeze. His fingers curled around mine and didn't let go. I was glad he didn't.

"Are you scared?" he asked quietly.

"Yes." I'd have to be seven types of insane not to be afraid of where we were going—and who would be there waiting for us. I had an extra reason to be terrified that had nothing to do with psychotic goblins. I'd be getting up close and personal with the Thief of Souls.

Piaras seemed to know what I was thinking and squeezed my hand reassuringly. "It'll be okay. We'll all be there with you."

That would have been a comforting thought, except for the gnawing fear that having my friends anywhere near me was as far from okay as it was possible to be.

The Guardians guided the gondola around the corner at the clock tower that marked the entrance to the Goblin District. I had always found it to be an inspiring sight. On a normal night it would inspire a better than average case of the creeps. Tonight it inspired that along with awe, intimidation, and a goodly dose of terror. Maybe it was the circumstances, though I imagine it was exactly the effect the Mal'Salin family was going for. No doubt Sarad Nukpana had a hand in the party decorations that met King Sathrik's guests as they made their way up the Grand Duke's Canal to where it flowed past the steps of the goblin embassy.

The buildings in the Goblin District were of arched stone and gleaming marble—both were dark and built to be as imposing as possible. At least that was my impression of goblin architecture. But for all I knew, goblins thought it was cozy and reminded them of home. Gates were of intricately twisted wrought iron, and the tops of most, if not all, ended in a sharpened point. The streetlights glowed a dim blue. Supposedly the lighting was for the comfort of sensitive goblin eyes. That may be the case, but in my opinion, the goblins just did it to discourage visitors. It worked. I certainly wouldn't come here for an evening out.

Apparently the goblin king's party planner was looking to maximize the effect tonight. Caged torches mounted on tall metal spikes were spaced at regular intervals on both sides of the canal. The torches blazed with blue flames easily two feet high. The long shadows cast from those flames gave the impression that the buildings were looming out over the canal—and over the guests' gondolas that traveled it. Mounted on the spikes were twin banners in the crimson and black of the House of Mal'Salin. Between the banners was a burnished shield that was easily an arm's span wide. The shields were emblazoned with the family crest that Piaras and I were all too familiar with—the double serpents surmounted by a crown. The crests were inlaid with red enamel that glowed with a life of their own. In the torches' light, the snakes on the crests seemed to writhe against the steel.

Then there was the warm greeting of the Mal'Salin royal guard in full battle armor standing at attention, illuminated by the blaze of the torches. They were spaced every twenty feet or so on both sides of the canal, and in addition to the usual curved daggers and sabers, each carried a slender spear with a particularly lethal-looking hooked blade at the top.

Piaras's hand had started to sweat. Or maybe it was mine.

"This was not a good idea," Piaras said from between clenched teeth.

"There's nothing wrong with the idea," I tried to reassure him—and me. "Just the welcoming committee."

I was determined not to be scared. The trappings of terror decorating the canal banks had Sarad Nukpana's name written all over them. Once again, he was only trying to frighten me so that I couldn't fight him. I wouldn't let him succeed.

But that didn't stop him from doing a damn fine job.

The steps of the goblin embassy extended down into the canal. As we neared the steps, the gondola pilots guided their boats into a single line. When their passengers had safely disembarked, they pulled away, making way for the next guests. I say safely, because due to both the costuming and masks, maneuverability and visibility were at a minimum for some partygoers. There were goblin footmen there to assist, but I wasn't about to take any proffered hands, especially if they belonged to someone working for the Mal'Salin family. I would rather risk going for an unexpected swim. I needn't have worried. Mychael jumped out first and gallantly offered his hand to me. And once he had it, he didn't let go. Considering where we were, I didn't mind.

Piaras stepped from the gondola by himself without a stumble. Just before we had disembarked, he had given my hand a firm squeeze, then stood resolutely, his jaw set. My little brother was growing up.

I looked at Mychael standing by my side—and kept looking. He was magnificent. Regal in the purple and gold of an ancient Pengorian knight, the paladin's surcoat looked almost black in the flickering torchlight, entwined vines and leaves finely embroidered in gold thread on the soft suede. Mychael's mask was etched gold, the perfect setting for those glorious blue eyes. The costume, the embassy, a king's masked ball. Mychael clearly belonged here. I didn't.

He caught me looking. I quickly glanced away.

I felt him raise my hand to his lips. "You're beautiful," I heard him murmur.

I didn't know what to say. I'd never been very good at compliments, especially those addressed to me.

He smiled and kissed my hand again, taking his time before draping my arm over his to escort me inside.

To get inside, all of the guests had to walk up the stairs flanked by yet more royal guardsmen sporting enough enameled steel to anchor a ship—or sink one. They didn't seem to mind the weight. They also didn't seem to blink. Eerie. Though I'm sure the Mal'Salins frowned on such displays of weakness. And when a Mal'Salin royal frowned, heads rolled, or so I'd heard.

At the top of the stairs, I saw a small goblin lady, her bearing regal, wearing a gown of the most ethereal fabric that I had ever seen. The color shifted and shimmered with the torchlight. Her hair and face were completely covered by a pale cloud of a veil that fell past her shoulders. Beneath that, she wore a mask as well. She reached out one tiny, gloved hand and placed it lightly on the arm of a goblin who was dressed as a jester, but he apparently had left his good humor at home. His bearing was straight, either from naturally good posture or tension. Considering where we were, it could have been both. I might not be the most nervous person here tonight, but I think I had the most reason.

The lady tilted her head to look up at her escort as he said something to her.

I knew her.

I tried to get as close to Mychael's ear as possible. Not easy in my hat.

"The couple at the door, the small goblin lady . . ."

"Yes?"

"A'Zahra Nuru."

"Are you sure?"

"Positive."

"Do you recognize her escort?"

"No, but he's probably one of the prince's courtiers. He's too short to be the prince."

"Well then, let's see if they get in."

I wasn't anywhere near as casual about it as Mychael, but on a positive note, at least I knew what the primari was wearing. Chances were once she was inside, she would be meeting Prince Chigaru. If I couldn't avoid my enemies this evening, it'd at least be nice to spot some of them before they spotted me.

The goblin primari gave her invitation to one of the guards at the door. He looked at it and then at her. He returned it to her and the door opened. She started to step across the threshold, then paused, glancing back over her shoulder. The beacon still vibrated happily inside my bodice. I fought the urge to cover it with my hand. I knew the gesture wouldn't do any good and would only draw attention.

A'Zahra Nuru paused a moment longer, then she and her escort entered the embassy.

Now it was our turn.

The guard gestured us forward. Mychael swept up the steps without hesitation. Piaras, Garadin, and I followed with Vegard and Riston Kirkwode, the dark-haired Guardian from Tam's place.

The guard scrutinized the invitation then our masked faces, each in turn. I hope the Count of Eilde, or his politics, hadn't bought us more problems than perks. The guard turned to confer with a superior. The officer was checking another invitation, and the guard had to wait until he was finished. Next to me, Piaras took a breath and held it. While he did that, I entertained myself by wondering which was closer—the dagger in my bodice, or the throwing knives in the hidden pockets of my gown.

Mychael waited seemingly without a care in the world. He even began humming a tune currently popular in the eastern kingdoms. He had nerve. The humming continued, and with it came a smile. It was contagious. A corner of the goblin guard's

mouth turned upward. He turned away from the still-busy officer and returned the invitation to Mychael.

"There's no need to keep you waiting, sir. On behalf of His
Royal Majesty, King Sathrik Mal'Salin, I bid you and your
guests welcome. Please enter."

Chapter 20

"It's not the song that matters, but how you sing it. Or in this case how you hum it," Mychael was explaining to an amazed Piaras. "A light and friendly tune to inspire light and friendly thoughts."

I really didn't care how he did it, I was just grateful that he had. I kept telling myself that there was probably nothing to the sentry's reaction to either our invitation or to us. But it would take more than my own assurances to convince my heart rate to return to normal. Call me insecure.

While we waited our turn to enter the ballroom, I took the opportunity to familiarize myself with the lay of the land. Others were obviously doing the same thing, but I was probably the only one, or at least one of the few, looking around in case I needed to make a quick getaway. The floorplan of the goblin embassy was similar to that of other great houses along the Grand Duke's Canal. The first floor was reserved for entry and less important rooms. Mermeia was prone to flooding, and no noble wanted to constantly have to rescue the ancestral portraits and Great Aunt Gertrude's favorite chairs from rising waters.

We were in a lavish reception area, with an imposing stair-case that swept up to a landing in front of a massive stained-glass window, again featuring the House of Mal'Salin crest. From there, the stairs split to either side to continue to the third floor, and the grand ballroom. All around us, guests were re-moving the outer cloaks they had worn to protect their finery. Piaras and I had left ours in the gondola. We had no intention of leaving the way we had come in. Since the count had been nice enough to loan us everything we needed for the evening, it would be rude to knowingly leave behind something we had borrowed. In my mind that also included returning the cos-tumes we were wearing without any unsightly slashes, holes, or bloodstains.

The lighting in the embassy was dim enough for goblin comfort, but bright enough so that the elven or human guests wouldn't bump into each other. As in Tam's place, the lighting was purely for theatrical effect. Playing tricks on the eyes with light and shadow.

I didn't like it one bit.

I wasn't just being paranoid. I was being watched. The black-garbed Mal'Salin guards and courtiers blended in all too well with the decorative shadows. They were watching me; but to be fair, they were also watching everyone else. And just be-cause the official color for Mal'Salin guards was black didn't mean there weren't watchful loyalists lurking around wearing silver gossamer or pink butterfly wings. I was certain the em-bassy was positively seething with those alert for troublemak-ers, and especially watching for me. While Sarad Nukpana hadn't requested that we attend the ball, I know he had to have been expecting it.

Garadin hovered by my side. Vegard was an oddly comfort-ing presence just behind my right shoulder. The blond berserker was as armed as he could be and not clank. If all hell broke loose at some point in the evening, as a Guardian,

Vegard was more than qualified to acquire any weapons he needed from one of the many Mal'Salin guards taking up useful space. I welcomed his company.

I leaned over to Garadin. "You'd think if Sathrik was that paranoid about someone trying to stick a knife in his ribs tonight, he would have just stayed home."

"Murder and intrigue are as natural to the Mal'Salins as breathing," he told me.

"Then Sathrik's in for the time of his life tonight."

I tried to locate A'Zahra Nuru without being obvious. Considering the vision restriction of wearing a mask, and the plumed velvet enormity that was the hat on my head, doing anything subtle was next to impossible. But I tried, and I looked, and I didn't see the goblin primari. That was good and bad. I didn't want to run into her, but I also wanted to keep anyone who I knew was after me in my line of sight. The beacon was no help. It just continued to hum happily. I would have liked to have shared its positive outlook, but my other senses that I had had for far longer, and trusted far more, told me otherwise.

I just wanted to find the Saghred before Sarad Nukpana found me.

"Are you ready?" came a deep voice close enough to touch.

It was all I could do to keep both feet on the floor.

It was Mychael.

"Don't do that!" I managed, once I got past my heart in my throat.

"Shall we?" he said, offering me his arm.

I hesitated, then placed my hand on top of his. "Let the fun begin."

As we made our way up the black marble staircase, I hoped that we didn't draw too much attention clumped together as we were. We were supposed to be the Count of Eilde and his new bride just home from their wedding and honeymoon in Rina. Accompanying them were her younger brother, Tamas, his tutor, and a pair of bodyguards. Fortunately there were others who were similarly grouped. I guess when most of your guests are from the aristocracy of various kingdoms, there will be more than your fair share of burly types looking uncomfortable in unaccustomed finery. That being the case, Vegard and Riston didn't look in the least bit out of place fidgeting with their embroidered collars.

Once on the landing, I saw that the portion of the window not taken up with the serpent crest was clear glass and gave me a good view of the gardens behind the embassy. The moon was on the wane, but still provided ample light. On the edge of the trees was a stone wall approximately head height.

Mychael paused next to me. "That's the outer wall of the temple ruins. The mausoleum is at the center."

The beacon thrummed against my chest, as if sensing an impending reunion, a little thrill of excitement to add to its happiness. As a result, my stomach experienced a similar sensation, though it was neither thrilling nor happy. My hand went to my stomach again. The wave of nausea wasn't a remnant from the gondola ride.

"Ocnus was right. That's the place."

Mychael was right, too. There were plenty of elaborately begowned and bejeweled ladies to keep me company. Next to some of them, my gown was downright plain. And those were just the guests waiting in the corridor to be announced.

That brought up another problem I had.

Protocol demanded that we be announced to the other guests before we entered the ballroom. For the duration of that announcement, every eye in the room would be fixed on us—and most of those eyes didn't belong to friendlies. Some of them belonged to goblins who had seen me and Piaras two nights ago. Not nearly enough time for us to have faded from their memory.

I was masked, hatted, and garbed in yards of velvet and silk.

I felt as naked as the day I was born.

"Is this necessary?" I hissed to Mychael.

"It is if you want to get into the garden."

I thought he'd say something like that.

"I thought you didn't want to attract attention," I reminded him.

"The wrong kind," he clarified. "Entering without being announced would be extremely rude to our host. That would attract attention that we do not want."

"Far be it from me to be rude."

Mychael wisely chose not to comment.

We stepped up to the threshold.

When we were announced, everyone turned and looked—and kept looking.

I felt like a mouse in a room full of hungry cats.

The ballroom took up the entire back of the embassy with floor-to-ceiling windows opening out onto a panoramic view of the gardens and the brightly lit harbor beyond. It was full of ships and was an impressive sight in the moonlight. I guess that was one of the advantages of being rich, you could enjoy a harbor view without any of the sounds or smells of the real thing.

Piaras stood next to me looking out at the view, and at the swirling riot of color as the guests danced. His mouth dropped open. I hooked a finger under his chin and closed it for him.

"Sorry," he said.

"It's a nice view," I told him. "Enjoy it while you can; we won't be staying long."

"Good."

While Piaras was enjoying the view, I noticed that more than a few noble ladies, both goblin and elven, were enjoying the view of Piaras. I glared a few of them down; a few more appeared to be more determined—or patient. I knew as soon as I left Piaras's side he'd have plenty of company. Company I was determined he was not going to have, and certainly not at an embassy ball crawling with Mal'Salins.

The glass that covered the south wall wasn't all windows.

There were also glass doors opening onto the terrace. From there, stairs led down into the ornamental gardens, and beyond that to the mausoleum. Tonight the doors were open to admit the cool, night breezes, but no one was on the terrace to enjoy it. Protocol had once again reared its ugly head. Until the goblin king had made his entrance, everyone was encouraged to remain in the ballroom. And being familiar now with the goblin sense of the dramatic, I was sure Sathrik Mal'Salin would want to wait until all of his guests had arrived, so that his entrance would have the maximum impact. That being the case, we were due for an extended wait. However, I couldn't see Sathrik cooling his heels in an anteroom somewhere until midnight. I know if I were throwing myself a party, I'd want to be there to enjoy it.

Once the goblin king had made his entrance, the count's bride would suddenly be in dire and desperate need of fresh air. Being from the provinces, it would be her first trip to her new home, and she would be understandably overwhelmed by all the pageantry and excitement. And as an elven lady of gentle birth, she could hardly be allowed to wander alone in the gardens at an embassy ball. After all, there were trees and tall shrubs. Apparently the upper classes considered close proximity to foliage a threat to a lady's virtue, even a married one.

Once in the shadows of the garden, we'd elude any wandering guards, and get on with the business at hand. At least that was the plan. I took a wait-and-see attitude about its success. It wasn't that any plan I had been a part of lately didn't work; it was just that they had a tendency to go off in unexpected directions.

A small goblin orchestra provided the music for the evening from a raised stage on the far side of the ballroom. The music they played was distinctly goblin—dark, dramatic, and faintly discordant. A tall, slender goblin crossed the stage to stand in front of the musicians. He wore a mask and costume, neither of which were elaborate or brightly colored, made of midnight blue velvet. His glossy black hair was pulled back with a single, silver clasp at the nape of his neck. He began to sing, without accompaniment at first, then with music evolving softly behind him. His voice was as rich and openly seductive as the formfitting velvet he wore.

Rahimat. Tam's nephew—and Prince Chigaru's spellsinger.

"Is that who I think it is?" Piaras asked, his voice a bare whisper.

"I can't imagine it being anyone else."

"But he works for the prince."

"He's also a spellsinger. A gig is a gig."

Piaras looked at me. "You don't believe that, do you?"

"Not for a minute."

I don't know what Prince Chigaru was thinking by having his spellsinger at his brother's party. The room was crawling with Khrynsani. If the spellsinger tried anything with his voice that could be perceived as a threat, his performance would be cut short—along with his life. Or perhaps he really didn't work for the prince. Goblins thrived on what they referred to as intricate alliances. I called it double-dealing, but their name for it sounded better. To hear Tam talk, it was a favorite pastime at the goblin court.

Piaras's dark eyes never left the stage. "He's about to do something."

"What?"

"I don't know exactly. It's very subtle."

I could feel it. I'm sure other sensitives in the crowd could feel it, too, but no one gave any outward sign. The volume of conversation did drop, so that the spellsinger's voice could be clearly heard. Maybe the kid just got tired of no one listening to him. Maybe.

Garadin had completed a quick circuit of the room and was making his way back to me.

"Prince Chigaru has people all over the place," I told him.

"Where?" He was calm, which was more than I could say for myself.

"The spellsinger, for one. He was at the estate in The Ruins night before last." I decided to leave out the part about Rahimat being Tam's nephew. Garadin already disliked Tam, no need to toss fuel on that fire.

"Then there's the primari and her escort," I added, "along with more than a few goblins not wearing black—any of whom who could be allied with either brother and up to no good."

"These are goblin aristocrats," Garadin pointed out. "Not many of them are up to any good. Like I said, there's nothing like an assassination to liven things up. No one would blame us for seeking the safety of the gardens. If things get too lively here, we'll have plenty of company to use as cover."

Out of the frying pan and into the fire.

Mychael appeared at my side. That was disconcerting. I didn't even realize he had gone. I had let myself be distracted. That wasn't going to happen again. The goblin spellsinger had just finished his song, and the musicians were playing the first few notes of a favorite Mermeian dance tune, with a dark goblin twist, of course.

Mychael held out his hand to me.

"It would appear strange if the count did not dance with his bride." His voice was low and for my ears only. "I also need to locate any Khrynsani in the room. A few turns around the dance floor should suffice."

I fought down a surge of panic. Not the life-and-death kind, but the die-of-embarrassment kind. It was ironic. I was surrounded by Mal'Salins, and I was afraid of dancing. But that didn't stop my mouth from being suddenly dry.

"I don't dance."

"You'll be fine."

"No, really. I don't dance."

"No lady of any court moves with more grace than you." He raised my hand to his lips. "Trust me, you dance. Your feet will be fine."

I took his arm. It wasn't my feet I was worried about. It was the shoes and the hem of the gown that would trip both of them.

"I'll keep Master Tamas company," Garadin said just loud enough that a Mal'Salin retainer passing close by could hear. "You two children run along and have fun."

Mychael merged effortlessly into the swirl of dancing revelers, and swept me along with him. My gown's wrist loop worked as promised, keeping my train off the floor and out from under my feet. Surprisingly, after the first minute or so, I had yet to land in a heap on the floor. With my nerves and complete lack of dancing skills, it was nothing short of a miracle. Either that, or Mychael was that good a dancer.

More than one goblin in the room wanted the necklace I wore around my neck, and were more than willing to take my head to get to it. Dancing next to them didn't seem to be the best way to remain inconspicuous. But at least I was moving, which helped me to feel less like a sitting duck.

Mychael's hand was firm against the small of my back; the other enfolded one of my hands. He drew me close and attempted to steer me in the direction he wanted to go.

"Raine?" he said softly.

I looked up at him. "Yes?"

"Some people find dancing enjoyable."

I couldn't help but smile. "I'm dancing backward, in a gown and shoes that aren't mine, in a room full of goblin nobles. This is as relaxed as I'm going to get."

He smiled back. "Then I'll simply have to make do."

After our first circuit of the dance floor, Mychael began humming softly along with the music. It was more of a countermelody, in a slightly different key, and less discordant. I found myself relaxing a little.

I knew what he was doing, and he did it well. Having been taught by Garadin, I knew that music makes a magic all its own. The goblin king would only have the best musicians performing for him. Their talent was apparent as their music's magic swirled with and in the air around the dancers.

Mychael was using the musicians to conceal a little musical magic of his own. It was similar enough to the tune being played to blend, yet different enough to do what he wanted— namely locating other mages in the room. I'm sure there were more than enough of them, but Mychael was looking for Khrynsani shamans. But there was only one Khrynsani whose location I wanted to know, and he was more than capable of hiding himself until he wanted to be found.

The song ended, and the dancers and those who were simply enjoying the music applauded politely. I wasn't thrilled with where we ended up when the music stopped. The royal dais and the goblin king's throne were only about ten steps to our right.

I also wasn't thrilled with the scrutiny I suddenly found myself on the receiving end of. I thought I recognized the interested parties. Unfortunately, the same thought had occurred to them. They were goblins. They were black-garbed Mal'Salin courtiers. Prince Chigaru Mal'Salin's courtiers. So much for whether the prince was going to crash his brother's party. One whispered to the other, and the pair started toward us. I don't think they had recognized me yet, but they wanted to get a closer look.

I turned toward Mychael. "Company," I said in a warning singsong tone.

"I see them." He took matters into his own hands—and me along with it.

Mychael gathered me to him in a kiss passionate enough to make me forget the goblins, forget the guests, and drop my fan. When I opened my eyes, I discovered it also had the equally desirable effect of making the goblins doubt they recognized me. A win-win for everyone. Anyone and everyone else who noticed were smiling indulgently at the love struck newlyweds.

I was a little short of breath. My corset wasn't helping matters any. No wonder fainting couches were so popular with the upper classes. I absently wondered if one was nearby. Mychael gently cradled my face in his hands. His eyes were darker than

I remember them being. I opened my mouth to at least attempt a protest.

"A valid tactical maneuver," his lips moved against mine.

"So that's what Guardians call it," I whispered breathlessly.

I felt him smile. "To deflect attention of one kind, attract attention of another."

"Works for me." Even better, it worked for Chigaru's courtiers. Apparently interrupting an intimate newlywed moment was in bad taste even for a Mal'Salin. One of them even bent to retrieve my fan for me before he scurried away in embarrassment. Mychael didn't release me; he just readjusted his hold. I liked the way he readjusted. I told myself he was just staying in character, and it was simply another valid tactical maneuver. I told myself that, but I didn't really believe it—and I didn't mind that I didn't believe.

There was movement on the gallery above as trumpeters stood in a flash of scarlet and black and blew a fanfare.

Mychael sensed what I wanted to do and anchored me to the spot, his arm firmly around my waist, his hand gripping mine. We must have looked quite the loving couple. But I knew he was right. Running would be suicidal. But that didn't stop every muscle in my body from wanting to do it. Especially when I saw King Sathrik Mal'Salin and the solitary black-robed figure that entered immediately behind him. Who would have thought Sarad Nukpana was the party type? The goblin king was unmasked and dressed in black and silver formal-dress armor. It was his party, so he could wear what he wanted.

Mychael pulled me even closer. "Be still and clear your mind." His voice was a bare whisper against my ear. "You're the Countess of Eilde, just home from your honeymoon. You're deliriously happy and honored to be here."

Delirious I could do, happy I was not.

Still, I took a breath and let it out slowly, willing myself to relax.

Mychael gave my waist a quick squeeze. "Happy, darling?"

"I'm getting there," I said from between clenched teeth.

"Good."

The goblin king and the Khrynsani grand shaman passed close enough to touch, though that was the last thing on my mind. I held my breath as they passed, and I was sure I wasn't alone. Something was wrong. Not really wrong, but different. Sathrik turned and seated himself on his throne, and the robed figure turned to stand at his left hand. I saw a shadow of a masked face beneath the cowled hood.

It wasn't Sarad Nukpana. I don't know how I knew, but I did.

I started breathing again.

"It's not him," I said softly.

Mychael squeezed my hand to let me know he heard.

The goblin king began to address his guests, but I didn't hear the words. Why would Sarad Nukpana send an impostor to stand at the king's side?

I knew the answer as soon as the question asked itself. He had more important things to do, a full evening planned. A stone of power to secure, a mage to torture. I shivered as the tension I'd just released was replaced by fresh fear. Tarsilia. She had to be close. What was happening to her?

There was applause as Sathrik concluded his greeting, and the guests began taking the floor for the next dance.

"Are you unwell, darling?" Mychael asked, as only a solicitous new husband could. "You're looking pale. Perhaps something to drink and some fresh air."

I nodded tensely.

We made our way to the bar nearest the garden doors. Garadin, Piaras, and the two Guardians were already outside. A tall, elegant goblin was moving toward us—moving just like the big, dangerous cat he was.

Tam.

His chosen garb for the evening was a dark goblin mirror of Mychael's own attire. The goblin primaru was every inch the Mal'Salin duke he used to be in a surcoat of midnight blue suede, with a mix of tooled gray leather and burnished steel armor beneath. Unlike most of the "knights" I'd seen on the dance floor, Tam's armor was authentic. I had a feeling he had something other than dancing planned for this evening.

"You encountered no difficulty gaining admittance?" Tam asked us once he was close enough to speak without being overheard.

"Just the expected," Mychael replied.

I didn't mention that I had expected worse—and I certainly hadn't expected Tam.

Tam looked down at me, or more to the point, at my bodice. "Nice dress."

"Thanks."

"Very flattering," he murmured.

"I didn't choose it."

"Who did?"

I tilted my head toward Mychael. "He did."

Tam glanced at Mychael. "You did?"

"I did."

Neither of them showed any emotion, but the tension in the air went up a notch. Wonderful. Just what I didn't need.

"I didn't expect to see you here," I told Tam. "The company not to your liking and all that."

"I've asked if he would assist us this evening," Mychael explained.

"How?"

Tam leaned in close to me. "To rescue fair lady from foul fiend," he said, his voice low and for my ears only.

Tarsilia. I breathed a little sigh of relief, then smiled at the irony.

"What?" Tam asked.

"She doesn't like you, you know." The "because of me" part I left unsaid.

Tam grinned. "I know."

"Trying to earn some points?"

"Couldn't hurt. And best of all, it would annoy the foul

fiend." He winked. "I take my fun when and where I can find it."

That was Tam.

He took my hand and gallantly raised it to his lips, though the lips-to-hand contact lingered for far longer than was gallant. "Now if you will excuse me, the other fair lady awaits."

"Good luck," I whispered. "And thank you."

"Luck to you, too." He glanced at Mychael, and an unspoken something passed between them. Tam looked back to me, his expression solemn. "But you won't need luck, you have your own brave knight."

Then he crossed the crowded dance floor and was gone.

I suddenly felt woozy again. "I could really use that drink."

"As my fair lady commands."

I sat in one of the chairs arranged around a column while Mychael went to get drinks for us both.

"My brother's taste in music is sadly lacking," came a voice so close to my ear I could feel his breath.

Prince Chigaru Mal'Salin's breath.

I stood, and he caught my arm in an iron grip.

"I thought Rahimat would be a welcome addition to this evening's festivities," he continued calmly as if we were friends having a chat.

Then Mychael was there.

"Come no closer, Paladin Eiliesor," the goblin prince said softly for Mychael's benefit and smiled fully for anyone who witnessed the exchange.

I felt a blade press against my ribs.

"I only require the beacon. Mistress Benares is no longer necessary."

Chapter 21

The goblin prince and I shared a dilemma.

We were in a room full of guards loyal to Sathrik Mal'Salin and neither one of us wanted to draw attention to ourselves. His grip on me, while tight, was such that it wasn't visible to anyone. I could have twisted free, but that would draw attention. And if he tried to stab me, I was definitely going to draw attention. Mychael was ready to attack if the prince so much as breathed wrong.

So there we were—all of us wanting to move, but none of us daring to. At least not yet.

Strangely enough, I was as relaxed as I had been all evening. Maybe it was that I'd been in a similar situation with the goblin prince before and I'd come out of that still breathing. Maybe it was the relief of something happening that didn't involve Sarad Nukpana. I didn't know. Whatever it was, the tension drained from my body. Prince Chigaru sensed the change and pressed the blade tighter to my side. That really didn't bother me either. With all the whale boning in my bodice and corset, he'd have had an easier job getting through plate armor. I even felt a little smile coming on.

"So, do you have a plan?" I asked him. I sounded almost cheerful.

My question and attitude took him by surprise.

"You will give me the beacon," he demanded.

There were definite advantages to having an absurdly tight bodice—and a beacon that refused to leave. I looked down just to make sure. Nope, nothing was coming up through that cleavage.

I almost laughed. "I'm afraid that's not physically possible."

His grip tightened. He had to have expected my response, but it didn't make him any happier to hear it.

He looked down to where the diamond chain vanished between my breasts. I didn't like that look one bit. Mychael didn't either. He took two steps toward us.

The goblin prince pulled me back against him. "No closer."

Mychael stopped. His eyes flicked to something just past my left shoulder. I was betting I'd only need one guess—Prince Chigaru's friends wanted to keep him company. Vegard was keeping me company, too—from a discreet distance. He stayed put, for now. Too much of a crowd would draw attention we did not want.

"You are wearing the beacon," Chigaru said. "You will remove it. Now."

"We've been over this before, Your Highness. I take the beacon off, I die."

He pressed the dagger harder against my bodice. "The same is true if you refuse."

He had me there.

"A lady dying in your arms isn't the kind of attention you want to attract," Mychael said, his voice soft and low.

Magic spun into the air at the sound of his voice. He risked detection, but with a dagger against my ribs, so did I. I wasn't going to die quietly. Mychael's casting was for the prince's ears only, but that didn't stop goosebumps from prickling at the back of my neck—though that could have been as much from the goblin's warm breath and the proximity of his fangs to my throat, as from Mychael's voice.

A slight figure appeared by the prince's side, on the edge of my vision. I didn't have to see her clearly to know who she was.

"There need not be violence." Primari A'Zahra Nuru's voice was quiet, but firm. "We can reach a compromise."

A quartet of the king's guards were beginning to look entirely too interested in us.

"But not here," she urged. "Into the gardens, quickly."

The possibility of being dragged into the bushes by a goblin prince was one of the reasons why noble elven ladies feared foliage. Who knew it'd happen to me?

"Or I could just scream now and save us all the trouble," I said. "Dying isn't agreeable to me, regardless of how or where it happens."

In an instant, Prince Chigaru shifted his grip from my arm to my waist, pulling me tight against him. The dagger's pressure never lessened. "Then we will all die at the hands of my brother's guards."

"Your brother has never seen my face," I told him, talking fast behind my fan. "Nukpana isn't here. No one has ever seen the Countess of Eilde. I'm safe. I can't say the same for you."

"Peace, both of you," Primari Nuru snapped. "All of you. We share the same goal; threatening each other does nothing to help us reach it. Please, let us all step outside."

In my experience, an invitation to step outside has never been a good thing. That it came from a goblin primari did nothing to change my opinion.

The king's guards making their way toward us through the press of guests might believe that I was the Countess of Eilde, but there would be questions, especially since I was in the immediate vicinity of a renegade goblin prince. His arm was locked around my waist. How much more immediate could you get? They didn't know he was the prince. Yet. But ordering him to remove his mask would change our status pretty quick. Questions or detention meant delays. We couldn't afford any delays.

"May we be of service, my lady?" one of them asked.

I sank back against Prince Chigaru's chest and weakly fluttered my fan back and forth. "Thank you, but no. A warm night and too much dancing." I offered a wan smile for their benefit. "And far too much excitement."

The guard glanced curiously at the prince. I didn't wait for his question.

"This gallant gentleman was kind enough to remain with me until my husband returned with refreshments. We're old friends." I reached up with my free hand and patted the goblin prince on the cheek.

I felt rather than heard the growl rumble low in the prince's chest. I took the hint and removed my hand, but I took my time doing it.

Mychael stepped in close, putting himself in the line of vision between the Mal'Salin captain and Prince Chigaru. "A Caesolian red always works wonders, doesn't it, my love?"

I smiled up at him. "Almost always."

I took the glass in one hand and Mychael's extended hand in the other. He drew me away, and Prince Chigaru had no choice but to release me. He sheathed the dagger behind his back and no one was any the wiser.

I took a healthy swig of wine as I stepped into the circle of Mychael's arms. "Thank you, darling. I feel better already."

"The cool air of the gardens will do you a world of good, my dear," the primari suggested, looking every bit like the gallant gentleman's maiden aunt.

I nodded. "I think that's exactly what I need."

Mychael held out his other hand to Primari Nuru, in courtly fashion. "Will you allow me to escort you, my lady?"

To the primari's credit, she didn't hesitate before placing her hand in Mychael's. The Guardian's hand closed over it.

The prince drew in his breath with a hiss. Someone didn't like his teacher's decision.

Mychael and I, along with the primari, led the way onto the terrace, followed by Vegard and Prince Chigaru. Four of Chigaru's goblin guards followed at a discreet distance. I recognized two of them from The Ruins. From the murderous looks I was getting, they remembered me, too. Once again I was going to be in a garden with goblins who didn't like me.

Being outside was a definite improvement. If there was going to be violence, at least there was more room for it. What made me feel even better was Garadin holding the door open for us, drink in hand, looking completely relaxed. I knew the truth. He was relaxed because he was confident. Garadin had a spell that could take out everyone on the terrace. Piaras and Riston were waiting near the stone stairs leading down into the gardens. Piaras recognized our new friends. He started to come to me, but Garadin's cautioning gesture stopped him.

"We need to leave the terrace, or disperse," I said to no one in particular. "Both would be nice."

"There is a gazebo in the center of the garden," Mychael said. "It should give us the privacy we need to reach an equitable solution. The others could wait within sight and earshot for security purposes. Is that agreeable?"

"I don't think that's agreeable to anyone," I said. "But right now, I'll settle for just getting off this terrace."

Under congenial circumstances, the gazebo would have been a perfectly lovely place for a quiet talk, or for two lovers to steal a few secretive moments together. Unfortunately neither description applied to us. Garadin, Piaras and the two Guardians waited near a small rose garden about ten feet behind us. Chigaru's guards were at a similar distance in the opposite direction.

In a rustle of gossamer fabric, the primari seated herself on one of the stone benches. Prince Chigaru stood behind the bench at her right shoulder, his dark eyes still on me. I opted to remain standing, my eyes more or less even with his. Somehow I felt safer that way.

"You should not have come tonight, my primari," the prince told the tiny goblin. "It is not safe for you here."

"And your safety is assured?" she shot back, though not unkindly. "You should not worry about me." She reached up and affectionately patted the prince's hand on her shoulder. "Has Mistress Benares agreed to assist us?"

"We were just getting to that," the goblin prince said.

"Perhaps I might help."

Getting to that? Might help? This was all too strange for me. The prince made it sound as though we had just taken a pleasant turn around the dance floor, and now I felt like I was about to be interrogated by someone's elderly grandmother.

I stood straighter, not that I had much choice in that dress. "You have a strange way of asking for help, Your Highness." I turned to the primari. "Two nights ago, he ordered a friend of mine kidnapped to use as bait to catch me. I was told he would be killed unless I cooperated. We were then tied up, and taken against our wills into The Ruins where your darling prince threatened my friend with torture unless I agreed to help him find the Saghred."

"Was any undue violence or coercion used against you or your friend?" Chigaru asked mildly.

I couldn't believe what I was hearing. I heard Piaras's gasp of disbelief behind me.

"Undue violence?" My voice went up a couple of octaves. I couldn't help it. "As opposed to justifiable?"

The goblin prince shook his head. "Merely necessary."

"The ends justify the means?"

He almost smiled. "Precisely. So you do understand."

"No, I don't!"

"Raine," Mychael said by way of warning.

I shot him a look, then took a breath and blew it out. I continued, but quieter. "Then tonight, His Most Serene Highness sticks a dagger in my ribs and says that unless I help him, he'll kill me. Perhaps this type of behavior isn't serious to a goblin, but we elves take that kind of thing personally. I know I do."

The look the primari gave the prince was the same one Tarsilia gave Piaras when she caught him sneaking cookies before supper. Then the tiny goblin shook her head and actually made tsking sounds.

"He acted out of concern for our people," she tried to assure me. "His methods may seem somewhat questionable, but his heart is in the right place."

I was flabbergasted. "He has one?"

"It might be an appropriate time to apologize, dear," Primari Nuru told the prince.

It was his turn to look appalled. I had to admit he did it well. He probably had a lot of practice.

He drew himself up imperiously. "For doing my duty as a prince of my people? For which I was viciously attacked." He shot a scathing look at Piaras.

Piaras responded with a low growl, but from the sounds of things, Garadin and the two Guardians kept him from joining us.

"For not taking into consideration the sensibilities of your guests," Primari Nuru helpfully clarified for him.

Prince Chigaru thought about that for a moment. Regardless of how he had considered us—guests or prisoners—it was clear that making apologies wasn't something he had much, if any, experience with. He looked at me and cleared his throat. Then he stopped and thought some more. I knew this wasn't easy for him, but unlike the primari, I wasn't feeling particularly helpful. I was willing to wait as long as it took. I resisted the urge to cross my arms and tap my foot.

The prince cleared his throat again. This time, words actually made it out.

When he had finished, it sounded like an apology. It had all the right words, and they almost sounded sincere, but somehow the phrasing was off. In the end, I don't think he accepted the blame for anything.

"Was that an apology?" I whispered to Mychael.

"It's probably as good as you're going to get." I could hear the smile in his voice.

"Should I take it?"

"It might speed things up if you did."

I took a moment to think, too. To my credit, I didn't take as long as the prince.

"Do you promise not to try to kill or torture me or my friends ever again?" I thought for another moment. "Or order anyone else to kill or torture us, or betray us to anyone who would want to kill or torture us?" I was proud of the last two. I think I was getting the hang of how the Mal'Salin mind worked.

Mychael leaned toward me. "Don't you think you're being a trifle excessive?"

I didn't even have to look at Chigaru Mal'Salin to know the answer to that one.

"No."

To the prince's credit, he responded almost immediately. "Barring betrayal on your part, or on the part of your friends— or another attack upon my person," he said with a meaningful glance in Piaras's direction. "Yes, you have my word."

"We shake hands on it now, don't we?" I asked Mychael, without enthusiasm.

"It is the accepted way to seal a pact."

I only had to take one step to be in the center of the gazebo. The goblin prince had to take two. I know; it was petty of me to notice. I extended my hand. He took it. I was almost surprised when he released it.

"Well, we've agreed not to kill each other," I said. "Now what?"

The prince answered. "We find the Saghred before my brother and Sarad Nukpana."

I blinked. *We?*

The prince's eyes narrowed. "We."

"And when we do?"

"That is what we must now agree upon."

"Any chance of you and yours going back to The Ruins and letting us take care of this?"

The prince's eyes hardened resolutely. "None whatsoever."

I shrugged. "I had to try."

Mychael spoke. "As Paladin of the Conclave Guardians, my duty is clear—restore the security of the Saghred to prevent its use. By anyone," he added meaningfully.

He'd get no argument from me.

"Mistress Benares is able to use it most effectively." The prince's tone stopped just short of being accusing. I saw where this was going.

"Against my will," I told him. "The last thing I want is a connection of any kind with something known as the Soul Thief. Sarad Nukpana is holding a dear friend of mine hostage. He wants the beacon and the Saghred in exchange for her release."

The prince bristled. "You are going to give it to him?"

"Of course not," I shot back. "And I don't believe for one second that he actually plans to keep his word. I'm here tonight to help Paladin Eiliesor recover the Saghred."

A'Zahra Nuru's eyes had rarely left me. They were now focused where the beacon lay beneath my bodice. I saw mild surprise mixed with relief in her eyes. The beacon fluttered against my skin in response to her attention. I waited for the inevitable request.

"Do you have a blood link to its creator?" she asked gently.

That wasn't the request I expected. Requests from goblins concerning the beacon usually began with "give" and ended with "now." I had to admit it was a refreshing change.

Mychael responded before I could. "That has yet to be established."

Not a lie. Not the truth, either. Apparently the paladin thought the fewer who knew my family history, the better. Considering who wanted to know, I agreed with him.

A'Zahra Nuru was still looking at me. "You do not seem to have experienced any adverse effects from its use."

It wasn't a question, so I didn't answer.

"What is your proposal, Your Highness?" Mychael asked the prince.

I welcomed the change of topic.

"The Guardians have failed in their duty," Chigaru said without hesitation. "The Thief of Souls is too dangerous to be left in the custody of your order. As long as it is, there will be a danger of it being found and misused by those such as my brother or Sarad Nukpana."

I'd heard enough. "Or yourself? To use against your brother?"

"The Thief of Souls cannot be wielded," Primari Nuru said. "It brings madness and death to any who try. You are the first known exception. The stone's very existence is an abomination."

I already knew all that, and really didn't want to be reminded with the rock itself probably less than a hundred yards away.

Mychael spoke. "In the nine hundred years since my order took the Saghred into our keeping has it ever been taken or used again for evil purposes?"

Prince Chigaru stood mute.

Mychael tactfully didn't directly mention the single recorded use of the Saghred—by the prince's own ancestor, whom the Guardians defeated. Subsequently, they took protective custody of the stone.

"Nine hundred years isn't too shabby a record, Your Highness," I said quietly. "Why don't you just let these gentlemen do their job?"

The prince was as still as the marble statues in the garden, his dark eyes on Mychael. "You question my motives because I am a Mal'Salin." It wasn't a question. He knew the answer.

"Yes," Mychael replied truthfully. "I do. But my main concern is for your present circumstances. You are still gathering allies with which to overthrow your brother. I wish you well and hope that you succeed. Your people will suffer under your brother's rule. But for now, yours is a young government in exile. You may have the means to acquire the Saghred, but you lack the experience and—no insult intended—the strength needed to protect it. There is also the temptation to use the stone, if not by you, then by your allies. You trust them to help you defeat the king, but can you trust them near the Saghred?"

The prince placed his hand on A'Zahra Nuru's slender shoulder. "When I first learned my brother's plans, I will admit the temptation to use the Saghred against him was strong. But Primari Nuru has convinced me that I must choose another way."

Good for her.

"Using the Saghred would only turn me into that which I have sworn to destroy," he continued. "It may take longer to defeat Sathrik, but my allies grow more numerous and stronger every day. In the end, I will prevail. If I do not, Sathrik would use the Saghred against our own people and yours. He must not possess it."

"Then we are in agreement," Mychael said. "Allow me to carry out the duty of my office unimpeded."

When the paladin stopped talking, the rest of us started holding our breath. To his credit, the prince seemed to give honest consideration to Mychael's words.

"Is there any assistance either I or my people might offer you?" Chigaru asked.

I started breathing again, and I think I heard A'Zahra Nuru do the same.

"Thank you, Your Highness," Mychael said, with a slight smile. "Yes, there is one thing I may need your help with."

I had to consider the possibility that Chigaru Mal'Salin may not have inherited all the personality defects his family tree had to offer. The primari thought the world of her prince. Tam trusted A'Zahra. I trusted Tam. Completing the circle shouldn't be difficult, but it was.

"Excuse me, Your Highness, but I have a question," I asked.

"Yes?"

"The Saghred isn't all your brother and Sarad Nukpana want this evening. Does your agreement to help Paladin Eiliesor extend to me and mine?"

"I understand that having you and your spellsinger at his mercy would please Sarad Nukpana and my brother. My brother and I have long enjoyed depriving each of what makes the other happy. Preventing my brother from capturing the two of you would greatly annoy him." He smiled. It was genuine, and it transformed his face with almost boyish glee. "This would please me."

It wasn't exactly the I'm-your-ally-now-and-you-can-trust-me answer I was looking for, but who am I to deny a goblin prince the simple joys of life?

Chapter 22

Only the Mal'Salin family would buy a house with a mausoleum in the gardens—and gardens that backed directly into The Ruins.

To tell you the truth, I couldn't tell that much difference between The Ruins and what the Mal'Salins referred to as their gardens. In the distance, I could even see a few pinpoints of light that looked suspiciously like fire pixies. It was disconcerting to say the least. I glanced at Piaras. A muscle in his jaw was starting to twitch. Looked like I wasn't the only one who had noticed.

The mausoleum was on what passed for a hill on the property, and that was where the now-tingling beacon wanted to go. I'd rather just go directly for Sarad Nukpana, but the beacon hadn't asked my opinion.

Chigaru Mal'Salin had agreed to help. I was hardly surprised. We were going after the very thing that he had been willing to torture Piaras for quite recently. So I think I could be excused a healthy dose of skepticism. On the other hand, Prince Chigaru had a perfectly good chance to kill us once and he didn't take it. That didn't exactly earn him sainthood status in my book, but sometimes a girl had to take what she could get.

I shot Mychael a look that I think fully conveyed the extent of my feelings and received a bare nod for my trouble. At least he was being cautious. The goblin prince and Primari Nuru were flanked by Vegard and Riston. The prince's four guards would keep their distance while keeping watch. A few people strolling in the gardens was one thing, but with Chigaru's guards, we more closely resembled a herd—and herds attracted attention. The prince had agreed. So far he was being the perfect gentleman. I hoped it lasted, but I wasn't going to hold my breath.

The beacon was likewise behaving itself, and I held out as much hope for its continued good behavior as I did for the prince's. The tingling had resolved itself into a quiet hum. It had let me know where we were going, and was now content to wait until we got there.

In a few minutes we would be surrounded by the dark, the damp, and the dead. I had never had the pleasure of visiting the Mal'Salin mausoleum, and would feel better about our destination if I knew more about it. I would also feel better if I could get my hat off my head. There was no way I was going into a cramped mausoleum wearing that hat. With a whispered apology to Mychael's cousin, I removed the hat pins and ditched the hat under the nearest bush. If I was going to die tonight, at least I'd die comfortable. I kept the hat pins and tucked them into the top of my bodice in between it and the corset. The more sharp, pointy things in my possession, the better. Then I removed the pins holding my hair up, and my hair came cascading down. I looked up to find that I had Mychael's complete and undivided attention. From his expression, you'd think I was standing there naked.

"So, how many of your family are interred in the mausoleum, Your Highness?" I asked, trying to shift attention to anyone but me. I felt Mychael's eyes following me. I wasn't sure whether to feel flattered or to run.

The goblin prince looked puzzled. "None. All Mal'Salins are entombed in our family citadel at Regor."

I didn't want to ask, but I had to. "Then these people are . . . ?"

He shrugged. "They came with the property. My great, great grandfather saw the mausoleum and had the house and gardens built around them. I believe the original owners were an old Mermeian family who have long since died out. My family would often spend summers here. When we were children, my brother and I would play among the crypts beneath the mausoleum."

Ick. Piaras's frozen expression told me he was having the same thought.

"Crypts?" I looked from the prince to Mychael.

"Yes, there is a small network of catacombs beneath the mausoleum," Chigaru told us both.

Mychael said nothing. I kept my own mouth shut, but I was thinking plenty—and most of what I was thinking wasn't suitable for polite company. Ocnus hadn't mentioned catacombs. Maybe he hadn't known. Maybe the little weasel had. Since Mychael and I thought Ocnus had told us the truth, we had let him go. His ship was probably halfway to wherever by now. I hope he was seasick. The only things worse than dead dusty bodies were dead dusty bodies in a dark tunnel. The beacon continued to hum happily. Apparently it didn't care about Ocnus or dead bodies in a dark tunnel, dusty or otherwise.

I heard a splash and the slap of something against a muddy bank. It wasn't small, and it was entirely too close.

"A small pond in the orchard," the goblin prince said calmly as if that explained everything. "I believe that was a serpent dragon, what you might know as a knucker. They prefer to feed in the night."

Other Mermeian nobles kept ornamental fish. Naturally, the Mal'Salins would be different.

Piaras was incredulous. "Your family keeps knuckers as pets?"

"They keep themselves, spellsinger. Like the temple ruins, the pond was already here. Oddly enough, the serpents did not occupy it until my family acquired the house."

Who said only opposites attract?

We were alone. No one had made any move to follow us. That was both good and bad. I didn't want anyone following us, but at the same time, I expected some kind of interference. The complete lack of opposition made me more than a little jumpy. Garadin's spell preparation on the terrace paled in comparison to the one he had ready to let fly at the first sign of a Khrynsani temple guard. I had knives that were likewise itching to go airborne, but I didn't want to inadvertently waste any on a waving tree branch. The wind was up, so there were a lot of those. My guard was also up, along with the tiny hairs on the back of my neck.

Vegard moved swiftly out of the shadows toward us. I relaxed my grip on the throwing knife.

"We're in position and ready, sir," he reported to Mychael. "Feroc and Hugh took out the wards around the outer garden walls. They weren't easy, but they weren't difficult either—and no sign of an alarm being given. Or Khrynsani guards. That has them worried."

"Sarad Nukpana does other things this night," Primari Nuru said. "He cannot spare the strength."

I knew the primari was right. "He wants me here," I said. "If you want someone in your house, leave the door open."

"Step into my parlor, said the spider to the fly," Garadin said.

I shot him a look.

"Sorry, I couldn't resist."

"Try harder next time."

We approached the temple and mausoleum from the back through the trees, hopefully out of sight of any goblin guards roaming the grounds. I still hadn't seen any. I liked this less every second.

The mausoleum was built of a smooth dark stone and was

only about thirty feet across. I walked into the center of the single room. Thankfully all of the vaults were still sealed. I was sure the crypts below wouldn't be as tidy. Various titles and first names all ending with the last name Ramsden were etched into the stone, and the most recent date I could see was from over a hundred years ago. I ran my hand over the wall's dark surface. It was cool and perfectly smooth. The canal that surrounded The Ruins was less than fifty yards away and flooding was common. I wondered how the crypts had faired. Hopefully we wouldn't be finding out.

"No one's here," I said, though I was still careful to keep my voice down. "Good."

"You expected someone?" Garadin said.

"If a couple of the guests wanted to be alone, this would be the perfect place."

Garadin thought about that. "Good point."

"Here?" Piaras asked, clearly creeped.

"It's not my idea of romantic surroundings either," I assured him.

The goblin prince looked around, then gazed outside at the moon and the clouds racing overhead. His black eyes glimmered in the faint light. "Actually these surroundings are very romantic." His voice was low and almost wistful.

I didn't know whether to feel reassured that he had romantic thoughts or disturbed that he was having them in a mausoleum—and while standing next to me.

"I cannot believe it," Primari Nuru was saying, her voice echoing faintly against the walls. "How could something that powerful be concealed so closely without our knowing?"

Mychael answered her. "The Saghred has remained hidden for nearly nine hundred years, Primari Nuru."

"How long has it been here?"

"Only the stone's Guardian could answer that."

"And he died centuries ago."

"Apparently that's come open for debate," I said.

The primari's dark eyes widened. "But that would make him—"

"Very old and very tired."

The prince spoke. "Sarad Nukpana knows the Saghred is in Mermeia, but I would give much to see his face when he discovers that he has been meditating next to it for over a year."

"Meditating?" I asked.

"According to agents I have in my brother's court, when the grand shaman is in Mermeia, he sits here for hours at a time. He finds the surroundings relaxing."

Sarad Nukpana sits with dead bodies for fun. Why wasn't I surprised?

"Raine?" Mychael was looking at me expectantly.

I took a deep breath. Right. It was my turn now. I relaxed as much as I could considering where I was and who was with me—and what I was looking for. I slowly walked around the mausoleum. It wasn't large, so it didn't take long. The beacon's vibration had increased in intensity when we'd come inside, but the signal wasn't getting any stronger, though if it didn't stop soon, my shoes were going to vibrate right off my feet.

I stopped. My feet and the stone floor beneath them were the only things that were vibrating. The mausoleum's dead were in the walls around me. The catacombs' dead would be under the floor, beneath my feet.

Crap.

I looked at Mychael and pointed down. "Guess what?"

He looked almost as thrilled as I did.

"Time grows short, Your Highness," Mychael told Chigaru. "Would you please show us the entrance to the catacombs?"

The goblin prince's expression was unreadable. "It would please me very much."

"Do you require more light?" Mychael asked.

Chigaru shook his head. "This is more than sufficient."

The goblin prince walked slowly into the corner of the mausoleum farthest from the house and ran a long-fingered hand along an upper vault until he came to what appeared to be several flowers carved into the stone. He pressed at several points, there was a faint click, and a panel below the flowers swung open into inky darkness.

The goblin turned to me and smiled as if from a private joke. "Your catacombs, Mistress Benares."

I knew there was a reason why I still didn't like him.

I had expected the entrance to the catacombs to be in the floor. It had never occurred to me that it would be hidden in the wall. The vaults in the mausoleum were stacked four high, one on top of the other, and covered every wall. The vaults concealing the entrance to the catacombs were fake. Where there should be four bodies interred was an incredibly steep and narrow stair leading down into the center of the hill.

Mychael held out his hand and stared at his palm. A pinpoint of white light flickered to life from the center of his hand, beneath the skin. It was no larger than a firefly. It spun, weaving a trail of light until a globe, the size of his fist, hung suspended above his open hand. It glowed steadily and seemed to solidify, the interior crackling with something akin to lightning. It floated down the stairs, then stopped, hovering, waiting for us.

Mychael indicated that the goblin prince should precede us. "After you, Your Highness."

Chigaru raised one elegant brow.

"You have been in these catacombs before," Mychael explained. "We have not. Rest assured, we'll be right behind you." He looked to Garadin. "Garadin, if you could remain here with Primari Nuru? Piaras, stay with Vegard. We won't be long. Riston," he said to the other Guardian with us, "you're with me."

"Sir?" Vegard asked uncertainly. He didn't glance at the prince. He didn't need to. Mychael understood.

"From the looks of things, there's not much room to maneuver down there," the paladin said. "Riston and his knives are a better fit. Just make sure there's a hole for us to come out of."

The blond Guardian grinned. "Count on it, sir."

"I am." He again gestured to the prince. "Shall we?"

Prince Chigaru descended the stairs. Mychael and I followed, with Riston at our backs.

The walls glistened in the globe's pale light, moisture trickling down the sides to collect on the uneven floor, making footing uncertain at best. The air was cool and damp. Somewhere ahead in the darkness, water dripped methodically into a pool. I gathered my gown up as best as I could. Mychael was directly in front of me. I aimed a dirty look at the center of his back. What I wouldn't have given for my old leathers and boots. Aside from our breathing, there was no other sound. The damp wasn't nearly as bad as the cloying smell of decay—or the unexpected silence. Not from the residents—I didn't expect any trouble from them. I did expect to hear or sense something from the Saghred. I suddenly felt faintly nauseous. Though that could be from being in such close quarters with centuries of Ramsden dead and a Mal'Salin prince.

The globe's light illuminated a white crust that shone in lines at differing heights along the rock walls. Salt. My subconscious knew what the lines meant, but my conscious mind didn't want to dwell on it. There were many ways we could die tonight, and I didn't want to add drowning to the list. The tide wouldn't turn for hours, and we certainly weren't going to be here that long. Knowing that didn't help. Fear was irrational that way. If I survived all this, I wasn't going to have to look far for fresh nightmare inspiration.

The catacombs couldn't be very extensive, at least I hoped not. There was only one tunnel with no branches that I could see in the dim light. Ledges had been hollowed out of the walls on both sides of us. These were packed with the yellowed bones of obviously more than one dearly departed, some to overflowing. A name and date was engraved on each ledge. Some were worn smooth with age and water.

"Thick as thieves down here, aren't they?" Riston remarked.

I grinned. I couldn't help it. It probably just meant I was on the verge of getting hysterical. "Makes you hope they all got along," I quipped.

The Guardian called my grin and raised me a wink.

"Riston, take the point," Mychael said softly.

"Sir." The Guardian slid his brace of throwing daggers around to his chest for quicker access. He flexed his fingers to warm them.

We hadn't gone far before my nausea turned into a wave of dizziness. I felt the Saghred's presence before I heard it. My breath came shallow and quick, my skin was clammy, my mouth dry. I tried to swallow, but couldn't.

"Stop. It's here."

A soft humming echoed through the tunnels.

Mychael looked sharply at me. He heard it, too.

"Raine?"

I dimly realized his voice sounded farther away than it should. It didn't bother me, and I think it should have.

"Fine." I felt myself try to breathe. I stayed on my feet, so I think I succeeded. "I'm fine."

I felt his arm slip around my waist. I don't think he believed me. I steadied myself, then stepped away.

"Down there," I said, forcing more air into my words than I had to spare. "Let's go."

The tunnel ended abruptly in a room only ten feet or so square. A white stone panel shone starkly in one wall on the edge of the globe's light. It was a burial vault in miniature. It was only about a foot square and oddly translucent, like alabaster. It also bore a striking resemblance to the containment box Quentin had found the beacon in—and the small box Mychael now held in his hands. The frosted surface was smooth and unmarked except for a small, circular section that had been carved out of the stone.

You didn't have to be too smart to know what was meant to go there.

Prince Chigaru stepped around Riston for a closer look. "That was not here before," he insisted.

"When was that?" Mychael asked.

"Three years," the goblin said.

Mychael and I exchanged glances. Plenty of time for a certain Saghred Guardian to do a little redecorating.

It took a lot of squirming on my part, but I managed to remove the beacon from my bodice. Prince Chigaru's eyes were instantly on me, his lean body tense with restraint.

I had one word for him. "Stay."

"Wait," Mychael told me. "Are you shielded?"

My shoulders slumped. "Do you really think that's going to do any good?" I sounded the way I felt. Tired.

His jaw tightened. "Probably not."

I knelt and put the beacon into the hollow. It grated against the accumulated salt, and some of it fell on the floor. That was all. Nothing happened. That didn't mean something wasn't different. It was, and it wasn't at all what I expected. I looked more closely at the white stone panel.

"What is it?" Mychael asked.

"Does it look more transparent to you?"

"No."

I looked again—then stared in wonder at what lay beyond.

"It does to me," I breathed. Then I became a part of it.

I was surrounded in pulsating light and movement. Flowing forms emerged from shifting colors, each separate and distinct. I realized with amazement turning to horror that the forms were alive. Most were faceless wraiths, their bodies pale and indistinct as they fled, terrified of me. Others didn't flee, but passed just out of arms reach, with faint cries and whispered pleas, held at bay as if by some unseen hand. The remaining ones were more solid, though their bodies were wasted as if from the ravages of disease. They didn't whisper or beg. They screamed in rage and frustration at not being able to reach me. Something stopped them from touching me, but nothing blocked their raw need. I tried to run, but the same force that held them at bay held me still.

I was inside the Saghred. The wraiths around me were all

that remained of those sacrificed or absorbed over the ages. Not just goblins, but elves, humans and dwarfs—though some were too far gone to be recognized as any race.

A lone figure came toward me and stopped just beyond arm's reach, silently staring. His elegantly pointed ears marked him as an elf, a beautiful pure-blooded high elf. His hair was silver, and his eyes were the gray of gathering storm clouds. Eyes identical to my own. A slow smile curled the corners of his lips. I could see why my mother hadn't cared that he was nearly nine hundred years old.

Eamaliel Anguis knew me and had been expecting me—all this time, all of my life.

"Daughter."

Like most fatherless little girls, I'd always imagined what my father would look like. What stood before me wasn't it. For one, I could see through him.

I couldn't move. I didn't even know if I was breathing.

"How?" I whispered the word, but it echoed in my head, not my ears.

He smiled. It was a kind smile, encouraging, patient. "How are you here or how am I here?"

My throat was too tight to speak. I just nodded.

"Because I needed to speak with you. Don't be afraid. You can see me and the others, but your body remains outside the Saghred, in the arms of your Guardian. You are safe."

"Are you alive?" I wasn't sure if it was in poor taste to ask, but I had to.

"The Saghred does not take life," he explained. "It absorbs it. I am alive, but on a different level than you are probably familiar with. Time is different on the inside."

I felt myself try to grin. "A couple of my formerly incarcerated Benares relatives say the same thing."

My father looked at me as if trying to fit a lifetime of seeing me into a few seconds. His gaze was so intense that I wanted to look away, but looking away meant seeing floating wraiths. So I kept my eyes exactly where they were.

"You're so beautiful," he managed. "Just like your mother."

Uncomfortable under his scrutiny—and even more uncomfortable at the mention of my mother—I brushed at one of the gown's jewel-strewn velvet panels. "This isn't how I normally dress. The goblin king's masked ball. We had to get on the grounds somehow. You might say I'm undercover. The gown and going to the ball wasn't exactly my idea." I stopped and tried to breathe. "I'm babbling, aren't I?"

He smiled. "Not at all. You found me, so it must be going well."

"As well as can be expected—at least for one of us." I could look right through my father and see the wraiths floating behind him. I winced. "You're the Saghred's Guardian. Isn't it supposed to like you, or at least not eat you?"

The corner of his mouth quirked upward. "Being here wasn't exactly my idea, either."

"I can understand that." I risked a quick glance at the wraiths, then lowered my voice. "Not your ideal roommates either, I'd imagine."

"All of those here were victims, some were more innocent than others. Few are actually evil; their greed and lust for power blinded them to the danger."

I thought of Ocnus. "Greed makes you stupid," I muttered.

My father nodded, a twinkle in his gray eyes. "Without exception. The more powerful you are, the more blind you are to your own greed—and its consequences."

Sounded just like Sarad Nukpana.

"Could you have found a less creepy place than a crypt to hide it?"

"Under the very noses of those looking the hardest for it. In a place they would disdain. It was perfect."

Apparently Sarad Nukpana liked it well enough to meditate upstairs. I decided not to mention that. The less creepiness I had to deal with, the better.

I held the beacon by its diamond chain. "I believe this belongs to you. Any way I can give it back?"

"Unfortunately, I'm in no condition to accept it."

Unfortunate was right.

I closed my hand around the disk. It was warm and oddly comforting. "Isn't it supposed to be attached to you forever or something?"

"I was ambushed by mercenaries, probably hired by the Khrynsani. I escaped with my life, but not with the beacon. The Khrynsani were close to finding the Saghred. Too close to risk leaving it where it was. To move the stone is to risk discovery. But to come in contact with the stone is to risk being taken."

"And you had to touch it to put it in the vault."

My father nodded.

"The stone wanted a snack before being put to bed."

He laughed, a rich silvery sound. "I never thought of it that way, but you're exactly right. When it hungers, it will feed."

"I know. Prince Chigaru told me."

My father's expression darkened. "A Mal'Salin."

"Yeah, yeah, I know. I take anything he tells me with a grain of salt—and one hand on my nearest dagger."

"As well you should, but in this case he didn't lead you astray."

"I know that, too. I get the feeling the Saghred's bad to know and worse to be around."

His eyes grew sorrowful. "As am I."

I drew a trembling breath. "Did my mother know that you were the Saghred's Guardian?"

"I tried to keep that from her as well. When you've lived as long as I have, you take and guard any semblance of a normal life that you can have. The Khrynsani had picked up my trail again—and they would soon find Maranda. I protected her in the only way I knew. I left her, drawing my pursuers with me."

I had a feeling where this was going. "Except they didn't follow."

His expression reflected equal parts anger and sadness.

"Not all of them. I only discovered later what had happened to her—and about you."

My mother, alone against the Khrynsani's best shamans. She had only been a marginal sorceress—like me. She hadn't stood a chance. Thanks to the Saghred, I wasn't so marginal anymore—and I was determined not to share her fate.

I blinked back tears. "Why didn't you—?"

"Try to contact you? So you could be hunted down like your mother?"

"I see your point."

"I kept watch over you, through trusted friends. Even they didn't know the connection. It was safer that way. But eventually, my secret was betrayed."

"Sarad Nukpana found out."

"And tracked you down. I did not want what has happened to you to happen. I am sorry, Raine. I have tried to protect you, but there was no other way."

I tried to shrug. I wanted to cry. "I'm none the worse for wear."

"None of this should have happened. I ask for your forgiveness."

"No one's been wronged," I managed past the lump in my throat. "No need to forgive."

A look of surprise passed over his flawless face, surprise and pride. "But your life, your family, friends . . ."

"I have a responsibility to my family—*all* of my family. Guarding the Saghred is your job; I'm thinking now that it's my job to help."

"You're very brave." Perhaps it was a trick of the light, but he appeared to be getting more insubstantial, if that was possible.

"I guess that makes me my father's daughter," I whispered.

He smiled. "And your mother's." He looked up and the smile vanished.

I looked where he was looking. I saw a gray void. He must have seen more.

"What is it?" I asked.

"He's here."

"What? Who?"

"Sarad Nukpana. He's here."

Damn.

My father was fading. "Go now."

I reached out toward him. "But I don't . . ."

I was on the cold dirt floor, in Mychael's arms, the small white stone box he had brought with us clutched in my white-knuckled hands. The lid was closed and the box glowed softly as if from within. The Saghred—and my father—were locked inside. So much for how the Thief of Souls earned its nickname.

"Who put—?" I asked him.

His face was impassive, but pale. "You did."

The door to the miniature vault was still in place. I didn't ask how. I didn't remember, and at this point I didn't care.

"They're alive," I told Mychael. "All of them." I didn't mention my father. I didn't know how to say it, and Prince Chigaru didn't need to hear it.

A light sprinkling of dirt and salt fell from the tunnel roof.

The goblin looked up. We all did.

"We must leave," the prince said, his voice low and urgent.

We didn't need to ask why; we all knew the dirt didn't fall by itself.

"Is there another way out?" Mychael asked.

"None that I know."

Mychael looked at Riston, and the Guardian ran silently down the corridor.

I wrestled my way free of Mychael's arms.

"Let me up."

"Can you . . . ?"

Standing by myself stopped his question. I wasn't dizzy or in the least bit weak. I was angry, more angry than I'd ever been in my life. And that anger steadied me more effectively than a sharp slap in the face. My mother was dead and my father was trapped for eternity inside a rock. No hope of help. No hope of escape. All because of the Khrynsani—and especially because of Sarad Nukpana.

Some magic users lost their concentration when they got angry. I wasn't one of them.

The goblin grand shaman was in the mausoleum above us. That Riston didn't return to report only confirmed it, but I didn't need to wait for confirmation. I could feel him. I could feel the fear he brought, the pain. He would wait, and then he would come after me. I would not die in a hole in the ground.

The only sound was the single word Chigaru had just hissed. Its simple eloquence summed up his opinion of our situation. I couldn't have agreed more.

With the Saghred clutched to my side, I started off down the corridor.

Mychael caught my arm. I wrenched it away.

"He's up there," I told him.

"Let me go first."

"Not this time," I said.

I ran to the foot of the stairs.

Sarad Nukpana stood at the top. He was smiling.

"There you are, Mistress Benares. I believe you have something for me?"

The goblin grand shaman almost sounded happy. I imagine he was. He thought this was going to be his lucky night.

I wasn't entirely certain he was wrong.

Chapter 23

The mausoleum was more crowded than it had been when we had left.

We had used one light globe so as not to attract attention. The Khrynsani had torches, a lot of them. They didn't need to sneak. They belonged there.

They also outnumbered us at least five to one.

Vegard lay unmoving on the ground, his scalp bloody, his ax still in his hand. More than a few motionless goblins shared the ground with him. The bloodied ones were probably Vegard's work, those with no visible marks of violence were probably the result of Garadin and Primari Nuru's attentions.

I saw why Garadin had called a ceasefire. A pair of Khrynsani temple guards held scythelike blades less than an inch from Piaras's throat. It looked like Piaras had made a magical contribution of his own, or tried to. I glanced at Mychael. His face was completely impassive. No clues there.

Sarad Nukpana held out his hand to me. I didn't have to ask what he wanted. I looked to Mychael. The Guardian didn't hesitate. He nodded once, tightly.

I did hesitate, and I certainly expressed my disbelief. "What?"

"Give it to him." Mychael's voice was perfectly level, utterly controlled.

There were two ways I could interpret that statement. One would be a lot more enjoyable. Unfortunately, I didn't think that was the one he meant.

"I am gratified to see you are being reasonable, Paladin Eiliesor," Nukpana said, his tone equally flat. He didn't know what Mychael was up to either. That made two of us. Garadin looked baffled, too. Apparently it was contagious.

I did a quick search for another option. It didn't take long, since there wasn't one. Give Nukpana the Saghred and I had nothing to bargain with. But if I refused, things would get ugly in short order, with more bloodshed a virtual guarantee.

So what I said was, "I'll make you a deal."

Nukpana sighed. "Another deal, Mistress Benares? This grows tiresome." He gestured and the two blades made contact with Piaras's throat. Contact, but no blood. They had been told to be careful. Nukpana wanted to have his cake and eat it, too.

Out of the corner of my eye, I saw Prince Chigaru move. If there was any chance I was going to give the Saghred to anyone, the goblin prince wanted it to be him. Primari Nuru's hand on his arm stopped him before the Khrynsani guards' blades could. From the look in their eyes, they wanted him to try it again. From Chigaru's expression, they'd probably get their wish.

"The lives of my friends," I told Nukpana. "I give you the Saghred, and you let them leave here. Alive."

He glanced at Chigaru with a half smile. "Does this assurance include the Mal'Salin in your company?"

"It does."

Prince Chigaru stiffened at Primari Nuru's side. Either he was surprised I didn't want Nukpana to kill him, or I'd just insulted him and committed yet another goblin social gaffe. I didn't have time to sort it out.

"Tell me why I should do this," Nukpana said.

I didn't expect the goblin shaman to keep his word, regardless of what he agreed to. But if I couldn't buy my friends' freedom, I could at least buy some time. I didn't dare risk a glance at Mychael, but I thought he'd agree that buying time was a good investment.

"From what I understand, you still need me," I told him. "The Saghred's not going to jump through hoops for you without me giving the word. Seeing my friends walk away from here would make me happy—and a lot more willing to cooperate."

Nukpana went through the motions of thinking it over. I knew he wasn't seriously considering agreeing to anything, he was just prolonging the game. The paladin of the Conclave Guardians, a Mal'Salin prince, a primari of the highest order, a former Conclave mage—these were prisoners the Khrynsani could only dream of. And then there was Piaras.

"No deals, Mistress Benares," Nukpana said. "But you may keep the Saghred. It is a lovely night and but a short distance to where we need to go." His dark eyes were shining. "A stroll in the forest with a beautiful lady. I cannot imagine a better way to end my trip to your city." He glanced at Mychael, a slow smile forming, fangs visible. "That is if the count does not mind me borrowing his new bride. I promise to keep her undamaged for as long as possible."

Sarad Nukpana could have meant any number of things by that, and I knew I didn't want to know about any of them.

Mychael didn't respond, at least not with words. He was utterly still, a dangerous stillness, so still that the only movement was the pulse in his neck. I felt the power he barely managed to hold in check. It was primal, and what it would have done to Sarad Nukpana would not have been pretty. Mychael didn't need his voice to fight Nukpana and the goblin knew it. The goblin also knew that Mychael couldn't risk it—at least not yet.

Nukpana half turned to an ornately armored guard. He wasn't about to turn his back on Mychael, hostages or not.

"Zubari, if you and your guards will take the paladin and mage to the compound. Mistress Benares, the witch, the prince, and the nightingale will be coming with me."

Where we were going wasn't anywhere I wanted to be.

The Ruins was my least favorite place in Mermeia, and for the second time in as many nights, here I was again. I wasn't familiar with this section, but seeing that it jutted against the Goblin District, there was a perfectly good reason why I had never made it a point to visit. It was darker and even scarier than the rest of The Ruins, if that was possible. Or maybe it was just the company.

The Mal'Salin family controlled the embassy compound, and I had assumed that for security's sake, Sarad Nukpana would want to stay there. It looked like he favored privacy over protection. But with the small Mal'Salin army surrounding us, I didn't think Nukpana considered security much of an issue.

A distraction or two would be good, but I wasn't going to count on any happening. I hoped we were being followed by some of Mychael's Guardians, but I've always tried to avoid counting on help I couldn't see. No doubt there were plenty of plans being formulated in many heads, but since I had no way of knowing if any stood a chance of going beyond the planning stage, I wasn't going to depend on any for help. This one was all mine.

Nukpana offered me his arm. "The footing ahead is uncertain."

Ordinarily I would have seen it as a gallant gesture of a distinguished gentleman. Tonight I would have rather taken the arm, or whatever, of a Magh'Sceadu.

"I'll take my chances."

He suddenly had my wrist. I hadn't seen him move. His grip wasn't painful, but I wasn't going anywhere, either. Never taking those black eyes from mine, Nukpana linked my arm through his. "I would rather you didn't." His voice was low and dark; apparently disobedience wasn't a familiar concept.

The trees around us were dark and silent. No shrieks, calls, or growls. No flickering lights. The first time I had been taken into The Ruins by Mal'Salin guards, I had deemed the creatures living there to be the greater of two evils until my captors proved otherwise. Tonight I knew better. The evil in The Ruins hadn't taken the night off. It was walking next to me.

Though walking into The Ruins gave me time to think. Not that I needed time, I knew what I wanted to do, which was more than I could say for the beacon or the Saghred. From the stone there was no sound at all. The beacon, on the other hand, was making the same happy, perky sounds that had been annoying me since we arrived at the embassy. I wasn't annoyed anymore. Now I just felt betrayed. Either the beacon knew something I didn't, or it didn't care who reunited it with its long-lost buddy, just as long as it happened.

From what I'd found out over the past two days, the Saghred would probably like nothing better than to demonstrate how it had gotten its nickname. I had a sneaking suspicion that was exactly what Nukpana had in mind. No doubt he'd like a little demonstration from the object he'd gone to so much trouble to get. And there was nothing like a spilled life to buy the life-long friendship of a soul-stealing rock. Spilled lifeblood to open it, and a soul sacrifice to tap its power, Prince Chigaru had said. I experienced an image of my father and the wraiths caught inside the stone. Nukpana needed me alive. He wanted Piaras alive. That left A'Zahra Nuru and the goblin prince. I didn't know which one he planned for the instant death or the prolonged one, but it didn't matter. Neither choice was acceptable to me.

I saw a gathering of stones ahead through the trees. It looked sickeningly similar to another rock altar in another part of The Ruins. Now I knew where we were going, but I still didn't know what I was going to do when we got there in a few minutes. Sarad Nukpana held all the cards, and I was left with a bad hand and an even less promising chance at a bluff.

I wouldn't bet on me, but plenty of others were.

Suddenly, I had an idea. And since the beacon was busy

being happy, I knew I had come up with it all by my lonesome. As far as plans went, it was simple, and simple was often best. In theory. Problem was, theories that didn't work had a bad habit of blowing up in your face. My plan also involved a couple of things I'd rather not do, like getting close to Sarad Nukpana—and even closer to the Saghred.

The first part of my plan was painless enough. It was a question. A question I now knew the answer to, thanks to my father. But Nukpana didn't know I'd met my father.

"Why me?" I asked Nukpana.

If I couldn't get a distraction, I'd take a delay. I didn't care about getting Nukpana to reveal the vast scope and sordid details of his evil plan; I just wanted to keep him talking. As long as he was talking, he couldn't start sacrificing. Tarsilia had always said, get a man talking about his favorite subject, and he'd forget just about everything else. I hoped she was right.

The goblin paused at the question. He didn't seem baffled by it, merely interested. "You are your father's daughter," he said, as if that explained everything.

I swallowed. "And blood links are the best kind for this sort of thing."

"Precisely."

"How did you know him?"

"Let us say we shared similar interests." He smiled. It could have been for any reason. "What interests me now is you."

Nothing called for a subject change quicker than having a psychopath interested in you. I forced back the lump that had taken up residence in my throat. "You didn't have the beacon. Nigel did. So how did you know the Saghred was in Mermeia?" If Nukpana wanted to chat like old friends, I could play along.

"Nachtmagus Nigel Nicabar should have chosen his words with more care—and been more selective to whom he spoke them. He acted unwisely. His indiscretion was his undoing."

Indiscretion and a certain goblin grand shaman. Neighborhood gossips didn't tie a rock around Nigel's ankles for a midnight swim, or kick that crate from underneath Simon Stocken's feet. But I didn't imagine Nukpana saw either as his problem or fault.

The goblin smiled. "And just before dawn this morning I ran into Ocnus Rancil. Apparently he was about to leave on an extended vacation." His smile broadened. "I persuaded him to stay."

I suddenly didn't feel so good. I'd never liked Ocnus, but I wouldn't wish Nukpana's persuasion on anyone.

"He mentioned that he had spoken with you and the paladin earlier," the goblin continued. "He also mentioned a name that I had not heard in quite some time—Tamnais Nathrach."

Now I really felt sick.

"Master Rancil told me everything I needed to know. In fact, he talked until he could talk no more. I have told His Majesty all about you. The Conclave Guardian's daughter who will be helping us. He is most eager to make your acquaintance."

Nukpana stopped at the edge of the clearing. The moonlight was just enough to see the trees on the far side, and more than enough to see the stone altar at the center. A quartet of Khrynsani temple guards stood at each of the altar's corners. When they saw their grand shaman, they came to attention.

Nukpana admired his guards' handiwork. "Good. All is prepared for us." He released my arm but not my hand, half dragging me into the clearing.

"I will take the Saghred now, Raine."

I made no move to hand it over. "Not until you let Piaras go."

"Very well." Nukpana spoke without turning, and without taking his onyx eyes from mine. "Kafele?"

"Your will, my lord?" asked one of Piaras's guards.

"Unless the Saghred is in my hands in the next five seconds, cut out the nightingale's throat."

Blades were drawn. Nukpana held out his hand. I gave him the Saghred.

His other hand released mine and closed over the top of the casket. "Was that so difficult?"

Not difficult for him, but breathing had suddenly become a challenge for me.

The moment Nukpana's hands touched the Saghred's casket I felt a power that had nothing to do with Sarad Nukpana. My father was talking to me. Not in the normal way two people talk to each other. There were no words spoken, no thoughts passed. It was more of a confirmation, an assurance that all of the Saghred's power was now mine for the taking. The box surrounding it contained those energies only as long as I wished it. I wasn't the only one who thought the world would be a better place without Sarad Nukpana.

That the goblin held it didn't matter. The Saghred—and my father inside—reached out to me, offering me the power I needed to destroy Nukpana, his Khrynsani, and anyone else I chose, in The Ruins, the embassy grounds, the gardens, and the house beyond if I felt like it. The stone's power seethed just below its surface. Waiting. Eager.

The air was charged with it. I was charged with it. Nukpana still held my hand. He felt and he knew.

His grip lightened into a caress. "By all means, Mistress Benares, show me your power," he whispered. "I have waited all my life to witness the Saghred's strength."

I certainly felt like destroying. The power was mine. I trembled with it. I could destroy Nukpana now, before he could hurt anyone else I loved. I knew it. So did he.

The power was also wrong, wrong in every way I had ever been taught. The Saghred would make me into what I wasn't. I wasn't like Sarad Nukpana.

"Learn patience," I hissed.

Nukpana acknowledged my choice with a bare nod. "As you wish. Bring the witch."

A pair of Khrynsani guards brought Primari A'Zahra Nuru forward. Her patrician features were expressionless, and even dwarfed as she was by the armored guards on either side of her, her bearing remained regal. No doubt she'd die the same way. My free hand closed on the dagger in the hidden pocket of my gown. No one was dying. Not on my watch.

Prince Chigaru shared my opinion, but not for long. The struggle was quick and fatal—quick for Chigaru, fatal for one of the guards. Three more sprang to take his place, and a vicious blow to the back of the prince's head ended the discussion.

Sarad Nukpana's eyes narrowed, the Khrynsani guard who struck Chigaru the new object of his disaffection. "If he is dead, you will take his place."

The guard dropped to his knees, desperately checking the prince for signs of life.

"He lives."

"Good. See that it remains so."

I pushed the Saghred's power down, then took a deep breath and slowly released it. I knew it wouldn't stay there for long.

Nukpana sensed it. "You are strong, Raine. Like your father."

The bastard actually sounded happy about that.

"I won't be your puppet," I told him.

"I don't want a puppet; I want a partner."

"Life's full of disappointments."

Nukpana held up his hand and the guards stopped. "Apparently you require a more personal incentive. Release the witch," he told the guards. His smile was slow and horrible. "Bring the nightingale."

I screamed and lunged for Nukpana. I was fast, but the guards behind me were faster.

Four big goblins grabbed Piaras. He tried to fight them, but there were too many. As they lifted him onto the altar, Piaras's voice dropped desperately to a dark, low register.

"Gag him," Nukpana snapped. "Quickly."

One guard gagged Piaras, while the other three held him down and shackled him to the altar.

My heart pounded, blood ran cold, mouth went dry. Anything and everything you'd expect to feel when you saw someone you loved about to be slaughtered. None of those things were going to get Piaras off of that slab, so I made myself stop doing them, every last one. If I panicked, I couldn't think, and if I couldn't think, a lot of people were going to die or worse—starting with Piaras.

"Don't." It took everything I had not to make that one word sound like begging. I would not beg. Nukpana would like it and I wasn't about to give him the satisfaction.

"What I do—or do not do—is for you to decide." Any pretense of civility was gone from his voice. He wasn't playing anymore. "You know what I require."

"I can't. I don't know how."

"But you do. In these very woods you destroyed six Magh'Sceadu, merely because they threatened your precious nightingale. I'm asking for a similar demonstration."

"Do I get to pick the target?" The words came out through clenched teeth.

The goblin laughed. "I could hardly enjoy the performance if I were vaporized."

"Scared?"

"Merely prudent." I felt his personal shields go up. He might as well have erected a fortress around himself.

"We all make sacrifices, Raine. I don't wish the nightingale's death either. Merely show me the Saghred. Show me the power, and we both get what we want." He looked over at where Prince Chigaru lay unmoving on the ground. "I think the prince and the witch will work nicely for your first demonstration."

I didn't move.

Tiny, pale lights appeared and flickered in the trees on the opposite side of the clearing. Each flicker brought them closer to us. Fire pixies. No doubt they considered the stone altar one big buffet. My job tonight was to make sure every last one of them went to bed without supper. The guards had probably rung the dinner bell the moment they chained Piaras to that altar.

"I am but a student, Mistress Benares," Sarad Nukpana was saying. "There is much to learn, and much to be accomplished. You will assist me in my work."

He placed the casket on the altar and opened it. Piaras seemed to stop breathing. So did I.

Nothing happened. The Saghred didn't steal anyone's soul. My father's ghostly hands didn't shoot out and wrap themselves around the goblin's throat. Absolutely nothing.

I expected something. From Nukpana's expression, nothing was precisely what he expected.

He lightly caressed the stone's surface. "Such a simple thing, is it not, Mistress Benares?"

My breath caught and my heart hammered in my chest. I actually felt the lightness of his touch, the warmth of him as if his fingertips had touched me, not the stone. I wondered if by controlling the Saghred, he could control me. That wasn't about to happen, not if I had anything to say about it. I tried not to think that I might not have any say.

"You still do not understand, do you?" he asked when I didn't respond.

His hand remained on the stone, and I felt a warm pressure heavy on the back of my neck. I didn't know if he was aware of the connection. I felt a shudder coming on and stopped it.

"You fear what the Saghred would give," he continued, "because you do not know the extent of its gift."

"I never considered madness a gift."

"Madness, or an unfettered mind?" His voice was soft and coaxing. "A mind without limits, free to do, to accomplish anything it can imagine. To be without boundaries. As the daughter of Eamaliel Anguis, you will have the honor of experiencing power beyond that of every mage on the Isle of Mid combined. Power the Conclave and their Guardian pets want for their own. Your powers will continue to grow. They fear that. I do not."

The stone gleamed in the moonlight and waited. Waited for the decision I didn't want to make.

A fire pixie glowed and fluttered near the altar. Either it was the same pixie that had bitten Piaras two nights ago, or it was her twin sister. Or maybe all fire pixies looked alike. I didn't know. I didn't care.

The grand shaman drew a dagger out of his robes. I'd seen its twin last night. A foot-long triangular blade, jewel-encrusted grip, pommel topped with a ruby the size of a child's fist. That one had been used to tack Nukpana's letter to me to the embassy gates. I was right; the crazies always carried spares. He put it on the altar next to the casket.

Piaras's dark eyes met mine, wide with panic and terror—and hope. A muffled sound came from behind his gag. He hadn't given up, not yet. He had no idea what I was going to do to keep him from taking that dagger through his heart, but he was hoping I knew.

I did.

The goblin grand shaman lifted the Saghred out of the casket and set it on the altar next to the dagger.

A male pixie clothed in blue flame darted in front of my face, then dove for my neck. I swatted at him, and he fled. Only after he had gone did I feel the sting. I touched my neck and my fingertips came back wet with blood.

The smell of blood, and the promise of more lured in more fire pixies. They were being cautious—all except Piaras's pixie. She fluttered around Sarad Nukpana and Piaras, glowing bright orange, eager to feed. Beauty, but no brains. She'd be better off taking her fluttering elsewhere. Piaras struggled in vain against the shackles that bound his wrists over his head.

Nukpana struck, one-handedly catching the pixie in midair, and crushing her the same way. He wiped the remains on the altar with no more regard than a swatted fly. The Saghred pulsed once with a nearly imperceptible glow. If I had blinked, I'd have missed it. Someone was awake—and hungry.

Sarad Nukpana's shields shimmered as he enhanced their

power even more. He was being careful. Nothing was getting through those shields unless he allowed it. I was familiar with what he was using—a circle to protect himself against the awakening Saghred, as well as spells, people, and weapons.

A small silver amulet wasn't a weapon—but I knew a way to turn it into one.

The goblin rested one hand lightly on the Saghred, and gestured me to him with the other, still bloody one.

"Release her," he told my guards.

"Sir, are you—?"

"I said release her."

"Your will, my primaru."

He gestured me to him again. "If you and the beacon would join me."

From what Mychael had told me, I should be close enough to the Saghred to remove the beacon without my usual brush with death. I pulled the diamond chain with the beacon over my head. I could still breathe and stand at the same time. Good. Mychael had been right.

I hoped my father was right, too.

Power makes you blind to your own greed—and its consequences. I didn't know if it would work. I didn't know if the backlash from Sarad Nukpana's shields would kill me. But with the goblin's breath close enough to fog the Saghred's surface, and Piaras about to be murdered for the sake of a sick experiment, it didn't matter.

I tossed the beacon to the goblin. "Catch."

The beacon passed through Sarad Nukpana's shields and into his waiting and bloody hand—shields that ceased to exist when he reached out to grab the beacon. The goblin's obsidian eyes widened in realization at what he had just done.

The Saghred, Sarad Nukpana, and blood to bind them—and no shields between them.

I didn't know if any of the blood on his hand was his, or if it was all from the dead fire pixie. The Saghred didn't care. A sacrifice was a sacrifice. And it was hungry.

A little sacrificial blood and a broken magical circle. The simplest magic was the best kind.

And greed will make you stupid. Without exception.

Tendrils of white light wrapped around the goblin's wrist like steel vines, anchoring him where he stood, engulfing his hand that still gripped the beacon, shooting up his arm to the shoulder, the light coiling and constricting, racing hungrily to consume his body. A high-pitched, strangled shriek came from inside the column of white flame that was Sarad Nukpana.

Then he was gone.

The Saghred's glow diminished to a single pinpoint of light. It winked out, leaving the stone cold and dark on the altar.

Chapter 24

After the Saghred consumed Sarad Nukpana, our guards remembered places they desperately needed to be. Apparently their
loyalty ceased to exist when their leader did. The fire pixies
likewise made themselves scarce. Within seconds we were
alone in the clearing.

As far as distractions went, it was one of my better efforts.
And as far as near-death experiences went, I was surprisingly
calm. Piaras was alive. I was outside the Saghred. Sarad
Nukpana was inside the Saghred. No one was here to keep us
from leaving. It wasn't everything I wanted out of this evening,
but I'd take it.

I cut the gag away from Piaras's mouth.

"Are you all right?" I asked.

He took a shuddering breath and nodded. I couldn't have
agreed more; air was in short supply for me, too. Stupid, tight
bodice.

I pulled one of the hat pins out of my bodice and went to
work on Piaras's wrist shackles. Fortunately there was only
one lock. I didn't want to take my eyes off the Saghred sharing

the altar with Piaras, but it wasn't like I had a choice. I heard a click and glanced up. A'Zahra Nuru had a dainty dagger in one tiny hand and had already picked the lock on one of Piaras's ankle shackles. I only had one lock to pick and I was still working on it. Not that I was competitive or anything.

"Thank you, Primari."

She smiled. "No, thank *you*, Mistress Benares."

I heard a groan from behind us. The prince must be waking up.

"Go, I'll finish," I told her.

She rushed over to the prince. If my luck held, he'd be able to walk, too. I had something else to carry. It was lighter, but a whole lot more dangerous.

The moment I unlocked his wrist shackles, Piaras sat up and pulled a stiletto out of his sleeve.

"I can get the last one," he told me.

And he did. Faster than I thought a lock could be picked. Piaras was very proficient, professional even.

He saw my surprise and flashed a quick grin. "Phaelan taught me."

I was going to have a long talk with Phaelan.

Piaras removed the last shackle and scrambled off the altar. "What did you do?" He kept his voice low so Primari Nuru couldn't hear. "Did you have to use . . . ?" He threw a quick glance at the Saghred.

I shook my head. "Just my brain." I grinned. "And some fatherly advice. Nukpana didn't expect either one."

The Saghred sat still and dark on the altar. "What's it doing?" he whispered.

I grimaced. "Digesting?"

"We're leaving now, right?" Piaras sounded like he'd prefer to be already gone.

"Just as soon as we can get that"—I pointed to the Saghred—"back in there." I indicated the box.

"Do we have to take it with us?" Piaras sounded as thrilled with the idea as I was.

"Afraid we have to."

"And you can't just pick it up?"

"I'm trying to avoid that."

"Probably a good idea."

"May I make a suggestion?" asked a cultured voice from behind us.

We both jumped. I'd forgotten about Primari Nuru.

"Please do," I said.

"As primitive as it may sound, a stick or small branch may be the solution. Turn the casket on its side, then use the stick to push the stone inside."

I blinked. "A stick?"

"The Saghred only responds to direct contact. You would not actually be touching the stone. You should not be harmed."

"Should not?"

Her half smile made her look almost girlish. "So the legends say."

"No disrespect intended, Primari, but if it's a legend, it's safe to assume those who wrote it are dead. Since I can't be sure it was from old age, and since I have blood on my hand." I paused, fighting off a case of the heebie-jeebies. "I've been in the Saghred once tonight. It spit me out that time, and I'm not about to try my luck again."

The goblin paled, no mean trick with her skin tone. "You were inside?"

I nodded. "And it's not a trip I want to repeat, especially now that Sarad Nukpana's been added to the welcoming committee."

Someone was coming toward us. Fast. And they had a lot of company close behind them. My first instinct was to run. But with the Saghred still on the altar, and not a stick in sight, running wasn't a viable option. Against my better judgment, I stayed.

It was Mychael and Garadin. There wasn't a mark on either one of them, which was probably more than could be said for the Khrynsani ordered to take them to the compound. Several Guardians were close behind. Vegard was one of them. He looked a little on the pale side, but he was upright. He looked around the clearing and grinned.

"Ma'am, you were supposed to leave something for us."

"Sorry about that. They left early." I nodded toward the Saghred. "I got the feeling they didn't like the company."

The big Guardian looked where I was looking. He went a shade pasty. "I can understand that."

Mychael looked like he wanted to do something along the lines of a rib-crushing hug. I was experiencing a similar urge toward him. He knew it. I knew that he knew. With the Saghred on the altar and more Guardians arriving in the clearing, I decided that we could always indulge ourselves later. First, I had a soul-eating stone of power to poke with a stick.

Mychael had a bare blade in his hands. I couldn't help but notice that it was Khrynsani. I'd imagine its previous owner no longer needed it. The Guardian looked around the clearing, not trusting what he didn't see. "Where's Nukpana?"

Using the smallest gesture possible, Piaras pointed at the Saghred.

Mychael raised an inquisitive brow.

"It wasn't pretty," I told him.

"No doubt."

"I'll fill you in on the details later."

"I wish you would." He locked eyes with me. "He didn't hurt you, did he?"

His eyes reflected concern, relief, and rage all at the same time, and I knew in no uncertain terms that if the Saghred and I hadn't taken out Sarad Nukpana, Mychael would have. I suddenly felt warmed to my toes.

"No, I'm good." I looked at the Saghred. "I'd be better if that was back in its box. Though at least I think it's finished what it's doing now."

"Where's the beacon?" he asked.

"Nukpana had it in his hand."

"It's inside, then."

I nodded.

"Then why's it still sitting out in the open?" Garadin asked, moving closer to the Saghred than I thought safe.

"Do you want to touch it?"

Garadin stopped. "Not really."

Mychael sheathed his sword. I didn't think that was a good idea either.

"Have you considered using a stick?" the Guardian asked.

Apparently he and the primari had heard the same legend.

"It's been suggested," I said.

"Then let's do it. We need to get out of here."

Mychael went and knelt next to Chigaru and A'Zahra Nuru. He touched the prince's temple and raised one of his eyelids to check the damage.

"He is not badly injured," the primari told Mychael. "He only needs time."

"Time's in short supply just now, my lady."

I'd really hate to survive this long only to have the Saghred slurp me up for dessert, but considering where we were—and who and what was out there—I had to agree with his suggestion to vacate the premises. But that didn't mean I had to like what I had to do before we left.

"I'll find a stick," Piaras volunteered.

I sighed. "And I'll poke the rock."

He found one. Quicker than I wanted him to. Now it was my turn. Mychael offered to do it himself, but I couldn't let him. This one was mine. I didn't want it to be, but that wasn't how things had turned out.

"There wouldn't happen to be any elaborate containment spells or extra-strength incantations I could use, would there?" I asked anyone and everyone who might know.

Mychael answered. "There are, but none that have been particularly effective. Personal shields have been the most often used." He turned to A'Zahra Nuru. "My lady, do you know of any?"

The primari was supporting a now half-conscious goblin prince. "I am sorry; I do not."

Great. I wondered if the poor sots the Saghred had inhaled for breakfast, lunch, and dinner over the ages had used shields, or just thrown caution to the wind. I was willing to bet most had been cautious, like Sarad Nukpana—right before they had been consumed.

No spells. No incantations. Just me and mine, poking at a stone with cataclysmic power with a stick. If I was the Saghred, I would have been insulted. Hopefully it wouldn't take any resentment out on me.

I turned the casket on its side; and wielding the long, forked stick like a rapier, made contact with the Saghred and pushed it neatly into the box. Point control was good for something. I closed the lid using the same maneuver. Power prickled up my arm, but other than that, the rock didn't seem to mind the contact. I shuddered, blew out the air I'd been holding, and picked up the box. The beacon was in the Saghred with Sarad Nukpana. In theory since I no longer had the beacon, I should no longer feel a connection with the Saghred.

No such luck.

"I really hoped I'd be able to get rid of this."

Mychael was looking at me funny. Not the good kind of funny. I looked down at myself. I wasn't glowing or anything.

"What?" I asked.

"The bond is still there."

He didn't ask it as a question. I wish he had. He knew it as well as I did. Must have been kind of obvious somehow. The power the Saghred had offered me to destroy Sarad Nukpana was still there, inside me, waiting just below the surface. Waiting for what, I wasn't really sure. Oh boy.

Mychael's lips set in a grim line. "Is it trying to influence you?"

"No. At least not right now. It feels more like a big dog with very big teeth on a very short leash." I grimaced. "A well-fed dog at the moment. Any idea how often it gets hungry?"

"Not a clue."

"Not what I wanted to hear."

His expression was unreadable. "We'll be taking it back to Mid."

That was good news, but I didn't need the Saghred's help to know his thoughts. That wasn't all Mychael wanted to take back to Mid with him.

"I would like it very much if you would come with me," he said.

I assumed since he asked nicely there wasn't a trip over his shoulder in my immediate future. Good to know.

"Because the Saghred thinks I'm its new psychic roommate?" I asked.

"Yes."

"Think someone on Mid could help me serve the eviction notice?"

"Probably."

I wanted to be rid of the Saghred, so that was a good reason to go to Mid, but it wasn't quite good enough. Not anymore. I walked over to where Mychael was and looked up at him, a challenge in my eyes and a tiny smile on my lips. "Is there another reason you want me to come home with you?" I asked softly.

A corner of his mouth quirked upward. "One."

"Does that reason have anything whatsoever to do with the Soul Thief?"

"Nothing," he murmured.

My smile broadened. "Can you answer me with more than one word?"

His smile melted into that boyish grin. "Maybe later."

Garadin cleared his throat. "Riston has boats waiting for us."

Piaras started. "What about my grandmother?"

"Not to worry, my boy," Garadin said. "She's safe with Tam Nathrach." He glanced at me. "Your primaru does good work." He only sounded slightly begrudging.

"He knew where Nukpana was keeping your grandmother," Mychael explained to Piaras. "We worked it out ahead of time that he would take a few Guardians, rescue her, and destroy Nukpana's workroom so he couldn't open any more Gates from Mermeia. Nukpana's overworked his shamans for the past few days, so Tam didn't encounter much resistance."

The Ruins were quiet as we left. I don't mean quiet as in serene. I mean silent in an unnatural and bad way. The only sounds we heard were the sounds we made, and I wasn't the only one who didn't like it. Blades were out. Crossbows were ready. I knew only too well you couldn't rely on footsteps to announce some of The Ruins' nasties. Too many of them didn't have feet.

There was one thing everything living in The Ruins had in common—a need for and an addiction to all things magic. And it didn't get more magical than the stone I carried clenched in my white-knuckled hands. If I could feel it through the casket, I knew that creatures, whose sole purpose in existing was the hunt for, capture of, and consumption of magic, were hot on our trail.

"Can we move faster?" I whispered to Mychael. The sound of my own voice was absurdly loud.

"What is it?"

"Company's coming."

The Guardian turned to where Chigaru was now walking unassisted. "Your Highness?"

"Yes?"

"Are you able to run, or do you require assistance?"

The goblin prince stiffened at the implication of help from anyone. "I can manage on my own."

"Glad to hear it." Mychael addressed everyone else. "Stay together, stay alert, but let's pick up the pace."

We did. And so did the things following us.

It was a race to the canal surrounding the island. And after what I'd been through over the past three days, it was a race I was not going to lose. Our exit point would still put us in the Goblin District, but if the Khrynsani guards' reaction was any indicator, there wouldn't be a welcoming committee. Or if there was, flashing the Saghred in their general direction should clear us a wide path. Unless someone had stepped in to fill Sarad Nukpana's boots in the past few minutes, the former grand shaman seemed to be the only one of his order chomping at the bit to get his hands on the Saghred. Nukpana's underlings were more enamored with the idea of having the Saghred than with actually having it in their collective face.

At least that's what I was counting on.

It had occurred to me that I was carrying the most dangerous thing in The Ruins, which by association made me the most dangerous thing in The Ruins. It had occurred to me, but I was doing my best not to think about it. It wasn't a distinction I wanted.

We actually got out of The Ruins without incident. I was nothing short of stunned. I kept expecting battle-armored Khrynsani or Mal'Salin guards to jump us at every turn, but it never happened. A pleasant surprise. I wondered if Sathrik Mal'Salin had any notion of what I had just done to his right-hand shaman. Would he care? I think he would. I was just lucky that way.

I made my decision before we even reached our borrowed gondolas.

Chapter 25

Sleep was easy. Getting there was hard. Try going to sleep with eleven pirates shouting overhead—and Sarad Nukpana whispering your name.

I was in Phaelan's bunk on the *Fortune* attempting to catch a few hours of sleep. Phaelan's crew was preparing to get underway. It wouldn't take much—either work or time. My cousin arrived in a port quickly, and was always prepared to leave the same way. An hour ago, a little wind manipulation by a weather wizard friend of Garadin's had nudged the *Fortune* out of her harbor moorings to just beyond the barrier islands where a pair of Guardian ships waited. The wizard had collapsed from near exhaustion from the effort. I could hear him snoring it off in the next cabin. Something else to keep me awake.

Mychael and I had talked before I'd turned in. Some of that talk I had liked; some of it I didn't. But we both agreed on one thing—my staying in Mermeia was out of the question.

While I didn't want to go there, the Isle of Mid was the only place where I could possibly get rid of my new soulmate. It was also an island full of power-grubbing mages, and I had a bond with a legendary stone of power no one had been able to wield and live—until me, until now. I'd be the most popular girl in town.

In an attempt at consolation, Phaelan told me that leaving Mermeia would make me part of a long-standing Benares family tradition: leave town until things cool down.

King Sathrik Mal'Salin knew about me. So did Prince Chigaru, who along with Primari Nuru had parted ways with us once we were out of The Ruins. One minute their gondola was there, then it wasn't. Mychael hadn't seemed concerned by it. I couldn't say the same. If they weren't making their own getaway plans, they were in deep hiding. As to Sarad Nukpana no longer being in control of the Khrynsani, I knew that wouldn't last for long. Nukpana might not be there to lead them, but one of his minions would claw his way to the top. And I was sure his replacement would be just as psychotic— and just as obsessive about me. It was the kind of attention a girl could do without.

Then there was the attention I was going to miss.

Tam had delivered Tarsilia safely to the *Fortune*. While Tarsilia and Piaras had an emotional reunion, Tam and I tried to have a nonemotional parting. I said we tried; we didn't succeed. I knew I had to leave; Tam knew I had to leave, but knowing it didn't make it any easier. Tam had a business to run. I had a stone of power to rid myself of.

In the end, words just weren't getting the job done for Tam, so he went for action instead. I've been on the receiving end of some heated kisses in my time, but none of the top contenders had ever involved me being slammed against a mainmast. I have to admit I liked it. A lot. The hoots and whistles of Phaelan's crew did nothing to discourage Tam's ardor. Quite the opposite. I think he wanted to make sure I wouldn't forget him. After that kiss, there was no chance of that. I thought there was a much better chance of Tam turning up on the Isle of Mid. Let's just say I wouldn't be surprised.

Garadin, Tarsilia, and Piaras were sailing to Mid with me. So was my cat, Boris. Once Garadin had drafted his weather wizard friend to help get us to Mid, he ran by my rooms to get Boris. Garadin was in a hurry. Boris did nothing in a hurry except eat. Garadin had to drag Boris out from under my bed. Boris had to claw the crap out of Garadin's arms. I'd only seen my cat once after we'd set sail, chasing a fat rat. Boris was on his ideal vacation. I couldn't say the same for myself.

Mychael had told me I was safe, but safe was relative. An armada wasn't enough to make me feel safe right now. Our trio of ships bristled with cannons and shielding spells. But what I feared most I had brought onboard myself. Not on the *Fortune*, but on one of the Conclave's ships. The Saghred was in Mychael's cabin, in its casket, under the strongest containment spells he and his Guardians could bind it with. Though it didn't matter where the Saghred was, because I heard it the whole time, whispering without words, a constant stream running under my thoughts. I tried thinking other thoughts to drown out the whispers, but all that did was make it harder to go to sleep. I could see this was going to be a problem.

I wondered if my father had lain awake at night listening to the voices, and later the temptations. Though at this point, I'd settle for a good night's sleep—and count on my own special brand of stubbornness as a defense. Garadin always told me I was stubborn as a rock. I never thought I'd actually have to put it to the test.

So far I hadn't experienced anything approaching the Saghred's full power. I didn't know what it would feel like, and I would really prefer to go the rest of my life without finding out. I just hoped I wouldn't wake up in a few hours craving coffee, sugar knots, and world domination. The last one sounded like entirely too much work, but that didn't mean I couldn't be tempted by the Saghred's other offers. I'd only heard a few, and I was sure there would be more.

I awoke to sunlight and sea air. Waking up meant I'd been asleep. Good for me. Nice morning, blue sky. The *Fortune* was under full sail and moving fast. I was alive. So were my friends. And most importantly, I didn't feel the urge to take over anything. Life was good.

I still heard voices, but this time they weren't coming from inside the Saghred. They were warm, living, breathing voices and sounds. Tarsilia speaking, Piaras laughing. Garadin knocking. Somehow I knew it was him.

I rolled over. "Come."

The door opened. Yep, it was Garadin. Nothing like getting a brand-new power from a soul-sucking rock to start your day.

"How did you sleep?" he asked.

I sat up, pulled the blanket around me and pushed what must have been some very scary looking hair out of my face. I hadn't bothered braiding it before I turned in. I was only wearing a silk shirt. A big one. It wasn't mine; it was Mychael's. It was also nice and comfy. With the Khrynsani probably on my tail, there was no time for civilized niceties like packing. I had some clothes onboard, but nothing for sleeping. Phaelan said he could find me some girl clothes, but I knew where those clothes had come from, and I'd rather not wear anything one of his nighttime visitors hadn't had time to put back on.

"I slept well enough," I said. "All things considered."

"All things?"

"The Saghred thinks I'm its new roommate."

My godfather didn't respond immediately. "You're the only one who can hear it. The shields are holding for the rest of us." There were the beginnings of dark circles under his blue eyes. It looked like he'd been helping with those shields.

"Apparently I'm not the rest of us," I said.

"I know. That's what I wanted to talk to you about."

"I figured as much."

He pushed off the door frame with his shoulder and crossed the cabin to the bunk. He sat on the edge near the foot.

"You might not want to do that," I told him. "Rumor has it I'm dangerous right now."

He halfway smiled. "I've always known that."

He leaned forward, elbows resting on his knees, hands clasped loosely in front of him. He sat that way in silence. I had a feeling he was gathering words he knew I didn't want to hear.

"Heard anything else from your father?"

I shook my head and sat up straighter against the pillows. "Just Nukpana."

That thought troubled him. It troubled me more.

"Anything now?"

"Not a peep from the grand shaman." I managed a weak smile, though there was no humor behind it. "Maybe he got tired."

"Maybe." Garadin bowed his head and looked at the deck. "I had no idea Eamaliel Anguis was your father. Maranda never mentioned him. I asked her. Once. She said she didn't want to talk about it, and I knew she didn't want me to bring it up again. So I didn't."

"Sounds like she was stubborn."

My godfather smiled. "Like someone else I know."

He lifted his head and looked at me then, and I found myself not wanting to meet his eyes. I knew he saw me—but he was remembering my mother.

"She loved you." His voice was soft and husky. "And I don't have that secondhand. I saw it myself."

If he kept this up, my long-promised screaming fit was going to turn into a crying jag. I could only manage a ragged whisper in response. "Thank you."

He was fighting his own case of the misties. He patted my knee under the blanket. "Mychael's a good man, and so is Justinius Valerian. We'll get this taken care of, girl."

I tried a shaky grin on for size. It didn't quite fit. "One way or another."

"No, just one way." He pushed himself to his feet and straightened his robes. "There's breakfast in the galley if you're interested. Piaras might have left something for you."

He stopped at the door. "Mychael isn't sending word ahead

to Justinius that he has the stone," he said quietly. "But I'm sure the goblins already have."

"Well, that'll just make the bad guys easier to spot," I said. "Anyone on Mid who knows we have the rock got their information through the back door."

Garadin met my comment with calm silence. The kind you had when you were right and you knew it—and so did the person who wanted you to be wrong. I chose to ignore it. I could think about it when we got to Mid. That gave me about four days to ignore my future.

I swung my legs over the side of the bunk. My muscles had other ideas. I winced. "I'll get dressed and be out in a few minutes."

My godfather nodded and left.

I took my time dressing, and then strapped on my blades. What threatened me most right now couldn't be hurt by steel, but I wasn't going to let a few days at sea get me out of a healthy habit. Once on Mid, I was sure I'd get ample opportunity to use both spells and steel. There were plenty of people there who wanted what I had, what I could do. That meant they wanted me.

I'm a seeker. I find things. Fate sure does have a warped sense of humor. Now I'm what the bad guys are trying to find. Most times people are glad when they find what they're looking for. Sometimes they're sorry they asked. If you ask me, folks should be more careful what they ask for. I cinched the buckle on my brace of throwing knives. Some things are better left unfound. Like me.

I'd had some sleep, I'd get some breakfast, talk to my friends, then I'd find my favorite place near the bow. Wind in my hair, spray on my face. A little sun and fresh air. A little happiness. I take my happiness when and where I can find it.

Explore the outer reaches of imagination
with Ace and Roc—don't miss these authors of
dark fantasy and urban noir
that take you to the edge and beyond.

Patricia Briggs	Karen Chance	Anne Bishop
Simon R. Green	Caitlin Kiernan	Janine Cross
Jim Butcher	Rachel Caine	Sarah Monette
Kat Richardson	Glen Cook	Doug Clegg